No Small Change

A Teapot Cottage Tale

Annie Cook

GW00778037

ISBN: 978-1-915889-94-2

Kerry, nothing means anything without you.
This book is for you, with all the love in the world.

Acknowledgements

There are people who have been in my orbit, throughout the process of writing and getting this book to print, who deserve a special mention.

Kerry Purvis, my amazing and endlessly tolerant husband, and my biggest champion, has supplied unwavering belief and encouragement throughout the journey. He has also provided copious quantities of tea and toast, especially on the days when I was so absorbed with Adie and her family that I'd literally forget to eat.

Rebecca Pockett, my absolute star, bravely read the first and roughest draft of No Small Change, back when it was called something different, and was so excited she brought tears to my eyes.

Liam Beale magically gave brilliant life to my incoherent graphic ideas without letting me drive him crazy, and Gwen Morrison from PublishNation brought the kind of enthusiasm and expertise to the project that no writer should ever have to do without.

I'm here because of all of you. Thank you, my darlings, from the bottom of my heart.

Chapter 1

The trouble with sat-navs, Adie fumed, is that they all-too-often lied. This one, the wretched stupid thing, was doing exactly that right now. It was lying through its teeth, or at least it would be if it actually *had* any teeth.

Somehow, through no mistake of her own - unless you counted blind obedience to a monotone-talking box attached with spit and a prayer to her windscreen as a 'mistake' - she'd managed to end up half a mile down an impossibly narrow, pothole-pitted dirt track. It looked like a road as far as the sat-nav was concerned, but it seemed to be leading precisely nowhere. As annoying and embarrassing as it was to have to admit it Adrienne Elizabeth Bostock, menopausal mess and newly disowned wife and mother (not to mention pilloried social pariah) really did seem to have got herself well and truly lost.

With her teeth clenched and her mouth compressed in a grim line, Adie stopped the car and contemplated the massive, spiky, paint-gouging brambles that flanked the ever-tightening track before her. It had dwindled to little more than the width of a cycle trail already. How much further could she realistically go? And, of course, there was nowhere to turn around. So that meant reversing. Around stupid blind bends and bushes. All the way back to the stupid main road. Adie glanced at her watch, tried to ignore yet another surging, suffocating hot flush, and gritted her teeth even harder.

With a frustrated sigh, and swearing like a slaughterhouse worker under her breath, she graunched the gear stick into reverse and started inching backwards. *And God alone knows how long this is going to take!*

Adie had a simple but important goal; to get to her first-ever house-sitting job at a place called Teapot Cottage in a town called Torley before the owners left for the other side of the world. She forced down her rising panic and wracked her brains to figure out where she'd gone wrong with the satnav's directions, but drew a blank. Instead, she took a couple of deep breaths and tried to hold

1

on tightly to the inner voice of reason – the one that told her nobody would die if she was an hour or two late. In fact, the voice of reason insisted, if she was an hour or two late, nobody might notice what time she turned up at all, except maybe the dog, who was no doubt desperate to be fed, and poo'd-n-wee'd-n-walked, before what was left of the daylight finally faded.

She checked her watch again. It was twenty to four. She promised herself that if she hadn't made sense of the directions in another twenty minutes, and assuming she had mobile phone reception in this God-forsaken place, she'd simply call her hosts, admit defeat, and ask for guidance.

She didn't think that would upset them greatly. They'd seemed very relaxed overall, about the house-sitting arrangement. They'd happily given precise instructions on where to find the key to their cottage and, by default, access to all their worldly goods, in case they *had* already absconded to the other side of the world by the time she arrived. But Adie thought it would've been nice if she could have made an entrance while they were still around. They could then perhaps bimble off to Australia for Christmas with a bit of peace of mind, having left everything they held dear - quite bizarrely, in her opinion - in the hands of someone they'd actually managed to meet.

The house-sit had all seemed perfectly doable and reasonable earlier in the week, when the plans were being made over the phone. But now, thanks to her apparent inability to find the place, even with the help of technology, she was beginning to wonder if she'd made a disastrous decision in plunging headlong into an arrangement she was only halfway confident she could even pull off.

It doesn't say much about my capabilities, does it, if I can't even find the bloody house?

Adie was a very reluctant free agent, this Christmas. Since the family home had been put up for sale, her now ex-husband Bryan had gone off in whatever direction he'd decided on (Adie tried to tell herself she didn't give a monkey's), and all three of her children were doing their own thing too. Not a single one of them was even vaguely interested her plans, or including her in theirs. As much as she hated the idea, and had done everything she could to avoid it, she'd ended up facing Christmas alone.

Her first-born daughter Ruth, who was barely speaking to her anyway, was in Italy with her gorgeous Italian wife, the well-known dress designer Gina Giordano, and their little daughter Chiara. They normally did the big Italian family Christmas every second year, but various events that included a recent pandemic, had derailed their plans more than once. Nobody could argue that it was well and truly time for Gina to go and reconnect with her people, and take her wife and daughter with her. Adie hadn't wanted to infuriate Ruth and Gina, or a noisy bunch of excitable Italian in-laws, by asking them to change their arrangements for her, so she didn't. After all, she was hardly in a position to ask for favours, especially over something as important as that. Knowing what the answer would have been, she'd decided that suffering in silence was infinitely preferable to being sworn at in Italian by the truly terrifying Gina.

If Ruth herself had suggested that they stick around to enable her abandoned, menopausally deranged mother to feel like someone cared enough to see her through her first Christmas alone, it would have been a different matter. But nothing was said, and Adie understood completely because plans are plans and her unfortunate position of 'persona non grata' within her family was, after all, her own stupid fault. But the timing really couldn't have been any worse.

Adie's younger daughter Teresa was also away, backpacking around the Sunshine Coast of Australia with a group of good friends she'd known since her school days. The date of their return home was open-ended. Teresa appeared to be in no rush to give up her freedom and join the workforce yet.

It was all fair enough, Adie knew. Ruth, Gina and Chiara needed time with their extended family, and Teresa deserved a chance to let her hair down before getting down to the business of deciding on her first career move. Adie's now settled but once wayward (and some might have said morally bankrupt) son Matty was a little closer to home, in Epsom, having his first family Christmas with his new wife and even newer baby, but his plans hadn't included her either.

"You do understand, don't you, Mum? We're just wanting to 'nest' this year on our own, for our first-ever Christmas in the new house. Why don't we think about getting together for a family do next year, when Teresa, Ruth and Gina will all be here? We could even invite Dad, if things have settled down?"

Over my dead body, Adie had seethed at the time, as she'd struggled not to choke on her raspberry gin and tonic. Even now, the very thought of Bryan's condescending presence inflicting an indelible memory-stain across *any* future family Christmas made her furious; so much so that she jammed her foot on the accelerator, shot abruptly backwards much faster than intended, and promptly smacked into a tree.

"Oh, dammit! This is all I bloody need!" She wailed angrily, banging the heel of her hand on the steering wheel. She took a deep breath, counted to ten, then flung the door open and got out of the car, at the same time as losing the battle to ignore the raging hot flush that was now doing its best to burn her alive.

And damn these stupid 'power surges'! When I wished for a 'hot body', this is NOT what I had in mind!

Fighting back her fury, she stomped to the back of the car to survey the damage. Luckily, it wasn't as bad as expected. A smooth, orange-sized dent stared defiantly back at her from the metalwork just below the back window, but thankfully the bent elbow of the renegade branch hadn't gone through the glass. The offending tree had been a small one. And the car was still perfectly driveable, thank goodness, with its bumper still intact. She could carry on with her journey, although there was still a long way to go back before she could expect to go properly forward again.

What an appropriate metaphor for my messed-up, train-wreck of a life, she muttered under her breath, as she stalked belligerently back to the driver's seat.

Adie had decided that house-sitting for three weeks in a quiet corner of the Lake District was a far better alternative to ending up at her much older brother Raymond's house for Christmas, with his horrible judging wife who she'd never got along with. Listening to (and pretending not to be hurt by) a barrage of sarcastic jibes about how thoroughly and permanently Adie had lost the trust of her family, and having to endure the terrible woman's spiteful remarks about how disgusting her 'tom-cat' son was, all just felt like more than she could stomach. Ditto the hours of mean-spirited gossip that would inevitably follow, about people she didn't even know or care about.

Chomping her way through her sister-in-law's overcooked turkey and lumpy gravy, and then being saddled with the washing up while her brother snored his head off in front of the millionth rerun of The Wizard of Oz, with an avalanche of gravy stains congealing down the front of his hideous Christmas jumper? No thanks. Adie and Raymond had never been close, and forced jollity at Christmas, spent with someone you shared absolutely nothing but a bloodline with, was just too grim a prospect – especially when part of the deal was having to suffer an insufferable spouse. And staying in her poky rented flat all alone seemed monumentally pathetic, especially as she didn't even have Creole for company. The ageing German Shepherd had stayed with Bryan after he'd thrown Adie out of the house, and although she had Creole on occasional weekends and holidays, Christmas wasn't going to be one of them.

But, as luck would have it, that had turned out to be a blessing in disguise. After meeting her glamorous friend Miranda for coffee one morning, and confiding her dread about being alone at Christmas for the first time in her fifty-two years on the planet, Miranda, (who was jetting off to Madeira for the holidays with a new and much younger man in tow) had made a rather interesting suggestion. She wondered if Adie might join a couple of house-sitting websites where people offered others the chance to go and stay in their homes to take care of their property and pets while they were away. She mused that if Adie could get a 'Christmas gig', that might just be the thing to get her 'out of her funk'. Miranda had a wonderful way with words, and she made house-sitting sound like a big adventure.

Adie wasn't entirely sure it would be that, but she had to admit that Miranda was right. She *did* need to 'get out of her funk', and this might just be a way of kick-starting the process. Because it really was going to be a process. Adie was under no illusions about the amount of time it might take to recover from a shattered 26-year marriage that was built on a foundation of lies - even if the lies were all hers.

As she continued to inch the car back towards the next hairpin bend, she thought back to last Christmas. They had tried so hard, as a family, to mend the cracks or at least ignore them for the festive season. Adie and Bryan were still in the house together, but they were living in different parts of it, coming and going at different times, rarely colliding, and being barely civil when they did.

Faced with the inevitable parting of the ways, the decision to have one last 'ordinary' family Christmas was brave and hopeful, but ultimately stupid. It had been a rip-roaring disaster of a day, an excruciating experience of walking on eggshells with everyone holding their breath, waiting for the axe to fall. Which, of course, it eventually did.

Bryan had chipped away all day, with his patronising glances and snide remarks about Adie being a liar and a fraud, manipulating her family to suit her own desires. By the time darkness had descended on Christmas night, after the mulled wine had been poured and the mince pies passed around, everything had finally fallen apart. All pretence had been over when Matty properly lost his temper and offered to tattoo the words 'intolerant asshole' back-to-front on his father's forehead, so he'd never be able to forget the fact. Teresa had then dissolved into an uncharacteristic flood of tears and became incapable of saying anything at all. An entire day of listening to their father openly and spitefully sniping at their mother had finally finished both kids off. Hurt and angry, they'd admitted defeat and rushed off into the night.

Adie hadn't blamed them one iota as she'd sat there wishing she had somewhere else to go, herself. For Matty and Teresa's own sakes, she'd been glad when they left. But she was bereft, being left to endure her husband's overflowing bitterness without a single buffer to mitigate the misery.

She understood Bryan's anger at the revelation that she'd had a baby girl at fifteen, had been forced to put her up for adoption, and had, in his scathing words, 'never bothered to tell anyone who had the right to know.' After secretly tracking Ruth down Adie had managed to persuade Bryan to sell the big family home he loved so much, at very short notice, and move everyone into the much smaller house she'd bought next door to Ruth and Gina, on the flimsy pretext of 'downsizing'.

She had then set about befriending the couple in an effort to be close in whatever way she could to her firstborn. She'd never told her husband the real reason for the move, or let any of her children know they each had a half-sibling across the fence line. She just hadn't known how, in the beginning, and the more time went by, the harder it became to tell the truth.

It only came out at all because of a freak set of circumstances nobody could have predicted in a million years; the kind of thing you really couldn't have made up. Her son Matty had been wrongly implicated in a woman's murder and had in the process been 'outed' as a moonlighting sex worker. Adie was still trying - and largely failing - to wrap her head around *that* particular nugget! After all, how exactly *do* you come to terms with the fact that your twenty-four-year-old son routinely shags women at least a decade older than you and gets paid for it? Adie was pretty sure nobody had written the manual for that, yet!

And whoever it was that first coined the phrase 'the truth will out' hadn't been kidding. Routine DNA samples had linked Matty with the half-sister he didn't know he had. In the most unnerving and random coincidence ever to be established by anyone, anywhere in the entire bloody world, the murdered woman had turned out to be Ruth's adopted sister. She had also been Matty's youngest 'client', at thirty-five. Most of the women he 'attended to' (for want of a more disturbing description) were roughly double that age at least.

It was all a gigantic, mortifying mess that took a lot of unravelling and explaining, but the long and short of it was that Adie had been forced to come clean about everything, and the revelations had left everyone well and truly shell-shocked with anger and disbelief. Bryan hadn't been willing to look her in the eye for almost a year now. Neither had 'grab-a-gran' Matty, albeit for very different reasons.

As far as Bryan was concerned, there was a lot to take on board, and a lot to forgive, and Adie understood that. But his resentment and nastiness had cut the family to the quick. As confused as Matty and Teresa were about everything, and as unready as they still were to talk about it in any real depth, they did at least try to understand. Sadly, their father didn't, and they struggled with that too. To say the family was a paralysed mess of anger, shame and confusion was the understatement of the century.

Matty's confused face was never far from her thoughts, nor was Ruth's outraged one, or Teresa's tear-stained one. And as for Gina, frighteningly ferocious in her desire to protect her vulnerable wife, she'd virtually torn Adie in half with her strident volley of insults, with Adie – for once – being profoundly glad she didn't understand Italian.

Again, here in her now-dented old banger of a car, stuck in the middle of nowhere and desperately grappling with the latest of the ferocious hot flushes that now routinely plagued her, Adie couldn't quite manage to stay ahead of yet another deluge of tears. There were simply no words to describe the agony of knowing how much she'd hurt the people she loved the most. Tears were all she had left. She hadn't known it was possible to hate herself so much, to cry as much as she had over the past few months, or to be so *sick* of crying. Some of her wretchedness was free-falling hormones, but most of it wasn't.

She blinked hard and forced herself to stop thinking about Bryan. Another emotional surge like the one she'd just had only intensified the heartache, and exponentially increased the likelihood of her poor little car being fully written off before she'd ever manage to guide it back to the main road.

Menopausal mood swings and everything else that went with them were the new 'normal' now for Adie, and she struggled to get used to managing her symptoms with no real idea how long they might last. Although Covid restrictions had initially prevented her from physically seeing her doctor, there had been a good long telephone talk about hormone replacement therapy. Adie had also picked the brains of various friends in the same hormonal boat, to try and weigh up the apparent choice between the increased risks of breast cancer or osteoporosis. She eventually decided against HRT.

Unfortunately, part of the deal of "flying solo" hormonally was being knocked sideways several times a day by 'power surges'. Weeping at the drop of a hat went with the territory too, and so did having to forcibly ignore far too many random and shocking impulses to punch innocent people in the face, and stave off the unfathomable urge to commit some seriously bizarre acts of homicide. Waking up at all hours was part of the fun as well, most times drenched and panicking, and fighting through the night to get her breath back.

She supposed that if her life was a bit less complicated, she might manage her symptoms a lot better. Her mood swings, in particular, were probably a lot more keenly felt than they otherwise might have been if everything else had been on a more even keel. Her doctor had said as much, and had stressed the importance of family support, but of course there was fat chance of that. As for the recommended 'circle of helpful and understanding friends', well that was just laughable. Most of Adie's so-called friends had effectively melted into the woodwork since her split with Bryan, having picked their camp by way of their absence. It was safe to say that her life wasn't exactly bursting at the seams with allies.

But even the isolation she was feeling, or the see-sawing state of her relationships and the ever-present worry about the future, weren't enough to convince her that HRT was a better option. Her doctor had assured her that she could change her mind at any point and go for the drugs but, so far at least, Adie had stood resolutely against her body being flooded with fake hormones.

I just have to get on with it, don't I? What's the alternative? Sitting in a sobbing, hysterical heap, waiting to be rescued or going completely mad?

She gave herself a mental shake and forced herself to focus. Reversing along this narrow, crater-riddled ribbon of 'road' was going to need all of her concentration.

Suddenly, a sharp, piercing whistle made her jump. Braking quickly, she glanced in her rear-view mirror to see a tall stocky man standing right behind the car with his hands on his hips. He didn't look angry, just a bit bemused, but she realised how narrowly she'd avoided hitting him. He had literally stepped up from behind the bend she was about to reverse around.

Really? People actually battled their way down this back-of-beyond track, with its lacerating thorns and ankle-busting potholes?

Momentarily forgetting about the size of her personal contribution to global warming, Adie slid her window down. "I'm so sorry, I didn't see you! Are you alright?"

The man peered at her, then nodded. "Oh, yes dear, don't worry, I'm fine. You don't look that great yourself, though, if you don't mind my saying so. Lost, are you?"

Acutely embarrassed, Adie wiped her weeping eyes self-consciously with the back of her hand, knowing she was anything but a 'pretty crier'. She hoped, against all odds, that her face didn't look as blotchy, shiny and clammy as it felt.

She sniffed hard. "Yes, sorry. But I think I *am* completely lost. I'm trying to find a place called Teapot Cottage, in a town called Torley, but the postcode must be wrong because the stupid sat-nav has brought me here. Right now I haven't a clue where I am."

The man stepped forward, and she could see he was in his mid-fifties. He had a distinctly windswept look about him, like he'd spent his whole life walking down remote country lanes in all weathers. Dressed in a domed-up Barbour jacket, scruffy jeans, wellington boots and a flat cap, he looked like the quintessential English farmer plucked straight from a country magazine, but with a lot more mud and unkemptness about him. He smiled kindly and nodded.

"Teapot Cottage. That's the Robinson's little place by Torley town. Converted old shepherd's hut. At the edge of Ravensdown Farm." He spoke very well, and his sentences were statements, rather than questions, indicating that he knew exactly where Adie was supposed to be going.

"Yes! That's it. Glenn and Sue Robinson. I'm their house sitter, but I haven't a clue how to find the place. I wanted to get there before they left, and I don't know now if that's possible, or whether I'll find it at all." She fought back her tears yet again. The last thing she wanted was for this kind stranger to write her off as the raving basket case she was trying so hard not to be.

But I can't be THAT lost, can I, if this chap knows where it is? It might've been nice if the Robinsons had mentioned the small matter of it being in the middle of bloody nowhere, and nigh-on impossible to find!

"Well, you were heading the right way, as it happens, so if you just keep going the way you were, for another mile or so, you should bang straight into it."

Adie looked dubiously at the disappearing track, and gnawed her bottom lip. The countryman laughed. "Yes, it's a tad narrow in places, and getting worse, since the row about who's meant to maintain it keeps rumbling on with no end in sight. But persevere, and you should get through alright. My brother-in-law comes up once or twice a year with a dozer and widens it out a bit, and I do the same. Makes life a bit easier for a few months at a time, but it's not our land so we don't do any more than that with it. Local authority clearly can't be bothered maintaining it. Makes me wonder what we pay our council tax for, but don't get me started on *that*."

Adie noticed for the first time that the man had a dog with him, a collie cross, possibly a working dog, since it kept out of the way and wasn't as friendly as most domestic dogs Adie had met.

"Are you a farmer around here?" she asked him.

He proffered a weather-beaten hand. "Yes, I am. Bob Shalloe, pleased to make your acquaintance. My wife and I own Bracefields farm. It straddles this end of Torley valley. Ravensdown, where you'll be staying, is on the east side. They have sheep and a few beef cows. Ours is all sheep, two hundred and fifty-four acres."

Adie took his hand. "Adrienne Bostock, just here for a three-week adventure. Very pleased to meet you, Mr Shalloe."

"You can call me Bob, my dear. Most people call me that, if not something worse. Only the dreaded bank manager calls me Mr Shalloe."

He winked at her, and grinned. "Three weeks, hmm? Well. You should call on us for a cup of tea while you're about. My wife Sheila makes a jolly good Parkin, and the best pot of black tea this side of the Lancashire border. She'll be glad to see you, if you come. You can get the directions from Mark Raven, at Ravensdown Farmhouse. It's the bigger place, further up the drive from the cottage. He's my brother-in-law. You can tell him you met me, if you like."

With that, Bob Shalloe tipped his cap and stepped back. Adie gave him a wobbly smile and the thumbs up, put the car into first gear, and doggedly proceeded. A mile down the track, which had widened again just a little, she realised she was still thinking about having met the upbeat weather-beaten farmer, his English gentleman's accent (which stopped just shy of being posh), and his offer of tea and Parkin.

Setting her jaw firmly against the tooth-jarring scraping of ferocious thorns against her car, she made her way around the next few bends in the track and then realised both Bob and the sat-nav had been true to their word. There before her - finally - was a real road, a proper tarmac one with white lines in the centre. And there, just over the crest, she saw a sign saying Ravensdown Farm, with a smaller one saying 'Teapot Cottage' tacked underneath it like an afterthought.

Almost weeping with relief, Adie swung into the long driveway and headed up towards a beautiful modern-looking stone cottage with multi-paned windows. In an odd sort of way, the little place seemed to be holding its arms out to her, and she had the oddest feeling that she couldn't wait to get inside it. If this really was Teapot Cottage, it was gorgeous, and a long way from being a mere 'shepherd's hut,' as Bob Shalloe had modestly described it. She suddenly felt her heart lighten, for the first time in months.

Maybe Miranda was right. Maybe this really is what I need right now. Maybe I can start to feel better here, for a few quiet weeks.

As she drew up in front of the cottage, which actually seemed to be smiling a welcome, Adie saw a tall, lean, red-haired man swinging bags into the back of a white Range Rover. He raised a hand to her in greeting, and called over his shoulder, in a broad Australian accent. "Sue, the house sitter's here."

An incredibly serene-looking woman came wandering out of the house, drying her hands on a tea towel. A small cappuccino-coloured cocker spaniel snapped excitedly at her heels.

The couple, who looked to be in their early thirties, both came forward, smiling from ear to ear. Adie switched off her engine and got out of her car, offering her hand in greeting, and marvelling at how 'at-one-with-the-earth' and joyous her two hosts appeared to be.

"Hi, Glenn, Sue? I'm Adrienne Bostock. Sorry if I'm a bit late, I had an interesting journey down a very tight track to get here and at one point I doubted whether I'd find this place at all!"

Sue laughed. "I bet you used the sat-nav didn't you? I'm so sorry, I never thought to explain. There's a much more hospitable route through the town, from the other side of the pass. That track's the old stockman's route that used to be the back road into the town, eons ago. I'm surprised it's even still marked as a throughfare." She gestured widely towards the direction Adie had come from.

"You just stay on the main road instead of turning off at Bracefields Top, that wonky little junction the sat-nav tells you to turn at. Keep going straight, then you get redirected and brought a much friendlier way! Ah well, you're here now, and not late at all, really."

Glenn piped up "Sue, why don't you show Adrienne around and go through stuff with her, while I finish packing the car, and we can get going?" Adie remembered from their email that they were headed to Melbourne for three weeks. They must be going home.

Sue led Adie towards the cottage. Its solid stone walls and timber window frames had the effect of the elegant 'shepherd's hut' blending seamlessly and beautifully with the land itself.

"Welcome to Teapot Cottage," she said. "We gave it that name after we found a banged-up old enamel teapot buried in the back garden, which we think must have belonged to the shepherds when they used this place for shelter at one time, before we converted it into a dwelling."

And what a stunning 'dwelling' it was! Two elegant multi-paned living room windows, both with seats in front of them, provided a panoramic view of the valley below. A cluster of buildings the colour of the same light grey stone nestled neatly at the bottom. Adie assumed it was Torley town.

The kitchen was cosy and just a little short of being cramped, with a rather daunting-looking bright red two-ringed Aga cooker commanding all the attention on one side of the room. It was the only cooking appliance in evidence in the kitchen. Adie's stomach lurched in panic at the prospect of using it, and she steeled herself not to appear as intimidated by it as she felt. The last thing she wanted was for the Robinsons to be worried that she wouldn't be able to feed herself!

The cottage seemed well-equipped, with an impressive array of pots, pans and utensils in different shapes and sizes hanging from iron hooks hammered into the low-beamed ceiling. A small bay window above a double Belfast sink looked out onto rolling fields at the side of the property where sheep grazed contentedly, here and there, and a small set of French doors at the other end of the room, beyond the dining table, opened out to a small, flagged courtyard enclosed by tall, evergreen hedges. Original old stone floors throughout the cottage's interior were adorned with bright rag rugs, giving the place an air of loved, lived-in cosiness. A fire had been laid in the grate and was waiting to be lit.

"It's all so lovely!" Adie exclaimed.

She followed Sue upstairs to what was to be her bedroom. It was a generous size, and she was delighted with the incredible view from the window, over the multi-coloured, contoured, patterned fields that looked like a patchwork quilt and swept down in a gentle curve towards Torley. From up here an elegant, narrow church spire could just be seen in the distance, in the setting sun

As the two women stood at the window, with Sue explaining how to find the footpath from the side of the cottage and across the fields that led down into town, a wet nose made its way gently and quietly into Adie's left palm. She looked down to the gentle face of the coffee-toned spaniel. He had the biggest, softest, most trusting brown eyes she'd ever seen.

"Well, hello! Aren't you beautiful" she said softly, sinking to her knees to put her arms around the dog, who sat patiently while she buried her face in his fur. When she looked at him again, he gently licked her nose.

"This is Sid," Sue explained. "He's a friendly happy chappie, most of the time. He's very food-focussed, so you can bribe him to do almost anything if you have a treat in your pocket."

Sue indicated a basket full of brochures, maps, and menus for the town's takeaway places. "We're food-focussed too! These places all deliver up here, which is great. I recommend the Chinese, the Flaming Wok. Great chicken Chow Mein from there."

"I'm sure we'll all be just fine", Adie reassured her, relieved that she sounded a lot more confident than she actually felt. "Is there a list of important numbers I might need, just in case?" She thought better of admitting that thanks to the peculiar and maddening phenomenon of what she'd started describing as 'menopausal sponge-brain', nothing got remembered if it wasn't written down.

"Yeah, on the fridge door. Plumber, vet, electrician and so forth. The power's usually good, but there are candles in the sideboard drawers, if the lights go out. The internet's pretty stable and the TV and satellite reception are fine."

Sue went on to say that Mark Raven, the owner of Ravensdown Farm, was on hand if Adie got stuck for anything else. "He's a bit rough around the edges, with the wickedest Lancashire accent you've ever heard, and he comes across as a bit of a grump, but don't let that put you off. He has a good heart. He won't see you stuck. The farm's just further up the drive, a couple of hundred yards or so."

Adie mentioned that she'd already heard about Mark Raven, after meeting his brother-in-law on the track on the way in.

Glenn poked his head around the door and grinned. "All under control? We do have to rattle our dags, if that's ok?" He looked apologetically at Adie. "Thanks for stepping in at short notice, Adrienne. We'd originally planned to have Christmas here this year, with friends we hadn't seen since before the pandemic, but Mum phoned last week to say that my dad's not well, and she's worried, so we managed to get a last-minute flight. It leaves just after midnight so we have to get our skates on." He looked pointedly at his watch.

"Sorry to love you and leave you," Sue sighed, rolling her eyes. "We had our plans all set, then everything changed, and it's all turned into a bit of a rush."

"Oh, I'm glad to be able to help."

Sue nodded. "Yeah, it's still a bit daunting, because that damn disease is still alive and kicking people's butts, and it really wasn't my plan to travel just yet. But we've got our vaccinations up to date, and we'll be as happy as Larry when we see the friends and rellies. We are looking forward to seeing our parents and hugging them all. Please call us over the next few hours about anything at all and we'd love an email update every few days about how the critters are, if you don't mind?"

"Of course," Adie confirmed, with a brisk nod. "Regular updates, complete with photos and video, are all part of the service." She was determined to sound competent, even though it was her first-ever house sit and she was actually a bundle of nerves. But, if this 'gig' went well and she managed to get a good reference,

15

perhaps there would be others. It might not be such a bad way to live for a while. She didn't have anywhere else important to be anymore, and nothing currently tied her to any specific place, unless she counted the short-term lease on the rather cramped and depressing flat in Guildford that she'd taken while she waited for the dust to settle on the rubble, as it were, and for the way forward to become a little clearer.

"Thank you so much, Adrienne. I know it's all in safe hands. Please enjoy everything here and do use up the perishables in the fridge. There's a hot tub out the back, and we've left it turned on for you, so I hope you've brought your swimsuit."

Glenn chuckled. "We don't bother with swimwear Adrienne, and you don't have to if you'd rather not. Nobody's gonna see ya skinny-dipping, way up here."

Sue jumped forward and gave Adie a quick hug, startling her a bit, but causing her to smile at how generous and trusting her hosts were. She was determined not to let them down.

Within minutes they were gone, tooting and waving as they made their way down the drive towards the main road, and from the living room Adie watched their car until it entered the Torley town boundary line and then disappeared from view. The light was fading fast now. It would soon be completely dark.

She lit the fire, made a mug tea, and took it to one of the window seats in the living room, where she sat looking out at the stunning view spread out in front of her, until the little lights of the town started twinkling in the distance. By the time she went to feed the chickens and put them to bed, her mind felt surprisingly soothed.

Total pitch-black darkness came quickly, so did the typical December-night chill. Adie drew the curtains and switched on a couple of lamps, which cast a gentle peachy warm glow across the room. With the fire blazing away, Teapot Cottage felt cosy, homely and safe. It was almost as if the house was *breathing*, not with sound, but with a gentle here-and-yet-not-here vibration; something definitely present, yet so light that Adie couldn't quite put her finger on what it might be, or mean. She wondered, briefly, if she was simply experiencing some kind of new hormonal symptom, or whether she really was losing the plot mentally, as she'd so often feared lately.

She pushed the idea out of her mind, telling herself quite firmly that she already had enough to worry about, without wondering whether or not she was staying in a haunted house!

It's all so cosy, all I need now is a tin bath in front of the fire, she thought to herself. Then she remembered the hot tub and hurried outside to find it, nestled neatly behind the cottage. Surrounded by high hedges, and with pretty solar-powered fairy lights strung all through the greenery like subtle stars, the tub had a distinctly enchanted feel.

Delighted, she lifted the lid, and the temptation to get in and have a soak grew too strong to resist. She quickly shed her clothes and stepped naked into the hot water. Immersed to her shoulders, she lay back and let the bubbles caress her, not caring that her hair was getting wet, or that she had no towel, or that she hadn't even considered making herself anything to eat, or that the fire might die completely in the living room grate.

A strange sense of peace enveloped her. All the anxiety she'd been feeling for months now just drifted quietly away, and for the first time that she could remember, her head felt clear of the fog that constantly clouded her brain. Jumbled thoughts, pain and confusion, sadness, despair, anger and haywire hormones had all held a vice-like grip on her for too many months. Lately, the roller-coaster of emotional and biological turmoil had repeatedly caused her to wonder whether she was going slowly mad, or whether she'd ever be truly happy again.

But here, on this night, content for once in her own company, Adie felt the beginnings of a new hope for something better. The solitude seemed peaceful and benign here, instead of oppressive and threatening, as it had felt almost everywhere else. She couldn't put her finger on it but something had tilted tonight, ever-so-slightly, on its axis. At last, finally, here was a glimpse of how life might be, going forward.

Might everyone find a way to forgive me, in time? Might I find a way to forgive myself? For once the possibility seemed real, and Adie quietly understood the significance of it. Four hours in, and the healing had already begun.

Chapter 2

Mark Raven stopped his tractor but left the engine running as he watched a small silver hatchback car weave its way slowly up the drive from the main road. He wasn't expecting anyone, and people didn't typically turn up randomly at Ravensdown Farm uninvited. But there again, some cheeky sods did feel they somehow had the right to ignore the four separate 'private property' signs along his driveway. They'd go on to park their cars directly outside his otherwise private house, if you please, before taking the public walking track that ran alongside the barn and wound around the upper levels of the farm, all the way up to the small historic Tor that had given the town its name.

Of all the things Mark hated the most about people's right of access across his land, in the ancient tradition that most other farmers in England had to put up with just as grudgingly, it wasn't that so many of them ignored polite farm signs, left important gates ajar, or dropped the remnants of their picnics all over the place. Those things were bad enough, but what riled Mark the most was the entitlement some of them felt they had, to just park in front of Ravensdown House, creating an eyesore for him to stare at from his living room windows and – more importantly - blocking the access to some of his fields. It never ceased to amaze him how many people were clearly capable of driving but apparently incapable of reading a series of signs that told them in simple enough terms what they could and shouldn't do. There had been a wonderful hiatus during the recent pandemic, when lockdowns had prevented most people from rambling. Visitors had been very few, and they'd mostly been local people, who knew how to respect a farmer's land. But things had gone back to normal, with ignorant fools from far and wide now returning in droves.

Mebbe I need to get a bloody gate up, an' stop t'buggers fer once and fer all!

He wondered if whoever was in the hatchback might be here to see his daughter Feen, although she hadn't mentioned expecting anyone. In fact, as Mark knew, she was still out anyway, having driven into Torley to meet her best mate, Josie Valley. The two had planned lunch and a girly mooch around the shops over in Carlisle.

He worried about Feen a lot, always feeling that she never got out as much as she should, for a girl of her age, and he was glad she'd gone to meet her friend. Ravensdown Farm wasn't as remote as many in the area were, but the place was still a fair hike from a lot of the social opportunities Feen should be freely enjoying at the tender age of twenty-two. Mark thought she should at least be dating by now, but there hadn't been a sniff of interest for well over two years from his daughter towards any of the young men in the district. Nor, to be fair, had any of them come knocking. The pandemic hadn't helped, but Mark suspected that even without it, the local pickings were pretty slim for romance.

Seraphine Raven was what most people - if they were being kind - would describe as 'an unusual young woman.' Those who were less than kind just called her crazy. She didn't have a harmful bone in her body, but a lot of folk did regarded her as pretty strange. An ethereal dreaminess prevailed upon her, more often than not, coupled with the strong affinity she had with the natural world, and the magnetic pull that plants, trees and flowers seemed to have for her. She also spoke in *riddles* more often than not, which either made people laugh or left them scratching their heads with confusion. Sadly, most folks who didn't know Feen well simply wrote her off, kindly or otherwise, as an oddity best kept clear of.

She didn't seem to mind too much. And as for meeting men, Feen seemed far more at home ferreting around for hemlock in hedgerows, or boiling up a foul-smelling poultice for someone in Torley town who had an ulcer on their leg, than she was sitting across a table having a drink and trying to make conversation with a bloke she barely knew.

That had all been fine and dandy for long enough, but Mark was surprised now, at how hard he longed for a sea-change. His beloved wife and soulmate Beth had died from bowel cancer eight years earlier, leaving him torn apart with a grief he thought he'd never fully come to terms with, and faced with the terrifying task of raising their decidedly weird only child alone. Acutely conscious of how inept he'd felt for such a Herculean task, he'd been dumbstruck at how deep the dread had been, that Feen would end up going off the rails somehow, or coming home in a heartbroken (or worse) condition thanks to some self-serving dead-beat. All he'd wanted to do was lock her away, out of harm's way, forever.

Mercifully his fear had faded, over time, as Feen had gradually grown up. All he wanted now, for the beautiful young daughter he was so profoundly proud of was love, and a family of her own.

He wondered again who was visiting unannounced. He wasn't expecting Feen back for hours yet. The little silver car wasn't hers, and it wasn't Josie's, unless she'd changed it since last week.

Mark waited for the car to draw level with the field he was working in, but it didn't, and he quickly realised it must have pulled up in front of Teapot Cottage instead. He recalled that the Robinsons had a house sitter arriving to take care of the place while they went to Australia to see their parents. *Is it today? It must be!*

He hadn't thought much about the Robinson's plans, but he'd been slightly alarmed when Glenn had asked him if the house sitter could go to him for help, if the need arose. Of course he'd said yes, but he did wonder if the 'middle-aged woman' who seemed to have landed was likely to be a needy sort. He hoped not. He certainly wouldn't see anyone struggle in a crisis, but he didn't have time to be at someone's beck and call over silly little things. Whoever she was, he hoped she'd be reasonably self-sufficient at least.

As he shifted the last of the hay bales into the corner of the field by the gate, his mind drifted back to his daughter. He hoped Feen was having fun with Josie. He recalled his own twenties, and how he'd almost never been at home. He'd had a great social life in Lancashire, with his beloved Beth, and with friends they'd known back then. They were always out somewhere, drinking, dancing, going camping, and such like. He hoped Feen still had all that to come, although he doubted whether she'd ever be much of a party animal.

It still defied Mark Raven to fully describe his daughter in any way that might do her justice, other than to say she had a unique perspective on the world that most other people couldn't relate to. She'd taken after her mother, who'd been psychic to some degree but had never been fully comfortable with the fact. Feen was more adjusted and receptive to the 'gifts' she had inherited from Beth. Mark couldn't really fathom Feen's ability to read minds and predict future events with no prior knowledge of the people involved. His sister Sheila probably explained it best, by saying that Feen could somehow access a 'portal' to a world most other people couldn't see into or understand.

When Mark had confessed to his wife how anxious he was about the impact on the child, of being so different, Beth had simply shrugged, saying that Feen just vibrated to a different frequency, that was all, and it didn't matter if nobody understood it, as long as they respected it and didn't judge her on being unable to help who she was. As simple as that seemed to Beth, it felt a whole lot more complicated and unfeasible to the down-to-earth and endlessly practical Mark, but it wouldn't have helped to have said so.

To give Feen full credit, she navigated life pretty well. She liked certain people, and tolerated others, but anyone she didn't like was usually left in no doubt about it, or the reasons why, because she didn't have much of a filter, and it did occasionally get her into trouble, as she was still learning to reign in her thoughts – and other people's for that matter – before blurting out whatever was on her mind about them. Mark had been left puce-faced and cringing with embarrassment on countless occasions after Feen had waded in on someone's private musings and unwittingly exposed them. She was improving, but she still had a long way to go before winning any awards for tact or diplomacy. She was still learning the full nuances of life being a lot more complicated for others than it appeared to be for her.

Beth's passing had ripped Mark's world to pieces. He hadn't been prepared for the force of his grief, for how much it had overwhelmed him, or for how long. Losing the one true love of his life had been brutal, but as he quickly discovered, being bereaved of his soulmate was only the beginning of his journey.

Friends and family had stepped up, rallied round, and done their level best to help Mark bring up his daughter, but his road had still been a sad and lonely one to walk. He'd lost count of the nights he'd lain awake, agonising over whether he was doing a decent job of raising his gentle, ethereal child to survive in the real world, when all she really wanted to do was run around in the forest with the birds and badgers.

But he'd managed it, and he'd been well rewarded for his dedication. Feen Raven was the absolute spit of her mother, so much so that his heart still sometimes momentarily stopped when she walked into the room. She was almost spookily beautiful, but she was also very clever, and gentle and patient – especially with him. That counted for something special, when a fifty-four-year-old man, stumbling inexorably towards old age, grumpiness and solitude, could be so well-understood and cherished by his only child.

Yes, Feen Raven loved to pick wildflowers and make herbal remedies with what she might find on the farm and in the forest. She loved to create woodland habitats for every creature that might conceivably want to make its home there, and she loved to sit in the low-hanging bough of a favourite tree and spend the entire day absorbed in a book.

But thanks to Mark she also knew how to change the plug on a table lamp, replace an electrical fuse or a washer on a tap, change a tyre, fit a new air filter to a tractor then drive it, paint a ceiling or a wall, and hang a picture. She could conjure up a feast fit for any decent restaurant, help a struggling ewe deliver a lamb, harvest hay, put a barn door back on its hinges and grow vegetables.

She was going to be just fine in the real world. She just needed to spend more time in it, that was all.

Mark hoped that today's girls' day out with Josie would lead to many more. Secretly, he was living for the night Feen might come home roaring drunk. It was a while since he'd had a good laugh, and that would probably do it.

Twenty minutes later, when he'd finished loading the newly delivered bales of silage into the barn, Mark finally parked his tractor and switched off the engine. It was good to get that job finished today, so the last of the animals' winter feed was all secure. As he was shutting the barn door, he heard voices carrying on the wind. Two car doors slammed, and he heard the unmistakable rattle of Glenn Robinson's diesel Range Rover as it started up. Clearly, the couple were on their way.

By the time he'd fed the dogs and was on his way back to the farmhouse, the light was fading fast. Mark could feel his muscles aching. He was acutely aware that he'd slowed down a lot in the last few years, and everything he did took a lot longer than it had when he'd been in his prime. His body was singing to him (well, more like howling at him) in all sorts of ways, reminding him more and more often, that he didn't still have the strength or stamina he'd had even just a couple of years earlier. The problem was, he didn't want to listen. He just wasn't ready for growing old.

I'm still only thirty, in me 'ead!

Ageing was a bastard. There were no two ways about it. He idly wondered if a trip to the doctor might be in order. His 'yearly MOT', as he described it, was very overdue. He vaguely remembered the last one as being pre-Covid. It wouldn't hurt to visit his old friend Doc Barnes for a check-up, just to be satisfied that he wasn't about to morph into a shambling human wreck just yet. Doc Barnes might even have a few suggestions for how he could ease the generalised aches and pains that were starting to besiege him more and more, at the end of the working day. Mark could probably even talk to Feen, and get her to make him one of her disgusting (but apparently effective) herbal tonics. Whichever way he looked at it, he wasn't the man he used to be, and it was time to admit it to people who could help him do something about it.

He stopped for a moment and watched as a few tendrils of smoke started spiralling out of the chimney at Teapot Cottage. The house sitter had wasted no time in getting the fire going, and he didn't blame her one bit.

Well, it's good to know she's capable o' that, at least.

As the shadows had lengthened in the dwindling afternoon, the air had turned decidedly nippy. Darkness had nearly swallowed the day now. Mark was looking forward to getting cleaned up and sitting in his favourite chair, getting warm in front of his own roaring fire, with a lovely hot pot of tea. Feen said she'd bring a chippie tea home, which he thought was an excellent plan, and he was surprised at how much he was looking forward to his chips and curry sauce, and hearing about his daughter's day out.

Chapter 3

The early morning brought dense fog. Adie was disappointed. She'd slept like a log after coming in from the hot tub and staggering upstairs to bed. She'd been looking forward to her first morning view from her bedroom window, but was gutted to find she couldn't see more than ten feet from the cottage in any direction, thanks to the misty cocoon it was wrapped in.

Stupid fog! She muttered under her breath. She was thankful though, that for the first night in more than a month, she hadn't suffered a saturating night-sweat. Waking up wet through, in the middle of the night, and having no choice but to get up and change her sheets and pyjamas and then try to go back to sleep, had become a wretched routine occurrence. Even when the kids were small, she'd never done so much washing!

She padded downstairs, and realised with a jolt that she was starving. Eating hadn't been high on her list of priorities for months now, and skipping dinner last night wasn't at all unusual. The fact that she had an appetite this morning, well, *that* was unusual!

Adie drew back the curtains on the miserable morning, and a soupy half-light filtered into the room. She filled the kettle and set it onto the Aga's right hotplate to boil, called a reluctant, sleepy Sid to come and attend to his morning ablutions, and then went to let the chickens out. Their enthusiasm at being freed for the day immediately lifted her mood and made her laugh. The cat, Mittens, was nowhere to be seen. Adie figured she'd show up, as cats are wont to do, when she was good and ready and not before.

Over a delicious breakfast of fresh scrambled eggs and some smoked salmon she'd found in the fridge, and a rich pot of coffee made with a gigantic aluminium stove-top percolator that looked like it belonged an Italian cafe, she decided that fog or no fog, she would walk down to Torley town. She would take Sid with her, and see what was on offer. She hoped there'd be a cafe, and a bakery or store where she could get some bread, which would be a jolly good start, and there might even be a newsagent where she could get a Sunday paper.

Adie quickly closed her eyes against an unexpected wave of emotion. One of the morning rituals she had always observed with Bryan was reading the Sunday papers together, over coffee and toast. Since the split, she hadn't even thought about a Sunday paper, and she suspected that even if she had, it might have been too painful a memory to indulge in. Even now, the thought of reading a Sunday paper brought a lump to her throat, but at least she *was* thinking about it. That was progress, surely?

To Adie's delight, little Sid was an absolute pleasure to walk. He was well trained and obedient, although she wasn't prepared to let him off the lead yet. The prospect of losing him in the fog was unthinkable.

The path was clear, even with limited visibility, and seemed to be a well-worn route for ramblers. Stiles were all well-maintained, fences were neat and tidy, and someone had put gravel down in several places where the ground beneath had turned to mud.

As she wandered along, Adie's thoughts drifted towards her husband. She knew she should have confided in Bryan right from the very beginning about giving birth to Ruth and adopting her out, when she was still more or less a child herself. He wouldn't have deserted her; she knew that now. In fact, had she been completely honest with herself when she should have been, she had *always* known it.

What she still *didn't* know, was what had held her back from ever telling him. Over the last few months of soul-searching, she'd trotted all the motives out for examination. Shame, embarrassment, anger at her parents for assuming they knew best, anger at herself for not being strong enough to stand up to them, fear of being judged for her anger, or condemned for abandoning her child, and endless other reasons or excuses for never having told her husband what had happened when she was just fifteen.

Even at the point when it became clear to Adie that she was about to lose everything, she still couldn't explain properly to Bryan exactly why she'd never told him. If she could have, she would have, and even if her marriage had still ended, at least he would have understood her.

Something had held her back. Even though she didn't know what it was, at least she recognised now that there had been some kind of barrier to making that big confession. That was a big step forward at least, but the same questions she'd asked herself a thousand times kept spinning around in her head.

Bryan was often distracted, nearly always focussed on work, and she *had* tried, at different times, to talk to him about 'big stuff'. She always did so in the hope that it might lead to a platform that felt safe to start the *really* big conversation, about the biggest thing of all. But Bryan usually cut her off at the pass, because – according to him - anything his wife might want to bleat about was always less important than what was going on in his job. He'd been grumpy whenever she tried to insist, so she'd got used to letting things drop. It was easier than trying to persevere with a preoccupied husband who clearly thought that unless something was important to *him*, it wasn't important at all.

But Adie's reluctance to confide in him about Ruth and all the subterfuge around moving next door to her, after keeping her a secret for the entire length of their marriage, had been more than just a fear that he might not listen. They'd been married for more than a quarter of a century, yet she'd never in all that time felt she could trust him with her secret.

Why not? What was it really, that stopped me from talking to him? What was I really afraid of?

As hard as she tried to understand her own emotional paralysis, she never came up with any answers. It still hadn't occurred to her that she shouldn't be so hard on herself. She still hadn't realised that the chronic insecurity and the deep sense of vulnerability that left her unable to explain herself to her furious and hurt husband, even at the end, had been a lot less self-inflicted than anything she'd already fretted about for decades. It had been caused, mostly, by the chemical imbalance that had stripped away her confidence as she started going through the change of life.

When Adie climbed the next stile, she was surprised to find herself and Sid in a car park at the back of a public house. Where had the time gone? Lost in her own musings, she also hadn't

26

noticed that the fog had started lifting too. A weak and watery sun was half-heartedly starting to battle its way through.

When she rounded the building and looked at the heavy sign hanging from chains at the front entrance, she burst out laughing. The pub was called the Bull and Royal, and it's cheeky sign depicted a highly indignant, stomping bull, angrily trying to shake off a crown that was wrapped around one of its horns. A chalk-board sign at the side of the door proclaimed the pub to be hiker and muddy-dog friendly, and invited bookings for Sunday lunch. Not all village pubs had survived the recent pandemic, but this one had, and was clearly a well-patronised and important hub for the town.

She glanced at her watch, and was surprised to see that she'd made it down the valley in less than twenty minutes. A cuppa at a cafe seemed more appropriate than anything bigger, so early in the day, so she made her way along the High Street, until she saw a cheerful little sandwich sign down Amble Walk that read 'Ye Old Torley Tea Shoppe.' The small quaint cafe had net curtains, and old-fashioned teacup sets on display at the front of the window. Trying not to cringe at the stereotype but feeling overjoyed that it was actually open on a Sunday, Adie opened the door, stuck her head around it, and asked if it was ok to bring a dog into the premises.

The woman at the counter was roughly Adie's age, and she beamed widely at her.

"Of course! Sid's a regular here. Please, do come in! I've been hoping you'd come. Sue comes in here quite a bit with little Siddy, and she did say she was getting a house sitter for when they went away. It's Mrs Bostock, isn't it? I'm Margaret Wilde, but people around here call me Peg."

She stuck out her hand, shook Adie's with real warmth. "Fancy a brew, then?" she enquired.

"Yes please, Peg. Earl Grey tea if you have it, with a bit of milk on the side. And those date scones look spectacular, so I'll have one of those as well, with butter please. I've had my breakfast, but all of a sudden I feel ravenous again," Adie chuckled, embarrassed.

"Well, that's no surprise, love, especially if you've come across them foggy fields. It's the air around here, it tends to spike

27

folks' appetites. The scones are home made, and the pies are too, if you wanted to take one home for your tea tonight. I've steak and kidney, minced beef and cheddar cheese, chicken and mushroom, or veggie. You can just bang it in the Aga for half an hour. You'll probably get two meals out if it."

Adie glanced at the chunky family-sized pies that sat in the cafe showcase. *Minced beef and cheese? What an odd combination!*

"Oh, they do look delicious! What would you recommend?"

Peg answered with no hesitation. "Minced beef and cheddar is my personal favourite, although there's folks around here that would argue black and blue for the others."

"They all look good, Peg. I'll take a beef and cheese. I'm curious to try it, and no doubt I'll get chance to sample the others while I'm here for the next few weeks."

"Yes love, and then you can make an informed choice on your favourite."

Peg winked at her then disappeared. She quickly came back with a tin bowl of water for Sid. She also gave him a dog biscuit, which he quickly crunched before settling down onto the floor with his front paws set out before him. Delighted, Adie though his good manners were probably better than most people's.

After she had polished off her tea and food, she watched Peg wrap a delicious-looking pie in heavy grease-proof paper and tie it with string before handing it to her with a flourish. So traditional! Adie was thrilled. Peg slipped Sid another biscuit as they left the tea shop, and at her insistence to come back soon, Adie assured her she would. She meant it too, having felt very welcomed and relaxed in Peg's charming little teashop.

Back out in the street, she located the local newsagent, and picked up a couple of Sunday papers, a word search puzzle book, and a small box of Belgian chocolates as a treat. She was amazed to find that her appetite was returning, and with so much force. Only now was she realising that she hadn't eaten properly for months.

The bakery was closed so she called into a fairly decent sized grocery store, amused by the self-important sign that declared it a 'supermarket'. She selected a couple of bottles of wine, one of tonic water and a hipflask of good quality gin. She also picked up two lemons, a decent packet of coffee, and a loaf of bread. The one carrier bag she'd brought with her was now completely full. With four bottles and the big pie, papers, coffee and bread, it was bulging and heavy, so regretfully she decided not to allow herself to be tempted by anything else. She figured that tomorrow would do, to drive into the town to stock up on other provisions. She had all she needed for today.

Adie also saw a hairdressing salon across the road, called 'Torley Tresses.' It was closed. She made a mental note to give them a call the following morning to see if she could, by some incredible fluke, get a pre-Christmas appointment. She was aware that she needed some serious help. Her brunette waist-length locks had always been her pride and joy, but her hair was such a mess right now, with its lustre all but gone, overwhelmed by lack of care. It had thinned a lot too, over the past year, probably as a symptom of her plummeting oestrogen levels, and she couldn't even remember when she'd last had it trimmed.

Even when salons had reopened, after the lockdowns, her appearance hadn't been high on her list of priorities. With customers stampeding to get their hair done again properly for the first time in many months, most salons had instantly been booked up for weeks in advance. Adie hadn't felt inclined to join the hordes and had more or less forgotten about her hair. It now looked distinctly drab, vaguely wild, and peppered with streaks of seriously unwelcome grey. Horrified, it dawned on her that her lack of interest in herself actually dated back to well before she'd even split up with Bryan.

When did I stop caring?

Behind her back, the more gossipy of her erstwhile 'friends' would probably be bitching that she'd let herself go in recent years, but she had to concede that they'd be absolutely right. Would they also be right if they were saying as well that no man wanted to stick around with a wife who didn't really seem to give a monkey's what she looked like?

Adie's mind had simply been on other things, and for far too long. Now, catching her reflection in the mirror above the counter in the salon as she peered through its closed door, she suddenly felt an overwhelming need to sort out the mess she'd allowed herself to become. It was time to start looking a bit more human and a bit less like she'd been dragged through a hedge backwards.

I'm going to get a full overhaul as soon as they can fit me in, maybe in time for the New Year or just after.

Halfway up the hill she had to stop for a moment and put her heavy bag down, as another hot flush swamped her. She took the opportunity to turn to look back at the little town. It really wasn't much more than a village really, but she felt sure its people would be proud of its 'town' status. They might be properly offended if she referred to it as a village. People in small places could be a bit precious about their environment. She'd have to watch out for that.

The rear of the Bull and Royal was still clearly visible, with many of the mechanics of the working business clearly in view. Barrels were stacked by the back door, next to two buckets and various cleaning implements. A mini skip overflowed with empty bottles, and a soggy crush of cardboard boxes over in one corner had clearly sat there through at least one good bout of rain.

Quite the metaphor for life, Adie mused. *Always more going on behind the scenes than what you can see at the front.*

She arrived back at the cottage gate panting. She was exhausted, and her fingers were painful and white with the strain of holding her heavy plastic bag, but she felt an amazing sense of satisfaction at having trudged for a full forty minutes uphill with a heavy load of shopping.

We did it, she thought gleefully, *although next time I might take two bags, to spread the load a bit and keep myself balanced.*

As she and Sid approached the front door she saw a small hessian bag, with a yellow smiley-face logo on the front, propped against it. On closer inspection she was delighted to find the most magnificent round Parkin cake! She beamed with delight. Bob Shalloe had evidently dropped by, or perhaps his wife had, and left her a welcoming gift. What a lovely surprise! Adie could smell the ginger and treacle wafting through the faded blue linen tea towel the cake was wrapped in, and her mouth watered. It was lunchtime!

After a large mug of coffee, a cold slice of the minced beef and cheese pie (which turned out to be gorgeous) and a hefty wedge of the Parkin, she felt quite sleepy.

This isn't like me, she thought, *eating for England and feeling all drowsy, but I wonder if I should just give in, and have a quick nap?*

It was Sunday, after all. Then she remembered the newspapers in her bag. She decided to get the fire going again, curl up on the window seat, and have a read.

It doesn't matter if I fall asleep, does it?

And that's exactly what Adie ended up doing; nodding off, safe in the gentle, cocoon-like embrace of the beautiful quiet cottage, replete with wonderful home-made food and lashings of hot sweet tea.

What woke her, almost an hour later, was being landed on most unceremoniously, by a very happy, purring little tabby cat, who had evidently decided it was time to come home. She head-butted Adie gently then started to trample the newspaper that had been lying half across her lap.

"Mittens, I presume?"

A sharp knock at the front door startled her. As she got up to answer it, yawning, she suddenly realised that a whole 24 hours had gone by since her arrival and in that time, she'd slept like a log, taken a hike, somehow managed to get her appetite back, and braved the purchase of a Sunday paper! What was even more astonishing was that she hadn't cried once since she'd arrived at Teapot Cottage. That had to be a record. Until she got here, she'd cried roughly a river a day.

Acknowledging these exponential leaps of progress, she grinned to herself. The smile must have still been playing around her mouth as she opened the door, because the tiny dark-haired young woman standing on the doorstep initially looked slightly anxious but broke straight into a wide and generous smile of her own on seeing Adie.

"Hello!" she cried. "You're the house-sitter, am I right? I'm Seraphine Raven, and I live up at Ravensdown Farm."

She gestured elaborately up into the air. "I want to gather some herbs from the hedges along the driveway before it goes dark, if that's alright, and I thought I should come and tell you first, so you wouldn't wonder who I was or what on earth I was doing Glue and Senn are used to me pottering about, but you won't be." She stuck out her hand. Adie took it, bemused, and shook it gently.

The diminutive girl – size six at best - had almost blue-black hair halfway down her back, in a long, straight, glorious curtain. She had the most beautiful blue eyes Adie had ever seen, framed by incredibly long, thick, sooty lashes. She carried a small wicker basket over her arm, and Adie noted a white cotton blouse with voluminous long sleeves, and a dark blue woollen pinafore over the top with a long full skirt and black lacing up the front of the bodice. A pair of ankle boots with buttons up the side completed the outfit, making her look like she'd just stepped out of a historical novel. All she really needed was a pointed hat.

She looks interesting, Adie thought to herself. *A bit like a white witch!*

"That's exactly what I am!" cried the girl. "A white witch! A lot of people laugh at me, but they still keep coming back for my terbal honics." Her eyes twinkled with good natured mirth.

Dumbfounded, Adie started at her. Seraphine stifled a giggle. "I read minds too! Actually, it's more like a fradio requency kind of thing. I just pick up on things sometimes, thought-waves, or something. But I don't catch everything, so please don't worry. Your thoughts are safe - well, mostly!" She giggled again.

Adie didn't know what to think, but she was aware that she was holding the door open and staring open-mouthed at this very odd little creature who had turned up from out of nowhere and had an incredibly strange way of speaking. She remembered her manners.

"Oh, hello, um – Seraphine? I'm Adrienne. Please come in."

The girl smiled and gracefully stepped through the door. "Only if you're not busy," she said more shyly now. "I don't want to intrude. And please call me Feen."

"You're not intruding, lovely. I'd enjoy some company for a bit, if you've time for a quick cuppa?" Even as she said the words, Adie marvelled at how eager she suddenly was for a visitor, after months of wanting to hide herself away from the world, wishing she would never have to speak at length to another human being ever again.

"Ooh yes, I'd love that! Thank you. Glue has some rooibos tea up the cupboard, I think. She usually makes me a cup of that whenever I pop in."

She slipped off her dainty little boots, put down her basket, and settled herself at the kitchen table while Adie located the rooibos and set about making a pot of tea.

A very pleasant three quarters of an hour was then spent, with Feen doing most of the talking, darting from topic to topic. It kept Adie a little on the hop, and caused her to struggle several times not to laugh at Feen's easy, natural, and very clever use of Spoonerism; transposing the consonants on a pair of words.

Feen was twenty-two, and lived at home with her father, Mark Raven, the owner of Ravensdown Farm, who Adie had already heard a bit about. She learned that he was widowed. Feen had lost her mother to bowel cancer eight years earlier.

"Mum being so ill made me think about how I could help her with things other than drugs", she explained. "Since I was a little girl, I've been fascinated by flants and plowers, but I wasn't very scientifically or academically minded, I'm afraid, so I could never have become a botanist or anything like that. It was all I could do to graduate from high school, to be honest." She shrugged her tiny shoulders.

"It's not that I was dumb or anything, but Mum being ill, well, that distracted me a lot, and not just until she died. My mind wasn't on my schoolwork for a long time after, either. But I've been making things like tandelion dea, and herbal poultices since I first understood what they could do. I got a lot of information from my andmother Gralice."

Feen went on to explain, "she's Mum's mother. She's in a rest home now, has been for years. Daddy found her a place fairly locally, after it became obvious that we couldn't take care of her properly at home anymore. She's quite doo-lally mostly, bless her, although on some occasions she's surprisingly lucid." Feen stopped for breath and then carried on.

"Anny Gralice is a white witch, herself. Mum had the gift, but I don't think she ever really trusted it, or used it as often or as well as she might have." Feen sipped her tea, pensively. "I think she felt it to be more of a hindrance, to be honest; a distraction she didn't really want."

There was no stopping the young woman as she talked, and Adie felt mesmerised, and more than happy to just sit and listen, as she rattled on.

"But I'm very lucky to have inherited a lot of tanny's gralent, which I'm so grateful for, as it meant I could help Mum. Some of the things I tried did make a difference, helped ease her pain, that sort of thing. She battled for three years but lost the fight when I was fourteen." Feen stopped long enough to take a good couple of swallows of her tea, before continuing.

"It took a long time for the fog to lift", she admitted, "but a couple of years after that, it finally did. Daddy struggled too, in fact he still does at times, but he's also very wise, and he'd been telling me for a long time, even before Mum died, that I needed to find a focus and do something for myself. So, I've trained properly as a herbalist and aromatherapist. I use flants and plowers, to make lotions and potions that do help a lot of people."

It transpired that Feen made a reasonable living from her work, as she had clients online as well as in the local towns. She also made a bit of flower-based jewellery from time to time, which Adie found intriguing, but Feen didn't elaborate on that. She admitted that some people did regard her as a bit of an oddity, but she seemed to be quite used to it and didn't seem to be unduly affected by it.

"When you're different, it's easiest just to accept that you are, and excuse people for being mean or dismissive, because it mostly just comes from an ace of plignorance." Feen explained, with a light shrug. "That's how I see it, anyway."

The young woman seemed remarkably relaxed, easy-going and philosophical. She had grown up on Ravensdown Farm, and all the locals knew her. By all accounts, few people minded her ferreting about in their hedges and gardens. Some found it amusing, some recognised it as valid work, and others simply ignored it. Nobody gave her a hard time, at least not to her face.

"Seraphine. That's a very interesting name," Adie observed.

"Yes, it's biblical, actually. It means 'fiery angel'! Apparently, I arrived lawling my bungs out and was quite a belligerent baby. It was Granny's suggestion that Mum call me Seraphine, so she did, although none of us were particularly religious. But I'm not at all biery or felligerent now," she added.

34

"No, I can see that" Adie chuckled. She felt very at ease with Feen, like she had already known her for years. Adie knew how flighty some twenty-two-year-old girls could be, but even with her air of irrepressibility, this one exuded a calm, peace and wisdom that was quite rare in someone her age. Adie's own daughter Theresa, at the same age, was far less self-assured and grounded.

"What are you looking for, in the middle of winter, in the hedgerows?" she enquired.

"Oh, you'd be surprised at what's out there at all times of the year!" Feen exclaimed, clearly warming to her topic. "Everything looks dead, but it's not really. I gather the lovely rat fosehips, after an autumn frost, for fea and tace-cream. There are hawthorn berries at this time of year, which are good for jam and for poultices that help inflammation, and tonic potions made with them help women's problems too, things like period cramps. There are also still one or two late sloes around, and of course they make good gin, but they come from the blackthorn bush, and the bark of the blackthorn makes a really good soat throother, in wintertime."

She went on to explain her belief that nature provided exactly what people need to help with general and season-specific ailments. Feen believed in the power of the earth and mother nature and that whatever diseases, illnesses and allergies existed, the remedies were also all present, but in many cases still waiting to be identified. The young woman's excitement and passion for her craft were plain to see, and Adie found it all incredibly interesting.

Feen had initially come across as quite literally away with the fairies, with what some might write off as 'mumbo-jumbo' about mind-reading and magic potions. But in general conversation she swung regularly and easily between that and some very intelligent, insightful and wise commentary about the human condition and how the world should be fixed. She was quite something.

She talked a bit about her father, Mark Raven. "He's a bit of a grump these days, to be honest. Etting golder does that to a man, I guess, especially one who's lonely. He really is, although he doesn't realise that himself, and he'd bite my head off if I suggested it to him." She grinned and rolled her eyes.

"But it doesn't help that he has to be cajoled into being sociable, these days. He's so wrapped up in the farm, he never thinks about anything else. He forgets his own birthday, most years, and I have to literally drag him to the pub for a pint and an ite to beat."

Adie could have listened to Feen for much longer, but the young woman suddenly looked at the clock above the Aga and jumped to her feet. She quickly drained her mug of tea.

"Yikes! I need to get going! I have doads to loo, and I'll lose the light before I'm done if I'm not careful."

Adie stood up too. "Feen, thank you so much for stopping by. It's been lovely to meet you, and I do hope you'll come again."

She really meant it. This lovely, fascinating little woman had been a delightful breath of fresh air, with her hilarious, clever penchant for Spoonerism. After swilling around in her own miserable company for far too long already, uninterested in really talking or listening to anyone even vaguely cheerful, Adie was amazed - and profoundly grateful - to be feeling so uplifted by this witchy little Feen.

Feen leaned against the front door jamb to pull her boots on.

"You were gently but very deliberately drawn to this place, Adrienne", she said unexpectedly. "It's no andom raccident that you're here. You are *meant* to be here. There's a very special vibrational energy here that comes directly from deep down in the earth. Ley lines", she added, almost to herself. Then she shook her head quickly.

"I'll tell you about them another time. But it's why you've been pulled here. You have healing to do, and this is where it will happen. You'll leave here feeling like a different person. If you leave here at all, that is.

"Oh, by the way, you're menopausal and quite fed up with it, aren't you? I can make you a potion that might help, if you like. I'll drop something off, in case you want to try it. Oh, and you must come up to the farm for coffee, sometime soon. You really must meet Daddy." She smiled gently and opened the front door.

Adie was again dumbfounded, and more than a little embarrassed. As excruciating as Feen's off-the-cuff, random reference to her change-of life was, she was more concerned with what else the tiny woman had said.

If I leave here at all? What's that supposed to mean? Am I destined to end up under the floorboards, or something?

But before she could say a word, or ask Feen what she meant by her mysterious remark, the tiny young woman had given Adie a quick but surprisingly strong hug, and closed the conversation. "I'll see you soon. Bye for now."

And in the next second, she had literally disappeared from the front door, mercurially, as if she'd never been there in the first place.

Chapter 4

With his sister's admonishing words still ringing in his ear, Mark hung up the phone. Bloody Sheila and her bloody insistence that the bloody Christmas party goes ahead again! Every year it was the same conversation, and every year he lost the argument. He told himself he should be used to it by now, never getting his own way with the women in his life, but he'd never been able to get to grips with how he always ended up feeling like he'd been firmly put back in his box, with the lid shut tight on him.

Mark Raven wasn't a pushover by anyone's standards, but he did know when he was beaten. He did recognise a lost cause when he was attempting to fight one, and this year (like every other year), he bowed to the inevitable and set about girding his loins for what was coming.

Before Beth had died, there had been a long-standing tradition at Ravensdown Farm that she and Mark hosted a party on Christmas night. Christmas lunch was exclusively for family, usually Bob and Sheila and their boy, and the parents that had still been alive and *compos-mentis* at the time, but later in the evening a party would take place for anyone who wanted to come.

The tradition was that everyone who came brought food for the buffet table, while the Ravens supplied the alcohol. Over the years the party became the focal point of many people's Christmas, particularly the other farmers in the area who were often too busy, even in the depths of winter, to make much effort with festivities at home. They appreciated the opportunity to be "Christmassy" without having to go to any real trouble, and since for many it was the only time of year when they really saw one another socially for long enough to have a decent catch-up, it was always a raucous and jolly affair.

As most people were leaving the party, they'd be muttering about what food they'd bring to the next one, a year ahead. The farm's kitchen fridges and freezers would be groaning under the weight of the leftover food until well into the new year. There was never any problem in polishing off the leftover alcohol though, because there never seemed to be quite as much of that.

Beth had adored Christmas. It was her favourite time of year, and she always went all-out, decorating the entire house fit for a magazine cover, welcoming people into her home with real enthusiasm and warmth, and setting up the "secret Santa" system for the annual party, where everyone bought a small unisex gift and put it in a decorated sack just inside the front door, so that everyone could receive an anonymous gift. For many of their guests it was the highlight of the evening, wondering what useful, silly or baffling gift they'd get, then trying to guess who might have bought it.

Mark had grown to love the Christmas party as much as everyone else. However, after his wife's death, his interest in socialising had more or less collapsed. He was happy to still have the occasional dinner with friends and family, either at home or down at the Bull and Royal or at the town's other pub, The Feathers, but that was about it. The first year after Beth had died, he hadn't invited anyone to a party. At the time, it had felt like it would be flying in his dead wife's face, the fact that she wasn't there anymore but the fun and games carried on regardless. It had felt profoundly wrong to Mark, to pretend to party away as normal, as if her death hadn't mattered.

But other people had other ideas. At precisely seven o'clock on Christmas night, that first year, he and Feen had sat by the fire in their armchairs reading, and feeling strangely at odds with the world at large but totally unable to explain why. Then, with no warning, four cars full of people had pulled up outside the front door, yahooing and tooting their horns. Sheila and Bob and a dozen friends and neighbours had barged into the house with enough food to feed an army, along with plenty of wine, beer and good cheer.

Despite Mark's protests and polite requests for them to go home again with everything, they would have none of it. Nobody was prepared to roll over and accept that the Christmas party had died with Beth.

"We will honour her memory!" Sheila had declared, "even if it's only this once. She's not here, but if she was, she'd want a bloody party, so we're 'aving one. Get that music cranked up, brother dear, and grab a tray of glasses, Feen!"

And so, a party had taken place. Feen had got on the phone and invited everyone else who usually came, saying she was sorry for the short notice, and they were to simply come as they were, without the need to get all dressed up.

In the end they'd had a crowd not far short of the usual, and most people had put on a party frock or clean shirt and trousers. There was no secret Santa that year, but nobody minded much. They ate, drank, danced and chattered and, to the last, every guest had told Mark and Feen how much they'd appreciated the party as a way of honouring their dearly departed friend, and enjoying themselves in her home as she would have wanted and loved them to do.

It was clear then, that the tradition established by Beth Raven was not about to fall over. The locals simply wouldn't let it die with her. At everyone else's insistence, Mark was 'forced' to have the party every Christmas night and over the past eight years, as much as a big part of him wished it could all just go away forever, he came to appreciate how much it had always meant to everyone, and how much it still did.

As Sheila had pointed out, it was one night. He could do his bah-humbug routine for the other 364 nights of the year, but not on Christmas night. That night, he had to be Mr Magnanimous, and be thankful for the people who cared enough about him and his family to want certain treasured traditions to remain.

And so, Mr Magnanimous he was. If he was honest with himself, he did enjoy the Christmas parties, particularly as Sheila had taken over the arrangements for them, with the help of her friend Peg Wilde who ran one of the local cafes. All Mark had to do was pay for the alcohol every December 1st, and come downstairs in a decent shirt and clean jeans on Christmas night.

It was always a poignant event for him. His heart had been lost to Beth from the very second his eyes had met hers, across the bar in a pub in the little-known hamlet of Whitewell, deep in the Lancashire countryside. She'd served him a pint of Pendle Witches' Brew, with a twinkle in her eye.

In that moment, he was lost forever, knowing there would never be anyone else for him but her; this gorgeous, blue-eyed, black-haired woman with the clearest complexion he'd ever seen, and the enigmatic smile that told him she already knew the broad-accented, salt-of-the-earth Lancashire farmhand far better than he'd ever know himself.

He still missed her like fire, but the pain of his loss had gradually receded. His life was simple now; uncomplicated. Farming, and being as good a father, brother, uncle and friend as he could possibly be to those who loved him; that was Mark Raven's lot now, and it was enough. He'd already had the love of his life. He recognised it had been more than many people were ever blessed with, and he was content to live the way he was, on the land, getting his hands dirty in an honest day's work, and sleeping not-too-bad at night. He had everything he needed. Having had the great true love, he wasn't selfish enough to expect to get even more of what some people never got to have at all.

Feen was a different matter, though. She didn't seem to mind that she didn't have a boyfriend, but Mark hoped with all his heart that she would one day get to wear the wedding dress she'd bought on a whim a year or so ago, on a trip around the charity shops in Whitby with Sheila.

He'd laughed his head off, at the time, at Feen's insistence that when the right man came along it was important that she already had the right dress. By all accounts, it was the most stunning dress she'd ever seen, and she'd literally been hysterical at the thought of leaving the shop without it. Sheila had understood immediately and had whipped out her credit card and bought it on the spot, which is exactly what Beth would have done if she'd been there.

Having laughed at his daughter when he heard the story, albeit with love in his heart, Mark had then been denied the opportunity to see the designer creation.

"You'll have to bloody wait now," Feen had snapped at him. "Laughing hyena, you don't *deserve* a peaky sneek!"

Certainly, she had plenty of time. Twenty-two was no age, these days. Many modern young women wanted a career first, and that was fair enough. Some wanted to sow a few "wild oats" of their own, and he supposed that was fair enough too. The days of a man expecting to marry a virgin had been gone a long time before he'd even started courting, himself.

41

The emancipated woman was a terrifying force to Mark, in many ways. He chuckled now, as he recalled a time, years ago, when he and Beth were camping, and a woman on her own was struggling to put up a rather complicated tent. Beth had warned him against riding in on his white charger, but he simply couldn't bear the thought of the poor woman having a hard time. Against his wife's better judgement, he wandered over and offered to help, and had been told in no uncertain terms that not all women were helpless and needing to be rescued, thank you very much, and he could piss off and mind his own bloody business, patronising git. Roundly chastised, he'd beaten a hasty retreat.

He hadn't meant to be condescending or dismissive of the woman's abilities. In truth, he thought her comments were fair enough. He'd never understood from the very beginning why women couldn't always have been treated with as much respect and given as many opportunities as men. He'd always wanted to help anyone who might be struggling, but he'd never been a chauvinist, and after seeing how hard his mother had fought, after his father had died, to try and keep the family farm going in the face of endless derision and criticism from most of the men in the district, he understood how important the fight for equality really was.

All Mark wanted was for his own cherished daughter to have the absolute best of every opportunity she could possibly want. If that meant waiting until she was thirty, or even forty, to have a husband and a family, after doing a load of other amazing stuff first, then so be it.

The one thing he couldn't bear was the thought of her never getting the chance to be a wife and mother, but growing old at Ravensdown Farm instead, boiling her bramble broth and nursing him into his dribbling dotage. She deserved better than that, and he was determined that she would eventually get it, even if he had to throw her out of the house himself and refuse to let her back in until she'd gone off and had enough adventures to make her see how big and exciting, and how full of opportunities, the world was.

Bloody Christmas party! 'Ere we go again. Sozzled mates passin' out on't bloody sofa, or in't garden! A shedload of food t'get through after't fact, ant' th'ouse smellin' like a brewery fer a week an' 'alf. He wasn't aware that he was mumbling aloud to himself, until he heard his daughter giggle.

"Oh Daddy, you funny thing! You know there's no use resisting, don't you? And can I just remind you how much you enjoy it all, on the night?" Feen smirked and poked her tongue out at him, then hesitated for a second or two before continuing.

"I asked Aunt Sheila yesterday if she thought we might start getting caterers in. It's a lot of work for her, and I know people bring stuff, but she always does such a lot of the cooking herself."

Feen put up her hands to ward off Mark's protest. "Before you say anything, I know she loves it, and she gave me short shrift, if you must know. She said how much she and Peg always look forward to the great Christmas cook-a-thon, and how much they've missed it. They're not ready to abandon their aprons and let someone else take over just yet."

"I should think they're bloody not, yer cheeky bugger. 'Ow old d'you think we *are*, for God's sake?"

"Ancient, Dad. Absolutely ancient. Muttering away to yourself, gnashing your teeth over the sospect of procialising, you sound about eighty-bloody-five!"

Mark pulled a face at her and she laughed. "And another thing. You need some new clothes. If you wear that blue and black checked shirt again this Christmas, I swear to God I'll be putting it in the bin on Boxing Day. And your jeans are all faded and horrible. We need a trip to Carlisle to get you dragged into the modern sartorial age, Daddy. I vote we go tomorrow, early. Braight after streakfast."

Mark looked at her, confused. "But you were wi' me when I bought that shirt, kid! Yer said it were nice!"

"It was. But that was five years ago! Now, since its millionth hot wash, it's all faded and just, well, *old*. And the collar is frayed. Have you even one decent jair of peans left?"

Mark thought for a minute and acknowledged that his daughter was right. He did need a bit of an upgrade, and even finding a simple black tie for a funeral would be a challenge and a half in Torley. Carlisle it would have to be. Grudgingly, he accepted his daughter's offer. He also knew he needed a haircut, which he would also get Feen to do in time for Christmas.

There were a few last-minute presents he needed to shop for too, because not everything he wanted to give as a gift could be bought online, and certainly not in the time left available. Feen usually took care of sending Christmas cards to everyone, and organising the presents for the rest of the family, but Mark always preferred to choose a decent card and gift himself for his daughter and sister.

Well aware that he only had a couple of days left to do it, and that Torley town didn't have much to offer, he conceded that a trip to Carlisle was probably his last chance to get them something nice. He wanted to get Feen some very large and heavy wind-chimes this year from a shop she adored in the city, and he had to think of a way to distract her, or lose her for half an hour, while he bought them and got them back to the car. Sheila had a penchant for beautiful bed linen, so he wanted to splurge and get her a feather quilt and a lovely Liberty-printed cover. It wouldn't matter if Feen was with him when he bought that. She could help him choose the best pattern.

He didn't relish the thought of charging around the town looking for clothes and Christmas presents just two days before the event, with the city bulging at the seams with no end of other frenzied shoppers on last-minute Christmas crusades. But of course, as per usual, he'd left it too late to do much else. As it was, he'd be wrapping his gifts at sparrow-fart on Christmas morning. It was the same every year. Somehow, despite his best intentions for it to always be different next time, it never was. It always became a last-minute thing.

Where does bloody time go? Last time I checked 't calendar, it were mid-November!

Chapter 5

Adie woke to the sweet sound of a sparrow calling from the tree outside her bedroom window. It was barely dawn. As she opened her eyes and turned over, sending a startled Mittens skittering off the bed towards the open bedroom door, she realised with a jolt that it just two more days to Christmas!

How did that sneak up on me? she asked herself. *That means I've been here three nights. Only three? It feels more like a week!*

Not that she was complaining. Far from it. She hadn't felt so much at peace for more months than she could count. But she did have to check the cupboards and make a list of anything she might need, and get it all today, because tomorrow was Christmas Eve and Torley's shops would likely be crazy-busy. The town might be closed for several days after that. Adie prayed that today they would still have at least some of what she hoped to buy.

After a hasty shower, some strong coffee and a couple of poached eggs on toast, she quickly attended to the needs of all the animals and then compiled a short list of food and drink to tide her over and perhaps even celebrate the festive season. It was incredible, she though, that after the last few months of absolutely dreading this first Christmas alone, she did actually feel a little like celebrating, even if it was by herself.

Maybe it won't be terrible after all. Maybe I'll actually enjoy being able to do as I please, and watch whatever I want on TV, on Christmas Day.

She apologised profusely to a crestfallen Sid, who had seen her lift her shopping bags from the hook on the back door, and was clearly hoping for a field walk. She promised him a decent walk later in the day, tried to ignore his look of utter dejection, and got into her car and drove into Torley town.

On approach from the road, which gave her an entirely different perspective than what she'd got when she'd walked in, she could see it was a very pretty town. As she searched for a parking space, she noted there were no dilapidated facades or empty shops. Most businesses had window planter-boxes with

45

cheerful, festive white and red crocuses sprouting from them, and they all had Christmas decorations and fairy lights in the windows. It was a charming town, clearly determined not to be diminished by a pandemic, and certainly not overshadowed by a cold wintry day when the sun didn't look like it was going to make it through the clouds. The dour and sombre sky didn't seem to matter much, with everything so bright and twinkly all around her.

All it needs now is a bit of snow, and it would be a proper chocolate box town! thought Adie, noting with relief that there was no charge for parking in Torley for the first two hours. She never seemed to have small change, for parking.

She found the 'supermarket' easily again, and picked up her list of essentials - plus a few treats, including a small Christmas cake and pudding, both reduced to half price, and a tub of brandy-laced custard to go with either or both. She then decided to call into the salon, Torley Tresses, to see how quickly she could get an appointment.

Expecting to be fobbed off until well after New Year, she was delighted to be told there'd just been a cancellation for later in the day, although it did mean a wait of about two hours, if she didn't mind that. They could even offer a manicure as well! Adie's ridged, chipped and brittle nails had turned out to be yet another casualty of the menopause and were in desperate need of some tender loving care. "They'll look a thousand times better by the time I've finished with them," the nail technician promised her. Adie took that to mean they were probably the worst the poor technician had ever seen.

Torley didn't have enough attractions to support two hours of 'pottering' time, but she could certainly go back to Teapot Cottage and drive back down later. She accepted the appointment and left the shop, thinking how lovely it would be to have a new hairstyle and a set of sparkly talons, and in time for Christmas, too! After the terrible trauma of the past twelve months, she felt determined look and feel a little different, this coming New Year's Day. New year, new start, she'd heard that people often had a makeover when their life had abruptly changed.

Maybe that's another metaphor, she thought to herself, *because whether I like it or not, it looks as if my life as I knew it is over. A new one has to start, and it's up to me to make that happen, whichever way I can.*

As Adie left the salon, lost in her own thoughts, she didn't see a heavy-set man with greying hair, who was carrying two large bunches of red roses. She literally crashed into him, sending his blooms to the pavement where they lay in a scattered heap.

"God, I'm so sorry!" Adie cried, bending down to pick the flowers up.

"Oh, don't be," came the gruff response. "They're all 'alf dead. I've just got 'em from't florist down there for me daughter." He gestured down the road with his hand.

As she helped him pick up the discarded blooms, Adie saw that they really were past their best. They were drooping dejectedly on their stems; most hadn't even fully opened. Sweeping aside the thought that few things were sadder than wilted roses, she smiled quizzically at the man as she handed to him the ones she'd gathered up. She was surprised at how blue his eyes were!

He evidently took this as encouragement to continue. "Our kid likes to boil' t petals for rose water. Some skincare thing, or one of 'er many 'medicinal experiments' as she calls 'em. I never remember which it is'. Florist keeps 'em back for 'er, the flowers that don't sell, and she gets 'em for next to nowt."

Adie grinned at his heavy Lancashire accent, which she found quite charming, in a ridiculous sort of way. Coming from anyone else she'd have wondered if it was deliberately exaggerated, but she suspected that she knew who he was.

"Her name's not Seraphine, by any chance, is it?"

It was the man's turn to look perplexed. "Aye, 'appen it is."

"Oh, I've met her! She's so sweet. She came to Teapot Cottage, asking my permission to rootle about in 'Glue and Senn's' hedges." Adie lifter her fingers to indicate inverted commas around her house-sit hosts Spoonerized names, chuckling at the memory of how they had been described. "She's a very interesting young lady!"

The man nodded. "Aye, that she is. Some folks say she's off 'er 'ead, but I think that's a bit 'arsh. She's just a bit dreamy, like, but not an 'armful bone in the lass at all. An' you must be the

47

'ouse sitter Senn and Glue were tellin' me about before they went. Feen did say she'd been to rattle yer cage."

"Oh, she was just delightful! And yes, I'm the house-sitter. Adrienne Bostock," Adie stuck out her hand, wondering if Mark Raven was affected with Spoonerism too, or if he just tended to go with his daughter's funny flow.

"Mark Raven," he said, shaking it. "'Ow long are you 'ere for, Adrienne? Three weeks, in't it? Senn and Glue 'ave gone now, 'ave they, to Aussie?"

Adie nodded, smiling. "Yes! A hot Christmas in the sunshine with family. Who could say no to that?"

He smiled, sheepishly. "Me! Not an 'ot weather fan, me, especially at Christmas. Seems a bit bloody weird to me, that; sittin' on a beach wi' a picnic. Sand in me butties, an' all that nonsense. No, lass. I like the cold weather at Christmas. Makes me enjoy me plum puddin' more."

Adie decided she liked Mark Raven. He was a no-nonsense man who called a spade a spade, and he clearly knew his own mind. And she felt he was right about Christmas needing to be cold. And she said so.

He nodded vigorously. "I tell yer what, Adrienne. If you've time, d'you fancy gettin' a brew across the street? Since we're neighbours, an' all? I've a meeting in town in an hour or so, but I'm just back from Carlisle shoppin' wi' Feen, an' I'm slightly ahead o' meself wi' a bit o' time to kill."

Why not, Adie thought. A bit of spontaneity wouldn't do any harm today, and he was her neighbour, after all. Besides, unused as she was to small-town social niceties, she worried that it might seem rude not to accept. It wasn't like she had to be anywhere else for the next couple of hours. She had her own time to kill, and it might be a useful conversation about what the area had to offer.

"Ok, lead the way," she shrugged, and Mark Raven promptly took her elbow in a slightly old-fashioned way which, to her own amazement, she didn't really mind.

They went into Peg's tea shop and found a table by the window. The cafe was surprisingly busy, much more so than it had been on Sunday when Adie had first found it. Peg beamed when she saw them. "Now *there's* a sight for sore eyes! She laughed. "Mark Raven, when did you last grace my cafe with your presence? I don't remember."

"Aw, away wi' you Peg! I were in 'ere only last week, woman, wi' you floggin' me two o' them bloody pies to take 'ome!"

Adie burst out laughing. "She's good at that. I had one wrapped up and in my bag on Sunday before I could even say 'feed me'! But they're good pies, aren't they?"

"Aye, they are that. No doubt she'll not let me leave wi'out forcing another on me today, but I can chuck it on't buffet table Christmas night and I'm sure it'll go like lightning." Mark chuckled and asked for a "big pot o' tea please, Peg, and two cups, lass."

Good job I didn't want coffee, thought Adie with a chuckle to herself. He's certainly assertive!

Mark then asked her if she wanted anything to eat, and she suddenly discovered she was ravenous again! Must be the country air again, like Peg said last time. There was a beautiful, deep quiche in the cabinet, with a wedge cut out of it, and Adie's mouth watered. Suddenly it seemed like the perfect lunch.

Peg came with the tea, and Adie ordered a slice of the quiche and salad. Mark Raven did the same. Adie noted that his hands were huge, like paddles. His clothes were tidy, and he was clean-shaven with a good shock of hair that was going more than a bit haywire around the temples. He was in dire need of a haircut, it had to be said.

Adie decided he was probably in his mid-fifties. Farming clearly kept him in good shape, as he didn't seem to have an ounce of fat on him, and he was quite nice looking, in a rugged kind of way, with the typical weathered face most farmers seemed to have. Not that Adie had met many farmers, as a city girl who had always preferred her men with a bit more 'cut and polish', but she'd certainly seen her fair share of Countryfile, and she also remembered Bob Shalloe, who she'd met just a few days earlier, which already seemed like weeks ago. He'd had that same weather-beaten look and demeanour. Men of the land; practical, down to earth, and they had to be, Adie supposed. She mentioned to Mark that she'd met Bob Shalloe, and he nodded.

"Aye, his wife Sheila's me sister. Bob's a good friend. That farm they're on, Bracefields, it went up for sale not long after I bought mine, so they grabbed it and moved up 'ere to take it on. We've 'ad our challenges around 'ere over't years wi' the weather an' foot an' bloody mouth, an' such-like, and we've 'ad to 'elp one another out a lot at different times, so it's led to a close friendship over't years.

"Been a bit 'arder for Sheila since me wife passed on, mind. She lost her best friend, as did a lot of people, but she's as solid as a rock, our Sheila. She's been a big 'elp to me wi' Feen, since Beth died. We're 'avin' 'em over for Christmas dinner, 'er and Bob. It's our year, mine and Feen's. We do turn-about, like."

He squinted at Adie slightly. "What about you, Adrienne? D'you 'ave plans? Yer most welcome to have Christmas dinner wi' us too, if you like? You don't 'ave to spend't day on yer own if yer'd rather not. It's our own lamb we're 'avin' wi' some of Feen's mint and chamomile jelly, or deadly bloody nightshade chutney, or summat." He chuckled.

Adie was touched by the gesture, but she knew she needed to have Christmas on her own this time around. It was an important rite of passage for her, the first Christmas without her family. It might be the shape of things to come, or it might not, but it was something she needed to do on her own terms. Accepting an invitation to have Christmas with strangers seemed like a bit of a cop-out.

"Thanks Mark", she said. "But I want to do the Christmas thing on my own, if you don't mind. Call it a significant part of a process of reconstruction. Moving forward with my life."

She wasn't prepared to say anymore, but she didn't have to. Mark reached over and patted her hand, lightly. "Yer needn't say any more, lass. It's all good. We all have our shyte to grapple wi'. But do come for a drink up at' farm Christmas night, if yer fancy it. It's just Bob and Sheila for dinner, about two o'clock we usually 'ave it. But a few others come for Christmas night drinks, from about seven. It's a bit of a tradition around 'ere. Beth started it, years ago, an' after she went I wanted to stop it, but our friends wouldn't 'ave that. They reckon't party keeps Beth in everyone's 'earts, sharing stories about her at Christmas, and who am I to argue wi' that?"

"She must have been very well loved around here." Adie observed.

"Aye, she was." Mark patted Adie's hand again. "So please come for that, if yer fancy. And bring a bottle if you've a liking for summat special, because it's basically just beer and wine we lay on." He gave her a cheeky wink. "I'll not be offended if you don't come. Christmas can be an 'ard day. I do know that. Just don't be lonely, lass, a'right? Not when you don't 'ave to be."

Adie felt a lump in her throat at this unexpected kindness. She wondered if any of her own family would even bother to call her on Christmas day, and here was a complete stranger inviting her into his home.

After lunch, Mark excused himself and went off to his meeting, telling Adie he hoped to see her at the party, if she wanted to see for herself what a motley bunch the local townsfolk turned into when a mince pie and a pint of ale were waved at them. He winked at her and refused her offer of payment for lunch.

After he left, Peg scuttled over. "He's a lovely man, Mark Raven. Most eligible bachelor in the county, but he's never looked at a single soul since his wife died. There's a lot of women around here that have tried to catch his eye and failed. But you never know." She winked conspiratorially at Adie as she cleared the table. Adie felt hot with embarrassment.

"He's definitely not my type" she spluttered into what was left of her tea. "Please don't get the wrong end of the stick, Peg."

The other woman grinned at her. "Oh, don't let his accent fool you. Country doesn't always mean bumpkin," she sang as she moved off. But Adie, still worried that she was in line for being match-made, gulped the last mouthful of tea and bolted for the door like a frightened rabbit. Peg intercepted her as she got there.

"Whoa! Adrienne, I was only joking! Mark's heart went with Beth and that's the end of it. He'll never look at another woman, and everyone knows it. I wasn't trying to infer anything, love. I was teasing you, that was all, and I shouldn't have done that. I don't know you well enough, do I? I'm sorry." Peg's voice was soft and her kind face was full of concern. Adie fought back tears, and Peg gently put an arm around her shoulder.

"I know it's a tough time for you", she said quietly, so nobody else could hear. "I don't know what's gone on, love, but I do know you're here alone at Christmas, and you're sad, so I can guess. But no harm will ever be meant to you here. I promise you that. The last thing I want to do is upset you, and if you ever want a tough old shoulder to cry on, you can always have mine."

Adie smiled apologetically. "I'm the one who's sorry, Peg. You didn't offend me. My moods are a bit erratic, that's all. It's that time of life, if you get what I mean."

Peg rolled her eyes and gave her a knowing nod. "Oh yes, I know all about *that!* All in the past for me now, thank God, but I sympathise. My menopause was hell. I could barely remember my own name for nearly two years, and how I never ended up slashing half my customers throats with the bloody bread knife, I'll never know!" Peg gave Adie's shoulder a quick squeeze and let her go.

"Anyway, I hope you will come to the Ravensdown drinks party Christmas night? It might cheer you up, and I'll be going on my own so I could use some intelligent girly company. Please say you'll come. I could pick you up on my way up the hill, if you like, at around seven-thirty?"

Adie nodded gratefully. Drinks where she could get to know a few more of the locals sounded nice. Mark Raven was no wolf in sheep's clothing (not that she'd thought of him as that, but it was nice to be reassured), and being able to walk into a party with a new friend instead of braving a room full of strangers on her own, and dreading the moment where everything went quiet as she walked in, sealed the deal. It was a marginally preferable alternative to sitting at home alone at Teapot Cottage, listening to the revelry over the back hedge. She would go, even just to put in an appearance. And maybe she and Peg would become friends. She did like the woman very much from her first impressions.

"Ok, see you Christmas night then. Merry Christmas, Adrienne."

"Merry Christmas, Peg, and please call me Adie."

So now there was a party to go to, and Adie suddenly panicked about what to wear. She hadn't even bought a decent dress with her, let alone anything appropriate for a drinks party. When she'd driven away from her flat, the last thing on her addled mind was whether she'd packed a party frock or anything nice to wear for Christmas!

She looked wildly about her, for any sign of a dress shop. Seeing nothing, she dived back into Peg's tea shop and called to her.

"Peg, is there a nice frock shop in the town?"

"Across the road. Back of the convenience store. Called GladRagz, and they also do shoes and handbags," Peg called back from the kitchen without coming out.

Adie soon located the store and went in. It was well-stocked, and when the shop owner introduced herself as Trudie Sangster and asked if she could help, Adie confessed that she needed a cocktail dress for a party, and a 'normal' one just for Christmas Day, but she had no real clue what she might want. She admitted that she hadn't even looked at herself in the mirror for as long as she could remember, and hadn't the faintest idea of what suited her now that she'd more or less lost her waistline.

After Trudie had asked her a few more questions about colour preferences, and acknowledged Adie's frustration and dismay at her changing body shape, she offered a number of nice choices, and helped her work out which styles and colours were now the most appealing to her. Her skin tone had changed a little too, and the colour palette Trudie chose to work with was far more flattering for Adie than it might have been even just a couple of years earlier. She discovered that colours she'd once never considered now looked quite nice on her.

Adie had never had a personal stylist or shopper, but today she felt that was exactly what she was getting, and all for free! It was a wonderful, indulgent experience. Trudie was so helpful, with attention to even the smallest details, like putting different pieces of jewellery Adie might like with the dresses she tried on, and thinking about the size of the heel on shoes she'd be comfortable wearing, in case she ended up dancing.

In the end, despite being pulled in a dozen different directions over choice, Adie settled on a lovely long-sleeved, knee-length dark navy merino sheath dress in a waterfall style, with just one electric blue, wavy diagonal stripe through it. She also bought the black shiny heels that had flattered her legs.

That took care of the party attire. A soft cashmere cowl-neck A-line dress, also to the knee, in a gorgeous shade of aubergine, ticked the box for Christmas Day, along with a pair of almost-flat slip-on shoes in roughly the same colour, with small gold buckles.

When Trudie offered Adie a long, delicate gold and silver chain necklace, as a suggestion to complete the ensemble, pointing out that she could also wear it to the party, she readily agreed. Adie knew she would wear the chain a lot - it would go with anything. As she left the shop, with her bank account significantly lighter, she wondered if she'd been too frivolous. But then she decided not.

It's Christmas, she said to herself. *So, Merry Christmas to me, with lots of love from me.*

Since it was likely the only gift she would get this year, she didn't think it was too much of an indulgence. In truth, it was way past time for her to concentrate on herself a bit. Her time with Trudie, trying on clothes, had both thrilled and dismayed her. It was lovely to be shopping, but it was also embarrassingly clear how much she'd let herself go over the past year while she wallowed in disbelief and self-pity about how her life had turned out.

Casting aside the images of lumps and bumps she hadn't previously noticed, Adie glanced at her watch and saw that she had just twenty minutes left before she was due at her hair appointment, and she needed to move her car. She decided that she may as well head to the salon a few minutes early, since there was little else left to do.

As she left GladRagz, she literally crashed into Mark Raven for the second time that day. This time it was *her* possessions that went flying. Mark instantly bent to retrieve them.

"Oh, God! I'm so sorry, again!" she wailed. He threw back his head and laughed so loud that Trudie came rushing out of her shop to find out what the commotion was. Hot with embarrassment but trying to make light of it, Adie gave a theatrical bow, then zoomed off towards the car park, her face flaming.

What is it with me and him? Are we destined to keep smashing into one another, everywhere we go?

At the salon, a stylist offered her a cup of coffee, and she settled down to wait. A few hair magazines were scattered on the table in front of her, so she idly flipped through them as she sipped and waited, until suddenly a picture of a model caught her attention. The model's hair was just gorgeous. It was short, barely to the jaw line, and was cut in a way that initially looked haphazard but on closer inspection had clearly taken considerable skill to achieve. The soft-curl style framed the model's face and flicked up in different directions. It was incredibly flattering. Adie couldn't take her eyes off it.

Her own hair was almost long enough to sit on, and it had been her pride and joy for more than twenty years. She loved how easy it was to work into different styles because of the length, and despite her many months of ignoring and neglecting it, it was still in fairly good condition, albeit with those fair few smatterings of grey. She took good care of it normally, but it had stopped being a priority since the bomb had gone off, so to speak. It no longer flattered her face the way it used to. She now noticed properly, for the first time, that her jawline was softer now, more fleshy and less defined; yet another symptom of advancing years.

But this new style, here in this magazine, this was really something special. It was something Adie kept gazing at and found herself wanting, more and more, as the minutes ticked by. It would mean losing well over a foot off her hair's current length, but it would be transformative, and very easy to maintain.

When she was called to the chair, she took the magazine with her.

"I want a radical change. Can you give me this?"

The stylist looked hesitant. "Of course I can, sweetheart, if that's what you really want." She lifted Adie's hair and caressed it a little. "But your hair is so beautiful. Are you really sure you want to cut all this off? It's not a decision you can go back on, once we make a start."

Adie nodded, decisively. "Yes, I'm certain. I'm going through the change, and I'm sick of feeling like a greying, lumpy old frump. My hair's got so much thinner, and I think the length draws unwelcome attention to my saggy jawline. My whole face has gone soft, actually. I seem to be morphing into an old woman with jowls! This should definitely help take the focus off that a bit, don't you think?" She pulled a face at herself in the mirror.

"I want a complete change, something that won't have me looking like a wrung-out string mop when I wake up after a night of hot sweats. Go for it. In fact, cover my eyes and don't let me see it until it's all done."

The stylist excused herself for a moment and came back with a woman who introduced herself as Madeleine Murphy, the salon owner. She gently asked Adie if she really was serious about cutting off her lovely long hair, and whether she would be prepared to donate it. Madeleine explained that an opportunity like this was so rare for the salon, to support a small charity a few miles away who specialized in making hand-made, real-hair wigs for people with cancer.

Adie's eyes filled with tears. "Well, if I had even the slightest doubt about cutting it all off - which I didn't, by the way - this definitely seals the deal. I would absolutely *love* you to cut it all off and let it help someone who needs it."

And with that, the process began, and in just under two hours Adie was transformed into a magnificent creature with fuchsia fingernails and a hairstyle that made her virtually unrecognisable to herself. With the flicked-up ends of her newly enriched and gleaming hair, and with all traces of grey at least temporarily gone, she looked a full ten years younger, and a lot like the woman in the magazine. The rumpled yeti she'd resembled that morning was officially gone for good.

Just wait until I get some slap on, she thought, relieved to remember that she had in fact brought her make-up bag with her. She had foundation and other cosmetic items, including a nice blue eyeliner pencil that would work really well with her new party frock.

And, and since a healthily-sprouting moustache was the last thing any self-respecting woman wanted, she'd also decided to have her very first top-lip wax. The pain of it made her gasp with shock and brought tears to her eyes, but she did feel a lot happier once the stinging stopped.

Her long locks had been carefully cut and wrapped in a gossamer-like netting, then reverently placed in a box to be sent to the wigmakers.

After receiving instructions on how to work with the new style herself, and purchasing an expensive set of tongs that would help to keep it looking fresh, Adie complimented her stylist and Madeleine on the Christmas decorations in the shop, explaining that she was house sitting in the area and hadn't had the opportunity to put any decorations up. She'd assumed Glenn and Sue would have some, but she didn't know where, and she didn't really want to go digging through their private stuff to find anything.

That was fine, she'd said to herself, since she wasn't really interested in the spirit of Christmas this year anyway. But looking at the little artificial tree and its twinkling blue lights, jauntily perched at the front of the salon's bay window, she suddenly wished she'd made a bit of an effort. Come Christmas morning, poor little Teapot Cottage would look and feel just a teeny bit Christmas-bare.

She thanked everyone profusely again for her transformation, and left the salon, walking on air. And the knowledge that her newly cut-off hair would benefit someone who was battling cancer was the best gift Adie could have had the chance to give to anyone. That was a gift, straight from her heart to a person unknown, and she loved the feeling it gave her.

"Merry Christmas," she sang out loud, unaware that she had done so, until a young man hurrying by wheeled round and said it back to her, with a salacious wink.

"Merry Christmas to you too, sexy!"

Back at home, Adie poured herself a hefty gin and tonic, and sat in the window seat, with just a few candles going, watching the twinkling lights of Torley town, down in the distance. After a cloudy day, the night had turned surprisingly chilly and sharp, with the kind of clear, starlit skies that promise a hard frost.

She now felt a little more ready to re-examine her rift with her family. She had no idea what Bryan was doing for the holiday. Was she *interested* in how her ex-husband was spending his Christmas? Adie carefully considered how she really felt. In previous attempts to come to terms with things, it had always been like poking her tongue into the cavity where a tooth had just been taken out. It felt raw, horrible and unbearably painful, but she couldn't stop herself from doing it, and it never really helped.

Every time she thought about how things had turned out, and how precarious and uncertain her future seemed, it brought tears, sadness and despair.

Tonight however, safely enveloped in the cosy, gentle, womb-like home of a virtual stranger, with nobody to share the night and the bed with except a cat and a dog, she found herself feeling slightly braver. And she *did* care what Bryan might be doing, but with a curious level of detachment she hadn't felt just a week ago, when she was accepting the Robinsons' urgent offer for this very house sit. She'd still been wishing then, with all her heart, that Bryan would phone or turn up at the door begging for them to talk or get counselling, or whatever else either of them thought it might take, to get their marriage back on track. She'd even thought that he could have come to this house sit with her, at short notice. But Bryan's absence, and his continued stubborn refusal to accept her calls or return her messages, had indicated that saving their marriage was of no interest to him.

As the evening drew out, Adie realised that without being fully aware of the process, she had in fact already started her journey towards accepting that her marriage was over. Perhaps that cavity the tooth had been torn from was actually starting to heal. Perhaps the way forward was revealing itself, and all she might have to do would be let it unfold the way it was meant to, in its own time. It was time for a new chapter to start and tonight, while the notion made her sad, it didn't make her tearful. That was a first.

It suddenly occurred to Adie that for the very first time, every member of her immediate family was in a different place for Christmas. Ruth was in Italy, Teresa was in Australia, Matty was in Epsom and Bryan was God-knows where. And then there was Adie herself, squirreled away in a tiny town in the Lake District that few people had heard of, and even fewer people knew how to find. All spending Christmas apart.

As she switched off the light, she thought about her two new dresses, hanging on the back of the bedroom door. Tomorrow was Christmas Eve. She would have a quiet day and evening, and there was a party the night after that. Christmas might mean messages, if she was lucky, from loved ones wishing her to be merry, and who knew what else might happen?

Chapter 6

Mark checked his watch as he hurried towards his meeting. He was surprised at how quickly the time had flown by in the cafe. He was even more surprised that he'd had the spontaneity to invite a complete stranger to have a cup of tea with him, and a woman, to boot. What surprised him even more than any of that, however, was how a 'quick brew' had somehow become lunch, and how much he'd enjoyed Adrienne Bostock's company, to the level where the time had got away on him completely. Now he was running late.

Mark Raven was never usually late for anything, and certainly not an important meeting involving finances. He'd invited Mrs Bostock (and he had noticed her wedding ring even though he hadn't planned to) to Christmas-night drinks at the farm. The fact that he had done so was simply extraordinary, and no explanation could account for it, other than the fact that she was his immediate neighbour, albeit a temporary one, and was on her own at Christmas.

I were bein' neighbourly. I couldn't 'ave a party wi' people paradin' past 'er door all night and not invite 'er, could I?

Satisfied with his own explanation, he put it to the back of his mind and concentrated on the meeting ahead. It was an important one, involving the sale of his mining shares. Mark's investment manager and long-time friend, Kevin Sangster, was a busy man and Mark didn't want to keep him waiting. He found himself jogging the last hundred yards or so to be there on time at Silver Dolphin Investments, Kevin's small but plush-fitted office above his wife Trudie's women's boutique, GladRagz.

He'd been surprised to get Kevin's call, which had come on the way back from his quick shopping trip with Feen in Carlisle. His friend had sounded a little worried, voicing his concern about the safety of Mark's mining shares which had been stable for many years now, quietly gaining value. Now however, thanks to some significant safety issues highlighted from a whistle-blowing employee, big problems at the mine site were causing the shares to wobble. Kevin wanted to show Mark on his big screen, how things were trending, and the two of them could discuss how best to react to the information. He'd wanted Mark to come in and see him straight away.

He entered the office after a cursory knock, and Kevin was instantly on his feet and coming forward with his hand outstretched. He laughed when he saw his friend out of breath.

"Now there's a sight I seldom see! What's got *you* running today, mate?"

"You, you daft apeth! Bein' on time fer you!"

Mark went on to explain how he'd been delayed after having an unexpected lunch with a strange woman.

"An' yer can drag yer bloody eyebrows back down from yer scalp, an' all" he growled good-naturedly.

As incredulous as Kevin was, at his friend having lunch with an unknown woman and actually divulging the fact, he shrugged it off and immediately got down to business.

"Mark, it's not looking good down there at the mine, I have to tell you. I've done some digging around to find out what's going on, and the news is bad." He took a deep breath. His expression was grim.

"It's not a new mining story, by any means. Two men nearly died as a result of a big collapse, which happened after serious shortcuts were made with non-compliant stability and safety materials. They hadn't been upgraded in years, and they just stopped holding up. Six employees working in the area of the collapse were injured, but the whole thing had been hushed up.

"The staff were given incentives to keep quiet, but one of the two most seriously hurt blokes has gone ahead and blown the whistle anyway, because he's realised - and rightly I suspect - that he can get a lot more in compensation than the mine would pay him in hush money, and he's likely to need every penny he can get his hands on. His injuries are life-changing, and he certainly won't be working down any mines again."

Kevin looked squarely at Mark. "There's a big storm brewing, and from what my sources tell me, the investigation is likely to find safety breaches so great that they're probably going to shut the whole operation down, and nobody knows for how long. It's very serious, and it's all about to blow."

Kevin went quiet, giving Mark a moment to digest the news. Then he said gently; "Mark, the shares will tank. Once this is all over the news, which is likely to be in the next couple of hours, they'll head south fast. They've lost five percent already today with the rumbles that have already started. I have no idea how low they might go. It all depends on how big this mess becomes. But I don't want you to take any chances and end up losing any more value on them. My advice would be to sell today. As in, right now."

Mark blinked at his friend. *Today? Right now? With no notice?* After nearly two decades of sitting pretty, the potential fall in the mining shares was an unexpected blow, to say the least. But then, that was often how the share market worked, wasn't it? News came in, good or bad, shares could rise and fall 'faster than a whore's drawers', to quote a phrase his father was once very fond of saying, and you had to move quickly, whether you bought or sold.

Mark had always known this in principle, of course, but thanks to Kevin's astute investment capabilities everything had seemed safe as houses for nearly twenty years. He'd never been in a position where he had to face the prospect of his shares plummeting or, worse, becoming virtually worthless overnight. It was a lot to take in.

He looked at his trusted friend. "So how much are they worth today?"

Kevin pressed a few keys on his computer and then spun the screen around for Mark to take a look at. A line graph showed long, steady line of growth over the past eighteen years, with just a few dips here and there indicating only minor fluctuations. But the tip of the upward-moving line had taken a sharp turn downwards, indicating a more significant reduction. Kevin gestured at the screen.

"Well, as you can see, they've gained a lot, over the years. But they're already dropping, and I can't guarantee they're not already in free-fall, Mark. If you sell the lot, right now, you'll get eight times the original investment, minus my commission, at the usual mates' rates of course. It would be a very tidy profit."

Mark was astonished. Indeed, it was a *very* tidy profit. Kevin had done surprisingly well with Mark's money. Mark had trusted him implicitly, never questioning his recommendations or ever looking too closely at his own portfolio. He had something of a head for numbers, that was true, but he knew he'd never be in Kevin's league, and whenever Kev gave him the thumbs up about his financial position and told him it was all looking good, Mark was always satisfied. He trusted his friend, and he felt that was good enough. His hunch had proved to be true.

He sighed deeply. "Kev, as you know that money were the in'eritance I got from me Grandad, and I invested it fer Feen's future. You're her Godfather and I know you 'ave 'er best interests at 'eart too. If I sell today, is there anywhere else I can invest it that will give us another good rate o' return for 'er?"

Kevin thought for a minute.

"Mark, does she even know about this investment?"

Mark shook his head. "The only one who knew owt were Beth. We made it to secure Feen's future, and the others were to 'opefully see us through our dribblin' owd age." He turned his mind away from the short, sharp pang of grief that suddenly rose in his chest.

"Then maybe you should just cash this lot in, and stick it in a deposit account for five years. She could have access to it when she was, what, twenty-seven? To be completely honest with you mate, with the markets currently so volatile anyway, I'm hard-pressed to know where's safe to put big amounts. Small bits of money yes, but my graphs look like a game of snakes and ladders. I'm not so comfortable gambling with the big stuff right now."

Kevin ran a hand through his hair, sighed, and rolled his shoulders back. He was clearly frustrated at not having any concrete answers for Mark. But he was an honest man, and Mark appreciated that.

"This is such a nice profit, Mark. My suggestion would be to protect it for Feen. Maybe keep the original amount back, to reinvest in a few smaller ventures that look relatively stable. Spread it around a bit, and we can see how it all builds. It might be a lot slower to get any significant gains, you need to remember that. Not everything's as lucky a strike as the mine shares have been, and of course your investment in the drug company, that's also doing very well, as are your other investments. Things have been building nicely. Quite a few are just stable, and I did transfer two or three that were heading south and locked them up in short-term stability that I'm monitoring all the time until they settle."

Kevin smiled at his friend. "You've an impressive portfolio Mark, and unless the whole world goes tits up overnight, you're sitting pretty on several million in realisable assets. You've also got your rental income from the farms and buildings you own. And thanks to Beth's life insurance policy, you own the farm outright, and we know what that's worth. You're a wealthy man. And when Feen inherits that lot, she's not going to want for much, is she?"

Mark shook his head. "Well, I plan to be around for a bit yet, thank you very kindly, and these minin' shares, that's money specifically earmarked for 'er future, and you know 'ow important it was to Beth an' still is to me. So, if that's yer advice, I'll take it. I trust yer. Just go ahead an' do whatever yer think's best."

Kevin gave him the thumbs up and turned his attention to his computer screens. In a few clicks, he had sold Mark's shares and both men sat back to watch as a very substantial deposit folded gently into Kevin's connected bank account feed. He turned and smiled reassuringly at Mark.

"You've done the right thing. I'll look around at secure investments for this, and I'll put it where I think she'll get the best return on it, over time. How *is* our gorgeous goddaughter, anyway?"

"Oh, you know Feen. Still ferretin' about in' t bloody forest an' dancin' around wi't foxes. Seems 'appy enough", he added, half to himself.

Kev nodded, pleased, and cocked his head on one side. "She's an enigma, that one, I'll give you that. But Trudie and I love her to bits, of course, and it's just as important to us as it is to you that she's financially secure. And tell me about this mystery woman you've just had lunch with."

Mark responded with a wave of his hand. "Oh, there's no great myst'ry, Kev. I collided wi' a woman in town. She were comin' out of a shop, and we crashed straight into one another. All Feen's manky roses went flyin', and it were quite funny, as it 'appens. Anyroad, we got to chattin'. Turns out she's the 'ouse sitter up at Robinson's while they've gone to Oz."

"What, up at Teapot Cottage?"

"Yep," Mark nodded. "I 'ad a bit o' time to kill so I thought I'd grab a quick cuppa at Peg's, an' I thought it'd be the neighbourly thing, to ask 'er to come along."

Kev's jaw dropped. He stared at Mark, who just chortled. "Kevin, for God's sake man, shut yer mouth. Yer look like a fly-catchin' bloody 'alfwit."

Kev shook himself. "Sorry, but I'm gobsmacked. You've asked a woman out. This is a matter for the national press. It's flag-flying, brass band stuff."

Mark shook his head emphatically. "No, it bloody isn't. It were't neighbourly thing, Kev, that were all. It were just a brew in a local café. But she were nice company, and she were starvin', as it 'appens, so we 'ad a bite to eat. There were nowt more to it than that."

With that, Mark stood to go. The two men exchanged goodbyes, said 'Merry Christmas', and Kevin assured Mark that he and Trudie would be at the drinks party on Christmas night as usual.

Outside, in the street, Mark happened to glance across the road at St Martin's church, where Beth's funeral had been held. On the day, people had spilled out from the entrance, onto the footpath, and into the road. Such were the crowds, the local council had come with barriers to divert the traffic while the ceremony took place. He didn't think there'd been a single soul in Torley who hadn't turned out for her. A moment of desperate sadness engulfed him, and he instinctively walked towards the church.

He wasn't a religious man, and he hadn't been in the church since the funeral. Eight long heart-breaking years. He was surprised by his sudden urge to go in there now but somehow it felt like the right thing to do. With a deep breath, he stepped in through the open doors, selected a pew, and sat down in the cool, quiet gloom.

Time had allowed him to adjust fairly well to his life as a widower, although in many ways his grief was still sometimes as raw and real as it had been in the days immediately after Beth's passing. It tended to come in waves, he'd noticed; all-engulfing ones, that often left him shaking, tearful and bereft. They were fewer and further apart now, after all this time, but whenever they hit him they were still painful.

A practical man, he wasn't overly given to bursts of emotion, but in those final months, as he'd watched Beth slowly but inexorably losing her fight with the cancer that ravaged her, he'd been dragged through every feeling imaginable.

The emptiness that had settled and stayed, in the wake of her death, became something he eventually grew to accept. It was more manageable now, outside of those random, sweeping tides that still stole in and threatened to drown him. In the beginning, there'd been nights when he didn't sleep, didn't even go to bed, knowing the sleep - the oblivion - he craved wouldn't come. There'd been days when he'd walked the farm until his legs felt like lumps of lead, hoping the physical pain would overtake the emotional anguish. Sometimes it worked, other times it didn't. There was no clear road map for grief, he'd discovered. It took you the way it wanted you to go, and took the time it needed to, and all you could do was go with it and try not to let it drown you.

They hadn't started a family for a while, as they were still very much enjoying getting to know one another, doing a bit of travelling, saving to buy the farm, then working on the house to make it halfway fit for a family, which it certainly wasn't when they'd first moved in.

They'd lived in one room while they sorted out the rest, with its rising damp, its falling plaster, smashed guttering and leaky roof. It wasn't fair to bring a baby into the kind of chaos created by the renovations. Both of them were out on the farm all day, and remodelling the house by night, for nearly two years before it was properly fit to live in.

It had been a mind-numbing exercise in time and money, with nothing of either left over to give to a baby, but when they finally agreed they'd done enough, they both stood back and acknowledged, as did all of their new local friends (many of whom had helped, long into many nights that had somehow turned into parties then deeper and more meaningful friendships) that they'd managed to make Ravensdown a truly beautiful home. At last, a family was possible.

Mark had never forgotten the kindness of the locals, when he and Beth had first arrived at Down Farm, as it was back then. He'd felt a bit pretentious, renaming it after himself, and he wondered what the local people would think of a cocky young man, newly arrived, still a bit green around the gills, setting himself up as some kind of lord of the manor. But as Beth had pointed out, renaming the farm had made it their own, and as the plan had always been to have a big family and have the beautiful big house as the family seat for the generations to follow, it was appropriate that they give it the family name.

As it turned out, Mark needn't have worried about appearing pompous. The people of Torley had readily recognised that the young, cash-strapped newlyweds were taking on a farm in a poor state of repair and a house that was even worse. They deserved a decent welcome and some good support to get the place ready for the family they wanted to have. The whole town had got behind their efforts, with other farmers lending machinery and supplying details for reliable and fast-working local firms, such as fencing and equipment suppliers, who wouldn't rip them off.

Other townspeople dropped by in a constant stream, with soups, casseroles and cakes, along with plastering trowels, paint rollers and wallpaper pasting tables. Many had even stayed to help plaster, retile the roof and redecorate the inside of the house. A distant neighbour had also turned up unannounced with a couple of friends in a flatbed truck with a beat-up old solid-fuel Aga sitting on it. Their extraordinary kindness and beaming smiles were just too hard for Mark to say no to, so he'd graciously accepted the rusting old wreck.

He'd helped the three men haul it off the back of the truck, utterly amazed at how blindingly heavy it was. He'd laughed at Beth, dancing merrily around it.

"Mark! Look! It's an AGA!" She'd virtually screamed with delight. Mark had inwardly cringed at the old heap of rusting iron and pitted brass, believing it to be a far more worthy boat anchor than a kitchen appliance. But Beth was so over the moon, he resolved to try and make it work. He spent nearly a month of late nights restoring it before installing it and proclaiming it vaguely usable. And it worked surprisingly well, for four brave, dogged years, until he was in a position to replace it with a brand new and much bigger gas-fired one. He'd sent the old one away to be fully restored and converted to gas by an expert and was keeping it safely wrapped up in a corner of the barn until it might one day be needed by someone else who was struggling to make a start in life.

The townsfolk had outdone themselves, and it told Mark and Beth a lot about the spirit of the community they'd moved to. Beth had lost little time in becoming part of the town life, throwing herself into running the local Barter and Trade Produce Market, as it was back then, and inviting endless streams of people up to the house for food and drink, long after the work on the house had been finished. She never forgot their kindness, and repaid it tenfold.

The people of Torley adored her in return. Her open-door policy was legendary, as was her sage ability to listen, observe and advise in both a practical and an almost spiritual way. Beth Raven quickly became an important part of the fabric of Torley town, and all who had taken her to their hearts felt the devastation of her death.

"Ah, lass," Mark mumbled quietly now, "what a gapin' bloody 'ole you've left. You know, I still come in sometimes, and open't door and expect to see you standin' there in't kitchen like you used to."

He braced his arms along the pew in front of him, laid his head on them and allowed his tears to fall. He wasn't sure how long he'd been sitting there, when he became aware of a figure standing by his side. He looked up to see the vicar looking kindly down on him.

"Hello Mr Raven," he said quietly. "Are you just having some time of reflection, or would you like to talk a while?"

Mark decided that it wouldn't hurt to give the vicar a chance. He'd been blinded by grief at the time of Beth's funeral, and vaguely recalled being rude to the man in response to his overtures of sympathy and support. He gestured for the vicar to sit, which he did.

Mark began. "I'm not a religious man, Vicar."

The vicar shook his head. "You don't have to be, to receive God's grace and comfort, Mr Raven. You're very welcome here. And you can call me Mike", he added.

"Then you can call me Mark. I'm a no-fuss type o' man, Mike. I like to just get on wi' things, y'know? My Beth, you took 'er funeral 'ere, eight year ago. It were eight full year ago, now."

"I remember", Mike said gently. "But it doesn't seem that long ago, does it, Mark?"

Mark shook his head. "No, it does not. In many ways it's like it were yesterday. An' in some ways I still feel frozen in time. Now an' then, I still feel as lost as I ever did, wi'out 'er. I'm functionin' but I still feel like bits o' me are missin' even after all this time. Beth really was me other 'alf."

To his horror, he felt tears prick his eyelids again. Mike covered one of Mark's hands with his own. It felt cool yet comforting. There was so much compassion in that touch, and Mark realised it was loving touch he missed the most; that unspoken reassurance that passed between two people who understood how one another felt, and sough to give and receive support, comfort and affection.

Feen, bless her beautiful gentle heart, was a hugger, and she would often hug Mark fiercely. He always responded, and he appreciated the affectionate connection he had with his daughter, but that was a different thing entirely from what he felt the need for now. He realised he longed for real comfort from someone who really understood the very bones of him. Quite simply, Mark missed being loved.

He said as much now, to Mike, who nodded but said nothing.

"I miss 'er so much. An' I know she'd want me to move on and' be 'appy. But thinkin' about maybe ever meetin' someone else, it feels disloyal. I 'ad lunch wi' someone today, just out o't blue, and it were nice, but that were all it were. Just lunch, and just nice, but even that feels like a betrayal o' Beth's memory." Mark couldn't believe how distressed he was now feeling.

Mike cleared his throat. "I knew Beth quite well. We had a lot of contact because of the market in the community hall, next door. It's part of the church, as you probably know. She wasn't a religious person either, and she never pretended to be, but I always thought there was something very spiritual about her anyway.

"I always thought she was one of God's messengers in disguise, even though she wouldn't have thought so herself. We talked a lot, over the years, about different things. Not so much about religion, but about life in general."

Mike chuckled, almost to himself. "She had some very refreshing perspectives on what was important in life, and I used some of them in my sermons, here and there, over the years. As you know, she used to organise a lot of the happy events here in the town, not just the barterers market. She was a wonderful woman. Very caring and kind. She had time for everybody, and she couldn't bear to see anyone unhappy."

He paused for a moment, then went on. "What do you think she'd say to you, Mark, if she were sitting here with you today?"

Mark wiped his nose with the back of his hand and sniffed hard. "She'd tell me to buck up me bloody ideas, stop snivellin' an' drownin' in snot, and get on wi' me life. She couldn't stand it when I were mopin' around about anythin'. It used to drive 'er barkin' bloody mad." He realised he'd sworn, twice, and quickly apologised. To his astonishment, Mike just laughed.

"I think you're right. I think the lady I knew would tell you to pull your socks up, *man* up, and embrace life again. You're still a relatively young man, Mark, with a lot of life left. I don't think Beth would want you to go through that, all the coming years, alone. I think she would want you to find happiness, love, again. She'd want you to live a full and happy life, d'you not think?"

Neither man spoke for a while, then Mike added, "What I believe is that all people who come to us are gifts from God. Some stay, some go. Some are here to enhance our lives, others are here to show us things we need to learn about ourselves or others, but whether they do us good or not-so-good, they are all gifts from the Lord. Your marriage was far too short, for you, but long compared with many. It was a loving and happy union, with a beautiful child to celebrate, and those things were bona fide gifts from the Almighty."

He patted Mark's hand and it didn't feel at all patronising. "Whether you choose to believe that or not is neither here nor there, Mark. It's the simple truth. In your marriage with Beth, you experienced a true, divine blessing. That is something you can thank God for, if you've a mind to, but no matter if you don't. He won't be offended, I promise you. He's not that sort of bloke."

Mark smiled wanly. The vicar went on to explain that while it was sometimes impossible for mere mortals to understand why God can so brutally take back His gifts, He was the kind of gentleman who would never take something away from anyone without leaving something equally valuable in its place. And that something wasn't grief, pain, suspension or misery. It was something far, far better than that. If God took away a gift, He gave another, and sometimes - as difficult as it was - all the mere mortals had to do was wait for it to arrive and recognise it when it did.

Mark was sceptical of Mike's religious logic, but he respected the man's perspective. He apologised for having been rude at Beth's funeral and Mike waved his apology away, without a word. His face was gentle, welcoming and open. He held no grudges or malice towards anyone, that much was clear. Mark didn't know when he'd ever seen another face so serene and full of faith and acceptance.

Mike sensed he had said enough. He patted Mark's hand lightly, and got up to leave. "You stay as long as you like, and you know where to find me if you want to talk again. I'll include you in my prayers. Take it easy, Mark. Be kind to yourself."

And then the vicar was gone. Mark stayed a while, considering what he'd said, and then stood up to go.

As he got into his car and set off for the farm, he was still thinking about Beth, and while he hadn't agreed with what a lot of what Mike had said, he realised he was right about one thing. Mark's marriage to Beth *had* been a blessing. And now that it was gone, it was something he could only cherish in memory.

Compared with other marriages Mark had been aware of that were fraught with all kinds of problems, he'd had a relationship with his wife that had been as close to perfect as anything could be. Yes, they'd had their struggles, but never with one another. They'd always been on the same side, weathering the storms and celebrating the triumphs of life together, as a solid unit.

They' rejoiced together when he'd been a finalist in the Young Farmer of the Year Award, not long after they'd got married, even though the hard, early farm days had been brutally exhausting, far more than either of them could have imagined possible, and there were nights when they'd been too tired even to speak. They'd rejoiced in Feen's birth, and they'd grieved together after Beth's miscarriage, two years after, with complications that meant she would never be able to conceive again, and their hopes of having a big family were dashed.

Yes, despite the hard graft, and some terrible disappointments that would have torn less-stable unions apart, he'd been incredibly lucky to have had a rock-solid marriage, with an extraordinary, amazing, beautiful, vibrant woman. He was luckier still, to have a daughter who was the spitting image of her. On some vague level, he'd always known how fortunate he was, but today, in the quiet church with the wise and gentle vicar, something had shifted.

Now, driving towards the home he still shared with the daughter who was so like her mother it sometimes hurt to watch her move, as much as Mark had always acknowledged the blessings of his wife and child, now he actually *felt* his marriage as the gift it had been, and felt the love he had for his daughter as real, and huge, and shining.

Back at home, sitting at the kitchen table with a cup of tea, he found himself struggling to figure out why he was feeling so suddenly out of sorts. After he'd left the church and crossed the street again back to where he'd started, he'd found himself once more colliding very roughly with Adrienne Bostock. Once more she'd apologised, then when she saw who it was, she'd gone beet red, mumbling that he probably thought she made a habit out of charging through shop doorways without looking where she was going.

He'd laughed, because it did seem completely ridiculous that they should literally have smashed into one another twice in one day after never having met before. Trudie had even come out of her shop to see what all the noise was about.

Adrienne had seemed to be in a proper hurry, so Mark had stepped to one side to allow her to pass. As she'd moved to go, she'd briefly turned, smiled at him, and lifted her bags. "A new dress for your party!" she'd said, before scurrying off.

"So yer comin' then?" He'd called after her, but he didn't think she'd heard him. The woman was a whirling dervish, and her mind already seemed to be somewhere else. He'd found himself feeling absurdly pleased that she would be at his party.

The significance of it escaped him though, as he sat there with his tea, wondering why he was feeling so oddly displaced within himself that he couldn't have explained it to anyone, to save his own life.

Chapter 7

Christmas morning dawned clear and cold. Adie was in the kitchen, very keen to make herself a cup of tea and take it back up to bed. It was still very early, barley half past seven and not quite daylight yet. While she waited for the kettle to boil she noticed a few little embers, miraculously still alive in the living room fire, which was usually as dead as a doornail in the mornings. The opportunity to get it going so easily felt as if Teapot Cottage had given her a special Christmas gift. She couldn't explain it any other way. Grinning at yet another of her fanciful notions that the cottage was somehow being deliberately kind to her, she quickly stuck some newspaper on top of the winking embers and threw on a handful of kindling. She blew at the fire for a moment or two, and was very satisfied to see the flames take hold.

Sid suddenly let out a high-pitched bark, which startled her. She heard a muffled thumping noise at the front door, which wasn't a knock, exactly, so she wasn't sure if she should go and open it. But her curiosity got the better of her, and she was hugely surprised to find an elaborate bouquet of flowers in a lovely glass vase sitting squarely on the rubber doormat, with a card labelled "Adrienne."

Who could they be from? Who even knows I'm here? Baffled, she picked up the vase and brought it inside. She ripped open the card and let out a snort of laughter when she read it.

Merry Christmas, Adrienne, Sidney, Mittens and Chooks!
Love from Glenn and Sue Robinson!
P.S.: there is a very nice bottle of brandy in the cupboard by the fire.
Feel free to drink the lot!

Adie was thrilled, but also mystified. How on earth had they managed to get this delivered to her on Christmas morning? She supposed they must have very good friends locally who would

72

agree to doing such an errand, on what surely had to be the most inconvenient morning of the year.

She realised she was overdue for sending 'Glue and Senn' another progress report about their house and critters, so she promptly threw some decent wood onto the fire and reached for her slumbering laptop, determined to ping off a ten-second email. She wanted to wish the Robinsons a Merry Christmas too, and thank them for their wonderful gesture that had made her morning. That way, her hosts could at least end their Christmas day knowing that their home and babies were all safe and well. But a sharp knock at the front door made her jump. *Good God! This place is like Waterloo station today!*

Adie was completely astonished to find Madeline Murphy, the owner of Torley Tresses hair salon, standing on her doorstep holding a small Christmas tree. It was the one from the shop. She laughed with real delight, and opened the door wider. Madeleine stepped through it, grinning, and handed her the tree.

"I know you said you didn't have any decorations, so I got to thinking. The salon's now closed until after New Year, so you may as well borrow the tree, since you like it. Maybe you could drop it back the on January 3rd, when we're open again?"

Adie giggled with delight at this wonderful, random act of kindness. "Yes, of course! Thank you so much."

Madeleine quickly checked her watch. "I have to go. I've a turkey to prepare, not to mention a hungry family to sling breakfast at. Merry Christmas Adrienne."

As she turned to leave, Adie said, "Wait! How did you know where to find me?"

"Easy! Sue Robinson's one of my best friends," Madeleine explained. "I knew you were here. I brought the flowers at her request, and I'd just gone back to the car to get the Christmas tree, but you'd shut the door!"

She raised a hand in a wave and started running towards her car. "See ya", she called, "and Merry Christmas! Your hair will look better after you've pulled a comb through it."

Adie laughed again, remembering her new shortened locks. They probably did look a bit like a birds nest. "Merry Christmas!" she called as Madeleine quickly turned her car around in Adie's driveway and tore away in a flurry of flying gravel.

Adie removed the cushions from one of the window seats, sat the little Christmas tree on it, and plugged it in. She hugged herself with real delight as the pretty blue lights winked into to life. The tree was about four feet tall, and it fitted just perfectly in its temporary home. She then cut the paper from around the gorgeous bouquet and placed the vase on the coffee table. The room looked complete, and it suddenly felt rather festive.

She found herself weeping gently, with profound gratitude. People were so kind here, and so ready with their time and resources, even at their own busy times. Already, just a few hours into the Christmas she'd been absolutely dreading, fearing she'd likely die from loneliness or wretchedness or both, she felt like she somehow mattered to some of the people in this little community. They had been so generous to her, it was truly humbling.

Remembering her need to reassure her houseowners that she hadn't burned their cottage to a pile of smouldering cinders, she quickly sent her email to them and finally went to get her longed-for cup of tea.

Back in bed, she checked her phone. Her heart soared, to see a missed call from Matty. He'd left a voicemail message wishing her a Merry Christmas. She rang him back.

"Hi Mum. Merry Christmas."

"Hello love. Merry Christmas to you too. Are you all ok?"

"Yep. Just having breakfast. Gonna be a quiet day, but that's ok. Millie has a cold, poor thing. We were up half the night with her, so we're all knackered. It's just as well we're staying put, really. Thanks for the presents, by the way, Mum."

Adie was sorry to hear that her baby granddaughter was unwell. She wished Matty and his family a happy and peaceful Christmas. Matty had apparently sent a parcel to her flat, which had probably arrived after she'd left. She assured him her neighbour would have taken it in and would certainly look after it for her until she went home. It was nice to know someone in her family had remembered her. Matty wanted to know if her house-sit was nice, and she told him it had exceeded her expectations, which it definitely had. She wasn't able to explain what it was about the place that had so effectively settled her turbulent emotions, so she didn't try. She also didn't mention anything about going to a party.

After the call, a quiet, cosy stillness settled gently over the house. Initially, Adie had thought the flowers at the front door were from Bryan, which of course didn't make sense because he wouldn't have the faintest idea where she was. But it was interesting, that her heart hadn't done anything when she'd found them. It hadn't flipped, lurched or swelled. In that briefest of seconds, when she wondered if Bryan had sent the bouquet, there hadn't been a reaction at all. And on learning they were from her hosts, she'd simply felt delighted. There was no disappointment, or self-censure for having guessed wrong.

Adie found it intriguing, how since she had arrived here at Teapot Cottage, just a few days earlier, she hadn't mourned much for her marriage at all. There had been periods of sad reflection, yes, but nothing like the howling, tearing grief she'd been drowning in for the months leading up to now. Her hormonal mood swings seemed to have settled a lot here too. Not for the first time, she wondered if perhaps her friend Miranda had been bang on the money, in suggesting a change of scene would work wonders.

She also had to concede that there may in fact be something in what Feen Raven had said, about the cottage having its own 'vibrational energy', whatever that really was. *Something* was helping to heal her, and considering the near-hysterical state she'd been in when she'd arrived, convinced that her life was over or would never have real meaning again, there had to have been some divine intervention from somewhere.

After all, nobody typically goes from being a basket case to almost total serenity and acceptance in less than a week, do they, unless they either had a bit of help or were nuts to start with?

Adie was fairly sure she wasn't nuts, and although her emotional turbulence was a continual challenge to be mastered, she felt she was actually dealing with things quite well here. She had to admit that this charming, healing little place that seemed to quietly hum to itself with a peculiar kind of joyful, gentle sweetness, had turned out to be exactly what her battered heart and soul sorely needed.

After handing Sid and Mittens their respective pre-arranged Christmas breakfasts of fresh chicken, Adie had a brief soak in the hot tub with a glass of prosecco. She then took a shower, blow-dried and tonged her hair back into its sassy new style, put on her nice new snuggly plum dress and flat shoes, and set about making herself some coffee and a favourite breakfast - mashed banana on toast with a bit-too-much-butter and a shake of cinnamon.

The morning passed peacefully, with a few festive texts popping up from different friends, and a happy video call from Miranda, who was sunning herself in Madeira with a champagne cocktail in hand. She was already slightly tipsy and giggly, and Adie laughed, truly delighted that her lovely friend was having a happy time, and grateful for the insight and push she'd provided.

She heard a heavy vehicle drive up the track about half past one, tooting its horn by the cottage as it went. *The Shalloes*, she thought to herself. *On their way to the Ravens for Christmas dinner.*

There had been no communication from Ruth or from Teresa, but time zones, phone signals and general Christmas busy-ness had to be considered. Adie figured she might hear something later from either of her daughters, and tried to shrug off her disappointment, for the time being at least.

She'd already had a look through the CDs in the shelf by the stereo. The Robinsons had surprisingly eclectic musical tastes, with a collection that offered everything from Enya to Motorhead, and she found herself picking an album by Sinead O'Connor. As the strains of *Nothing Compares to You* filled the room, she found the tears coming again. This old favourite was such a sad song, and a haunting one, and never had it been more poignant than it was right now.

As the pain of loss returned, Adie found herself sobbing almost uncontrollably. She replayed the song over and over, allowing the grief to come tumbling out, which she knew it had to, if she were ever to rebuild her life in a healthy, positive way. What kind of life could she possibly have, if she continued to try and live with this much pain and sadness bottled up inside?

After a full hour of cathartic crying and reminiscing, she felt herself gently coming to understand that it was time; to acknowledge and accept that her marriage to Bryan was now behind her, and she had to find a way to move on. Drifting along and hoping for a miracle just wasn't an option anymore.

Her husband was gone, her kids had independent lives, and it was time; to start really thinking about herself, and what *she* wanted from a life that was now headed in a new direction. Here in this little house that somehow felt almost magical, the prospect no longer seemed so terrifying. The idea of being in full control of her own choices didn't feel so scary. It was time; to stop fighting the process, and embrace the quiet transformation that had started taking place within her soul.

Adie's outpouring of grief quietly came to a natural and comfortable stop, and she then put on a more cheerful CD - an old favourite from Bon Jovi. The red-eyed panda look (or the 'two piss-holes in the snow' look, as Bryan used to say) was anything but flattering. She went upstairs and bathed her puffy eyes and face. When she came back down, she scooped up a reluctant Mittens and danced around the living room with her, singing "Livin' on a Prayer" at the top of her tone-deaf voice.

"Take my hand, we'll make it, I swear. Oh-oh, livin' on a prayer." Mittens managed to struggle free and bolt away, and Adie giggled out loud.

Who'd have thought I'd be singing and dancing on Christmas Day, even if it was only with an unwilling cat?

Mid-afternoon, a call came in from Ruth, and Adie's heart leapt as she answered it. Ruth sounded like she was on the moon. The call was all hissy with interference and kept cutting out, which was frustrating, but the communication was manageable - just.

"Adie! Happy Christmas! I'm sorry it's so late in the day. There's no phone signal at Gina's uncle's place up in the hills. It's a nightmare trying to communicate with anyone! I've had to drive halfway up a mountain to get any reception at all! I didn't have a hope of trying to make anything work down there. We're literally in the middle of nowhere. I can't even pronounce the name of the nearby town. Are you alright?"

"Hello, Ruth. Yes, I'm absolutely fine, don't worry. Happy Christmas to you too."

"It's raining cats and dogs here, Adie. How's the Lake District? How's that cottage you're staying in? Not too damp and chilly, I hope?"

"Oh, no, not at all! It's warm and cosy, with a lovely open fire and a stunning view of the valley. And a hot tub, of all things! The local people are nice. All very friendly. In fact, I've been invited to a drinks party tonight."

Adie felt a tiny pang of guilt, admitting she had an invitation to go out. She wasn't sure whether Ruth might find it offensive that she was 'already getting on with her life' again, so soon after the hand grenade she had thrown into the middle of her family had blown everyone's world to smithereens.

"I'm not sure whether I'll go", she added, self-consciously, thinking about the lovely dress hanging on the back of the bedroom door. All of a sudden, for no apparent reason, her confidence had nose-dived again, and she was back to the all-too familiar feeling of trying not to burst into tears, for the millionth time.

"A party? Oh Adie, do go! Have some fun. You have to start living again, you know. Please say you'll go."

"I don't know, Ruth. I'm not sure whether I deserve to have any fun."

"Oh, Adie, that's ridiculous! Of course, you do! Look, events have certainly shocked us all. There's no denying that, but we can't change anything now, or pretend that none of it happened, can we? We have to move forward and take each day as it comes until we figure out how we really feel. But staying in on Christmas night, and depriving yourself as some form of self-flagellation, well that won't help anyone, will it? Please, promise me you'll put on a really posh frock and go to that party."

"Well, I haven't got a *really* posh frock, but I've got a fairly nice one that will do the job," Adie admitted. "So yes ok, I will go. As long as you don't mind."

"Why on earth would I mind?" Ruth demanded. "It's not my place to even *have* an opinion, let alone voice it! Look, Adie, you need to forgive yourself, ok? I've forgiven you, so you must forgive yourself. I was desperately upset, of course, but I'm not anymore. I've had some counselling, to process all this, and I'm in a much better place with it all now. It's what I called to say, mostly, apart from 'Merry Christmas' from us all here, of course. I know you probably didn't expect to hear from me."

"No, I didn't", Adie confessed. "I'm so glad you rang." She felt the depressingly familiar tears pricking her eyes again. So much for feeling like she had a handle on things! *When will I ever get off this ridiculous emotional see-saw?*

Ruth spoke again. "Adie, you have to stop beating yourself up about everything. You can't keep living in anguish. We're all only human, and we only ever do what feels right at the time, which is what you did. I don't agree with how you chose to handle it all, and I'm entitled to say that much, but I've never been in that position myself, to really judge. I can only imagine how difficult it must have been for you."

Ruth's voice crackled and waned, and Adie had to strain to hear her daughter. "It's not my place to second-guess what was going on in your head, Adie, or tell you what you should have done instead, because who else can truly know how you felt about anything? But I do know it had to be horrific for you. Giving me away in the first place, even though you were still more or less a child yourself, must have been a devastating choice to be forced to make. If you felt even an ounce of what I feel for Chiara, who I didn't even give birth to, it must have torn you apart to have let me go. And I can't imagine what it must've been like, dealing with that all by yourself, for all these years; to have been too ashamed and afraid to tell any of us. To have settled for what you were prepared to, in order to be closer to what you needed."

Adie was deeply humbled by Ruth's perspective. She thought she'd never be forgiven by the daughter she'd tracked down, moved next door to, and deceived for a long time in an effort to simply be closer to her. Ruth hadn't known she'd been adopted, and Adie hadn't felt it to be her place to tell her that, or to admit to the fact that she herself was Ruth's natural mother, until circumstances forced her into it, but the long-carried burden of deceit had been crippling. Ruth acknowledging that, well, it meant everything.

"You're right Ruth, of course, and I'm working through everything too, here on my own. I'm doing ok actually. I've been pretty knocked around by the menopause and its horrible symptoms, which hasn't helped my state of mind, but I feel like I'm gradually getting to grips with everything. A week ago, I wasn't sure I'd ever be ok again, but now I think I just might. And I will go to the party, I promise. Please give my love to Chiara and Gina."

Ruth assured Adie she would pass on her Christmas wishes and rang off.

Adie was pensive. Counselling? Laying your life bare to a complete stranger, while you tried to hack your way through the hurt and confusion and make sense of everything? It wasn't a comfortable thought to her, but she was vastly relieved (and humbled yet again) that Ruth's process had helped her to reach a place of forgiveness and acceptance.

Ruth had initially rejected all Adie's attempts to explain. Communications had been impossible at first, then frostily civil, and lately slightly more friendly. There had been a gradual thaw towards cordiality, but Adie hadn't known whether that was the best she could ever expect to have with her daughter.

Now, after Ruth's call, she felt more hopeful. It felt like a significant breakthrough. It was big progress, and for the first time, Adie felt that maybe - just maybe - she and Ruth would continue to move forward to some kind of positive relationship. And maybe Adie could consider getting some professional support, herself. Uncomfortable or not, perhaps it really would help, to talk to an objective stranger who wouldn't judge her. It was something to think about, at least.

At seven o'clock, Adie began to get ready for the party. She could hear different vehicles going past the cottage on their way up to the farm. Her face was still slightly puffy from her long bout of crying. Nobody here knew her well enough to really notice that about her but she still took extra care with her make-up, to camouflage the fact as best she could. Satisfied with the result, she then tweaked her hair a little, and slipped into her lovely new dress.

She checked her reflection in the long mirror on the back of Sue and Glenn's bedroom door. Her legs looked pretty good in the black patent heels, with her new sheer tights which had just a little hint of sparkle. She couldn't quite ignore her softened jawline or the fact that her torso had lost the feminine definition it had before the menopause. Her hitherto hour-glass figure now looked more like a straight sausage in a sack, but she thought she could have looked a lot worse, as a fifty-two-year-old cast-aside wife with a shipwreck past and no idea whatsoever about where she was going in life. She gently chided herself.

Come on, old tart. Time to shelve all that negative thinking, for one night at least. Let's go have some fun!

At seven-thirty sharp there was a knock at the door, and Peg stood there, smiling, wearing a fake fur coat worthy of a Hollywood movie. It was spectacular, a real vintage piece, with a generous fake fur collar that covered the shoulders entirely, and deep fur cuffs. Peg had put her hair up in a messy bun and with chandelier-like earrings dangling from her lobes, she looked a bit like Patsy out of Absolutely Fabulous.

"WOW!" both women exclaimed at once. Adie had forgotten that Peg hadn't seen her since her radical hair transformation. She giggled. Peg was gaping at her. "Oh my God! How amazing do you look?" she cried. "Loving the hair!"

"Thank you!" Adie laughed. "I was in need of some serious TLC, and a radical change was in order! Madeleine Murphy's trusty assistant and nail technician at Torley Tresses overhauled me. They had their work cut out for them, make no mistake, but thanks to their heroic efforts, I look human again, and a lot less bedraggled, although I must admit the hair is a still bit of a shock every time I look in the mirror!"

"It must feel great, though? All short and sassy, so much easier to work with?"

Adie nodded. She told Peg about donating her hair to the cancer charity, and Peg beamed. "That's so kind and thoughtful! What a wonderful legacy!"

Adie grabbed a bottle of wine from the kitchen table and came back to the door.

"Let's go. And Merry Christmas, by the way!" Peg linked her arm, and as Adie pulled the door closed behind her, she felt, for the first time in a long time, a small but distinct thrill of anticipation.

Peg parked her car in one of the few remaining spaces left in the crowded driveway at Ravensdown House. Looking up at the place, Adie was amazed at the size of it. She was expecting a more modest farmhouse dwelling, more in keeping with Mark Raven himself, perhaps - practical and functional with little in the way of frills or embellishments.

This house was something else. Even in the dark she could see it was a very substantial dwelling. It was a two-storey, completely symmetrically built homestead. Made of stone, it comprised of a solid square centre flanked by two impressive gabled wings, mullioned lead-light windows, and gentle amber light pouring from every single one. One of the two bay windows downstairs had a huge Christmas tree in front of it, complete with multi-coloured lights and an assortment of interesting vintage glass baubles.

The effect was like a Christmas card. It was magical. The house looked cheery, warm and welcoming. The big, heavy wooden front door was furnished with metal hinges and hobnails, with a large holly wreath covered in berries and tinsel hanging above the round knocker in the centre of it. The whole effect was like something out of a story book.

Adie said so to Peg, who nodded and gazed up at the house. "Yes, it's a beautiful old place. It was in very poor shape when Mark and Beth took it on, nearly thirty years ago now, and it needed a lot of repair. It's got at least five double bedrooms, I think. It's a long time since I was here for anything other than a Christmas party, so my memory's a bit hazy. But it's certainly a gorgeous house."

"Were you friends with Beth?" Adie asked.

"Oh yes! For many years. I used to mind Feen from time to time, when Beth and Mark had other events to go to. It used to be a very social crowd, around these parts, but a lot of it fell by the wayside after Beth died."

Peg's voice became thoughtful. "It was strange, really. It was almost as if she was the glue that held everyone together. Even if the Ravens weren't the instigators of a party or social event, they'd always show up for one. The Christmas party's pretty much the only bit left of the old social scene now, and if Mark had his way that would stop too, but we're all hanging onto it, in Beth's memory. She gave so much and expected so little. This yearly remembrance is important to a lot of people. It's nice that we can do it again. The pandemic kept everyone at home for far too long, didn't it?"

The party was already in full swing, with at least thirty people milling about, chatting among themselves. Adie was pleased to recognise Trudie Sangster from GladRagz Boutique, standing over by the fire, and assumed that the tall, sandy-haired man stood next to her with his arm around her waist was her partner. A massive dining table dominated one side of the room, heavily laden with food. A very big, rich-looking dark-fruit Christmas cake with berry-laden holly wrapped round it occupied the centre of the table, and there were sparklers sticking out of it, waiting to be lit.

It will look amazing when they light those, thought Adie to herself.

"Wow! What a feast!" she exclaimed.

Peg grinned. "Yeah, there's always a good spread laid on. There'll be more food in the kitchen too, I expect. Beth always used to make sure there was plenty. The Ravens started off providing everything but as the party got bigger each year, she switched it to 'bring a plate' to take some of the load off, and everyone's pretty obliging. Sheila Shalloe still provides a lot of it. She's amazing. She cooks and bakes like a demon. Puts me to shame, she does!"

Adie turned to Peg in dismay. "Oh, God! I didn't realise! Mark never said anything about bringing food. All I've brought is one pathetic bottle of wine! What was I thinking?"

"Don't worry," soothed Peg. "I've got two steak pies, two family-sized festival quiches, three dozen sausage rolls and a dozen date scones in the car, which we'll have to take through to the kitchen, since the buffet table's already full. That's plenty to add. We'll all be bloody exploding with food. And Mark lays on a lot of booze. So don't you worry about there not being enough of anything."

Adie grinned, and followed Peg back out to her car. Peg's relentless determination to feed the masses knew no bounds. Neither did Sheila Shalloe's, by all accounts. Clearly, if there was one thing people wouldn't suffer from around these parts, it was hunger.

Peg handed Adie a carrier bag and said, "You can give that to Mark, let him think it's from you, if you like. It's just a few boxes of Christmas crackers, for the table."

Back in the living room, Feen suddenly appeared in front of Adie, resplendent in a long, blood-red, vintage velvet ball gown with puffed sleeves, and pair of old, battered black ballet shoes that were tied to her ankles with ribbons, and which appeared to be the genuine dancer's article. She wore a delicate tiara threaded with bright green tinsel, to top it all off, and the overall effect was stunning. She gave Adie a dazzling smile and gave her a quick hug.

"Adrienne! You came! I was really hoping you would! Daddy said he'd invited you. I'm so glad you're here - and your new hairstyle looks completely divine! It's beautiful! That's a lovely dress too. You look futterly abulous!" The young woman's warm enthusiasm was touching.

"Thank you. So do you. Your dress is amazing. You look like you've just stepped out of a film set." Adie returned Feen's hug. "I keep forgetting I've had all my hair cut off. I always get a bit of a shock when I see myself in the mirror, or when someone mentions it," she laughed.

Feen was smiling and steering Adie gently towards the Christmas tree, which still had a few wrapped gifts beneath it.

"I've got you something for Christmas. It's only little, but I hope you like it." She bent down, selected a small parcel wrapped in gold paper with a bright blue gauze ribbon tied around it in an elegant bow.

"I know it's unexpected. Please don't be embarrassed", she added, as she handed the parcel to Adie. "It's just something little I really wanted to give you."

Adie excitedly unwrapped Feen's gift and found a beautiful pair of earrings nestling gently in blue tissue paper. They were tiny white, yellow-centred daisies set in clear, teardrop-shaped resin bubbles, wrapped up the sides with delicately plaited thin strands of silver. Adie gasped.

"Oh, Feen! These are so beautiful! I've never seen anything like this before. Wherever did you get them?"

Feen blushed. "Well, I made them, actually. It's a hobby. I'd have done forget-me-knots instead, if I'd known you'd be wearing a bless with drue in it."

Adie decided she loved Feen's adept and almost unthinking switch of her consonants. Spoonerism was so clever, and so funny, when used well.

"No, Feen, the daisies are absolutely perfect, truly. I'm far more casual than dressy, normally, and these will go with everything in my wardrobe. How wonderful of you! They are really beautiful, thank you so much!" Adie hugged Feen tightly, overwhelmed by the young woman's thoughtful kindness. She couldn't believe that Feen had made these exquisite little earrings – and especially for her, as well!

She looked more closely at them, nested in their paper. Along the bottom of each earring, the woven strands of silver had been pressed into a tiny flat piece with a '925' stamp set into it, and she could see by the fixings, the clarity of the resin, and the unblemished purity of the tiny blooms, that Feen's work was of excellent quality. She allowed her new little friend to put them on for her and she admired them in the mirror over the mantelpiece. They went well with Adie's new, shorter hairstyle.

"It's one of the nicest gifts I can ever remember getting."

Feen beamed. "Well, thank you. I'm so glad you like them. I won't monopolize you, Adrienne, as I'm sure there are plenty of other people here who'd love to do just that, but would you like to take a quick look at my workshop?"

Adie accepted the invitation with real delight, and before she knew it, Feen had taken hold of her hand and led her away to a room on the other side of the big hallway. It was a medium-sized room with plain cream walls and heavy purple damask drapes that covered what Adie remembered seeing from the outside as a lead-light bay window.

There were several lamps around, including an angle-poise lamp on wheels with two separate heads, and a few trestle tables set at different points around the room, which also had a fireplace, although there was no fire lit tonight. An easel had been set up in one corner, with an A2 sketch pad propped against it. Around the walls were a series of photographs. Some were pictures of flowers, others were pictures of trees, and there were more than a few dotted in amongst them of an attractive, smiling woman with strikingly similar features to Feen's. Adie assumed it to be Feen's mother, Beth Raven, although it didn't feel appropriate to ask.

Against one wall was a massive symmetrical sideboard, clearly an expensive antique, with heavy carving across the front of its two cupboards and many drawers. It looked to be walnut. The wood was rich and beautifully grained, and polished to an incredibly high sheen. It was extraordinary. Adie wasn't into antique furniture at all, preferring much more modern lines and styles, but there was no denying the absolute beauty of this sideboard. It was a work of art.

"What a piece of furniture!" she exclaimed. "It's magnificent!"

"Yes, isn't it? It was Granny's. I've restored it. She'd always used it and it was showing a lot of tear and wear. I've always loved it. In fact, I used to take out one of the shelves and hide in one of its cupboards when I was really small, whenever we went to visit her, and she always had to come looking for me in there. She brought it with her when she came to live with us, and when she went into the home, in one of her more mucid loments she told me she'd dragged it with her purely so I could have it."

Feen stopped, took a breath, and cleared her throat. "I attacked the whole thing with an electric sander, ripped and stroiled it, and repaired some of the dovetailing on the drawers."

Adie smiled to herself, completely unable to muster the vision of the tiny Feen wielding a sanding machine.

Feen walked over to the sideboard and pulled out one of the drawers. It was filled with tiny bottles of essential oils. Another drawer contained a variety of herbs, all neatly labelled, and a number of larger bottles of different oils and creams. In one of the cupboards was a good selection of interesting botanical books, and folders with hand-written labels which clearly contained Feen's notes.

Another set of drawers contained a selection of small jars of dried flowers, different beads and jewellery fixings and a neatly arranged set of small tools. In the cupboard on that side sat a variety of reels of wire, a couple of small soldering irons, various pairs of short and long-handled tweezers, and a large, heavily carved oak box, which Feen lifted out.

As she opened the lid, several little drawers slid forward in concertina-style, and Adie could see some of the jewellery Feen had made, nestling in the little pockets within each drawer. There was a breath-taking assortment of earrings, pendants, bracelets and brooches, in a variety of colours, shapes and sizes, all set in clear, lustrous resin like Adie's daisies. Some of the nicest were tiny, simple but perfectly formed fern leaves in beautiful shades of brown, orange and green. Adie was enthralled. Every last piece was a stunning work of art.

"You made all these?" she said in astonishment.

"Yes," Feen said simply.

"But why are they all hidden away, Feen? They deserve to be worn, all these gorgeous pieces!"

"I know", she admitted shyly. "I keep meaning to do the Christmas Daft Fair in the town, but somehow I never get around to signing up and committing to do it."

Adie sensed a lack of confidence in the young woman.

"Well, they need to see the light of day," she insisted. "In fact, may I please choose something to buy from you from this collection, for my daughters?"

Feen blushed again. "Of course," she said quietly. "Choose whatever you like, Adrienne."

It didn't take Adie long to choose a few pieces. She picked out a pair of exquisite green fern earrings and a matching bracelet she knew would be perfect for Teresa. A stunning teardrop-shaped sunflower pendant seemed equally perfect for Ruth, and she chose a more elaborate piece for Gina, Ruth's wife. That one was a series of seven small connected, cascading round discs with tiny red and orange carnation-like blooms inside them that looked like fire. It was impressive, a real statement piece, and Adie knew it would suite Gina's flamboyant nature. A small pair of earrings with similar colours, for Matty's wife Marie, completed her list. It might be a long way off, but she was hopeful that the time would come when she could give her gifts to the women in her family, and have them accepted in the spirit in which she'd offered them.

She insisted on paying Feen well for the pieces, which she knew were top quality. They negotiated a price that Feen was embarrassed by, but which Adie thought was entirely appropriate for unique artistic jewellery. Feen insisted she take the pieces now, and pay her later, so Adie accepted them in pretty presentation boxes, and promised Feen she would return the next day with the cash to cover the cost.

As they were about to leave the room, Feen hung back a little. Adie raised her eyebrows at the young woman, who then said, "I wonder if you'd like to see something else?"

"Of course!" Adie had already decided that Feen Raven was full of delightful surprises, but she was literally lost for words when Feen stepped back, bent down, and peeled back the sumptuous dark red rug beneath her feet. Underneath it was the most incredible, tiny-tiled circular mosaic of different flowers and leaves, all laid out in beautiful hues of pink, purple, green and cornflower blue. It must have been eight feet in diameter. The flowers included bluebells, daffodils, hydrangeas, and pink rose buds. Woven throughout the entire circle was a long, sinuous vine of green leaves. The centre circle of the mosaic was done in pure white tiling with gold edging and a red heart at its centre. It was one of the most beautiful things Adie had ever seen.

"Oh Feen! My God! Why do you keep this covered up? It's just stunning, so beautiful!" Adie gasped. She couldn't help herself. She felt somehow drawn to the mosaic, like she could stare at it for ever and never get tired of it. It really was the most glorious thing.

"It's my Intention Circle," Feen said shyly. "I created it to use for manifesting good intentions. Healing, creating good fortune, that sort of thing. I keep it covered until I need to use it. That helps keep it pristine and special."

"What, you *made* this?" Adie was awestruck. It was, indeed, incredibly special.

Feen nodded. "Mum and I did it. Well, she helped to design it, I mean. She was too ill to actually get down on the floor, but...." Feen nodded over at a small armchair with a delicate patchwork quilt draped over it. "That's where she'd sit, giving me direction as I put it all together. I fanaged to minish it before she died. She got to see it completed, which I'm so glad about."

Adie was slightly embarrassed at her own lack of knowledge. "So how does it work?"

Feen explained. "I generally cast spells on it, or meditate, or visualise healing, that sort of thing. While meditating I sit directly on the heart, and close to it when I'm using the centrepiece as the arena for manifestation instead."

Adie was slightly lost, understanding little about anything 'new age', which she supposed this was. She admitted as much to Feen, who just shook her head and smiled.

"That's ok. Not everyone gets it, but it's my thing. I always feel connected to Mum, too, when I'm working with it. I feel like her spirit is in it, somehow. She placed positive spirit into it while she watched me build it. I'm quite sure of it."

Feen hesitated for a moment before continuing. "You probably aren't familiar with the concept of vibrational healing, or energy medicine, as it's also called. A lot of people think it's more of a 'woo-woo' type of thing than anything that actually exists, but let me assure you, it's quite real."

She chewed her lip thoughtfully for a second, as if trying to work out how best to explain it in simple terms to a complete novice, as Adie had to admit to being.

"Everything is matter. Energy. All things emit frequencies and all living things are affected by them, Adie. As living beings, each of us is a mass of electrical and magnetic energy, and we're affected in different ways through different frequencies. It's proper science. Physics, in its most basic of terms." Feen was unable to contain the enthusiasm in her voice as she continued to explain.

"In a nutshell, this circle sits over something that's called a ley line, which runs through the farm. Ley lines are straight lines that connect important and sacred sites, and large and small energy vortexes of electromagnetic energy, across the world. The ley line here runs through to the tor at the top of the hill behind the farm from beneath the town. It runs all the way down through the Salisbury Plain, through Stonehenge, and for thousands of miles beyond, well into different countries. Teapot Cottage sits on it, as does this farmhouse." Feen grinned at Adie. "That's why Mum fell in love with this little pocket of the planet, and why the cottage feels so special too. It's because it really is. Most people who hang around here for long enough feel something deeply positive and affirming here, but most of them can't describe it, or even understand what it is," she murmured, almost to herself.

Feen's narrative sounded strange, but she spoke in simple, matter-of-fact terms, as if she were describing a shopping list. She didn't for one moment appear deranged or deluded. She'd simply shown Adie an integral part of her life, and Adie felt honoured by the young woman's generous and trusting invitation to take a peek into the ethereal world she inhabited.

The notion of vibrational energy intrigued Adie, and so did Feen's simple view of life. She vowed to try and learn more about it. After all, *something* profound and potentially wonderful was happening to her within the walls of Teapot Cottage, but it was beyond her current capacity to describe what it was. Maybe it was time she delved a little deeper. Learning more might mean she'd get to spend more time with her charming and enigmatic little neighbour. And there was nothing wrong with that!

Chapter 8

It looked as if most of the usual suspects had rocked up again this year, and the girls had done yet another great job with the food. As Mark looked around at all the happy, animated people in the room, he conceded once again that the Christmas party probably was a good idea. It was good to catch up with friends he really liked and never seemed to see enough of.

He was, by his own admission, uncharacteristically jittery tonight. Frustrated with himself over his own nervousness, he'd had to make a conscious effort not to let anyone see it. He was also very reluctant to admit to himself that he'd taken more care than usual with his appearance, wearing a new blue shirt that matched the colour of his eyes and having insisted that Feen took the best care she'd *ever* taken, in cutting his hair last night. She'd given him a Christmas gift this morning of a very upmarket, fresh-smelling aftershave, which he'd indulged in a liberal splash of tonight, after shaving more carefully than he'd done in years. He was a bit worried that he'd gone overboard with the aftershave, and he'd also been glancing at his watch more often than usual, and keeping a closer eye on the door than he normally would.

Feen had pulled him to one side, and quietly told him; "don't worry, Daddy. Just calm down a bit. She'll be here! You can stop acting like a cat on a hot tin roof."

Mark was used to his canny daughter knowing his innermost thoughts, even when he didn't fully understand them himself, but he still tried to play down the fact that he'd been quite looking forward to seeing Adrienne Bostock. He tried to shrug it away.

"Feen, if she comes, she comes. If she doesn't, it's no big deal, honestly!"

Feen had just smirked in that maddening way she always did when she was privy to something he hadn't cottoned onto himself, before turning on her heel and walking away.

Daft bugger's got wrong end o't stick, as usual.

Thanks to his inability to quell his jangling nerves, he'd let himself be distracted with more than a couple of inane conversations, hoping it would take the tension out of him. It had worked up to a point, but he couldn't deny the sudden rush of relief he got when Adrienne finally walked into the room.

She looked amazing, after quite a radical transformation from when he'd seen her two days earlier. The beautiful long hair was all gone, but he admired her short new style. She was wearing a very pretty dress too. He decided that she looked a bit cheeky now, which he liked, and he thought she scrubbed up quite well.

Feen pounced on her more or less immediately, but Mark hadn't minded. It was enough that she'd turned up. He knew he'd get the chance to speak to her eventually. Finally, he could start to relax and enjoy himself.

He was perfectly happy, too, mingling among his guests, until the wife of one of the famers who leased some of his land remarked in passing that the heavy gold drapes in the room were looking a little faded. She thought the room might benefit from being redecorated.

He must have looked a little taken aback by her comment, because she immediately flushed beet red and hastily apologised for being critical, before promptly scuttling off towards the buffet table. Mark watched her go, and blinked. Nobody else had ever said anything to him about the state of his house, so he immediately found his sister and asked her what she thought. He was more than a bit surprised at how swiftly she nodded her head.

"Yes, Mark. It needs updating. You're stuck in a time-warp with this 'ouse. Its twenty-five years since you decorated it. The sun has all but killed the wallpaper in 'ere, and them curtains are only fit for the bin, really."

"So what, yer tellin' me the room looks scruffy?"

Sheila had nodded again. "It does. Scruffy is a very good word for it. Dated might be another, so might tired, dilapidated, faded, jaded, take your pick. And that applies to the whole house, Mark, not just this room. It's time you chucked some new paint and paper at the place."

Mark was mortified. "Well, fer God's sake, woman! Why 'aven't yer said anythin' before now?"

Sheila shrugged. "It hasn't come up in conversation, and I don't spend much time up here, do I, these days? It's your house. You have to decide what to do with it. But it could do with a tart-up. Don't ask for the truth if you don't want to hear it, brother dear."

Mark was dumbstruck. But, as he looked around him, he had to admit that the house was looking a bit tired. Neglecting the place was probably just a by-product of being determined to keep busy on the farm after Beth had died, but the habit had taken hold, to the point where he'd become more or less oblivious to his surroundings.

He suddenly felt like he was waking up after a long sleep, and noticing his home with fresh eyes. To his dismay, as he took an objective look around the big living room, he could now see that the curtains *were* all faded at the edges, the wallpaper *was* all bleached across the middle where the sun had poured straight onto it for more than twenty years. The carpet *did* look threadbare in the doorway and in front of the hearth, and the light fittings *did* look hopelessly old-fashioned.

He immediately accosted Feen and demanded to know why she'd never mentioned it either, that the house was in dire need of redecoration. She'd gazed at him thoughtfully, before replying.

"It's a mess, yes. But the time to do it is definitely coming. Don't worry about it for now, Daddy. It will be done next year, and you'll be happy with the results, I guarantee it."

So, Feen had something up her sleeve, then! Mark was relieved that she apparently had it in hand. He had no real idea how he might want the place to look. Interior design was never his thing. He knew he was good at many things but being stylish wasn't one of them. Decorating had been Beth's domain; she was the one who knew how things should be. Left to his own devices with trying to make the poor old place look better, it was a pretty safe bet that it would probably end up looking a hundred times worse. He realised with a jolt that when he and Beth had gone on the hunt for paint, wallpaper and soft furnishings, Feen hadn't even been a twinkle in his eye! Sheila was right. No wonder everything looked dated and worn out.

If Feen could take care of it without his input, he'd be happy. He just hoped she wouldn't turn the place into an interior woodland, or some kind of witches cave with the fluorescent yellow eyes of God knows what staring out at him from every corner. He could probably cope with a crystal ball or two, and other strange ornaments dotted about, and even some questionable wallpaper themes if it came to it, but he figured he'd have to draw the line at artistically created cobwebs in the corners of every room. At the very least, they'd have to be less obvious than the real ones that were already there!

He wondered again why she'd never said anything about the state of the place, because it hadn't got like this overnight, had it? Decay was a gradual process. Surely she must have noticed it? It baffled him that she'd never drawn his attention to it, but there again, he hadn't seen it himself, so how could he blame her if she hadn't, either?

Ah well, mebbe kid's not said owt because she's always 'ad a mind to get on wi't job next year.

Inwardly though, Mark cringed. As thankful as he was for the farmer's wife having drawn his attention to the state of his house, he now felt mortified. He usually wasn't overly concerned with people's opinions, but the last thing he wanted was for any of his friends to feel sorry for him, or wonder if he'd decided to just give up on the home he'd worked so hard for, and let it go to rack and ruin now that Beth was no longer here. Did they all think he was still so submerged in his grief, almost a decade on, that he was oblivious to the state the place was falling into? It would really bug him now, he knew, until something was done about it. He shook himself mentally.

Oh, fer pity's sake, man. Get a bloody grip! It's decoratin'! There's worse things to be worryin' about.

And something else *was* gnawing quietly away at Mark. If he was honest with himself, he was trying very hard not to think too hard about Carla Walton, a woman here at the party who he'd unwisely agreed to go out with a couple of times. He was wishing with all his heart that she wasn't here tonight. He couldn't have avoided inviting her, since the Christmas party was common knowledge and it would have just been mean, to have omitted to tell her she was welcome. But he was starting to feel that any kind of involvement with her, even a casual one, was a big mistake. He didn't really have any feelings for her, and he could never understand why he'd ever said yes in the first place, to going out for dinner with her, and then to a movie on another night soon after that.

Maybe it had been a random spark of loneliness, or gratitude that someone was interested in in a grumpy, greying farmer, enough to want to share a meal. That must've been what had prompted him to agree to it. He'd also felt that refusing would be rude. He had no idea at all, what the expectations, boundaries and behaviours might be in the 'dating world' these days!

But that first evening out had led to another, and now Carla was pushing for more, and it worried Mark a lot. She clearly now felt there was something between them, and he knew that from his side at least, there never would be. Since she'd more or less ignored him whenever he'd tried to explain that he wasn't in the market for romance, he knew he needed to be a bit more blunt in setting the record straight.

He winced at the thought of having to spell it out. Carla was probably lonely, and maybe a bit vulnerable too. Not everyone was resigned, like he was, to a loveless life. She might be on the wrong side of fifty as well, but she still had hopes and dreams, and Mark knew he'd have to let her down as gently as he could. He still didn't know quite how he was going to do it, but he did know that tonight couldn't be the night, with it being Christmas and all. Early in the New Year though, he would have to grow a pair and figure out how to pull the pin.

His courtship with Beth had been straightforward. It had been love at first sight, and a kind of *knowing,* and he couldn't have described it better than that. They both just knew, from the moment they met, that they were meant to be together, and so they were. Nothing about it had seemed complicated or wrong. They just fitted together, like two pieces of a puzzle, right from the very start.

Before meeting Beth, Mark had been on a few dates with a handful of girls, and he'd enjoyed himself, but he'd never broken anyone's heart and no one had ever broken his. He'd played the field a bit, had some fun with girls who were willing, but there was never anything serious about it. The worst that had ever happened to him was being stood up, and left hanging around in the street outside a movie place where he was meant to meet a girl he'd liked. He'd been furious, but only because he'd already paid for the tickets. After half an hour of waiting, he'd decided that it didn't make any sense to waste both of them so he'd gone in and watched what was left of the film on his own. His pride had recovered quickly enough, and he'd soon forgotten about the girl.

He and his friends were all so young, back then, and settling down had been the last thing on most of their minds. They were all more interested in travelling or finding a decent job than following in the footsteps of their parents' generation and getting married young and starting a family straight away. It was a new world, with new opportunities for young people. Marriage, mortgages and babies were definitely on the cards, but still a few years into the future, for most of them.

The young Mark had wanted all that eventually, but he hadn't been remotely ready for falling instantly in love. When it happened, he'd been astonished to realise that settling down was suddenly the obvious and comfortable thing to do. It was proof, in his mind, that you just had to meet the right person. When you found the one you really clicked with, who shared your dreams, you doubled the energy and passion required to realise them, and everything else fell into place.

The modern world was a scary one. He remembered a conversation he'd once had with Beth, on one of their wedding anniversaries, before she'd got sick. She'd said something along the lines of being glad she'd met him when she did, because she couldn't imagine being with anybody else, or being on her own. He'd agreed and said that he was really glad he wasn't "out there" in the crazy mixed-up world, as it was even way back then, trying to find someone to settle down with.

It were bad enough in yer teens an' twenties, hopin' a lass might like yer, an' gettin' tied up in knots if she didn't. Bein' "out there" now, at this time o' life, is a thousand times more terrifyin'.

Now he was pushing fifty-five, and widowed from the woman he once couldn't imagine living without. It was just as well he wasn't in the running for romance. It would all be just too complicated now. The couple of 'dates' he'd recently had with Carla had made that crystal clear. There was a lot to be said for a simple life, and on the random occasions where the loneliness of being on his own started to bite a little, he usually shrugged it off, figuring it was better to be alone than tied up with the wrong person. He knew Carla was the wrong woman to be involved with, but it hadn't occurred to him that there might still be a 'right' person, out there in the world for him.

Chapter 9

When she re-entered the party with Feen, Adie was surprised to be immediately swooped upon, by a woman of about the same age as herself, who almost demanded to know her name. Adie disliked her immediately, with her icy demeanour, her heavily made-up face with its over-bright, car-crash lipstick, and the brittle smile that didn't reach her eyes. She wore a short, low-cut, black satin dress that was at least one size too small. It clung to every curve, leaving little to the imagination, and not in a flattering way.

The woman didn't bother to introduce herself, electing instead to initiate her conversation by pitying Adie for having been "caught in the clutches of that mad Seraphine" who "can't even utter a sensible sentence", as she put it, with no trace of humour. Her remarks immediately put Adie on the defensive, and when she then went on to ask several intrusive questions about where Adie was from, where she was staying, and how long she intended to stay in Torley, she found her hackles rising.

Although appearing polite and attentive, the woman's smiles were completely insincere. She seemed highly strung, jittery and almost angry, and Adie felt very much on edge with her. There was no denying her attractiveness, but her green eyes were cold and watchful, almost reptilian in their lack of warmth, as she sized Adie up. Adie looked around to try and catch Peg's eye, hoping to send out a silent plea to be rescued. Mercifully, the woman abruptly lost interest in her and ended the conversation with a tight laugh, saying she hoped Adie wasn't in the market for romance, because there was none to be had in Torley.

As she walked away, Feen appeared again, and Adie almost sagged with relief. The young woman handed her a glass of wine and grinned apologetically at her.

"Sorry Adrienne, I could sense what was happening over here, and I was really trying to get to you! But Daddy has weirdly chosen tonight to have some sort of midlife crisis about redecorating the house, of all things, and then Uncle Bob was banging on about his bloody sciatica, and I couldn't cut him short and barge off."

She nodded toward the retreating back of the woman who had accosted Adie. "So, you've met the lovely Carla Walton, then. The 'ice maiden', I call her. Horrible creature. She's been trying to wheedle her way into Daddy's affections for a few months now. She thinks she's laid claim to him, not that he's having a bar of it."

"Well, I wouldn't want to speculate of course, but I think if he was looking for love he'd be barking up the wrong tree there," Adie murmured, now aware that Carla's conversation had been a thinly veiled warning to Adie to keep her sights clear of the other woman's prize.

"You're absolutely right. She's a proper cold fish. She makes a good show of being all cordial and friendly, but it's not just the Botox that stops her from smiling. She hasn't got a warm bone in her body. She's as ruthless and crass as they come. Fancies herself as lady of the manor, and doesn't care who knows it."

Feen giggled. "The funny thing is, Adrienne, she makes no secret, even to Daddy, about the fact that she doesn't like me. She isn't smart enough to see that she's spoiling her own agenda, since he'd never have a bar of anyone who didn't like his family. She's selfish to the point of being utterly clueless about what matters to him the most. She'll hoist herself with her own petard soon, which won't be a bad thing for him, or me for that matter. Mum would spin in her grave at the thought of Carla sinking her fangs into him."

Adie nodded. "She'd have every reason to, I think."

Feen went on to say, in a more thoughtful tone, "I wouldn't mind Daddy meeting *someone*, though. He's a nice man, and he doesn't deserve to be lonely. But he's never looked twice at anyone since Mum died. He loved her so much, you know. He went to pieces when she went. Threw himself into the farm and other things, and that's how he got through it."

Adie nodded. "I'm sure it hit you all very hard. A *lot* of people loved her, from what I've heard."

Peg showed up at that point, and Feen wasted no time in telling her that Carla had already been across to spray her territory, as it were. Peg rolled her eyes.

"No change there, then. Sassy, gorgeous thing like you, Adie, I'm not surprised she's marked your card. She's even warned *me* off the good Mr Raven in the past, not that she needed to. Since my Andy died, fifteen years ago now, I've gone through the change and lost all interest in men." Peg took a long swig from her own wine glass, and carried on.

"Not that I mind. I've had the happy marriage, and the mind-blowing sex. I've been there, seen it, done it, worn out the bloody t-shirt, and that's it. I'm a happy little singleton now, quite at home and content with my three cats and no sexual fireworks, apart from the battery-induced kind now and then, when I've remembered to put damn things on charge."

Feen went bright red and made a quick excuse to dart away. Peg and Adie both cracked up laughing.

"Well, I don't think she was expecting that!" Adie sputtered, trying not to choke on her drink. "There's nothing like a couple of old bags talking about their sex lives to send the younger generations skittering for cover."

"Oh, she's young yet, bless her, but one day she'll be having those conversations herself. She just can't imagine being sixty-two quite yet." Peg chuckled, prompting Adie to try yet again not to choke on her drink. Sixty-two? Peg looked ten years younger!

Carla heard them laughing and shot a 'daggers' look at them both, which only made them laugh all the harder.

As the evening went on, Adie found herself enjoying the party immensely. She met Trudie's husband Kevin and got a chance to chat to Bob Shalloe again, and meet his wife Sheila, so she had the opportunity to thank her for the gorgeous Parkin. Sheila offered to email her the recipe, which she accepted.

"I'm not much of a baker to be honest, Sheila, but I'm definitely going to give that one a try. The Aga terrifies me, though!" she confessed. "All I've done is reheat things in it, so far. My Christmas lunch was a ready-meal lasagne! I haven't the faintest clue how to regulate the thing. I'm used to a big gas range, eight hobs, three ovens, all thermostat controlled with quick dials for on and off!"

Sheila grinned. "Oh, don't be afraid o't Aga, love. It's easy-peasy when you know 'ow to use it. It's all about coordination. Shall I come over and give you a lesson on using it? Day after tomorrow? I'll give you a ring to sort out a time. Truly, once you know what to do with it, it's a piece of cake!" She laughed at her own joke, as did

Adie. Sheila also had a Lancashire accent, but it wasn't as broad as her brother's.

"Yes, please, that would be really helpful." Adie nodded, hoping that the random hot flush currently creeping across her body wasn't making her as red in the face as she felt.

Mark Raven tapped her on the shoulder. She was delighted to see him, and finally have a chance to thank him for the party. He'd been busy talking with different friends each time she'd looked over to see if he was free. He waved away her thanks.

"Yer welcome, lass. I'm glad yer decided to come. I didn't recognise yer when you walked in, mind. You've 'ad yer 'air done."

"Yes", Adie laughed, flattered that he'd noticed, "But so have you! And I bought a new frock and a pair of shoes. You had me in a bit of a scramble at short notice." She found herself, to her great surprise, having to actively resist the urge to ask him if he liked her new hairstyle.

Mark smiled broadly, and she was immediately taken with how it transformed his weathered face into what felt like a ray of warm light. She noticed for the first time how neat, white and straight his teeth were.

At that moment, Carla descended, placing a proprietorial hand on Mark's arm. She barely looked at Adie but beamed an exaggerated smile at Mark who flinched ever-so-slightly, although Adie doubted the other woman would even notice, let alone be rebuffed by it.

"Well, there you are, darling! I've been looking everywhere for you! Come with me, I want to show you something."

With that, and with no acknowledgement whatsoever to the fact that Mark had been in a different conversation, she all but dragged him away, which he allowed with a look of polite resignation. It was clear that he didn't want to go anywhere with her, but he was too much of a gentleman to refuse her and appear rude to both women in the process.

Adie felt a spark of irritation. *Seriously?* She'd waited all evening to speak to Mark. He was her neighbour and her host, and she just wanted to have a friendly conversation with him and wish him a Merry Christmas, which she still hadn't done. But the plainly possessive Carla had other ideas.

Ah well, so be it, she shrugged to herself. *Maybe I'll have another chance later.*

Adie hadn't intended to stay long at the party. Her initial intention had been to put in appearance and leave early, since she didn't expect she would enjoy herself or be good company. But to her great surprise she was having a lovely time, and she really didn't want it to come to an end. Christmas night, affable and genuinely interesting people to meet and chat with; what was the hurry to go back to Teapot Cottage and spend the rest of the evening alone?

Someone started playing music, and a few people started dancing. Bob and Sheila Shalloe were having a 'wiggle', and a few others decided to join in. Abba gave way to Queen, then when Madonna's Material Girl started, Feen grabbed Adie and drew her into the growing group of dancers.

"Daddy plays Madonna all the time," she laughed. "Fantasising about her is his guilty pleasure, and has been since the eighties. He sings to her music while he works in the barn, but don't tell him I told you!"

Adie felt a bit self-conscious, trying to remember the last time she'd danced, and wondering how silly or old-fashioned her 'moves' might look, but as happy songs from the past kept coming, she loosened up a little more and moved in time with the music. She didn't even notice Mark Raven reappearing, until he asked if he could cut in on Feen who happily stood aside.

"Hello again," Adie smiled. "Merry Christmas! I forgot to say it before."

Mark rolled his eyes. "More like yer never got bloody chance. I'm sorry about that. She's a strong character, that Carla. A bit 'ard to say no to, at times. Merry Christmas to you too, lass."

He grabbed her hand and spun her around, and she almost lost her footing. He caught her as she stumbled, and she was aware that Carla Walton was glowering at her again, from the side-lines.

The music slowed a little, and she found herself in Mark's arms. His hold was light as he moved her around, but it was firm and confident, and it felt very nice. Adie found herself in no hurry to bring that to a close, which surprised her. She noticed that Mark wasn't much taller than she. At five feet five in her stocking feet, Adie calculated Mark to be about five feet ten.

Perfect! She thought to herself, then jumped. *What am I thinking?*

She pushed all rogue thoughts of height-compatibility out of her mind and concentrated on the music, finding that Mark was quite a good dancer. He must have danced a lot at parties with Beth.

Of course, he did! They'd been the life and soul of everyone's parties, hadn't they?

They chatted while they danced, with Mark talking about the various tasks that needed doing on the farm in the coming days. "No rest fer't wicked", he chuckled. "This is it. One day off, one night o' drink an' dancin' and back to the grind in't mornin.'

But he was smiling. He didn't seem to mind everything getting back to normal so quickly. Adie was pretty keen for the festive season to be over too. It would be good to start a new year, in a new place, hopefully with a different perspective. It certainly felt now as if the future might be less scary. Not for the first time she marvelled at how a simple change of environment could have such a positive effect on the state of mind.

"You love farming." She said it as a statement, rather than a question. Mark nodded.

"Aye, I do. It's in me blood. Can't imagine doin' owt else, to be honest. I love the land, the changin' seasons, 'ow everythin' looks different every day. And the animals are simple creatures, an' I like that. Y' know where you are wi' a sheep or a dog. Can't say't same about many people, in my experience. It's good honest graft, farmin'. I'm knackered at the end o't day, mind, but most days are good 'uns."

As the music changed again, and became more upbeat, Carla reappeared and tried to wrangle Mark away to dance. He was having none of it.

"I'll catch up wi' yer a bit later Carla." Mark was polite, not-quite dismissive, but not exactly warm to Carla. He was clearly determined to reject her advances. Adie cringed inwardly as the other woman glared squarely at her then turned on her heel and marched off.

"She's very keen on you, I think", she said mildly.

Mark sighed. "Aye. I've told her often enough, to look elsewhere. She's a persistent bugger, I'll give 'er that."

That was all he said, and Adie was wise enough not to press. *It's none of my business anyway*, she thought to herself. As a fly-by-night house-sitter who'd be leaving again in another couple of weeks, it was hardly her place to judge the love lives of the people of Torley, even if some of them *were* on a straight path to nowhere.

As the night wore on, people gradually started leaving. Most of the early departers were other farmers, who all had a pre-dawn start. Boxing Day was just another day on the farm to them, with animals or crops to tend, and plenty of work to keep them busy. A few had expressed relief that they didn't have farmhands to feed and pay on a Bank Holiday, but most were aware that it also meant more work to do themselves, so they were keen to get home to bed.

Peg came over and asked Adie if she wanted a lift back down the hill, but Mark chipped in and said he'd see her home himself.

"*Good*, thought Adie, *because with everyone leaving, there'll be nobody left to help with all the clearing up.*

Offering to help would be the least she could do, she reasoned, after being given such a lovely evening's entertainment in return for one measly bottle of mid-priced wine.

An hour later, everyone else had gone, including a clearly resentful and frustrated Carla, who had been trying every trick in the book to be invited to stay, but whom Feen had virtually dragged to the front door and pushed unceremoniously through it with a very firm "goodnight."

With the last of the dirty pots and cutlery stacked into the dishwasher, Adie looked around for her bag.

"It's safe in my bedroom," Feen piped up. "I'll fetch it for you. I made you a tonic too, a herbal remedy you might like to try, to help your hormones settle a bit. You might find it helpful."

Mark gestured for Adie to sit back down, in one of the comfortable armchairs.

"Nightcap?" he enquired.

"Just a quick one then, I know you have a busy day tomorrow. I don't suppose you have a Baileys, do you?" Adie responded hopefully.

"Aye, we do indeed. Funny, that. Baileys were Beth's nightcap an' all!"

"Oh." Adie didn't know what else to say. She felt uncomfortable. Mark noticed and shook his head. "Don't worry, lass. I'm a big lad and it's been a while now. I can pour a nice lady a nice Baileys wi'out gettin' me kecks in a twist over it."

Feen reappeared with Adie's bag, and a small jute carrier bag containing a small bottle of green and rather unappetising-looking liquid, and the pieces of jewellery Adie had chosen from her collection a few hours earlier. Feen glanced at Adie's glass and tactfully asked for a Baileys as well, and the three of them sat quietly with their drinks.

Adie broke the silence.

"Mark, Feen. Thank you so much for tonight, for inviting me. It's been really special, and I've had a far better day and night than I ever could have hoped for. A Christmas to remember."

She raised her glass. Mark and Feen raised their glasses too, and echoed Adie's sentiment. "A Christmas to remember."

Mark had poured generous measures of liqueur, so when Adie had finally finished her drink, it was nearly half past one in the morning, and she really did feel it was time to leave.

"Shall I walk Adrienne home?" Feen asked her father.

"No, lass. You get on away to bed. I'll see Adriene home."

"Guys, you must call me Adie from now on. My friends call me that."

Feen smiled and gave her a warm hug. "Adie it is, then. I'm glad we're friends. Goodnight, and I'll see you soon."

She then looked down at Adie's feet and promptly declared that her lovely shoes would be completely ruined if she tried to walk down the muddy, puddle-ridden gravel driveway in them. She produced a pair of wellington boots with roses all over them, for Adie to wear instead.

Mark laughed. "Fair point, you'd either ruin't shoes or break yer bloody ankle, an' then I'd 'ave to carry yer."

Adie grinned at the image that conjured up for her, and gratefully accepted the boots, promising to return them the following day when she came over with Feen's money.

"No rush", the girl waved an airy hand as she left the room. Nothing much seemed to bother her, except for maybe Carla Walton, who had clearly struck a nerve more than once as the party had progressed.

The night air was cold, and Adie realised she'd also come up without a coat. It wasn't far to the cottage, but she was chilly, and she shivered. Mark immediately swept off his jacket and draped it across her shoulders. Gallantry was a rare thing these days, she knew. Giving up his coat was the sort of thing Bryan had done, many times in the past, and she allowed herself to acknowledge a twinge of grief, a tiny but poignant moment of sad reflection, at the loss of her marriage.

As they made their way down the drive, Mark spoke up.

"Thank you for your 'elp tonight, Adie, and for comin'. You were a proper breath of fresh air in that 'ouse, and that's been sorely needed. Us lot, we've all gone a bit bloody stagnant of late, even before that pandemic came an' buggered us up. You've caused quite a stir tonight. It'll give the neighbours summat to talk about for a bit, any road, the bright little bluebird that came to Ravensdown's Christmas party an' 'ad me dancin'."

"Oh, Mark, it was a *lovely* party! Such nice people, your friends, all of them. You must keep having the Christmas party. I know you'd rather not keep doing it, but please don't stop. In fact, wherever I am this time next year, I think I'm going to get in my car and come back here for this. So, you'll *have* to have it again next year!"

Mark had taken her arm, without her really noticing, and he now gave it a squeeze.

"It's a deal," he said decisively. "You come back, an' I'll 'ave the bloody party. Wi' bells on! An' next time you'll not be doin' any cleanin' up."

As they approached the edge of the entrance to the cottage, Adie suddenly jumped, and gasped with shock. She could hardly believe her eyes. Teapot Cottage's lovely little front lawn, next to the driveway itself, had been completely mashed up, like a large vehicle had driven over it several times.

"Oh no! Look at that!" she cried. "What a mess! Who would do something like that?" She looked at Mark in horror. The once pretty patch of lawn was now a massive, muddy pile of churned up earth. What would Glenn and Sue think, when they arrived home in a fortnight and saw that?

Mark stared at it in silence for a moment or two. Then he spoke, quietly. "Bloody 'ell! It's a right mess, in't it?" He shook his head. "Some bugger must o' bin blind drunk an' driven over it on't way down. I didn't think anyone had been pissed enough to end up doin' summat like that, to be fair, but I could be wrong. Most around here are dead against drink drivin' but you never know who might've 'ad a skinful and then got behind the bloody wheel."

Adie felt like sobbing. Mark tried to reassure her.

"Don't worry, lass. I'll pop down tomorrow mornin' and smooth it over, it'll not take ten minutes wi' a bobcat an' some britches-arse-steam. We'll see what we can make of it then. Might 'ave to get some sod from somewhere up on't farm and relay't grass, but there's plenty up there. Its fixable, Adie. It's a small thing. Don't give it another thought tonight. Get on in to bed."

He squeezed her arm, and she felt reassured. This unflappable man would sort it out. He said he would, and she believed him. He was quietly solid, a reliable rock. He said what he meant and he meant what he said, and that was good enough. She wasn't sure what 'britches-arse-steam' was, and it didn't seem like the right time to be asking, even though she was itching to. Maybe there'd be a chance another time.

She slipped off Mark's jacket and handed it back to him. The air felt freezing, so they quickly said goodnight and she let herself into the cottage. Sid was excited to see her, and she slipped off Feen's wellies, sank to the floor with her back against the sofa, and buried her face in his warm fur. For once, she let him lick her face. He was such a lovely, affectionate dog. Even just in a few short days, she'd grown quite fond of him.

It had been a delightful night, until she'd seen the lawn. Someone had virtually destroyed it. Had it been deliberate? Adie felt sick to her stomach. She couldn't bring herself to think anyone would want to do something like that to Glenn and Sue's property. They were, by all accounts, a well-liked couple in Torley. She couldn't imagine who might wilfully inflict that kind of damage upon them in their absence. Mark was probably right - it was likely just an unfortunate, drunken incident. Whoever had been responsible probably wouldn't even remember it tomorrow.

Still, that didn't stop Adie from feeling thoroughly unnerved, and compelled to check once again that the chickens were safely locked away. She also made sure that Mittens was safely asleep on the window seat, and that all the doors and windows were firmly locked shut, before she finally went upstairs to bed.

Chapter 10

The thrum of a heavy engine woke Adie, just before dawn. Startled, she wondered what on earth it could be. Yawning sleepily, she tiptoed to the window and peeked around the curtains. Through the pre-dawn half-light and the swirling early-morning fog, she could just make out the shape of a bobcat excavator. It was going gently to and fro, flattening the ruined lawn into some semblance of smoothness.

Good God, she thought to herself, realising that Mark Raven was making good on his promise from the night before. *He doesn't waste any time! It can't be much past six in the morning.*

To her surprise, however, it was closer to half past seven. She quickly changed into jeans and a jumper and hurried downstairs. On opening the front door, she could see that the ground was indeed smooth again, albeit without its lovely grass top from yesterday. As she approached the grader, she called out, in fear of otherwise looming out of the fog and giving Mark the fright of his life.

He let the bobcat's engine idle.

"Sorry Adie", he shouted. "I didn't mean to wake yer, but these bloody machines make the noise they make, and that's that."

"It looks much better," Adie observed, looking at the muddy but now smooth surface

"Aye. I've some sods to lay down, 'opefully they'll take, and I've brought a few stakes and string, to put around it all and keep everythin' off it fer a bit. Give it best chance, like, fer middle o'winter." He gestured to a small pile of grass-topped sods that he had brought down from the farm.

He must have dug that lot up in the middle of the night, bless his heart.

"Will you stay for a cup of coffee?" Adie offered.

Mark thought for a minute, then nodded.

"Aye, that'd be grand, lass. I've plenty to do, but nowt that can't wait another 'alf hour."

He slipped off his boots at the door, came padding through to the kitchen, and pulled out a chair and sat down. As Adie poured the coffee, she asked how early he'd had to get up to start repairing the carved-up patch of lawn.

"I were up at six, like every other mornin'. I've seeded it, and if them sods take alright as well, it should start lookin' a bit more like its old self in a few weeks. It'll take longer than that, mind, for it to go back to what it was, since it's winter an' all. But it'll be fine. I've put a rope around it all, so hopefully it'll grow again grand."

"I can't thank you enough. I feel so bad about it."

"Well, yer shouldn't," Mark said in his matter-of-fact way. "I know, it's not your 'ouse, and that makes it worse, but what's done is done. The Robinsons are good people. They'll understand. Sometimes, shit 'appens. And nobody got 'urt. That's more important than a bit o' mashed-up grass. No-one's goin' to bend their arses about it, if you'll pardon me French." He shrugged his shoulders.

At that moment Mittens chose to appear and jump straight into Mark's lap. He patted her surprisingly gently with an enormous hand.

"Allo, little 'un. You behavin'?"

They chatted for a while, and then Adie remembered that she needed to see Feen and pay her for the jewellery. She told him she had chosen some lovely pieces for her family, and that she believed Feen had real talent. He nodded.

"Aye, she does. Feen's a lot cleverer than most around 'ere give 'er credit for. Her big problem's not 'avin' enough confidence to step out into't world independent, like. Beth dyin' hit 'er pretty 'ard. She was just at that age, you know? Goin' on fifteen, wi' all that adolescent stuff goin' on wi' 'er body and 'er 'ead. She needed her mother to 'elp her find her way, but her mother were gone."

"It must have been incredibly hard," Adie observed.

Mark nodded again. "Aye, it were. Sheila's 'elped a lot, over't years, an' it's just as well, since I'm no bloody expert on teenage girls. One minute they're all over yer like a rash, the next they're screamin' in yer face an' slammin't doors on yer. I were all at sea, wi' Feen. She's settled down alright now, but for a while there I never knew whether I were Arthur or piggin' Martha."

Adie laughed, remembering how things had been with Teresa. She told him she had a daughter the same age as Feen, and admitted that Teresa had been just as difficult to manage, growing up.

They talked a while about the rollercoaster ride of raising daughters, and it was a comfy, easy conversation. Mark was nice company, and his conversation was educated and informed, even with his broad Lancashire dialect, which Adie found reassuringly earthy, real and funny. He had a good sense of humour too.

Mark Raven was a rough and ready man of the land, pragmatic to a fault. There was nothing hidden about him. What you saw was what you got, and Adie had the impression that if you didn't like what you got, he would simply shrug and walk away from you, and never give you a second thought. This was a man who had no time for appearances or for playing games with people. He was straight-up, and he expected everyone else to be. She suspected he would never stay for long where he felt out of place, just for the sake of appearances, unlike so many phony people she knew from what now was already starting to feel like a long-ago past life.

When the coffee pot and cups were all empty, Mark stood up, saying he had a ton of work to do, and needed to get going. Cheekily, he offered Adie a ride up to the farmhouse on his knee, in the bobcat, and she accepted with a smirk, in a 'what the hell' moment that was quite unlike her. There was a first time for everything, she supposed, picking up her purse and Feen's wellington boots as they left. The ride was decidedly bumpy, but mercifully short. Mark's knee was comfortable enough for the duration but Adie wouldn't have wanted to go much further.

Declining Feen's generous offer of breakfast, she settled her payment and returned the wellies, and headed back down the hill. As she did so, she heard Teapot Cottage's phone ringing, and she hurried to answer it. She was delighted to find that it was Sheila Shalloe, ringing to arrange a time to come and show her how to work the Aga.

*   *   *

A couple more days passed, quietly. A heavy, low, freezing fog persisted, making it too difficult to try to get down to the town across the fields, so Adie was content to take Sid up and down the drive to the main road for his walks. It was probably a good half a mile there and back, she reasoned, so it was still a decent walk for herself and the dog, especially if she did it twice.

The chickens were busy as usual, and their eggs were starting to accumulate, so Adie decided she would make an omelette for lunch with what bit of cheese remained, and some chives from the herb garden at the back of the cottage.

No snow had come yet, which was disappointing. The Ravens and the Shalloes were vastly relieved, of course, and Adie knew they wouldn't be the only ones. She also knew, from a conversation she'd had with another farmer's wife at the Christmas party, that too much snow rendered the town virtually inaccessible from both roads in and out, which made things difficult for everybody. Snow was something no farmer could escape being anxious about. Still, Adie secretly longed to see the fields covered in a blanket of pristine snow, even if it was only for a day.

Be careful what you wish for, a little voice inside her gently whispered, and she told it to bugger off.

A couple of nights later, the phone rang for only the second time since Adie's arrival, and she almost jumped out of her skin. She was surprised to hear Sue Robinson's voice. Sue sounded strained, and when she began the conversation by saying she was sorry to disturb her but there was a big problem to be handled, Adie's heart sank. Fearing that Sue had somehow heard about the damage to the lawn, and was phoning to give her early notice, she pulled up a chair.

Great. Getting sacked from my first ever house-sit probably means I'll never get another. She swallowed a lump in her throat and braced herself.

But the reason for Sue's call was far different and it meant exactly the opposite, for Adie, of being fired from her house-sitting job.

"Adrienne, we have a situation out here that puts us in a really difficult position. Glenn's Dad has just been diagnosed with an

110

aggressive form of leukaemia. It's terminal, I'm afraid. The doctors have only given him three to four months."

Adie heart plunged. She conveyed her dismay and condolences and asked if there was anything she could do.

"Well actually, Adrienne, there may be. That's why I'm calling. Glenn wants to stay here for the duration, which is understandable. But he's not in good shape emotionally, so I'm very reluctant to come back to the UK and leave him. And I'm very fond of my father-in-law too, of course, so staying here feels like the right thing to do for us, as well as for him. You know, until the end? We want to spend and cherish every moment we have left with him, now. Glenn's Mum also needs a lot of support to prepare and deal with what's coming, and there's really nobody else close. Glenn's an only child."

Sue took a deep breath. "Adrienne, we wondered if there was any way you could stay on at the cottage for a bit, just until we can organise someone else to take over when you'd absolutely have to go, whenever that would be?"

Adie was stunned. This was a truly unexpected development. While she'd had it clear in her mind that she'd be leaving mid-January, she didn't have any concrete plans beyond that, other than to go back to her rented flat. Her diary wasn't exactly bulging with commitments. Coffee with Miranda could certainly be put on hold for a while, and if the whole Christmas experience had been anything to go by, she wasn't much needed by anyone in her family. What did she have to lose, by staying on for another week or two? Aware that she had gone quiet, and that Sue was waiting for an answer, she spoke up.

"Well, yes. I can certainly stay for a couple more weeks, of course."

Sue heaved a sigh of relief. "Adrienne, I know you have a life to get back to, but it would be amazing if you could do another fortnight. That would give me time to advertise for someone who could go and stay longer term. We'll pay you, incidentally, to look after things for however long you're able to stay."

A life to get back to? Ha! If only you knew! Adie thought to herself.

"Sue, I'll be happy to stay on until you can make other arrangements, and you don't need to pay me."

111

Sue explained that her father-in-law's illness was a massive shock to the family. Nobody had thought it was anything particularly serious, since Glenn's Dad had played it down and not talked to a doctor for all the time he was feeling unwell. Typical of his generation, he hadn't wanted to make a fuss. He thought he was just a little under the weather, but in the run-up to Christmas, he had become a lot sicker very quickly.

The results of the tests had come in just this morning, devastating the family, and throwing them into a complete tailspin with only a miniscule scrap of future time to spend together. Glenn had immediately arranged a leave of absence from his job, and Sue's work as a life-coach was all online so she could keep up with her clients, as much as time zones would allow.

Sue insisted that if Adie was to stay on, for whatever length of time she could manage, it would be regarded as a position worthy of payment, for her commitment and for the responsibility of taking care of everything they cherished at home. When Sue asked if she would even consider staying for the whole, open-ended duration under the agreed terms Adie found herself throwing caution to the wind and saying yes, without a scrap of hesitation, effectively boxing herself in with no chance to talk herself out of it.

Sue was over the moon at that. Astonished at her own impulsiveness, and at the lack of her usual penchant for procrastination, Adie wasn't sure whether to laugh or cry about it, but she was very pleased to find herself 'gainfully employed' and more than happy to take some of the pressure off the poor Robinsons. Sue was clearly relieved, as the tone of her voice became a lot less formal when they went on to discuss and agree on various other housekeeping matters.

On the basis that the Robinson's trust in her was being extended, Adie decided to come clean about what had happened to the lawn. She felt it only fair, after learning from bitter experience that honesty had to be the only policy, whether it was comfortable or not. She'd had enough of secrets.

But Sue was less interested in the fact that her lawn had been damaged than she was in the fact that the Ravens had had another Christmas party. She wanted to know who had turned up, what time the party had ended, whether Adie had met some interesting people, and what she thought of the Ravens in general. She also wanted to know what the gorgeous little Feen had worn to the Christmas party. It seemed that 'Glue' and Feen were very good friends!

She was also philosophical about the lawn, dismissing it in the same way Mark had, as a drunken mistake on somebody's part, and grateful that he'd already put it to rights. She remarked that even though Mark always swore every year's Christmas party to be the last, it never was.

"He hasn't said that this year," Adie laughed. "In fact, he's promised to have it next year, as long as I come back for it."

"Well, crikey! You must have made a big impression, for him to have said that! Either that, or he's going soft in his old age!"

After she finished talking with Sue, Adie sat looking out the window for a while, marvelling at how randomly and gently her life was changing, without any warning at all. It just seemed to be headed in a direction best known to itself, for now at least, so Adie decided that she had nothing much to lose by going with the flow for once. It occurred to her that she now had to make a trip back to her flat to pick up some more of her personal things, since what was in the small bags she'd brought to cover a three-week stay would no longer be enough. There would need to be a mail redirection too.

Then there was the job of telling the kids, and a few friends, but Adie decided she could do that by email, and deal with any questions the same way. She wouldn't call anyone. They could call her if they wanted to, but she wasn't going to start conversations with anyone except Miranda, about her plans. She was in no mood to explain herself. If the kids and Bryan didn't like it, they could all bloody lump it. They seemed to have no problem staying away and getting on with their own lives, so they could hardly castigate Adie for doing the same, could they? And, like Ruth had said in her call on Christmas Day, at some point Adie had to forgive herself for being human and fallible. She had to hang up the cloak of guilt and self-pity, and start getting on with her life. This small new opportunity strengthened her resolve to do just that.

Mittens came and jumped into Adie's lap and started purring, and trampling the throw she'd wrapped around her shoulders. Even with the fire going, and the Aga and the central heating, she felt only just warm today. She hadn't been aware that there was such a thing as menopausal *cold* flushes too, until her doctor explained it. Most of the time she wasn't bothered by cold surges, but today seemed to be one of those rare times when she simply couldn't get warm.

There was still no talk of snow, but Adie still clung to her secret hope that there would be a little. Imagine how lovely it would be to be sitting in the hot tub with it magically drifting down around her!

She stroked the little cat. "Well, Mittens my love, you've got me for a bit longer. In fact, you all have," she announced to the view beyond the window. "Torley, you'd better get used to me! At least for a while."

As Mittens settled on Adie's lap, she found herself nodding off. There were few things more therapeutic than the sound of a purring cat. It was the last thought that entered her head before she drifted off to sleep.

* * *

After a couple of days, during which she had baked a batch of muffins and a bacon and egg pie, cooked a roast chicken and a small complement of vegetables, Adie felt that she had at last mastered the Aga.

Sheila's patient guidance had been so helpful. She had also shared her own similar menopause experience, with its sleepless, sweaty nights, maddening memory lapses, and worrying gaps in confidence and concentration. It was good to be able to sit and talk face-to-face with someone who had the empathy and time to really listen, who really did understand the bizarre evaporation of self-assurance, and the endless bouts of uncontrollable weeping that seemed to go with the territory of going through the change of life. Sheila reassured Adie a lot, about all of it, and suggested she ask Feen for some more herbal remedies and tonics aimed at easing some of her symptoms. Feen had been supplying Sheila with them regularly for a couple of years now, and she believed they really did help.

After such a heart-warming visit, Adie decided to invite Sheila and Bob over for a thank-you meal on New Year's Eve, if they weren't already busy, now that she knew she could probably cook them something that wouldn't be a burnt or undercooked disaster.

As luck would have it, the Shalloes didn't have New Year plans, and were delighted to be invited to dinner. Adie decided it would be rude not to invite the Ravens too, so she quickly jogged up to the farm to ask if they could make it. Mark was nowhere to be seen, as expected, but as she approached the front door of the house, she caught sight of Feen. The young woman was bending intently over a table in her workshop. Adie gently tapped on the window.

Feen opened the big front door with her characteristic wide smile, and invited her in, gently batting away her apologies for arriving unannounced, and reassuring her that she wasn't too busy at all to be disturbed. She ushered Adie through to the large but warm and welcoming kitchen.

Adie had decided, on the night of the Christmas party, that this kitchen was the best room she'd ever seen in her life. A huge, heavy, battered pine table dominated the room. It would seat eight people comfortably, ten at a push. Stone walls were peppered here and there with iron rings, hooks and other metalware.

Huge, polished ceiling beams ran from one end of the room to the other, and an Aga three times the size of the one at Teapot Cottage dominated the end wall. It was a beautiful rich dark blue, with gleaming polished brass handles and hotplate tops. Above it was a big old-fashioned drying rack, from which a couple of faded tea towels and several dried bunches of assorted flowers, herbs and grasses were hanging. The kitchen cupboards were plentiful, with richly varnished teak doors. The entire room was like something out of a home and garden magazine. Adie had fallen instantly in love with it.

Feen insisted on making a pot of fresh rosehip tea, which Adie had never tried before. It was delicious. Feen didn't seem at all surprised that Adie would be staying on at Teapot Cottage until probably the middle of April. She merely nodded and smiled gently. She was very excited by Adie's invitation to dinner, though, and warmly accepted for herself and her dad. She seemed very happy at the prospect of sharing the table with her aunt and uncle as well. They were quite a close bunch, it seemed.

"That would be lovely, Adie! Thank you so much! How nice to have that to look forward to! Will you let me ding a bressert for us all?"

She offered to make an Eton Mess, with home-grown raspberries she had in one of the big farm freezers. Adie accepted her kind offer and told her to come and get some eggs from the cottage for the meringue. Feen laughed, saying they had hens of their own, with eggs coming thick and fast, and she suggested Adie take hers, which she'd admitted were piling up much faster than she could eat them, to the local Farmers Market on the following Saturday morning.

It was in the church hall, and a few traders in the area used it as a small source of income, selling cakes, jams and jellies, and various other items such as farm-produced sausages, bacon, butter, cream, eggs and vegetables. Peg Wilde usually had an assistant manning a stand with baked goods from her cafe. One woman apparently made a killing selling nothing but bunches of rhubarb, and another farmer's wife offered large wood-fired pizzas and foil-dish portions of home-made macaroni cheese, which always sold like hotcakes, and if you weren't in line for one or the other by half past ten, you'd usually missed out.

Adie thought it would be great fun to do the market. She would probably only have about thirty eggs, but Feen offered to join forces with her and sell some of the farm's root vegetables and a few berry syrups. Feen knew the market's organiser and promised to phone and book them a place. Adie thought she might make some of her mother's orange and ginger marmalade recipe to sell as well and resolved to add the ingredients for it to her shopping list. She asked Feen if she had any jars going spare, and to her delight was given ten, all with decent lids.

So that gave her almost a week to get organised. Despite Feen having warned her that the market was fairly small, and nothing to get excited about, Adie found herself really looking forward to it. It was a strangely satisfying thing to contemplate, offering

116

people something home-made and home grown. She had only ever been to a handful of farmers markets herself, as a committed city-dweller who never had much time to even think about organic food, let alone go looking for it. The closest she'd usually got in the past was to buy something from the supermarket with an organic label on it, at roughly twice the price of the non-organic alternatives. It was usually only bought as a special treat, or as a last resort when there were no better-priced choices to be had.

Now, having met a few farmers and realising how hard they worked, Adie humbly appreciated how much of a commitment they had made to their land, to the wellbeing of their animals, the quality of their crops and produce, and to the lifestyle it provided for them and their families. There was a real-earth wholesomeness to this little community that Adie found refreshing and real.

It occurred to her too, that maybe in the course of rebuilding her life she could also rebuild her attitude to her own health and wellbeing, which had never been much of a priority while she was raising her family. Bryan's and the children's needs had always been more important. On some level she had always known she should pay more attention to herself, but self-care had never been convenient. There just never seemed to be enough time to go dress shopping, or to indulge in a massage or a facial, find an exercise class or even talk to anyone about which vitamins and minerals her ageing, hormone-depleted body might benefit from taking.

This could be the start of a whole new revolution, she thought to herself as she made her way back to the cottage.

After adding a more few bits and pieces to her shopping list, she found her car keys and drove towards the town. It was a case of necessity, and since walking along the track or even the footpath at the side of the main road seemed too dangerous in the dense fog, driving seemed to be the least hazardous option. Down in the town the visibility was a little better, and she managed to park the car without any problems.

Wondering why hot flushes never seemed to appear when she actually wanted them to, Adie decided she needed a cup of something hot to warm her up. Peg was busy when she walked into the cafe but gave her a wide smile.

"Hello, love. It's bloody freezing out there, isn't it? Is it coffee you're after, or tea?"

Adie requested hot chocolate, and a date scone.

"Sit yourself down, I'll bring it over."

A couple of minutes later, Peg brought a tray of steaming mugs and fat scones, and sat herself down.

"I'm due a break so I'll take it now, since you're here."

The two women ate, drank and chatted, mostly about the Ravensdown Christmas party, and a little about how good it was that the café was regularly busy. Peg hadn't been entirely sure she would even be able to reopen, after the recent pandemic. That had been an anxious time for all of the local businesses, wondering whether they'd be able to go back to trading as they had before. Bleakly, it had seemed that the local undertaker's, Frost Funeral Services, had been the only business to thrive during Covid. But the town had bounced back well, with most traders surviving to reopen, largely due to the dedication of the townsfolk themselves, who were determined to support local businesses to get back on their feet.

Adie mentioned that she'd invited the Shalloes and the Ravens over for dinner. She also told Peg about the new arrangements with the Robinsons - that she would be staying on at Teapot Cottage until at least the end of March. Peg beamed and excitedly grabbed hold of Adie's hand.

"Oh, that's *fantastic* news, Adie! Not for poor old Mr Robinson, of course, because that's just tragic, and right after Christmas as well! That poor, poor family. But how lovely that we won't be losing you just yet!"

Adie went on to talk about doing the Farmer's Market next Saturday with Feen. The other woman smiled.

"Well, you're not wasting any time getting involved with the local life, that's for sure! It's great, Adie. You're finding out for yourself what I told you. Although we're a small community here, we're a friendly one, and there's always room for a happy new face, love."

Peg seemed genuinely pleased that Adie was finding her feet in Torley.

What a nice woman she is, she thought to herself. *I hope once I do leave, I can stay in touch with her.*

She bought what she needed in the town, including some pretty blank labels for her jars of marmalade from 'Patchwork & Pen', the local stationery and craft shop that was twice as big as it looked from the outside. Adie then wandered across to the church hall to get her bearings for the following weekend and see what other activities they might run there.

A noticeboard beside the door advertised a variety of events, all printed on official church hall paper. Among various activities that seemed mostly aimed at entertaining small children, there was a women's free-dance class on Tuesday mornings, quilting and dressmaking on Wednesday nights, and a yoga class on Thursday nights.

Hmmm... not too sure about the yoga. Can't really see myself sitting stock still on my squishy bum with my legs wrapped around my head.

Someone had tacked an independent, hand-written notice to the board with details of a Friday night film club meeting on it; 'not too heavy or intellectual', it promised. Liking the sound of that, she noted the phone number, and decided to commit to trying the Tuesday morning free-dance class too. The idea of being here for a few months suddenly felt exciting. It gave Adie a buzz of anticipation she couldn't remember having felt, for a very long time.

Chapter 11

In the barn, Mark noticed an irreparable bulge the size of a fist in the sidewall of one of the tractor tyres. Sighing deeply, he set about removing the tyre, cursing quietly to himself about the cost and inconvenience involved in fixing it. A lot of things had become harder and slower to get now, ever since the pandemic that had turned the entire world on its head. Most things were a lot more expensive too. The price of tyres would make his eyes water, he was sure, and he supposed he could thank Brexit too, and the unfathomable, God-awful war in Ukraine, for the triple whammy that had forced the price of everything through the roof. The need to replace the tyre didn't help his already grumpy mood, brought about through contemplating his own mortality after the Robinson's news, which had rattled him more than he'd care to admit.

In the months after Beth had died, he'd spent a lot of time wondering about the randomness of cancer and other illnesses, and what his own future might hold. There had been a lot of financial planning done, to legally secure his daughter's future in the event that something untoward might happen to him, and before the pandemic he'd started having more regular check-ups with his doctor, which he'd never seen as a priority in the past. That, he'd already decided, needed to start happening again now that seeing a doctor wasn't such a challenge anymore. He needed to stop procrastinating about it too, because look where Glenn's poor dad had ended up, after putting things off! With Beth gone, Mark owed it to Feen, to be as healthy as he could be, and for as long as possible.

He was profoundly grateful for the closeness of his family, and for how well-loved Feen would always still be, if anything happened to him. But he was still a long way from being ready to fall off his perch. The news that Glenn Robinson's father was dying from leukaemia and would be gone in all too short a time had left him desperately upset.

Bloody 'ell. The owd bugger's not much older than me!

It was a sobering thought that from the day of diagnosis, a man less than a decade ahead of him in age could be gone from the world in a matter of months.

Mark had never met Glenn's dad, and he didn't even know Glenn all that well, but he felt keenly for both men. It was a terrible thing when anyone died before their time, and Mark knew only too well how big a hole it would leave in the lives of the Robinson family.

Feen knew Sue pretty well, but Mark had only ever had superficial conversations with her, and not much more than that with Glenn at different times. He was surprised now, at how much the news of their impending bereavement had affected him.

I must be goin' soft in me owd age.

Every tragedy has a silver lining though, and for Mark the fact that Adie Bostock would be staying around a while longer was nice news. She seemed like a good woman. Troubled, yes; he could feel a certain sadness around her. He could only speculate at what had happened in her life. He knew she had grown-up children and that she'd been separated from her husband for about a year, but he didn't know any of the details.

It was none of his business, but he was quite concerned that she was unhappy. One thing he'd learned was that some stuff, you didn't get over. You could only come to terms with it, which wasn't the same thing at all. With some stuff, the best you could hope to do was find a place in your head where you could live with it. He hoped that whatever demons Adie was dealing with would have been safely squared away by the time she had to leave, and now that she had a bit longer, he hoped the extra time would help her heal even more.

Adie was nice to have around. She always had a wave and a smile, and she seemed to get on quite well with Feen. By all accounts, the invitation to dinner tonight was to show off her newly acquired skills with the Aga at Teapot Cottage, and to thank Sheila for showing her how to get to grips with it. Cooking dinner for a group of virtual strangers was a generous thing to do, especially on New Year's Eve, and Mark was looking forward to it, as was Feen, who had promised his favourite pudding as her contribution. She had also promised to mend, wash and iron his favourite blue and black shirt into a vaguely respectable state.

It was always nice to sit around a table with Bob and Sheila too. Outside of the usual predictable farm talk, the Ravens and the Shalloes always had plenty of funny family stories to rehash, and Mark thought Adie might enjoy hearing some of them. The family were a fairly self-deprecating lot, who'd never taken themselves too seriously, and who were usually well-able to laugh at themselves when tales were told around a table, especially when one or three bottles of wine might be involved. Adie may even have some interesting stories of her own.

He was still troubled about what had happened to the lawn in front of Teapot Cottage on Christmas night. He hadn't mentioned it to anyone else, and while he repeatedly tried to tell himself that only he and Adie knew about it, he knew he was wrong. Someone else knew, alright. The person who'd mashed up that lawn knew *all* about it. Devastation on that scale hadn't been an accident. The damage was total. The entire lawn had been churned to a muddy wreck, and that hadn't just been a drunken mistake by someone who couldn't see where they were going.

Mark never got so drunk at a party that he couldn't keep an eye on who else was drinking what, and then expecting to drive home. He and Feen were both responsible hosts, and there'd been many a Christmas night when one of the Ravens had swiped the keys off friends who'd believed themselves capable of driving when clearly the opposite had been true. Following on from her mother, Feen had spare beds made up every year to point people at, to head off their temptation to drive home drunk.

The truth was that nobody at the party had been in the kind of state to have accidentally ruined an entire lawn well off a driveway. It had been a deliberate act of savagery. Someone had turned the wheel wilfully away from the drive, towards the lawn. Then they had driven over it, reversed, driven over it again, and repeated the process several times.

That was no accident. Mark knew it, and he suspected that deep down Adie probably knew too. He'd tried to ease her dismay and assure her it had to have been a mistake, and she'd accepted it without further comment, but whether she actually believed it was another matter.

That destroyed lawn had bothered Mark all night, so much so that when he'd gone down early on Boxing Day morning to fix it, he'd taken a few photos of the tyre tracks before getting stuck in and levelling it off. He had an idea about what had happened, but he wasn't about to say it out loud.

Carla Walton had a mean streak, and he hadn't missed her animosity towards Adie at the party, especially at the end of the evening when everyone was leaving and Feen more or less shoved Carla through the door and slammed it in her face, while Adie stayed behind to help clean up. That would not have gone down well with the other woman at all.

As unwilling as Mark was to consider it, Carla trashing the Robinson's lawn in a fit of pique was the only explanation that made even the slightest sense. But while he was willing to place a small bet on the tyre tracks being a match for Carla's father's four-wheel drive, he was still reluctant to cast blame where there was no hard proof.

He also didn't want to poke a hornet's nest. Even though he'd been out with Carla a couple of times, he didn't know her well enough to predict what she might do if he accused her of wilful damage, even if the tyre-track 'proof' was right there in front of her. As outraged as he was, on Adie's behalf, sometimes it was better to let a sleeping dog lie.

But I will 'ave to do summat about the woman. She means well, I suppose, but she's just not fer me. Too intense, too much like bloody 'ard work, even if I were lookin' fer a dalliance, which I'm not. I should go an' see 'er, I suppose, call 'er off, tell 'er fer once and fer all, I'm not interested. I 'ave to man up, it's as simple as that.

It was a tricky situation for Mark. He'd been made aware, over the last few years, of his appeal to unattached women of a certain age. Friends had started ribbing him gently (after what they all probably assumed was a 'respectable' period of mourning his dead wife) about being the most eligible bachelor in the Lake District.

He supposed there might have been some truth to the notion that he might be a catch for someone, but he wasn't really sure why. He kept to himself, divulged very little about his financial status, and wasn't even capable of pretending any airs and graces. If anyone had asked him to describe himself, he'd just have called himself a bog-standard, middle-aged farmer who was greying around the temples, spreading slightly around the middle, and more than a bit set in his ways. He'd been good looking enough in his younger years, or at least that's what people had always told him, but that was a long time ago, and his face was weathered and lined now. He was acutely aware of how his features kept changing as they aged (and not for the better, in his own opinion), and he was more or less resigned to the fact that he'd long since passed his peak.

Mark didn't openly encourage women's attention because he simply wasn't interested in having a relationship. Beth had been the one true love of his life, and as he'd said many times; *when yer've been lucky enough to 'ave had that, nothin' in the world would measure up to it, so why would you even try an' go there?*

He was baffled that someone like Carla Walton would be attracted to him. She was pleasant enough, on the surface, but she was strong, opinionated, territorial, and passionate in ways that were actually quite off-putting. She'd tried more than once to seduce him, and had made many lewd comments in that regard, but he just hadn't felt a pull to her. To Mark, the prospect of sleeping with a woman who wasn't his wife was frightening enough in itself. He simply couldn't contemplate having to fake an attraction he just didn't feel, for someone who could either swallow him whole or chew him up and spit him back out, depending on how the mood took her.

He'd managed each time to rebuff Carla with excuses, but it never seemed to put her off. It was almost as if she was biding her time, believing he'd come around eventually. He'd known from the start that he wouldn't, but he wasn't sure how to make it clear without causing embarrassment and offence, so he'd said nothing.

It occurred to him now, that his passivity had probably just added fuel to her fire, making the challenge of 'conquering him' all the more alluring, and in some peculiar way it was probably leading her on in ways he didn't want. He definitely had to sort it, for once and for all.

Carla also had a real edge about her, a presence that you just knew could cause real hurt if you went up against it. Brittle. That was the word for it, Mark decided. Carla was brittle. Feen had words for her that were far harsher than that, which surprised him. Normally his gentle daughter didn't waste much time commenting on the worst of people, even though he knew she always could see or feel it. But Carla Walton was something else again.

Feen had called her a tormented soul, and not in a good way. "That woman is a bitch, and a vicious one at that", she'd said, more than once. "She wants to clink her saws into you, Daddy, and please don't take this the wrong way but she's actually less attracted to lovely you, than she is to your also rather lovely house and your standing in the community."

She astutely advised Mark to never let the woman know how much he was worth, proclaiming that he would never get rid of her if she knew.

It was good advice, but Mark didn't need it. It was nobody else's business how much money he had, and besides, giving someone that kind of knowledge never helped when it came to deciding whether they liked you for yourself or for what they could get from you.

Mark knew a lot of people thought he was a bit of a 'two-bob' (in his own words), or 'nice but dim,' as the saying went. He kept to himself, and his accent didn't help some folks' opinions of his intelligence either, but in truth it suited him well to let them think he wasn't particularly bright. It meant they left him alone, and that was all he really wanted. He had his family and his friends who knew him well, and he told himself he didn't want or need anyone else.

It never even occurred to him that he was a fit, healthy, attractive man, who some might've said was still in the prime of his life. He didn't imagine he deserved another chance to find love again. It hadn't really resonated with him that he was lonely, let alone that he could do anything about it.

As far as Mark was concerned, no woman would ever hold a candle to Beth, and if Carla Walton thought she was in with a chance, she was sadly mistaken. Taking her out had been an error of judgement, an over-positive reaction to being invited out somewhere after everyone had been locked away from one another for months, and nothing more. He needed to tell her as much, before things started to get out of control, because if it had been her who'd ruined the Robinson's lawn, it meant she was a lot more invested in pursuing a relationship with him than he'd first thought. And, if she could do something like that in a jealous rage, what else might she be capable of, if things didn't go her way?

Again, Mark hoped he was wrong. But the notion that the Robinson's mashed up lawn had been Carla Walton's handiwork was a message his gut kept quietly but insistently telling him, and he thought it was time he started listening to it.

Chapter 12

On the morning of New Year's Eve, the fog finally lifted and the air was crisp and clear. Adie decided to take Sid across the fields, in the opposite direction from the town. It meant going further uphill and behind Ravensdown Farm, but she reasoned it was time she saw a bit more of the area, and on a crystal-clear day like today the views from higher up would be even more spectacular than the ones from Teapot Cottage. It was too good an opportunity to ignore.

Had she really been in this lovely place for less than a fortnight? It felt like much longer. Adie already felt a sense of belonging in Torley, and she recognised already that the next three months or so she was now going to spend here would likely set her path for the future. Thanks to her time in such a peaceful, healing environment, she would leave with a much clearer sense of purpose.

Although she still had no idea what the future might hold, she was no longer afraid, the way she'd been when she'd first arrived. A calm sense of inevitability had enveloped her from the very start of her time here, quietly but effectively replacing the fear and dread she'd been feeling. Whatever would be, would be. Now, rather than feel paralysed with fear by that notion, Adie was strangely comforted by it. She was also vastly relieved that her menopausal symptoms had waned to the point where most were hardly noticeable. There hadn't been a single saturating night sweat to fret about, and her urges to wring the neck of the nearest passer-by, however innocent they might be of anything, had thankfully disappeared completely. Even her flushes had been less severe.

It's this place, I'm certain of it. I just can't explain how comforted and nurtured I feel, in this wonderful healing house. I've never experienced anything like it before, this feeling of being perpetually hugged and healed and encouraged by something I can't even see. Exactly how I've got to where I am in my head now, it feels like so much bigger than just the passing of time or just being in a different place. It really feels like some kind of evolution is occurring for me here, within these walls.

Adie pulled on her walking boots and grabbed Sid's lead. Eventually, after a steep and steady climb that left her short of breath, she found herself at the lovely little Tor at the top of the hill behind the farm. As expected, the view was absolutely stunning. The town seemed like a tiny, huddled speckle of stone dwellings, with nothing identifiable except the church spire. Off in the distance, at the bottom of the long, high hill that flanked Torley from the west, was a glistening lake. It looked small, almost like a puddle, from up here.

I wish I had some binoculars, she thought to herself. *I must see if there are any at the cottage. If so, I'll come up here again and bring them with me.*

A whistle made her turn, and as she did so, a young collie dog came barrelling towards Sid, who was wagging his tail fit to fall off. The animals clearly bore one another no threat, and quickly started to tussle and growl, in friendly play. Just as Adie was wondering where the dog had materialised from, Mark Raven came striding over the last rise of the hill. He stopped, in surprise, as she waved her hand in greeting.

"Bloody 'ell. It's Adie an' Sid! Now I know why't bloody dog ran off!" He chuckled. He had clearly scaled the hill himself but was not even vaguely out of breath.

"So, you've found't best view from't farm, then! Welcome to't world famous Tor, " he drawled sarcastically.

"Yes, it's gorgeous! I feel absurdly happy up here, like I want to roll about on the ground kicking my legs, like these crazy dogs, and I can't even begin to explain why! What's that lake?" Adie pointed to the puddle in the distance.

"That's the Bassholme Reservoir," Mark said. "If you come across 'ere", he said taking her by the arm and guiding her across to the other side of the slope, "you can see right up to't Scottish border."

"Oh, it's so beautiful! I want to build a house right here!" Adie exclaimed.

Mark laughed. "You'd not be sayin' that if you saw what it's like up 'ere in a gale or in't snow. Not a scrap o' bloody shelter, this far up! You'd be blown to Kingdom come!"

As they started walking down the hill again, Mark whistled for his dog, which this time obeyed him and came to heel.

"What's his name?" Adie asked.

"Jinx," Mark responded. "He's only young yet, I'm still trainin' 'im, really. He's got the makings of a good 'un, but a new dog always takes a lot o' work. They still get a bit distracted, like, the collies. But I'm gettin' there, wi' 'im. Seems to enjoy playin' wi' that daft bloody Sid."

On the downward walk, the two dogs continued their happy tumbling and tussling, and the ever-playful Sid was in doggy heaven, with a boisterous friend to play with. Mark was apparently looking for a couple of sheep that had strayed from the herd. Just one dog would be enough to round them up when he found them, and he thought it would be good practice for Jinx.

He thanked Adie for her dinner invitation and said how pleased he was that she'd be around a while longer.

"End o' March, y'reckon?"

"Yes, it's looking like that, or possibly even into mid-April," Adie confirmed. "Of course, now I have to arrange to go back to my flat in Guildford, to pick up some more of my stuff. I brought enough for three weeks, but certainly not for three months."

Mark asked her when she needed to go, and she said the sooner the better, really. They walked together in silence for a minute, then he said;

"Well, if yer can wait until weekend, I have to go to London meself, to do some business. I were in two minds about takin' the train, until I looked at the cost of it. They want an arm an' a bloody leg, so I'm drivin' down. I could take yer down to Guildford in't Range Rover an' bring yer back. You could fit a lot more in that than in your little 'atchback."

"Oh, I'd love to, but I've arranged with Feen to do the Farmers Market next Saturday!" Adie was dismayed.

Mark thought for a moment.

"Well, if we got goin' straight after, say midday or summat, we could be at yours by teatime. I can 'ave me meetin' on Monday mornin', and then come an' fetch yer around lunch time. We could be back 'ere Monday night. Would that suit? Feen could do't chickens and feed the cat and the dog. She's done it enough times in't past, on the odd day."

Adie considered this for a moment. She had to admit she hadn't been too thrilled at the prospect of driving herself all the way down to her flat and back again in one long round trip. But a couple of nights at the flat would give her time to choose properly what she wanted to bring back with her and do a bit of dusting at least. With Feen taking care of things at Teapot Cottage, hitching a free ride seemed like too good a chance to miss.

She gratefully accepted Mark's offer. He smiled and gave a quick nod, and that was that.

They parted company at the lower gate, Adie heading along the path back to the cottage, and Mark towards the lower field, in a renewed attempt to find his two separated sheep. He confirmed that he and Feen would be at the cottage for dinner at seven sharp, and she deliberately ignored the little flare of warmth that blossomed in her chest.

I'm sure it's not anticipation, she told herself. *I'm sure it's just another hot flush.*

* * *

Adie's meal was virtually ready before everyone turned up. She'd found a string of fairy lights in the upstairs hallway cupboard and had strung them up above the kitchen window. The effect was soft and lovely. Perfect for New Year's Eve! She had also called Heavenly Blooms, the local florist, to request a glorious bunch of heavy-scented Christmas lilies that had started to come out just in time for new year. Fiona Frost, the shop owner, had been kind enough to deliver them, and they were now sitting in a square glass vase at one end of the worktop.

None of Adie's guests were vegetarian, so her menu would start with a seafood mornay, served in the lovely scallop shells she'd found tucked away at the back of Sue Robinson's plate cupboard. Then would come a beautifully rich chicken, ham and leek crumble, accompanied by a medley of fresh green beans and cubes of roasted squash. Adie intended to round off her meal with amaretto-soaked figs that she would serve with ice-cream and, of course, Feen's promised Eton Mess.

She was particularly pleased with the mornay and the crumble, since they were the first Aga experiments to be inflicted on guests since Sheila had been over to show her how to regulate and time everything. She was thrilled that she'd managed not to burn a single thing. The mornay sauce that gently smothered the scallops was bubbling beautifully, and the crumble's savoury topping was appropriately crisp and perfectly brown. Adie had also set three different cheeses off to one side with a selection of crackers, home-made granary toast squares (again baked in the Aga) and a bunch of green grapes. A bottle of white wine was chilling in the fridge, and one of Chianti sat open and breathing on the table, next to five of Sue Robinson's sparkling crystal glasses. A couple of gently flickering little tea-light candles made the table look welcoming and cheerful.

Adie had done her hair, put on a little light make-up, and changed into her nice aubergine Christmas Day dress. She kept her slippers on though, because they were just too comfortable, and she reasoned that none of these down-to-earth guests would mind in the least. The fire in the living room was blazing and inviting, and the lamps threw their soft, warm glow across the room. Adie was pleased with the result of her efforts, and quite excited at the prospect of entertaining; hosting a dinner party for delightful people she hoped would become new friends.

She heard a car draw up, which was almost certainly the Shalloes, since she expected Feen and Mark to simply walk down to the cottage. As she opened the door, she was handed a second bunch of lilies by Sheila, who hugged her like an old friend. Bob hugged her too, and just as Adie was about to close the door again, she heard Feen's voice.

"Hold up! We're here too!"

Feen and Mark stepped into the room, and Adie caught the faint whiff of Mark's cologne. Just like she'd noticed it at Christmas, it was only slight, very subtle, but fresh and clean smelling.

Ooh, that's nice, she thought.

Mark was wearing dark blue denim jeans, and a black leather jacket with a dark blue and black checked shirt underneath with its collar open. She noticed a light smattering of hair on his upper chest, just visible at the top button. The tiny Feen was swathed in a very lightweight emerald-green and purple tartan woollen shawl dress that was fastened at one shoulder with an antique silver and amethyst pin in the shape of a thistle. She looked exquisite, as always, and she handed Adie a huge, covered bowl of Eton Mess. Mark raised his hands with a bottle of wine in each, and he set them down on the kitchen bench.

Compliments came readily for the food, and the wine and conversation flowed freely. Nobody asked any intrusive questions but Adie felt comfortable enough to open up a little and explain a bit about her circumstances; that she'd made a big mistake that had hurt her family and ended her marriage. She didn't supply many details, but she did divulge that forgiveness was thin on the ground, especially from herself, and she was trying to move on, with the house sit as the first real move towards that.

She noticed that Feen was watching her intently throughout this small confession, but not with any judgement. The young woman simply wore her usual, slightly enigmatic smile, and after Adie had finished speaking, Feen reached over, took her hand and silently squeezed it. Adie squeezed gently back.

Bob Shalloe piped up. "Ah, we've all made mistakes, Adie, old girl! Of course we have. I've found the biggest disappointment about growing up is you don't stop *stuffing* up! It's funny how we spend most of our childhood longing to be adults, but nobody bothers to warn us in advance that we have to clean up our own mess, and the mistakes we make as grown-ups somehow always seem to be so much worse than the ones we made as kids."

Adie grinned, in spite of herself. "That's so true. It's probably got something to do with the fact that when we're kids, someone else usually takes over and sorts it all out. Being responsible really sucks, sometimes!"

Sheila chimed in earnestly, leaning forward to make her point. "And we do 'ave to forgive ourselves. Few things are so bad that anyone should 'ave to live a life crippled by guilt or remorse, Adie. Bob's right. We're all human, and we don't always make the best choices, even though they might feel like the right ones at the time."

She shook her head sadly. "We've none of us a crystal ball, love. All we can do is learn from our mistakes, however horrible or tragic, and try to do better next time. If people don't forgive you, well, it's their shit to deal with, if you'll pardon my French, and I think – in fact I *know* - that the ones who love you will understand in the end."

Sheila then went on to explain how she and Mark had grown up in rural Lancashire, on a smallholding that ultimately had to be sold when their father unexpectedly took his own life and they subsequently discovered that he'd gone bankrupt without his family knowing. She described how hard it was to leave the family home, after a long battle to try and keep the farm going before admitting defeat and having to find somewhere else to live. It was a long time before she could forgive their father, and start properly grieving for him, but the family had to move on and find their own way. She and Mark both worked and saved to make their dreams happen, and they'd both met their respective spouses in the process. Sheila met Bob through an old school friend whose dad still ran a farm. Bob was a young labourer there, and friendship had soon turned to love after Sheila had gone to stay with her friend for the weekend, and Bob had suggested they keep in touch.

With a merry twinkle in her eye, Feen then took on the story of how her parents met.

"They fancied one another straight away. Mum told him she was a descendant of one of the Wendle Pitches, which was true, by the way. It was love at first sight. They were married within a year, and the rest is history."

"I think she only married me fer me name," Mark chortled. "If I were Mark bloody Smith, I wouldn't 'ave 'ad a look in."

"And here you are, Feen!" chuckled Sheila. "Another descendant! And you've definitely inherited your mother's witch's gene."

Mark and Bob rolled their eyes, but neither denied the fact. Beth Raven had named her only child in a very special way too. Seraphine Raven was quite a unique name, and it definitely suited this intriguing young woman who had such an ethereal, mysterious quality about her.

"I do love *your* name," Adie smiled at her. "That's quite witchy, just there!"

Her guests all nodded, and agreed that Feen's name did indeed confirm how special she was, and that Beth had known it in her heart, had seen it in her baby's eyes, long before anyone else ever did.

Mark then chipped in too, telling Adie how he and Beth had been looking for a smallish farm to buy locally, but there hadn't been one that suited their budget or their plan to run sheep and a few beef cattle. When a property called Down Farm came up for sale, here in Torley, they came up to have a look at it. Beth was almost beside herself, utterly convinced that despite its inflated price tag, they simply had to live here, and nowhere else would do. She wouldn't be swayed, so they made it their mission to find a way. And with a lot of haggling and compromise, they managed the stretch to buy it.

The big old house had been virtually derelict, but luckily the bones of it were still solid enough for the bank to give them a mortgage. The restoration of the house became their shared labour of love, and there was no arguing over how magnificent it was now.

The farm had come with more acreage than Mark initially wanted, but he leased a few fields out to another farmer, which initially helped them out with income for the expensive work needed on the house and farm, both of which had been neglected for a long time. Beth's mother had eventually retired and moved up to live at Ravensdown with Mark and Beth and had only recently gone from living in the big house, into a family-run, cosy care home in nearby Keswick. She was incapacitated now, and ill with dementia, so it was simply too difficult for Mark and Feen to meet her increasing needs at home. According to Feen, her grandmother still had many clear and lucid phases, though they were sadly becoming fewer and shorter, and with more time between.

Bob then picked the story up again, saying he'd been a farm labourer for a long time but he also had dreams of having his own place. After getting together with Sheila, they also looked around for something they could buy. They'd almost settled on buying a property on the edge of Beaconfell in Lancashire when Mark heard about Bracefields, a farm on the opposite side of the valley to Ravensdown, going up for sale. The vendor had been a friend of Mark's and had given him first refusal, so Bob and Sheila had the inside scoop. They leapt on the farm without hesitation. So, just a couple of years after Mark and Beth had moved to Torley, Bob and Sheila followed suit, along with Mark and Sheila's mother, who lived happily with the Shalloes for nearly twenty years until she died peacefully at home in her bed.

Adie learned that Bob and Sheila had a son, Peter, who'd recently completed a farming degree at the Royal Agricultural University in Cirencester. He was intending to settle somewhere locally, if possible, on a smallholding of his own, but was currently 'whooping it up' in Thailand with a few mates. Adie mentioned that Teresa was doing something similar in Australia, having already completed her economics degree. She was hoping to find a job, preferably in London, when she eventually returned from her frolics abroad.

At around eleven, the conversation dwindled slightly. Everyone was starting to feel a bit tired after so much lovely food and rather a lot of wine. The evening felt like it was drawing to a natural, comfortable close. A short while later Bob and Sheila left, departing with hugs and more compliments about dinner, but saying they just wanted to be at home together to see the New Year in, as was their custom, and with Sheila forcing a very reluctant promise out of Adie (who was horrified at herself for having made it) to meet her at the church hall yoga class on the following Thursday night. It seemed she might be sitting in a corner with her legs wrapped around her neck after all!

Feen also quickly excused herself, saying she had a few 'bings to do before thed.' She gave Adie another of her trademark, surprisingly strong hugs, thanked her for a 'fabulous' dinner. She wished her Happy New Year, and was gone from the cottage like lightning, leaving Adie marvelling once more at the speed at which the little creature was always here and gone again, like a moonbeam you could only wonder if you actually really saw before it disappeared.

That only left Mark still at the table. He started to get up also, but Adie stopped him.

"Please, don't feel you have to go. It's not midnight yet! Although, I suppose it's already late enough for you," she added, suddenly remembering he would probably be up at the crack of dawn, with a million jobs to do. Most days seemed to be like that, for him.

She chided herself for being selfish and wanting company to see the New Year in. But it had been such a lovely evening. She didn't want it to end, or to be facing a new year by herself. Christmas alone was one thing, but it felt right to want to welcome a new year with a friend. It was all she could do not to say it aloud.

Expecting him to wave her request aside she was astonished, and quite relieved, when he sat back down again.

"Well, you'd best get kettle back on, then", he said simply.

It felt good, having this nice man in her kitchen. As she bustled about making a fresh pot of tea, Adie turned to him and smiled. "I do very much like your sister, and her husband. They're kind and generous people, with big hearts."

Mark nodded in agreement. "Aye, that they are. They've had their fair share o' heartache, make no mistake, but they keep ploughin' on. What else can yer do?"

Adie let out a short, humourless laugh.

"Oh, I don't know. Buckle, maybe? Go into hiding? Wallow in self-pity, and let yourself drown in your own pathetic, self-inflicted drama?"

She bit her lip, aware that too much wine had loosened her tongue, but she felt unable to stop herself from continuing. "It's what I've been doing. Feeling sorry for myself, acting like my life was over. I've been so pitiful. When Bob first met me on the track when I was looking for this place, I was in floods of tears. Did he tell you that? And I wasn't crying about being lost. I was crying because that's all I was *capable* of doing. The classic, cliched, mid-life-crisis woman, bursting at the seams with hormones and hysteria." Adie shook her head and ploughed on.

"Being lost was just the final straw, that day. It had all but finished me off. But coming here has kicked me out of my bubble, and I needed it. I was a basket case before but, haywire hormones and the change of life aside, it's not easy to bounce

136

back from having your world blown apart, even if you *did* detonate the bomb yourself."

Mark looked at her kindly.

"I don't know so much about menopause, other than seein' our Sheila struggle wi' it at times, but I do know about 'eartache, lass. Believe me, I do."

Of course you do, thought Adie. *You watched your wife being eaten alive with cancer, you're watching your mother-in-law being ravaged by dementia and you were left to raise a decidedly odd and challenging child, all by yourself. You've been to hell and back too.*

He cleared his throat. "Look, Adie, I don't know what's gone on, an' I'd never dream o' pryin', because it's none o' my business. But you seem like a good woman. A *strong* woman. Whatever it was that's 'appened, it won't define the rest of yer life, lass. Not unless you want it to."

And with that, Adie promptly sat down and started spilling her story. She told Mark every wretched detail about how she'd arrived at where she was right now.

She described the profound frustration, then the terrible, tormenting sadness, of her husband's inability to overcome how he felt about her secrets and lies, and the agony of her marriage dying. She recounted how hard she had battled for almost a full year, to come to terms with it, before finally giving up and making the painful decision to move on.

She also confessed that she was still a long way from being ready to make peace with the fact that her son had been making a living as a male escort, having sex with women older than herself.

"I haven't been able to get anybody in the family to talk much about that, despite my attempts to get them to, and I suspect I'm not the only one who's still trying to come to terms with it, Mark." She shook her head, sadly. "Call me old-fashioned, or unenlightened, or whatever, but it's disgusting to me! It's embarrassing beyond belief, but he's my son. I don't know how to feel about any of it."

To give him full credit, Mark listened intently, without saying a single word. By the time Adie had finally run out of steam and fallen silent, she was crying again, and only then did she notice that Mark had taken hold of her hand at some point in the process and was gently stroking the mound of her thumb with his finger. He spoke softly.

"Oh, lass! It must feel like a right mess. But don't be cryin' anymore, now. Don't be so bloody 'ard on yerself! Yer've made mistakes, and it's cost yer dearly. But yer've done what you could, Adie. Yer've tried, to make it better, in the best way you knew 'ow. It's not your fault that yer 'usband couldn't see that, or that no bugger else wants to talk about anythin' that matters to yer.

"Yer've said yer daughters are tryin' an' yer son's comin' round to it. And he's kept it in 'is pants since 'e met 'is wife, a'nt 'e? So, that's a bloody good start. I know your marriage were important, and I know yer love yer 'usband. And 'e could still come around 'imself, in time. I'm really sorry it's all so painful for yer."

Adie looked at him, suddenly realising something that was only becoming clear to her now, here in Teapot Cottage's warm, cosy kitchen.

"That's the thing, Mark. I do still love my husband, but not in the way I did. I'm absolutely amazed at myself for saying it, and its only just occurred to me now, talking through the whole sordid mess you couldn't even make up as a story, how I really feel. But the truth is, I don't want him back. Not now. It's only a couple of weeks since I was praying with all my heart that he'd come and find me and beg me to go back."

But if he showed up here right now, doing just that, I wouldn't go back. I've moved a long way forward with all this, especially since I came to this place.

She gestured expansively at the cottage. "I dunno how to describe it, Mark, but since coming to Teapot Cottage, something's just kind of *shifted*. In *me*. It's like I've turned a corner, and it's hard to describe how it even happened, because it wasn't a conscious part of my process. It's kind of snuck up on me, that I feel like a different person, in this little house." She grinned, embarrassed.

"I know, it sounds completely bat-shit crazy. But Feen says there's a spiritual energy here, and I think I'm starting to believe that, because I've undergone such a profound change, that I once

138

would never have imagined could really happen, since I first walked through that door. It's happened so quietly, and so fast, I can only attribute it to some kind of divine intervention." She gently blew out the air she'd been holding in her lungs.

"Yes, I miss what Bryan and I had, and I'm grateful for all the good times, because there were a great, great many, and we've got two wonderful kids together, and I wouldn't change that for the world. But *something's* changed. I just know I couldn't go back now. And that's really what my grief is about now, if I'm honest. The certainty that it's really over, that this is how it's ended up, for me and Bryan. Everyone I loved got so hurt, and I was the cause of all of it, and I guess not everything that gets broken can be fixed."

Mark sighed deeply and shook his head. "Guilt can be cripplin', Adie. It robs yer of yer joy, and it stops yer from gettin' past everythin'. Sheila were right when she said you 'ave to forgive yerself, and she should know."

He then went on to explain to Adie that Bob and Sheila had had a daughter, Amanda, who'd died of meningitis when she was seven. Sheila had thought her little girl was simply trying to get out of going to school, by complaining of feeling ill, and Sheila had made her get on the bus and go. For the rest of her life, she would wrestle with the burden of guilt, knowing that if she'd listened more, and acted differently, if she hadn't put her on that bus to school, Amanda might still be alive.

"I know she wouldn't mind me tellin' yer. It's no great secret. She'd want yer to know if it would 'elp."

Adie was horrified. At dinner, Sheila had talked passionately of the need to forgive oneself, and now she understood exactly why. It was about so much more than what Sheila and Mark's own father had done to his family by leaving them homeless and destitute. It went far beyond simply trying to make Adie Bostock feel better about herself and her stupid choices. That poor woman had lost her little girl. What a terrible, unimaginable thing to have happened.

Adie thought of all the times she had sent Teresa to school when the child was complaining of a sniffle or a tummy ache in a bid to have a day at home. Most kids did it at some stage, and most parents knew when their kids were genuinely ill or simply pushing their luck. But how often were they wrong?

Adie remembered one time where she'd sent Teresa to school once with a 'tummy ache', believing it to be a hoax, only to have the school on the phone two hours later, asking Adie to go and collect her because she'd thrown up all over her desk. She empathised completely with another mother's simple but ultimately cataclysmic error of judgement. A wrong decision, with no thought of consequences, until the worst ones came and tore her world to pieces.

"So, yer see, Adie," Mark continued gently, "we all 'ave our mistakes to answer to. We all 'ave our demons to wrestle with. But it's not what 'appens, it's 'ow we deal wi' it that matters. Be kind to yerself. Yer movin' on, an' it's time yer did, an' there's no need to feel guilty about that. It's the natural way o' things. We're not meant to stay stuck or static. We're like ships, lass; built fer open sea, not fer 'angin' around in't bloody harbour."

He let go of her hand as she reached out to grab a square of kitchen roll to dab at her eyes with. Then he took hold of it again, and she let him.

"Adie, you're in the right place. Feen does reckon you were drawn 'ere, for a reason, an' I think she were right. You were drawn 'ere, to this nice little cottage, to 'ave the breathin' space yer need to get better. An' it's 'appenin'. Yer turnin' a corner. Whatever the magic is around 'ere that Feen keeps bangin' on about, it's workin' for yer. Just let the process run the way it wants to." He sighed heavily, again.

"After Beth died, I just 'ad to take each day as it came, and deal wi' what it brought me. It were bloody 'ard at beginnin'. It still is sometimes, even after eight soddin' years, but at least I can get up in a mornin' now. I didn't even want to get out o' bloody bed, for more than a year, but I 'ad to, fer't young 'un, because she needed me. And, after a time, it started to get better, an' one day I realised I 'ad a handle on everythin' again. I were in a different place. I still miss Beth wi' every breath I take. I always will, I suppose, but I've moved on from the early devastation. An' it's ok for you to do that too. Time's a healer, Adie."

It's true. He's right. Life pushes us forward whether we want it to or not, and it's only when we kick against the process that we start to have problems.

Mark glanced at his watch, and quickly stood up. "Eh up! New Year's rollin' in! We need a glass o' summat!"

Adie noted that it was now almost midnight. Mark poured the remaining contents of the last open bottle of wine into two glasses and handed one to her. They went to stand in one of the living room windows. On a whim, Adie turned the lights out, and the room was only lit by the fairy lights in the kitchen, the little blue ones on the Christmas tree, and the glow from the fire in the grate. It was a surprisingly clear night, and the lights of Torley town twinkled, down in the valley.

"Happy New Year, Mark," Adie said softly. "Here's to new friends, and new beginnings!" She lifted her glass, and Mark did the same.

They drank their wine, and watched a few fireworks as they punctured the sky above Torley town. After a few minutes, Mark cleared his throat, apologetically declaring that he really did have to go.

They said goodnight at the door, and Mark gave her a hug. "Happy New Year, Adie, and thanks for a really nice evenin'. It's been as near as dammit perfect." He gave her a kiss on the cheek, and then he was gone. What a lovely friend he was turning out to be!

Oh damn, I keep forgetting to ask him what 'britches-arse steam' is!

Adie quickly took Sid out for his late-night ablutions, aware that he'd waited well past his usual ten o'clock time without complaint. After loading the dishwasher and switching off the remaining lights, she prepared for bed with a heart full of gratitude for this remarkable little town, its people, and the wonderful healing energy of Teapot Cottage. Tomorrow – now today - was not just a brand-new day, but a brand-new year. Suddenly, everything seemed possible.

Chapter 13

As predicted, the Saturday Farmers Market had been a lot of fun. It wasn't as busy as Adie had expected, and it was still very quiet in the town generally, so soon after the Christmas festivities too. There were a handful of stalls and quite a few people milling about, though, and Adie had made ten jars of orange and ginger marmalade during the week. She was thrilled that by eleven thirty on Saturday morning she'd managed to sell the lot.

Customers had mostly been locals, most of whom knew Feen, and Adie's brain was awash with all the names and conversations that had peppered the morning. Again, she marvelled at how friendly people were, especially those she'd already met at the Raven's Christmas party. They greeted her like an old friend, and didn't seem remotely offended that she couldn't remember most of their names.

One less-friendly encounter had been with Carla Walton, who had shown her face briefly, to buy some cut flowers. She didn't come by Feen and Adie's stand but glowered at them both from across the room. Feen had deliberately avoided acknowledging Carla, but Adie had made eye contact and raised a hand in greeting, only to be met with a cold stare, before the other woman abruptly turned on her heel and walked out of the hall without purchasing anything.

Not so friendly then, she mused to herself, and shrugged it off.

With midday approaching and just half a dozen eggs left to sell, she was grateful when Feen waved her off, saying she'd take care of selling them, and suggesting that she text Mark to tell him they could set off for Guildford an hour early. Adie tore up the hill in her little hatchback, marvelling yet again at her luck. She couldn't remember when she'd last had such a long run of good fortune. There really did seem to be some kind of magic surrounding her, which kept showering her in fairy-dust. The cottage, the sweetness of the animals, and the genuinely kind people who had drifted into her life all felt like blessings and balm to a troubled heart.

I'm starting to sound like Feen, thinking about fairy dust and magic, she laughed to herself as she pulled up at Teapot Cottage. Mark was already there, waiting in his car, so she raised a hand in greeting, then scurried into the house to collect the small bag she'd packed to take with her.

Mark had thoughtfully made a stack of cheese and tomato sandwiches and a flask of very good coffee, so Adie gratefully munched and sipped, and settled back to enjoy the drive.

He was a good travelling companion, easy company, and he made her laugh. They shared lots of stories about favourite holiday places, bands they had seen, what was on their bucket lists, and what they'd do if they won the Euro millions lottery.

Mark told funny stories about the various mishaps that had happened at the farms in the area. His broad accent made the stories all the more hilarious. He talked about a local farmer who'd had the bad luck of having one of his sheep spooked in the field, which had then run through his yard gate, in through his open front door and into his living room, where it promptly had a pro-lapse all over a brand-new carpet. His wife had been screaming and calling her husband all the names under the sun, and the insurance company had grudgingly paid out nearly a thousand pounds to have it replaced, but only after the aggrieved farmer had threatened to rip it up and haul it into their office. Adie was nearly crying with laughter.

Farming was hard work, but it seemed to be liberally peppered with good times. Mark also confessed to being a real softie about his animals. His wife had been equally devoted to their welfare, and he shared a cherished memory with Adie, of Beth walking up the field towards the house in the pouring rain, with her hair plastered to her face, and carrying three baby lambs who had just lost their mother. She was going to ensure they survived, come hell or high water, and they did.

"I'll never forget how she looked that day", he said softly. "She were a slight thing, like Feen, but she 'ad real grit about 'er. She weren't goin' to let them lambs die. She hand-reared the buggers, gave 'em bloody names, and that were the end o't notion of sendin' 'em to't slaughter. Pets, they ended up, and we still 'ave two of 'em now, old ladies, soft bloody things they are!"

Adie smiled. She liked the sound of Beth Raven, and she said so.

"Aye, she 'ad some spirit, that's for sure. Weren't afraid of owt. She fought that cancer bloody 'ard, too. She were brave, right to't last. Braver than I'd be."

Adie doubted that, but she didn't say it.

When they eventually arrived in Guildford, it was dark. As they drew up at Adie's flat, she asked Mark where he was staying. When he told her he had booked a hotel she was surprised. For some reason she'd thought he'd be staying with friends. It hadn't occurred to her that he might be staying alone in some anonymous hotel.

She suggested he stay with her instead. She had a perfectly decent spare room, with a comfortable bed already made up, since she'd always had half an idea that Teresa could decide to turn up at any moment. Adie assured Mark it would be no bother at all to have him there. He protested but she insisted.

"It will be nice to have the company" she said simply, and with that, he agreed.

Sunday dawned chilly with frost; a typical mid-winter's day. Adie woke early to a grey half-light and decided that since Mark was evidently still sleeping, she would walk up to the local shop and get some bacon and eggs. She knew he appreciated a good fry-up.

She arrived back at the flat with her shopping and a couple of Sunday papers, which she also though Mark might appreciate. She had coffee on, and breakfast on the table, by the time he surfaced from the shower. *It must have been the smell of frying bacon that woke him up*, she thought to herself, and laughed out loud when he admitted that indeed it was.

After a leisurely breakfast, during which they both somehow fell into a pattern of reading amusing or unbelievable bits of news to one another from the papers, Adie decided she needed to take a shower, so she excused herself and went to do just that. Half an hour later, when she came back down, she found Mark had done the washing up, and had brewed another pot of coffee.

As they sat together, amiably sipping, the doorbell rang. Adie went to answer it, and was completely stunned to see her ex-husband Bryan on her doorstep.

"Hello Adie", he said, looking pointedly at Mark's sleek black Range Rover parked in the drive. "Got a new car, have you?"

"No," Adie replied. "It belongs to a friend."

Bryan pulled a face. "I've been driving by every day for almost a week, and your car's not been here. I came by last night and finally saw some lights on, but it was very late. So, I thought I'd come back this morning. Can we talk, please, about us? I think it's time."

Adie shook her head.

" I have a friend staying, Bryan. Now's actually *not* a good time."

Bryan blinked at her in astonishment.

As well he might, she thought to herself. *After months of pleading with him to talk about the state of our marriage, and him point-blank refusing, no wonder he's surprised that I'm refusing now!*

Abruptly, Bryan pushed roughly past her into the tiny hallway and into the kitchen.

He took one look at Mark, sitting at the table in his stocking feet, with hair still wet, a cup of coffee in one hand and a newspaper in the other, and promptly exploded.

"Oh right, Adie! A *friend*. I can see exactly what kind of 'friend' you've got here. This is all rather cosy, isn't it? Jesus, woman, you haven't wasted much time, have you?" His voice was tight, his jaw set.

Adie struggled to remain calm in response to Bryan's anger, as her own threatened to boil over with what was, these days, an increasingly familiar force. She spoke quietly.

"Bryan, it's not what it looks like, and even if it was, it's no longer any of your business. You gave up the right to tell me how to live when you refused to listen or speak to me for almost an entire year after you threw me out of our home. If I have moved on, it's because I have every bloody right to."

Bryan sneered at her. "It's been a difficult Christmas. I've missed you. I came here to try and work things out. I came to see if we could talk about fixing our marriage. But I can see that's now a redundant concept and I've wasted my time." His tone was cold, as cold as it had been since the split.

Adie felt sad. Not bereft, not panicked, not desperate. Just sad. She sighed, heavily.

"Yes, Bryan. I'm afraid you have. You don't get to pull the strings anymore. Not after I've begged and begged you to sit down and talk with me, for months and months, and you wouldn't even acknowledge I was alive. Now, because I've stopped begging, and you can see I've not been here, and I'm out having a life, you've decided you now want to talk." Adie shook her head.

"For you, it's all about gaining the upper hand, Bryan, and that's not what our marriage should ever have been about."

"Well, that's the pot calling the kettle black! Like you didn't have the upper hand all through the lying years? And a bloody sly one, at that."

Adie quietly asked him to leave.

Bryan looked at her in disgust, but he made no move. He was furious and made no effort to hide it.

"I can see exactly why you've stopped begging, Adie. Well, you certainly haven't let the bed get cold, have you?"

Adie closed her eyes. *What? It's been nearly a year! And you can think what you like. I don't owe you any explanations. Not anymore.*

"You need to go Bryan, please," she said more firmly. Again, Bryan didn't budge, but kept glowering at her, with his hands on his hips.

Mark had laid down his mug and paper and stood up. He'd made no move forward and had stayed silent, but he hadn't taken his eyes off Bryan. Now, he came forward, just a couple of steps.

"The lady said she'd like you to leave. 'Appen you should do that."

He spoke gently, but Bryan's answering laugh was harsh and grating.

"Don't worry, mate. You're welcome to her, and she's anything *but* a lady. Twenty-six years I was married to this old slag, and she really wasn't worth it."

"Don't say that," Mark said. "In sayin' that, yer regrettin' yer kids. Don't d'that. None of it were their fault, were it?"

Bryan turned and looked squarely at Mark. At six feet three and seventeen stone, he was taller, considerably bulkier and more powerful than Mark. Adie prayed he would control his vile temper.

"What the fuck do you know about my family, you north-arsed, inbred halfwit?" he demanded.

"I know enough." Again, Mark's voice was quiet.

"Enough? Enough to know that only two of her kids are mine as well? Or at least I think they are. God knows how many others might be out there too, and who their fathers might be." Bryan's laughed harshly again. He looked Mark up and down, as if he were something he'd trodden in.

"I should beat the shit out of you, you bastard, for screwing my wife."

Mark didn't flinch or waver. He just kept staring at Bryan, with a completely neutral expression on his face.

A violent rush of pure hatred suddenly coursed through Adie. She stepped forward, and didn't even try to keep the anger out of her voice. "I'm not your wife anymore, Bryan. We're separated. And I'll soon be making that official then filing for divorce. Now for the last time, get out, before I stick a fucking fork in your chest!"

Bryan sneered at Mark, and left, pushing past Adie and sending her stumbling backwards as he went. He slammed the front door so hard the glass rattled, and Adie prayed it wouldn't break. Mercifully it didn't.

The sound of squealing tyres pierced the air as Bryan's car left the kerb. Then silence settled.

"Are you alright, Adie?" Mark came forward and put a hand on Adie's shoulder. She was struggling to get her breathing under control. Tears pricked her eyes.

"Yes, thanks", she said in a slightly wobbly voice. "I'm fine. I'm so sorry about that, Mark. I never expected in a million years that he'd show up here, *ever*, let alone today!"

"No, I'm the one who's sorry. I shouldn't 'ave stayed. I 'ope I 'aven't made things worse fer yer, with 'im."

Adie reassured him that Bryan's appearance at the flat had been the last thing she'd ever expected. She was still happy that Mark had stayed over, and she told him so, adding that him being around didn't make a blind bit of difference to what was left of her relationship with her ex-husband.

"If I even had the slightest doubt that it was over, I don't have it now", she said decisively. "Coming in here, shouting the odds like that. He's behaved like a Neanderthal."

Mark sighed. "Well, if you really do think it's over, that's good I suppose, sad as it all is. Look forward now, lass. If you've decided you do want a fresh start, don't keep lookin' back. There's nowt that way for yer, now." He thought for a moment.

"Tell yer what. D'yer fancy goin' out to lunch? My treat. But only if yer promise not to stick a fucking fork in me chest." His eyes twinkled with humour. Adie could tell he hadn't judged her, and she managed a shaky grin.

"Yes, please. That sounds like a nice idea."

Lunch would be a welcome distraction. Bryan's visit had really rattled her. His arrogance and sense of entitlement were breath-taking. It didn't bother her much that he'd got the wrong end of the stick about her relationship with Mark. They *were* just friends, and it *was* none of Bryan's business anymore, what she did or who she did it with. What did upset her was the timing, and his assumption that she'd still be waiting with open arms.

Was a year long enough to have waited? Should I have given him longer? How much longer? How long is long enough?

She realised that the house sit at Teapot Cottage had shifted her paradigm more than she'd first though. If she hadn't gone to Torley, if she'd stayed at home, would she still be wallowing in her own grief? Most likely. Would she have welcomed Bryan's arrival and willingly gone back to him? Probably.

But time and distance had given Adie a new perspective and a different focus. In her heart, she knew that a year *had* been long enough, and she was surprised once more to realise that she really had moved on, quite a lot in fact, while being more or less oblivious of the process occurring.

Mark had made a few phone calls, during her musings, and he had efficiently arranged a taxi into in the centre of London. Adie was absolutely thrilled to find herself being whisked to the top of The Shard. She gaped at Mark.

"My God, I've been wanting to come here for ever! How the hell did you manage to book a table here, for the same day? It's almost impossible to do that, especially on a weekend!"

He grinned and winked at her. "I know a man who can pull a couple o' strings."

Adie was astonished but delighted. She was excited too, that from their table, they could see all across London. The grey morning had given way to a clear winter's day, with no clouds or haze to mar the view.

They chatted, as the waiter went to get their drinks, but Adie's thoughts kept drifting back to Bryan's visit. She felt compelled to apologise again to Mark, for the unpleasant encounter.

"For the record, I need to say that you saw the absolute worst in him, today. Before all this, he was usually fairly mild-mannered, and he's not a violent man by nature. Stubborn and opinionated at times, yes, and with a nasty temper when he did get riled up, but he never used to be violent.

"I know he threatened you today, but please don't think that's who he is, because it's not. I've seen him lose his temper very infrequently, over the years, and it was always a big thing when he did, But he never lost it with me. At least, not until everything blew up. Since all that, he's been a different person. I don't know who he is anymore, but threatening you today was the last straw for me, Mark. It's not ok for him muscle into my space and act like that towards me or my friends."

She went on to apologise for threatening to bury a fork in Bryan's chest that morning, and chose to ignore the cheeky smirk that spread across Mark's face, that he didn't even bother to try and hide.

"You've seen the worst in me too, today. I'm so sorry, Mark. I think it must be my hormones. They're all over the place right now, and I do occasionally have these random thoughts of doing serious harm to people who piss me off."

She grinned as the smirk quickly fell off Mark's face and he looked alarmed instead. "Oh, don't worry. You're as safe as houses. You'd have to do a lot to make me as mad as he did this morning. Stupid sod. Him, I mean, not you," she added. Mark chuckled, then shook his head.

"As I've said before, lass, my knowledge o't change o' life is more or less limited to what Sheila's been dealin' with," so I know it can be 'ard, but I dunno what else I can say about it that

149

would 'elp yer. But as fer yer 'usband, I reckon I do know a bit more about that."

He looked at Adie kindly, and his voice was gentle. "He thinks 'e's a man scorned, Adie. He saw summat this morning that really 'urt 'im. He's put two an' two together an' made five. We know that, but 'e doesn't. And he's reacted like any man would, under't circumstances."

"He'll never believe another word I ever tell him, after everything that's happened, not that it really matters much anymore." Adie felt a deep rush of sadness.

"Maybe not. But you've no control over what 'e chooses to think, lass. You're who you are, you're still who you've always been, and 'e should know you too, after all these years. If 'e can't get past what's 'appened, that's not your fault, Adie. That's summat 'e's got to take responsibility for, and work on, 'imself."

Adie knew Mark was right. She shook off her guilt, as best she could, determined that Bryan was not going to ruin her day.

"Well, I'm not going to let what happened this morning spoil our lovely lunch. You've brought me to this amazing place I've only ever dreamed about coming to, so I'm going to enjoy it! Bring me a fork!"

Chapter 14

Well, by 'eck! That bloody Bryan, Adie's ex-'usband, he were a piece of work weren't 'e?

Mark was partly sorry he'd been there when the man had shown up unexpectedly at her door like that, and partly relieved he'd been there to back Adie up. To be fair, Bostock probably wouldn't have kicked off like he did if Mark hadn't been there, but it could still have been an unpleasant encounter for Adie anyway.

The last thing Mark wanted was for things to be difficult for his new friend, especially if it was him being around that got her into trouble. The two of them were innocent mates and nothing more, but Bostock had clearly thought otherwise. It was fair enough too, Mark had to admit. The man shows up and finds his ex-wife having breakfast with a man sitting there all comfortable with his feet quite literally under the table. Sat there in his socks and wet hair, reading the Sunday paper, Mark must've looked like he owned the place.

He was acutely aware of how upsetting that must have been. He'd have thought the exact same thing himself, if he'd been in Bostock's shoes, so he chose to let the insults pass over him. For all his bluster and ill-will towards them both, Bryan Bostock was clearly a man who was hurting very much.

While Mark had never had to face being betrayed through infidelity, he had certainly felt his share of pain and bereavement for what was lost. He understood how grief could make a man react. Some might weep, others would throw punches, still more - like Bryan - would tough their way through it with intimidation or verbal abuse. It was par for the course, and Mark had tried to explain as much to Adie. It wasn't that he presumed to know her husband better than she did herself, it was just that he knew how difficult it could be for women to see a man's perspective. Just as difficult, in fact, as it usually was for a man to see a woman's view of the world. How the two sexes managed to get along, once they'd got together, was an absolute miracle.

He laughed to himself at Adie's not-so-idle threat to do serious harm to Bryan with an eating iron. She certainly had a bit of feistiness about her, when the occasion presented itself. He thought that was rather lovely, not that he'd ever dream of letting her know.

A lot of effort was needed, to keep relationships on an even keel. Mark had learned as much from his own wife and daughter. Beth had always been patient and eloquent in trying to explain how she felt about things, preferring respectful adult discussions to angry self-righteous fights, but Feen's adolescence had been a different experience altogether. That had been long and hellish, and as Mark tried to shield his wife from the worst of it while she battled her cancer, then continued to deal with it, *and* his daughter's deep, raging grief over the death of her mother which only compounded things, he felt like he'd been on the hop for most of his life.

Later, when Feen's moods had settled down, he'd managed to establish more positive communication with her. He'd painstakingly adopted his wife's diplomatic approach, and over time it had helped him find a way to get along with Feen. As she matured, she'd become a bit more like her mother; willing to discuss how she felt, instead of screaming in his face or withdrawing to her room for days on end. The two of them had continued to grow closer over time, and Mark had forced himself to stop worrying about what his daughter would make of his thoughts, since he wasn't a mean-spirited man and didn't feel he had any 'dark' or worrisome notions that he needed to shield from anyone.

Pulling his thoughts back to the present, he was grateful for how readily Feen had taken to Adie Bostock and he'd seen at his own Christmas party how she'd treated Carla Walton after the woman had been so unfriendly towards Adie. He also appreciated that Feen understood many things about Adie that he had yet to be privy to. While he couldn't profess to understand what really went on in women's heads, Mark knew that Feen was a good judge of character. If she liked Adie Bostock, it was good enough for him to like her too. And he decided that he really, really did.

One thing that baffled Mark completely though, and made him fight the impulse to run screaming for the hills, was the prospect of dealing with a menopausal woman. His sister Sheila was going through the change too, and there were days when Mark thought she was completely bloody bonkers, in what she said, did or thought. There were days when she'd do nothing but weep, others when she'd do nothing but sleep, and there were countless occasions when she'd bitten his head off for no good reason.

He understood it was a biological *and* an emotional thing, and Sheila had tried to explain to him more than once how bewildered and out of control it often made her feel, and how her mood swings were even a struggle for her to understand herself, at times. He sympathised, and offered what support he could. He'd talked to Bob about it, who'd said that giving Sheila as much reassurance as possible that she was ok and would stay that way, would be a big help, because she was losing her confidence in herself. She needed to *feel* understood, even if she wasn't.

Beth had never made it to menopause. Mark wasn't sure whether to be sad or relieved that he'd been robbed of helping his wife through that particular journey.

Adie's frustration and anguish at her husband's hard-line and consistent rejection of her weren't hard for him to understand, though. And now Bryan Bostock had to face the inescapable fact that he'd shot his own foot off, by refusing his wife's year-long process of pleading with him to talk to her. The man had allowed his umbrage to take the driving seat and all it had done was push poor Adie past her ability to wait.

It's a bloody 'ard road if the person you think loves you most can't forgive yer for stuffin' things up. What were 't stupid bugger's problem? Pride?

Adie's husband had been wallowing, pure and simple. He'd made the situation all about himself. He was the 'victim'. Admittedly, he had every right to be angry and hurt that Adie hadn't confided in him for all that time and yes, she'd manipulated the family in ways they had every reason to be outraged about. But Bryan had allowed his own pride and anguish to smother his ability to forgive, or be objective. He'd simply left it too late to change his mind. Adie had given him enough chances. As Mark's mother-in-law Alice had often observed, in her more lucid moments, you can only wait so long for a bus before you decide it's time to walk.

In his opinion, Adie had taken her marriage as seriously as anyone could. If her own husband couldn't even try to understand what she'd felt compelled to do, and why, it wasn't much to rebuild on.

Mark had no idea if she'd done the right thing. It wasn't his place to judge her. He only had his own experience of marriage to go by, and he liked to think that if Bryan had loved Adie as much as Mark had loved Beth, he would have tried earlier, and tried a lot *harder*, to put his umbrage aside, and try to communicate, understand, and find a way of righting the ship before the bloody thing simply sank without trace. It was such a terrible shame that after twenty-six years, two grown up children, and a wealth of good times and happy memories together it looked like Adie and Bryan would struggle to salvage even a civil line of communication, let alone their broken marriage.

Mark had explained to Adie before they left the flat that he needed to stay in the city that night, at a hotel where he was having his breakfast business meeting the following morning, because it would be more practical to do that than leave well before dawn to get there in time. London traffic drove him crazy, he explained, and Adie understood fully, bless her. She insisted on him putting his bag in the car right away and declared that she would find her own way back to her flat after lunch, saying she did it all the time, could do it with her eyes shut, and it wouldn't be a problem at all.

He could tell she meant it. He appreciated her understanding, and it also meant she would have more time to herself, to think a little on her encounter with Bryan, and finish her packing and do anything else she might want to do in the area before heading north again. She might have neighbours to update, or a bit of personal shopping to do. Mark too would have some time to himself. He had some reports to look over before tomorrow's meeting, so a quiet afternoon, a quick dinner and an early night would suit him well.

After their lunch, Mark walked Adie to London Bridge tube station, where they said goodbye and agreed that Mark would be back at the flat by midday on Monday at the latest. Adie gave him a quick hug, and promised to have everything packed and ready to go. She offered to make the coffee and sandwiches for the return trip since Mark's rinsed-out flask was still sitting on the draining board in her kitchen.

As he waved her off, Mark was surprised at how much affection he had for his new friend. He felt protective of her, especially after the encounter they'd had with her ex-husband that morning, and he hoped Bryan wouldn't bother her again. He had a funny feeling however, that if he did, she'd hold her own.

He realised he was already looking forward to the return journey. Adie was good company. Her conversation was witty and intelligent, and he liked her sense of humour. Unlike the other women in his life, she wasn't in any way aloof, dreamy or distracted, and he found that refreshing. She also wasn't hell-bent on snaring him as a husband either, with the kind of thinly disguised attempts so many other women had made at trying to get him interested, including that hellcat Carla Walton. Despite what she'd so recently been through, Adie was direct, warm and honest, as far as he could tell. What it must have meant for the poor woman, to hold on so hard and for so long to the secrets of her past, he could only begin to imagine.

*　*　*

Monday morning dawned grey and dull. It was a typical dreary London morning in mid-winter, with the bleak sky mirrored in the gloomy expressions of people trudging past the window of the hotel restaurant, presumably on their way to work.

Mark glanced at his watch. He was half an hour early, but his desperate need for decent coffee had driven him down to breakfast ahead of time. The instant stuff they provided in the rooms was horrible.

He'd been given a table on the other side of a tall bamboo screen, so he needed to keep a look out for Kenny Lee, the Korean guy he was meeting, and be ready to stand and wave him over, otherwise he wouldn't be seen.

Mark had prepared for his meeting, with all the necessary paperwork ready for the purchase of some new farm equipment, heavily discounted from an importer, but the trip to London had felt like a good idea, because the importer had other things that he thought Mark might be interested in hearing more about. As Mark and Bob were both always keen to invest in the upgrade of the farm's equipment, some of which was getting a bit old and decrepit, Mark agreed to make the journey. The effort of making face-to-face connections and break bread with a solid supplier could shave thousands of pounds off the bill for new stuff and pave the way for more later. Relationships did still count with some people in the business world. Mark had decided it was worth putting Kenny up at The Dorchester, one of the best hotels in London, and he figured it made sense to stay there himself.

Over at the restaurant entrance, Mark caught sight of a couple coming in. The man looked vaguely familiar, and as they came closer, he realised to his abject horror that it was Adie's ex-husband Bryan Bostock. He was literally dumbstruck at the coincidence.

What? Yer bloody kiddin me! This is bloody London, wi' six million people in it! What are the soddin' chances o' this?

Bostock was holding hands with a woman who looked at least fifteen years younger. Clearly, despite berating Adie for 'moving on', he hadn't wasted much time himself. The woman was stunning, with her silver-blonde hair cut in an impossibly neat, jaw-length bob. Her make-up was immaculate, and her clothes were elegant, well-cut and expensive. Even Mark could see that.

I guess that's what yer'd call 'high maintenance', he thought to himself.

He quickly hunkered down in his chair, praying he wouldn't be seen by Bostock. To his utter dismay, the hostess sat the couple down directly on the other side of the bamboo screen. Mark could have poked his fingers through it and almost touched them. Instead, some sixth sense made him take out his phone and quietly press the record button. He wasn't sure the couple's conversation would be meaningful in any way, but he didn't want to miss it if it was.

The woman spoke. "Thank you for inviting me to Monday breakfast again, darling. It's been ages, hasn't it? I've really missed coming here, especially during that God-awful pandemic when we weren't allowed to do anything at all. And you've been so bogged down for months now with all the new work. But here we are, finally, back at the good old Dorch, and it's so nice not to have to be all illicit and sneaky!" Mark heard her giggle. "I do miss those days a bit though, if I'm honest. Being out in the open is wonderful, and so is the fact that you've finally dumped that silly wife of yours for good, but being your dirty little secret was so exciting sometimes, and *very* sexy!"

Bostock drawled a lazy response. "The Dorch does the best breakfast in the city. Why break a seven-year habit?"

The woman giggled. "Well, five if you take Covid out of the equation. Anyway, I'm really looking forward to Paris! I'm already packed! We can have dinner at Maxims and visit Montmartre, maybe have our portraits done by some starving artist!" She sounded excited.

Bostock sighed. "Nicki, I can't take you with me. Not this trip. I'm sorry."

"What? *Again*? Are you fucking kidding me, Bryan?" There was silence for a few moments, then Bostock spoke again. His voice was wheedling now. He was in the doghouse and he knew it.

"Nicki, please don't look like that. I know you were looking forward to going. But I'm only taking one day to get over there and back again this time, so there's no point in you coming with me. Next time I go, it will be for longer. Five or six days, maybe. We can have a nice hotel, indulge in some proper French cuisine, sleep late, make lots of love, and see the city properly, I promise."

The woman's voice was waspish now. "You've been promising me ever since you got the contract with this company, four years ago now at least, that you'd take me to Paris. Every time you've gone there's been some excuse for why I can't come with you. First it was too hard to hide it from your pathetic, clinging vine of a wife, now it's time constraints. This is bullshit, Bryan. I can't believe you! What the fuck am I even *doing* here?"

Bostock sounded contrite. "Nic, I'm sorry, truly I am. I just don't have the time to spend right now. I've got to just get over there, have a very long and boring meeting, and get straight back. I'm so committed to everything, I can't justify any real time off. Not for a few months yet. This trip, you'd see nothing. It wouldn't be fair, darling."

"Commitment? Don't make me laugh! What about your commitment to *me*?" Nicki snapped. "I was committed to you, the faithful mistress for six damned years! You talk about how inconvenient it is for me to be waiting around for you for a few hours in Paris? What do you think I've been doing for the last six fucking years? Seven in total, Bryan, waiting in the wings while you endlessly dithered about whether or not to leave your wife, even after your kids went off to uni! I was your ridiculous cliché for long enough, and even now when we're supposedly no big secret anymore, you're *still* fobbing me off! Don't you think it's about time I got what was owing to me in return for my long and faithful commitment to *you*?"

Mark heard Bostock sigh heavily. "Nic, I'm as committed to you as you are to me. I always have been! It's just work. Project management. You know what it's like at the moment. It's absolutely manic, with everything still in post-pandemic take-off. We'll make a solid plan for Paris, for later in the year, I promise. Maybe we can go to Rome as well. Would you like that?"

Mark heard the sound of a chair scrape back, and he felt rather than saw Nicki stand up. She hissed at Bostock.

"That's what you said last year. You didn't mean it then, and you don't mean it now. You can stick your 'promise' up your arse and choke on your bloody breakfast for all I care. I'm leaving. I'll find my own way to work."

With that, she stormed out of the restaurant and, as unhappy luck would have it, she virtually collided with Kenny Lee, leaving Mark with no choice but to stand up and let himself be seen as he waved Kenny over. Mark was aware of the shock and dismay on Bostock's face, but he refused to make eye contact until Kenny was almost at the table.

Then, he looked the other man squarely in the eye. He said nothing, but he let his expression convey that he had heard the lot. Bostock looked completely dazed - and very worried. *As well 'e bloody might*, Mark thought to himself.

He shook his head very slightly at the other man, then turned his attention to Kenny. He switched the record button off, on his phone, and settled to have his meeting. Within seconds, Bostock had risen and left the restaurant.

After Mark's business had drawn to a close, he made his way to his car, with a heavy heart. Sitting in the driver's seat, he hesitated before starting the engine. What he'd heard had upset him and he knew it would be devastating for Adie. His blood boiled at Bostock. What a selfish snake he was, to allow his wife to carry the heavy burden of guilt for her mistakes, accusing her of destabilising their family as a result, when he'd been sneaking around with another woman behind her back for more than half a decade!

Mark's fist itched to connect with Bostock's jowly face. He really did feel like knocking the bastard's teeth out.

But Mark now felt a burden of his own. Should he tell Adie what he'd heard? Would a good friend do that? Should he be the bearer of news that would break her heart all over again? Or should he keep the terrible knowledge to himself, and allow her to keep feeling the unfair weight of her own mistakes while Bostock would receive no blame for being unfaithful in their marriage? From what Mark had seen and heard of him, it would suit the man well, to keep appearing like the injured party, the betrayed, manipulated and lied-to husband. Mark found that unacceptable. Despite her own mistakes, Adie deserved better. There was no denying that.

The dilemma weighed heavily as he drove back towards Adie's flat. But, as it turned out, being the bearer of bad tidings wasn't the only thing he had to confront. As he turned to sweep into Adie's driveway, he found himself slamming on his brakes, on finding another car, a red Porsche Boxster, parked there.

He found space to park in the street, walked past the Boxster, and heard its engine ticking as it cooled down. Adie's front door was open. Immediately, he recognised Bostock's voice. He stopped to listen, before he was seen.

"I don't know what you're talking about!" Adie was saying. She sounded angry and frustrated. "What lies? What lies would he tell me about you? He doesn't even know you! You're not making any sense, Bryan."

"I'm telling you, Adie. He'll pretend he does. I've met blokes like him before. He'll tell you he's heard something about me, or he knows someone who knows me, and he'll spin you all kinds of bullshit that he reckons he's heard. You mark my words. You can't trust him. Get rid of him, Adie. He'll poison your mind."

Mark took a deep breath and walked into the house. Bostock turned and sneered at him.

"Well, look what the cat dragged in."

159

He sounded nonchalant enough, but Mark could read his eyes. There was real fear there, and the man was trying to communicate as subtly as he could, that Mark should keep his mouth shut. But Mark had no intention of doing any such thing.

"What's 'appenin' Adie?" he asked gently. Adie shook her head in bewilderment.

"I don't know. I really don't. Bryan's just showed up here, proclaiming that you intend to poison me against him. It doesn't make sense."

Bryan rolled his shoulders. "I've just been telling Adie that you're a nasty piece of work, and that she shouldn't trust you."

Mark looked at him in disbelief. "*I'm* a nasty piece o'work? *Me?*"

Adie burst out "Will someone tell me what the hell is going on around here?"

Mark nodded. "Aye lass, Bryan'll tell yer, in a minute or two." He looked at the other man and jerked his head towards the front door. "A word outside, if yer would. Now."

Bostock laughed. "You want me to step outside? No problem." He made a show of starting to roll up his sleeves.

"Stop this nonsense, both of you! You're like a couple of silly little schoolboys" Adie snapped.

Mark put his hand on her shoulder. "Adie, just gimme a minute. Bryan and I need to 'ave a chat about summat. It'll not take long."

With that, he turned and left the flat. Bostock followed him out and had the grace to close the front door behind him. He sneered at Mark again.

"So, big man - what's the plan? You're not gonna tell Adie about my little indiscretion, are you? I've already paved the way for that." He looked triumphant.

"No, Bryan. Yer goin' to tell 'er yerself. Right 'ere, right now, today."

Bryan laughed again. "Oh, okay, halfwit. Right-o then!" He stood gloating at Mark with his arms folded across his chest. Mark sighed, took out his phone, and started playing back the recording he had made in the restaurant. Both Bryan's and Nicki's voices were clearly audible. The colour drained from Bryan's face as Mark watched him. He stood, stock still, suddenly looking helpless and panicked.

Mark stopped the recording. His voice, even to his own ears, sounded low and deadly. "I've emailed it t'meself, mate. So, you can smash me face in, an' stamp on me phone if yer want, but the bloody evidence will still be there. So, get yer fat, lardy bloody backside into that flat an' confess everythin'. Tell 'er, or I will."

Bostock bit his lip and tried another tack. "Well, some 'friend' you are! If you were really her 'friend', why would you play her that recording? Why would you break her heart like that?"

Mark's expression never changed.

"Because she doesn't deserve to be carryin' the can for everythin' by 'erself, yer cheatin', lyin' piece o' shyte. It's suited you, a'nt it? To play the injured party? But that's not strictly true, is it, Bryan? Adie made big mistakes and one way or another it's caused yer marriage to fail, or so you'd like the world to think. But it weren't so clever any road, were it? Because you? You were an unfaithful fuckin' snake, and if that marriage 'ad been as 'appy as you always tried to tell 'er it was before *she* went an' ruined everythin', yarda bloody yarda, yer would've kept it in't family, instead of sowin' it about wi' a bloody mistress."

He stepped forward, almost daring Bostock to hit him, but the other man stood silent. "So, man up, an' get in there an' tell 'er. Because if I end up tellin 'er, she'll take you to the fucking cleaners, an' I'll champion that. If you do the decent thing, if you still remember 'ow, she might go a bit easier on yer - over't divorce, like."

Bostock just stood looking at the ground, clearly outtrumped. Mark waited for a full minute, while the other man digested the ultimatum, then he ran out of patience and stepped forward, grabbing Bostock by the scruff of the neck. The other man put his arms up in surrender and the two men walked back into the flat, with Mark pushing Bostock in first. Adie was standing in the kitchen with her hands on her hips. She looked angrier than Mark had ever seen her.

"Right, you two", she said grimly. "Somebody tell me what the bloody hell this is about, or I swear to God, I'll throw you both out and never speak to either of you again." She sounded furious; in fact, she was shaking with anger.

Mark cleared his throat. "Bryan's got summat 'e wants to tell yer, Adie. I'll leave yer to it. Please gimme a ring when yer ready to leave. I'll just be around't corner. Two minutes away." He smiled apologetically at Adie and turned and left.

As he sat in his car, he felt a surge of sadness. His lovely friend was about to have her world shattered again. It would be painful, he knew. The shock would be immense. But Adie needed to know the truth. He'd watched her beat herself up so badly, about the way her marriage had ended. She needed to know that she wasn't the only one to blame, that the responsibility for the foundations not being strong enough to survive the onslaught wasn't hers alone.

It was desperately unfair of her ex-husband to let her go on feeling that she'd single-handedly destroyed a happy marriage. And it certainly wasn't fair for him to get away with what he'd done. A six-year affair was more than just the "indiscretion" he'd tried to pass it off as. Six years wasn't just a passing temptation. It was a long time. It was a real commitment to infidelity; a conscious choice, to cheat for that long.

An hour went by. Bryan's car remained in Adie's driveway, and she hadn't called Mark. It was another half hour after that when he saw Bostock leave. The man pulled out of the driveway and headed off in the other direction. Half an hour after that, Mark's phone rang. It was Adie.

"You can come and get me", she said simply, and hung up.

The door to the flat was still open, and the chilly air had seeped in. The place felt cold and utterly devoid of the ambience it had in the beginning. Adie had moved her bags and boxes to the door, and they sat ready to be loaded into Marks car, which he had now backed into the driveway. She was sitting at the kitchen table. When he came in, she gave him a weak smile.

"I've made the flask of coffee, and some egg and bacon sandwiches. I've wrapped them in foil so they'll stay warm for a bit."

"Are you alright, lass?"

Mark could see that Adie had been crying, but he was relieved she was composed now. He'd been dreading finding her hysterical, as he wasn't sure how he'd handle that. But he needn't have worried. As if she could read his mind, she sought to reassure him.

"I'm fine, Mark, please don't worry. I'm only sorry you had to be dragged into this awful mess. All you did was give me a ride down here and back again, and that was all you were supposed to do. I never wanted you to be put on the spot like you have been."

Mark was touched by her heartfelt apology. He waved his hand in dismissal.

"Let me get this lot into the back o' t car an' we can get goin'. Is there owt else yer need to do before we set off?"

She laughed lightly. "Other than find a certain bit on the side and bury a fucking fork in her chest? No, Mark. I'm ready to leave. More than ready. My only regret is that eventually I'll have to come back. It would be nice never to have to, to never see this place again, now that he's walked in here and tainted it. Thank God it's only rented." She sighed deeply, and her bottom lip wobbled.

"This little flat was mine, Mark. It isn't much of a place, but it was my private space. Now, all I'll ever associate it with is him, in here, confessing his dirty little secret, and grovelling and begging for forgiveness himself. He told me it wasn't me, it was him, the usual stupid clichés. Not that any of that matters, now." She chewed her bottom lip, thoughtfully.

Mark didn't know what to say. Instead, he started picking up the bags and boxes and loading them into the car. When the job was done, he went back into the flat and helped Adie on with her coat. She picked up her handbag, threw her keys into it, handed him the coffee flask and the sandwiches, then stepped through the front door and pulled it shut behind them.

For the first hour, on the drive back, neither said very much. Mark turned on the radio and tuned into the traffic report, pleased to note that the planned route home was clear. He didn't try to make light conversation, which would have seemed insensitive, and he certainly didn't feel it was his place to initiate a heavy discussion. He left Adie with her thoughts, knowing she needed time to process what she'd learned from her husband, and she seemed content to remain quiet.

Chapter 15

As their journey back to the Lake District got underway, Adie realised that as devastating as it had ended up being, the weekend had passed in a flash. After returning from her lovely lunch with Mark the day before, she'd done a bit of shopping at a nearby mall and gone for a long walk in the park while there was still enough light left in the day. She'd then made a very light throw-together dinner and spent the evening deciding what she wanted to take back with her to Teapot Cottage.

She'd managed not to dwell too much on Bryan's visit yesterday, but it had been harder than usual to switch off and fall asleep last night. This morning, while she was waiting for Mark to return, she'd put the finishing touches to her packing and done a bit of housework, trying not to choke on the surprising amount of dust that had built up in the flat in the time she'd been away.

Adie had also made a few phone calls, one of which was to Ruth, to see how she and her family were after their Christmas trip to Italy. Another call went to Miranda, who promised to come up to Teapot Cottage for a weekend very soon. Adie laughed at her friend's astute observation that she sounded like an entirely different person from the one who had hightailed it out of Guildford in a saturating mist of misery just a couple of weeks before.

Adie had accumulated enough stuff to fill Mark's Range Rover. One box contained wellington boots, hats, gloves and scarf, along with a couple of heavy coats. She'd also included a favourite patchwork quilt, a couple of jigsaw puzzles, some framed photos, a few books she hadn't yet got around to reading, and some other bits and pieces that would make Teapot Cottage feel a bit more like home for the next few months.

She had managed to catch up with her neighbour who had handed her a few parcels which she hadn't opened, preferring to do that back at the cottage. One was from Matty, as promised. Opening a gift from her son would be something to look forward to when she was back in her new temporary home. It would form part of the good memories she knew she would have of Teapot Cottage when her stay was finally over, and she inevitably returned to Guildford for once and for all.

Now more than ever, it seemed important to Adie that she make the absolute most of her time in Torley, and she'd planned to say as much to Mark, as soon as he returned. He had been incredibly kind and generous with his time and resources. She enjoyed spending time with him and Feen, and she hoped their friendships would continue long past her time in Torley. She hadn't forgotten her promise to return for the next Christmas party.

The second unexpected arrival of her ex-husband at the flat in as many days had taken her even more by surprise than the first. When the doorbell rang, she'd expected to find Mark on the doorstep, earlier than arranged. To see Bryan standing there with a face like thunder was incredibly alarming.

What he'd started saying had confused Adie totally. He told her he already knew Mark, and that Mark would tell her vicious lies about him that weren't true. The whole story had sounded preposterous, and she wondered for a brief moment whether Bryan had taken drugs. He made no sense whatsoever. When Mark arrived, and more or less frog-marched Bryan out into the courtyard, everything started to get even cloudier. Adie knew better than to try and get between two big, angry, fighting men, but she was furious, wondering what the hell they were playing at.

When she found out, it took a little while for it all to sink in. Apparently, Mark had run into Bryan in what could only be described as the most freakish of coincidences. He'd then overheard a conversation that had left him in no doubt about what Bryan had been up to, namely having an affair for several years - since well before Adie's own deceptions and secrets had come to light, in fact. Mark had for some reason seen fit to record that conversation and use it as leverage to force Bryan to confess everything to his wife. Adie still didn't know how she really felt about that, but Bryan did tell her everything. He sat there at her kitchen table and tearfully spilled his guts in a way that simply made her deeply sad, rather than angry and resentful.

It seemed there had already been deep cracks in their marriage and she'd been completely oblivious to them. Bryan had been excellent at covering his tracks. She'd never suspected a thing. Never for one moment, in all the years he'd been unfaithful, had she ever wondered where he was, all those nights and weekends when he said he was working. She'd taken him on trust.

Maybe she hadn't been the wife he'd really needed. When she suggested that as a reason, in seeking to understand Bryan's choice to be unfaithful, he'd been quick to reassure her that it hadn't been her fault. He admitted that it was cathartic and constructive to finally be confessing his own reprehensible behaviour instead of constantly dredging up the energy to keep flinging mud at Adie, and he had acknowledged that he'd behaved like an arrogant bastard who thought he could keep his cake and eat it. Well, that was one thing he *did* happen to be right about.

He said he was sorry, and when Adie had asked him if that was because he genuinely was, or whether it was simply because he'd been outed as a cheat and a liar, he'd hastened to tell her how ashamed he was of his own behaviour, including allowing Adie to be seen as the sole instigator of their marriage falling apart.

What was just as uncomfortable for Adie to hear, though, was Bryan confessing how confused and hurt he'd been that she'd never told him right from the outset, that she'd had a baby girl and adopted her out before they'd even met. He felt like she'd never trusted him, and he couldn't figure out why. He was angry about that, and about the fact that she'd moved her oblivious and trusting family around like pieces on a chessboard, purely to suit her own desires. He left her in no doubt about how much that had hurt him.

She also knew that deceiving his family over a period of years would have been no more comfortable for Bryan than her own deceit had been for her, and she knew from bitter experience the relief that always followed the revelation of burdensome, hurtful secrets.

Bryan ended the conversation by telling her she could have a divorce on grounds of adultery, and he wouldn't contest it. There would be no need for a fight over the assets because she could have whatever she wanted if she left his pension intact, and he would agree. The lawyers would have an easy time of it all which would of course keep the legal costs down. Bryan also said that he forgave her for keeping him in the dark and manipulating the family, and hoped she could one day forgive him his selfishness too.

It was a lot to take in. But Adie was curious to find herself feeling more philosophical than angry at the way everything had unfolded, and there was undeniably a massive relief in no longer having to bear the burden of being the only one at fault. Two wrongs didn't make a right, but knowing Bryan's affair had put their relationship in jeopardy even without Adie's contributions of lies and deceit, and well before it in fact, took some of the burden of guilt away from her.

They would probably have fallen apart anyway, in time, since Bryan had been unable to say when she'd asked him, if he was in love with the woman in question. He'd certainly been committed enough to keep seeing her all the way through the Covid pandemic when he wasn't supposed to be going *anywhere* outside of what was regarded as 'essential work'.

Adie didn't ask him who the woman was, only if it was someone she knew. She was relieved when he said it was someone she'd never met; a woman he'd met through work. He was still seeing her, that much was clear, and since it had been a full year since Adie had left the family home, the situation appeared to be less about the illicit thrill of having a clandestine affair than it was about him genuinely enjoying that relationship.

Adie looked over at Mark, who had been lost in his own thoughts for some time while they'd been driving. Their silence wasn't as comfortable as it had been on the way down, and Mark seemed to be at a loss for how to break it, so Adie decided to do the honours.

"It's ok, you know. It was all very civilized, in the end. I know why you did what you did, and it's ok."

Mark looked over at her. His eyes were full of kindness. "Are *you* ok? I can't imagine 'ow much of a shock it must've been, to 'ear all that. An' I know it's none o' my business really. But I'm fond of yer, Adie, an' I can see the 'urt and the guilt you've been carryin'. It were an unfair burden anyway, lass, but I couldn't just sit back wi' what I knew an' say nowt, and let you carry on wi' it, when 'e was as much to bloody blame. I couldn't stand 'im lettin' you think it were all down to you, lass."

"I know", Adie sighed. "And it is your business. It became that when he threatened you."

Mark reached over and patted her hand. He let out a mirthless chuckle. "What do folk say, about bein' in't wrong place at wrong time? Or mebbe it were right place, right time. Either way, it were a hell of a coincidence, ending up in't same hotel in a place as big as London. An' I still don't know if tellin' yer was the right thing or not, but it felt like the *only* thing I could do, Adie."

Adie wondered about the timing and place, herself. It had been on her mind ever since Mark had got to the flat and it had become clear that the men had ended up in the same London hotel for breakfast at the same time on the same day. Was that just one of life's extraordinary and random coincidences? Or was it the hand of fate that had put them both there on purpose? Was some divine intervention responsible, the universe working behind the scenes to engineer an outcome that eased a heavy burden, using certain people as receivers and messengers to aid the process? Had Mark been one such messenger, divinely engineered into position by fate?

Believers of Universal Law would have said a resounding 'yes' to that. Advocates for karmic justice would agree that the universe sorts everything out in its own peculiar way, in its own time. If you just step back and allow the process to naturally occur, without trying to force anything, you get the right result.

Instinctively, Adie knew that Feen would believe that. Feen never foisted her own beliefs on anyone else, but she was a devout believer in Universal Law. The trust she had in all things naturally and spiritually driven shone out of her every pore.

She'd no doubt find the notion of her own father being used as a Universal angel hilarious, but she would declare without hesitation that this situation had evolved exactly as it was supposed to. She would believe with all her heart, that it was all precisely what the universe had ordained.

And now here Adie was, in a car with an incredibly wise and kind man who had her interests at heart yet expected nothing big of her in return. He was simply taking her back to Teapot Cottage - her healing place – and she just couldn't wait to get back there. She had all her favourite things with her now, and she started to feel a real sense that the body blows had ended. The worst really did feel as if it might be behind her now, and maybe that even included the wretchedness of the menopause, and all the turmoil that came with it.

Maybe there really was something in Feen Raven's way of seeing the world. When certain things happened the way they did, it often prompted you to at least *consider* the karmic wheel, whether you actually believed in it or not. Some synchronicities were simply too powerful to ignore. It did feel like this had been one of them, and maybe going with the flow was the key to riding out the storm and staying on your feet after it ended. She sighed and smiled gently at Mark.

"I'm so sorry you've been caught up in all this ugly nonsense, Mark. I'm sure you never imagined you would be, when you offered me a simple lift down here and back." As predicted, Mark waved her apology away. She could see he wasn't affected by anything that had happened. In fact, she suspected, he might even be pleased for her that she had a resolution of sorts.

It would take a lot more than Adie and Bryan Bostock, and their pathetic marital dramas, to shake a man like Mark Raven. That much was clear. He was like the proverbial rock, capable of weathering all manner of storms with no erosion at all.

"Bryan's not going to contest a divorce, and we've agreed to do it with minimal legal involvement. He's told me I can file on grounds of adultery, he'll admit to it, and the whole thing should rumble through in a straightforward way."

Mark nodded in response, clearly still at a loss for what else to say.

Adie decided to lighten things up a little. "I'm so glad we're on our way back. I expect you're relieved to be going home too? London's a pig of a place. In fact, you know, I think I'm done with it, and with Surrey. I'm pretty sure I don't want to go back and live there anymore. Too much rush and bother, too many sad memories. There's not much I want there now that I couldn't get just by visiting. I think, once the house sit is finished, I'll look for a quieter home. I like your end of the country better, I think."

Mark nodded. He refocused on Adie with a light smile.

"Aye, I'd not live anywhere else, even if I 'ad the chance. It's 'ome. I think Feen feels the same. I can't see the lass ever movin' away, at least not proper, like. There's summat special about Torley, and its people, that makes yer feel at 'ome there."

She nodded. She suddenly couldn't wait to step back into the gentle, warm embrace of Teapot Cottage, make a cup of tea, sit in a window seat, and rest her eyes on the magnificent view of Torley valley.

* * *

They took a restroom stop, an hour or so later, but when Adie got back to the car, she found Mark distraught on his phone. He clicked off as she got back into the car. His face was ashen.

"What? What's happened now?" she cried.

"Adie, that were Feen on't phone. She's 'ad to take Sid to't vet. E's goin' t be ok, by all accounts, as she found 'im in time, but the vet thinks 'es been poisoned."

Adie looked at him in horror. "*Poisoned?*" Her mind reeled.

"Aye." Mark's expression was serious. "'E were vomitin' an' all floppy, when she found 'im this mornin', so she took 'im straight down in your car. Vet says it looks like poison. Reckons it were meat put through't door overnight."

Adie went cold. "What? Are you sure? My God! Poor Sid! Are you sure he'll be alright?"

Mark nodded. "Yes. They're keepin' 'im for a day or two, to make sure, but vet thinks 'e'll make a full recovery. I'm sorry Adie. It's not nice news on't back of everythin' else, I know."

She found herself blinking back tears. "Who would do such a terrible, heartless thing?"

Mark said nothing. Adie was upset, but furious as well. The poor little dog. What had he done to anyone? The thought of him in pain and suffering was too much for her to bear. Tears filled her eyes then spilled out and ran down her cheeks. "I shouldn't have left. If I'd stayed, it wouldn't have happened. He'd be safe."

"But maybe not, Adie. Maybe it still would've 'appened, while yer were sleepin' or summat. You were never to foresee anythin' like this 'appenin'. I can't remember a time when owt like this 'as ever 'appened before."

"It must be me then. I'm the newcomer here. Someone must hate *me*."

Adie asked him if anything else had been said. He thought for a moment then nodded, reluctantly.

"Well, you may as well know all of it. If it's what we think, it'll all be comin' out, any road, an' soon enough. Feen told me Carla was 'anging around outside the church 'all, on Saturday. She saw you race off, and she followed yer. She saw us leavin', then she went back down to't hall and 'ad a right go at Feen about it. Reckoned we were 'eadin' away for a dirty weekend. She made quite a scene, as it goes."

"Are you saying *she* did this?" Adie was incredulous. Was the woman completely, certifiably mad, to have tried to kill someone else's dog, out of jealousy towards Adie?

You'd have to be insane to do something like that, she thought furiously.

So, the body blows weren't over quite yet then!

"I don't know, lass. It might just be a coincidence. But I'm goin' to 'ave the tyre prints checked on 'er car. If they match the ones that ruined the lawn at' cottage, I reckon we might 'ave a bit of a situation to deal with."

Mark went on to explain that he'd taken photographs of the tyre marks on the ruined lawn before proceeding to fix the damage. He didn't know if they might be useful or not, but decided it was better to be looking *at* them than *for* them.

Adie grappled with the notion that her friendship with Mark could make another woman so deranged as to inflict such devastating criminal damage to an innocent dog. Surely not. Surely, she wouldn't stoop to doing something so heart-breaking and cruel? *Would she?*

Poor, darling little Siddy. And poor Feen, having to deal with the other woman's tantrum in a public place, AND finding poor Sid and having to deal with that too.

She voiced her concerns to Mark who shook his head.

"Don't underestimate our kid, Adie. She might be a slight slip of a thing, but she can more than hold 'er own wi' that one. An'

171

I know what yer thinkin'" he looked sideways at her. "An' don't you bloody dare!"

Adie *had* been thinking that maybe she should just cut her losses, find someone else for the Robinsons and leave, to avoid any more hurt to the people, animals and property she cared about. It amazed her that Mark understood that, without her having said a single word. She looked across at his profile. His jaw was firmly set.

"We'll get to't bottom o' this, Adie. I think Carla might be involved, because as much as I rack me brain, I can't think of who else would do summat like this. Nobody else 'as anything even resemblin' a motive. Think about it. The lawn were damaged after't party and who were there, and upset? And little Sid bein' poisoned; again, who were makin' a scene just a day before it, and who were upset? An' who knew you weren't at 'ome? If it's a coincidence, lass, it's a bloody strong 'un."

"So she may have done the lawn too? Maybe that was an accident, like you already said," Adie said feebly, trying very hard to deny a link between the two incidents, but failing.

"Aye. Mebbe. An' before this, I might've chalked it up as that, too. But I'm askin' meself now, an' I think the two might be connected. An' if they are, I reckon it's Carla."

Adie sighed. "Maybe it *would* be better, safer, for everyone if I chucked it in and went home."

"No!" Mark's reply was firm. "We need to make sure we're on the right track. As strong as it is, a hunch in't enough. But if we can prove it were Carla, there's no need for you to think about leavin'. Don't let 'er think she can win and drive you out o' town by bullyin' an' bloody violence. Both incidents are criminal matters, Adie. We'll get it sorted."

He went on to say that he had instructed Feen not to touch the outside of the front door, especially not the letterbox hatch. As they sat in the car, he telephoned the local Torley police and spoke to Colin Fairways, a Senior Sergeant and very good friend since they days when his daughter had been going through chemo at the same time as Beth, and reported Sid's poisoning formally as a crime. Fairways assured him that since it was a "slow day at the office", he'd get a couple of officers to go and check out the property straight away, and take what fingerprints or other evidence they could find. Mark also emailed across to him the photographs of the ruined lawn, in case they might be of help. When Fairways had asked why that particular matter hadn't been reported, Mark had told him everyone had initially thought it was the result of a drunken accident after his party, and only now were they wondering about a possible connection. Fairways conceded that was fair enough.

Adie was now completely on edge, and desperate to get back to Torley. She wanted to see everything for herself - Sid, Feen, Mittens, the chickens, and the cottage. She believed Mark's reassurances that all was well there, but she knew she wouldn't rest until she could see it for herself.

Darkness had already fallen as they approached Torley town. Mark drove straight to the vet surgery, and Adie jumped out of the car and went rushing to the door. There was still a light on inside, although the surgery had officially closed.

The vet, David Thornely, explained that Sid was going to be fine. He was just a bit sore from his stomach pump, and he was on a rehydration drip, but he was comfortable and sleeping now. He showed Adie through a door off to one side of the treatment room, and she saw Sid immediately. He was, as the vet had said, sound asleep, and breathing normally. She burst into tears once more, this time with relief.

Dr Thornley confirmed that Sid could be collected in two days' time. Apparently, the poison hadn't had chance to enter his intestinal tract. Feen had got to him just in time. It felt like a miracle to Adie. She could only imagine how worried and wretched poor Feen must be feeling.

On some visceral level, Adie knew that Carla Walton was the culprit. The woman disliked Adie, and she'd made it very clear. She wanted Mark, but he didn't want her. As bitter a pill as that may have been for Carla to swallow, she was completely off base in assuming so much about Adie's relationship with him. They were friends, pure and simple. She found it interesting though, that Carla had assumed something else and so, for that matter, had Bryan.

Why were relationships so complicated? And what did this horrible, sinister set of developments mean for Mark and Adie's friendship?

173

Feen told them the police had turned up more or less immediately after Mark had called them, to take a statement from her. She had taken them down and let them into the cottage, where they'd examined the area just inside the front door, below the letterbox hatch. They found traces of blood just below the hatch and on its shelf, which suggested that raw meat had been pushed through it to land on the floor at the bottom of the door. Photographs and swabs had been taken and they'd asked Feen to get Mark to contact Sergeant Fairways as soon as he got back. While Mark was putting the call through, Feen made a pot of tea and laid out three cups. She looked at Adie squarely.

"You know, it might seem awful of me to say such a thing, but I really hope the police *can* prove it was Carla Walton that did this. I know she's responsible, and I know Daddy believes that too. But if it can't be proved, it means she won't be dealt with, and we still can't put this behind us. I think it would be just horrible if the person behind these awful, cowardly things wasn't brought to justice, because we'd never feel safe from something happening again."

As they sat around drinking their tea, two uniformed police officers arrived. They informed Mark and Adie that they had examined the front door and were arranging to get several sets of fingerprints checked. They had also found a muddy footprint in the soil under the window next to the door, that they'd matched with one of Carla Walton's Nike trainers. And they had also matched the tread on the tyres of her father's truck with those in the photographs Mark had emailed to them. It seemed fairly clear that she was their culprit and when pressed, she had admitted being at the house, and looking through that particular window, to see if anyone was there.

It was highly unusual for the police to be able to establish a case and wrap it up in the same day but Colin Fairways had been fully committed to getting the matter resolved as quickly as possible for his friend, and as he pointed out, Carla wasn't exactly what they'd call an experienced or clever criminal. Believing herself to be effectively boxed in by the evidence the police hinted they already had against her, she'd made it easy for them. Spooked and scared after they'd called her bluff, she'd readily caved and confessed to both acts of criminal damage.

Adie almost felt sorry for the woman, barking mad as she seemed to be. Love sometimes made people do crazy things, she knew that all too well. Unrequited love could send them a bit round the bend. It was no excuse, and the poisoning of darling little Sid would be difficult to forgive, but Adie did understand it.

* * *

She collected Sid two days later. He threw himself at her, yelping with sheer joy when she picked him up, and David Thornley was clearly delighted too, that the little dog had made such a good recovery. Adie was grateful that it was possible for people to attend surgeries again, after hearing stories of dogs dying or being put to sleep while their owners couldn't even be present, during the lockdowns imposed in the recent pandemic. She couldn't imagine what that must have been like for them.

Carla was to appear in court two days later.

"I guess the best we can hope for is that she'll be punished appropriately and be horrified enough at her own actions to never want to even contemplate doing something so heinous again," Adie remarked.

Feen blinked at her. "Well, you're a much petter berson than me, for thinking that. Giving her the benefit of the doubt for changing, I mean. I just think she's as mad as a fabid rox and ten times as bloody dangerous."

Adie pulled a wry face. "Feen, I've seen people change. I know it's hard to believe, and sometimes it takes a mighty catalyst, but maybe this is Carla's. Only time will tell."

She resolved to try and put the whole sorry encounter to the back of her mind for now. Sid was fine, that much was clear, and she still had to process everything that had happened with Bryan. What a strange and surreal 48 hours it had been!

Chapter 16

Mark was facing a long day clearing the gorse and rampant blackberry from the bottom two fields closest to the road, and he wasn't looking forward to the prospect one bit. It was horrible stuff, gorse; as vicious as the day was long, and almost impossible to get rid of once it took hold.

It wasn't raining or foggy for a change, and Mark was determined not to waste a day of near-perfect conditions for the job. Weather waited for no man and neither did nature's various forms of persistent pestilence. Feen would be helping him today, which he was grateful for. She was pretty good with the tractor and the mulcher.

As he pulled on his heavy leather gloves and tossed another pair to his daughter, Mark knew he needed to set some time aside – and soon - to really explore how he felt about everything that had recently shaken his normally calm world upside down like flurries in a snow globe. Maddeningly, they didn't seem to be the kind that would simply settle of their own accord.

The pair quickly got underway with tackling the gorse, but even as the bushes grew steadily smaller and the pile for burning ever larger, all Mark really wanted to do was stop. Unusually for him, he really had to dig deep to keep going and get the job done.

When the work was finally completed, and the blazing bonfire of crackling, burning bracken and gorse they'd painstakingly cleared had died to little more than a small pile of smouldering embers, he finally gave in to his urge to go inside the house and sit quietly with his feet up, in his armchair. He couldn't continue to ignore his overriding need to get the events of the past few days into some kind of perspective.

He left Feen to put the tractor back in the barn and went inside to make a pot of tea. He knew she understood that he had things on his mind. He was grateful to her for being wise enough to keep her own thoughts to herself about his, and leaving him alone with them.

Normally, Mark was able to square things away fairly quickly, no matter what life threw at him, and just get on with whatever he had to do, so he was a bit surprised at this unsettling need to consciously sit and actively process recent developments. What was that all about? Why was he finding it so hard, to get past this poisoning thing, and to push Adie and Feen's panicked, tear-stained faces out of his mind? And why did he have to fight so hard to stop himself from physically hurting Carla Walton when he'd gone to see her?

The poisoning of Sid, and Carla's subsequent confession, had rocked the little community of Torley. Most of the townspeople had been horrified at what Carla had done, and after she was convicted and given 120 hours of community service, they'd rallied around the Ravens and Adie, with cards, calls and flowers. They were keen to make the point that the bad apple in their midst did not reflect how everyone else behaved or felt.

Mark had kept himself busy all week, determined to keep it all from crowding his mind and sending him round the twist, but things were not squaring themselves as neatly away as usual. Finally, a time of reckoning had arrived. As foreign as the concept was to him, he knew he needed to be an active rather than a passive part of the process of these particular bugbears being properly put to rest.

Part of that, he decided, was confronting Carla Walton about the nasty things she'd done to Adie, *not to mention almost killing that poor innocent little dog.*

He wasn't sure what someone had to have missing, in their make-up, to be capable of something that cruel. He knew that women were often vindictive towards other women, in all sorts of unfathomable ways, and for all sorts of unfathomable reasons. And the concept of jealousy, he did understand. But to use an innocent animal in such a heartless way was impossible to accept. Mark felt lucky that he'd had such an important and timely wake-up call about just how dangerous Carla Walton could be if she didn't get her own way. If he had gone on to develop feelings for her, and things didn't end up working out the way she planned, the situation could have become very sticky indeed for him and his family.

He really didn't want or need that kind of drama. Even without what Carla had done, he knew she didn't have many friends in the town. He knew there wasn't a scrap of love lost between her and Feen. He also know that his sister Sheila hadn't warmed to her either.

Feen meant everything to him, and the promise he'd made to her mother, on her deathbed, still held true. He would protect her from harm in every way he knew how, for as long as it took. Exposing her to the venom and spite of an unhinged woman like Carla was the worst thing he could ever do, and he decided that if anyone ever did come along to spark his interest, it had to fit for Feen too. However much he might one day want it, romance would never happen with *anyone* without his daughter's blessing.

Carla had been cringingly apologetic when he'd gone to see her at home, unannounced, and he hadn't pulled any punches with her.

"I'm not one fer usin' me fists willy-nilly, Carla, but I do 'ave to say that if you were a man, I'd knock yer fuckin' block off."

Carla had been too distraught and tearful to reply. Usually compelled to do whatever he could to comfort a weeping woman, Mark had remained stony and unmoved by her histrionics. He'd stood his ground. *If she thinks I'm some kind o' pushover, the crazy bitch can think again.* If they were crocodile tears, he wasn't having a bar of it.

"Stay away from me, an' stay away from my family an' friends. If yer come anywhere near any of us again, for any reason at all, I'm likely to forget yer a lady. Are we clear, Carla?"

Eventually she'd managed to nod. He hadn't said another word but had turned on his heel and walked away, slamming her front door behind him, to make his final point.

On the way home, he'd struggled to maintain the cold composure he'd shown in front of her. In truth, his emotions were red hot, and close to boiling over. Feeling unusually overwhelmed, almost like crying, he'd had to pull into a lay-by at the side of the road, to get himself under control. He couldn't figure out why he was so rattled. All he knew, in that moment - all he could have told anybody - was that if anything else happened to upset either Feen or Adie he wasn't sure he could keep his hands away from the neck of anyone who caused it.

That's when he knew there was something much bigger going on than a 'simple' role of worried father and friend. He just wasn't sure he understood exactly what it was.

* * *

The following morning, as Mark sat down at the kitchen table, he noted how cheerful Feen was. A small smile played around her lips, as was often the case, and as usual he dared not ask why. Sometimes the girl's thoughts were better left 'un-prodded', in his opinion, having suffered on more than one occasion from a desperate embarrassment over something she'd revealed about someone, that he'd rather not have known about and kicked himself for asking about.

His daughter was humming and smiling, as she set his coffee down in front of him. A plate of scrambled eggs and toast swiftly followed and as she sat down to her own identical breakfast, she looked up at him, grinning. Mark allowed his curiosity to win the toss, as he so often did. He was nothing, he supposed, if not predictable.

Ok, kid. Best tell me what's on yer mind, then.

She tried to look nonchalant but failed.

I know you as well as you know me, lass. I think you've forgotten that. Granted?

Feen inclined her head. Mark struggled not to laugh and was about to actually speak out loud, and say something cheeky, when she swiftly got in first; trying to sound casual, but clearly a lot more interested than she wanted him to think.

"Granted. Ok, Daddy, so, how was your date last night?"

Mark had taken Adie over to Carlisle to the Performing Arts Centre to see a touring production of the musical, Chicago. They'd had a bite to eat first in a very nice Italian restaurant he'd promised her she would love, and he hadn't been wrong. The food was authentic and lovely, and Adie had said she would have made it a regular haunt in a heartbeat, if she was going to be sticking around. The place was just around the corner from the theatre, so the evening was a leisurely affair with no need to rush anywhere.

"It weren't a bloody date! 'Ow many times do I 'ave t'say it? We're just friends, Feen. It were a dinner and a show wi' a friend. That's all. And it were nice, thanks. Good food, good show, good company. End of."

Feen was openly smirking again, and with a heavy inward sigh, Mark had to accept that he probably wasn't going to shut her down as easily as he wanted to; not about this.

"*What*, fer God's sake?"

"Ah, methinks the gentleman doth protest too much!"

Feen faced him with a wicked grin and shook her head. "No soughts are thacred, Daddy. You know that already. So, c'mon. Spill. You like her, don't you! And I don't just mean like her, I mean you really, *really* like her, don't you?"

Mark put his hands together and placed them under his nose, against his lips. He stared at what was left of his breakfast, unsure of how to answer. Feen waited, cocking her head and raising her eyebrows. She still wore the infuriating smirk. Eventually he cleared his throat.

"I do like her a lot, yes. But we're just friends, good ones, I might add, but that's all it is, Feen. Nowt to get excited about."

"Are you sure about that?" Feen prodded gently.

Mark nodded vigorously. "Yes, I'm sure, but even if I weren't, she's leavin', in't she, in a few more weeks? There's no future in it, Feen, even if I wanted one, which I don't, by the way."

Even to his own ears, Mark's voice sounded unconvincing, but he chose to ignore that. He hoped that now Feen would too, and let it go, but to his deep dismay, it didn't seem like that was going to happen.

"I don't believe you. I think you're in love, Dad, and I think you're just too chicken to admit it to yourself." He looked up at her in surprise. She wasn't smiling anymore.

He looked at her as squarely and seriously as he could. "Feen, I don't know what yer thinkin' lass, but trust me, there's nothin' 'appening between me and that good lady except friendship. I don't need owt else, and I don't *want* owt else, and neither does she." He put as much finality into his tone as he could muster, and his daughter finally took the hint, putting her hands up, as if to ward him off.

"Ok, ok, if you say so. But you don't fool me, even if you manage to fool yourself. And you dight moo that, but not for much longer, I don't think. I don't think she can fool herself for much longer either," she added, almost to herself. She looked up and caught Mark's eye. She smiled lightly at him and went back to her own breakfast. He finished his, took his cup, plate and cutlery, set it down in the sink with a bang, and left the kitchen without another word.

Out in the barn, he found himself literally unable to concentrate on the task he'd set himself, of mending an old generator. It was a simple enough job, but his mind just wouldn't focus on it. Feen's words were still ringing in his ears. *I think you're in love, Dad.*

How ridiculous! The very notion of it! Well, if that was what he was going to get, for simply taking a female friend to dinner and a show, he wouldn't bother again. It wasn't worth the grief, of everybody assuming there was more to it than what it was, and thinking it was ok to give him a hard time about it. *The barefaced bloody cheek o' that!*

Mark tried to summon up a decent level of righteous indignation at being falsely accused of something so silly, but it wouldn't come. And if he had to make a concentrated effort to be angry and still couldn't manage it, what did that say about his state of mind?

Observations like the one Feen had just made could be incredibly damaging, if heard by the wrong ears, but as crazy as he'd found the suggestion, he simply couldn't shake the feeling that while he most certainly absolutely, categorically was not in love with *anybody*, thank you very much, there was a certain sadness that niggled away at him whenever he thought of the time when Adie Bostock would be leaving Teapot Cottage to start a new life somewhere else.

He was going to miss her when she went. Over the weeks she'd been at the cottage, he'd got used to having her around. She was such easy company. She made him laugh, he made her laugh (a fact which always made something swell warmly inside him a little whenever it happened), and they enjoyed one another's company.

It was nice, having a female friend, after all these years with no womanly company. Carla Walton had tried in her own way to get his attention. A few other local women in the town had made half-hearted attempts to do the same, all the while knowing that Mark Raven was known throughout the land as a one-woman man, and just because that woman was gone, it didn't mean she was forgotten.

Beth Raven had left big shoes to fill, and he doubted if anyone could ever measure up to her. No; the thought of opening his heart to someone else was out of the question. Most people knew that, but Feen had plucked at the string that had tied his heart up, and it was now in danger of coming loose.

That wasn't what Mark wanted. And even if it had been, why would the likes of Adrienne Bostock, with her city lifestyle and everything new to look forward to in her life, look twice at a bloke like him? He was a rough-sawn man of the land, with dirt under his fingernails more often than not, and without a scrap of spit and polish, who lived about as far from London as most of the people who lived there would ever want to get. What could he offer to someone like her?

No, Adie's time here in Torley was temporary. It had only ever been that, and there were better things in store for her when the time came for her to move on. It wouldn't take her long to build a new life, and her time at Teapot Cottage would soon become a part of her past, a memory for her to look back on. He'd be lucky if she even remembered him, a year from now. The early remark about coming back for this year's Christmas party, well…

Mark suspected they both knew it wouldn't happen. He was a philosophical man, but he was genuinely surprised at how sad he felt about that, along with everything else that saying goodbye was going to mean.

Maybe there was a lot to be said for being on your own. If you didn't let yourself get too attached to people, they couldn't hurt you when they left.

Chapter 17

Surrounded by some of her own cherished things, and without the prospect of an early deadline looming, Adie found herself settling a little more into Teapot Cottage. After the date of her initially agreed departure sailed by, she found herself establshing a routine that typically consisted of an early morning walk around the Ravensdown boundary lines with Sid, a leisurely breakfast, completing errands in the town, having coffee with Peg at her shop, and then spending the afternoons reading, or baking cakes and scones and making marmalade or jam for the Saturday Farmers Market, which she decided to start doing on a regular basis. Feen didn't want to do the market regularly, so Adie found herself liaising directly with the warden at the church hall, to book her weekly stand.

The money she made from her offerings of eggs, jams and cake was never going to make her rich, but it was enough to cover her costs and pay for a few luxuries, like having her hair or nails done at Torley Tresses or selecting something nice from Trudie at GladRagz. As the weeks passed, she got to know Trudie quite well. The boutique owner regularly came to the market for her fresh produce, and had placed a regular order with Adie for a dozen fresh eggs each week. She'd also started attending the Thursday evening yoga class with Adie and Sheila.

To Adie's enormous surprise, she was thoroughly enjoying yoga. She was also enjoying the friendships she was developing with Sheila, Trudie and Peg. All four women were of similar age. They met for morning coffee at Peg's café once a week, usually on a Friday, and conversation was always lively and interesting. Discission usually turned at some point, even briefly, to the frustrations they were all experiencing, to varying degrees, of trying to manage their haphazard hormones. Peg, who had already gone through the change, was able to give some sage and rational advice, which the others appreciated. It was nice to be reassured that they weren't all going stark raving mad in various different ways.

"I wonder if that's why Bryan went off me," Adie mused, at one of their meetups. "You know, why he had an affair with a younger woman. Because, apart from all the biological and emotional ups and downs I've been having to grapple with, I've more or less had to accept that I'm completely uninteresting to anyone at all, really. I've felt invisible for years now, even to my husband and kids, like it hasn't mattered for such a long time whether I was even around or not." Adie looked at her friends, to see if what she was saying made any sense to them.

"Do you know what I mean, by that? That when you reach a certain point in your life, people just stop noticing you? I feel like I've become chronically insignificant, like nobody would be interested in anything I have to say, so there isn't much point in speaking." She was vastly relieved to find all three of them nodding.

"I mean, I'm not feeling sorry for myself, or anything silly like that. I do just wonder though, about how I managed to become so *irrelevant*, without even realising it had happened. Maybe Bryan just stopped finding me interesting. I mean, I'm still the same person I always was. I'm just older, but somehow, that seems to mean I've kind of morphed into a non-person. I must've lost my appeal by the time I was forty-five. That's when his affair started. The one I knew about, anyway."

Sheila nodded her head agreement. "Adie, I totally get what you say about feeling irrelevant. I feel that way too, so much these days. One day, when I went into Carlisle, I was feeling a bit invisible myself. I decided to actively try and catch someone's eye – anyone's at all - so I could give them a smile, and maybe even get one back. I just wanted to feel validated, I suppose, like I still existed, like I was still *real*. But I didn't exist for a single person on the street. Not one person even looked at me, let alone smiled back."

She went on to explain. "I've had quite a rough time too, with the change, and my mother was the same, so I think there was a bit of 'eredity in there, which didn't help. Feen's 'elping me a lot, but it's still difficult, especially on days when I can't understand why all I want to do is cry, or smack Bob around the back of the 'ead with a frying pan, just because the poor bugger swallows his food too loudly. I'm sure the poor sod hasn't a bloody clue what to do with me, 'alf the time. I often feel like I'm fading slowly but surely into the woodwork, so I know exactly what you mean. But Adie, you're a very 'andsome woman. You're anything *but* invisible, and if that was your ex-'usband's excuse for cheating on you, it's a bloody poor one."

Adie smiled gratefully at her new friend. "Well, you didn't see me when I first arrived in town! I had lifeless, greying, ramrod-straight hair so long I could almost sit on it, shapeless baggy pants and jumpers, and I never bothered with a scrap of make-up. It was almost like I'd given up on myself without realising it. I think the expression most used would be I'd "let myself go to rack and ruin," and as for poor old Bob, who *did* see me that first day I arrived here, weeping fit to burst, God knows what he must've thought."

Sheila grinned. "Oh, don't worry about Bob! He's long since accepted that most women of a certain age are soggy basket cases at least some of the time."

Peg was nodding thoughtfully. "Yeah, you know, I wonder if that whole 'fading into the woodwork' thing is a circular process, like some kind of self-fulfilling prophecy. You start getting older, you becomes less noticeable because society only seems to favour the young. People start ignoring you, so you give up trying to be seen and then, hey presto, you never are. I've given up on being noticed too, really, but I sometimes wonder how faded and shabby I really am these days. Do I still have any sense of style or am I just seriously deluded that I still look halfway decent?"

Adie burst out laughing. "Are you kidding? I'd kill for that fur coat and those crystal earrings you rocked at Christmas! I could never pull that off in a million years! There's nothing faded or shabby about you, Peg!"

Peg shook her head. "Before Andy died, he once told me that he was afraid of getting old. We were only in our late forties when he died in a car crash. I never understood what he meant about fearing getting old until I started the change, and confronting myself in the mirror, all spready and shapeless, all jowly and drab. D'you think Bryan had the affair because *he* was afraid of getting old?"

Adie nodded at her friend's question. "Yeah, I'm sure that was a big part of it. It's such a cliché, isn't it, falling for a much younger woman to shore up their waning masculinity? I guess men really do fear getting older too. But they just seem to handle it differently, don't they? Without the interference of hormones that randomly behave like ricocheting bullets, of course"

She lowered her voice a little. "I lost interest in sex, and I now know that's a menopause symptom too, but at the time I never thought much about it, or how it would affect him. I guess that wouldn't have helped."

Did Bryan start to feel old and invisible? Did I contribute to that? I wish he'd talked to me. He was always attractive to me, even at the end. Did I fail somehow, to let him know that? Would it have made a difference, if I had? Or would our secrets have ended us, anyway?

Trudie piped up, then. "I've been quite lucky with my menopause, so far at least. My mum had a terrible time with hers, but I wonder if her attitude sabotaged her a bit. She saw the change of life as the end of everything. She often said that because she was no longer fertile she only felt like half a woman, and I thought that was really sad. So I made the conscious choice to embrace the change, when it started, and not see it as the end of something, but as the start of the next phase of my life, which I decided could be a lot more interesting, and would certainly be a lot less stressful, since I've struggled with my periods for decades. And I never managed to get pregnant, despite all attempts," she confided.

"Adenomyosis, sadly. Couldn't be sorted, we had to give up trying, didn't fancy IVF, and we never felt quite ready to adopt. Then I woke up one morning and realised that my time for wanting any of it had passed." She shrugged, and compressed her lips into a thin line.

"To be honest, it's a relief to be reaching the end of all that drama," she confessed. "Kevin's been brilliant. I couldn't have wished for more support. And I do think making the decision to see menopause as a positive transition has helped me. My symptoms have been fairly light, so far, touchwood!" She knocked her knuckles on the table.

Adie agreed. "Yeah, I think mindset definitely has a lot to do with it. How you feel about yourself to begin with too, maybe. I do feel better since I had my hair done, and you got hold of me and started to restyle me, Trudie! I'm not such a tragic fashion wreck anymore, and the yoga is toning me up. I've probably dropped a few pounds and I feel loads better. And you always look amazing, by the way!"

Trudie laughed. "Well it's a conscious effort every day, make no mistake, but I wouldn't be much of an advert for my own fashion store if I let myself morph into a bag-lady! I agree with you though. That notion, that we stop being relevant, in the eyes of the younger generations, it's pretty hard to swallow, and for men too, I suppose. We just handle it differently. Women internalise and blame themselves for everything, while men's reactions to ageing are to go out and reinforce their masculinity by pegging someone half their age. Whichever way we rebel against it, the reason is the same. We all just hate getting old."

* * *

Slowly but surely, Adie was establishing a place in the Torley community. Once she had read all the books she'd brought with her, she joined the town's tiny library, and initiated a successful book drive to get people to donate any recently published books they had that were in good condition. To her great fascination and pleasure, she found that the people of Torley were quite diverse in their interests, if their donated books were anything to judge by. Some of them were quite an eye-opener, and part of her wished she could have worked out who'd donated the well-thumbed book on sex addiction, the in-depth psychological profile of Vladimir Putin, and the rather alarmingly-titled 'Fascism for Beginners'!

The townsfolk were very generous in letting the library have their books. Adie had spent an entire day driving round, picking up donations, and each time she did, she was offered a cuppa and a biscuit. At the end of that day she'd sank into the hot tub, awash with tea and full of cake and exhaustion, but with a very deep sense of satisfaction.

On her collection rounds, a couple of residents had also expressed their heartfelt wish that a few more book clubs would start up in Torley. Adie had come to realise that as friendly as the townsfolk were in general, there were a number of people who lived alone and who didn't appear to have as much social interaction as they really wanted. They felt isolated, and clearly craved more company. They wanted to keep feeling connected to their community, but they needed some help to make it happen.

Adie thought the book clubs idea was a jolly good one, and there was also scope for increasing the profile of the local film club, she realised, since the library boasted an interesting assortment of DVD's and many more had come in as the result of the book drive.

That might be of more help to some who perhaps didn't enjoy reading, or whose eyesight made it more of a challenge than a joy. She resolved to talk to Peg and Trudie about it, thinking they might offer some useful perspective. Peg told her that someone in the town had started a movie club a while back, but it had become a very private affair, involving a few people who wanted to keep it exclusive. "They were probably academic types", she'd said darkly, as if that was something to be ashamed of, and Adie had laughed at Peg's reverse snobbery.

So, a notice had gone up in the newsagent's window that anyone interested in joining a light-hearted book club could call Adie's number. Within a couple of days, she had nineteen contenders, including a long-retired schoolteacher who had an impressive multi-volume collection of classics and plays that he'd paid for with his own money at a time when the school had no spare funds to provide extra books for the pupils.

It might be fun to read the classics again, she thought to herself, and when she floated the idea past the other hopefuls, they all agreed that it wasn't such a bad place to start. The prospect of plays was also intriguing and gave rise to a discussion about eventually starting an amateur dramatics club in the town.

Another happy development for Adie was her growing friendship with Mark. She was always delighted to see him, which had started to become a more regular occurrence when the weather was kind enough and she spent more time out in the fresh air with Sid, on the various trails around the farm. Mark was very often out with the sheep or scooting around on his quad bike.

He always made time to come over to her and stop and chat for a few moments. She'd got into the habit of looking for him whenever she was outside, and she usually found him, which made her wonder if he was keeping an eye out for her as well, as he went about the busy business of farming. Most days, they managed to find one another in short time, and have a quick chat. Whenever that happened to be around a lunch time, one would invite the other in for a cuppa and a bite to eat. Feen was usually about, if Mark invited Adie into Ravensdown, and was always happy to throw a sandwich and some soup together for them all.

January gave way to February, and the weather stayed cold. Some days were spectacularly crunchy, crisp and sunny, with hoar frost on the hedgerows, but much of the time the valley was shrouded in freezing, pea-soup fog - the kind that perpetuated and accumulated in layers. Adie often found the weather a lot clearer up on the Tor on those murkier, soggier days, but of course there was no view to be seen through the mist that hung like a shroud below the summit.

As the weeks passed, she knew she had to start thinking about where she might move to, since her time at Teapot Cottage was flying by. The problem was that she wasn't sure where she should be looking. None of the familiar places she'd known all her life felt like a good place to set up home.

Guildford no longer appealed, nor did the prospect of running into any of her former 'friends' down there, some of whom – she now knew – had known about Bryan's affair all along, even as they sat at her dining table eating her food, drinking her wine, and pretending they gave a damn about her. The only way she'd want to see any of *them* again was to have the chance to tell them exactly what she thought of their two-faced, phony lives. It must be exhausting, to keep pretending to like someone while all the time laughing or pitying them behind their back. She wouldn't be 'busting her arse', as Mark had so eloquently put it, to spend time with any of them again.

Already, she knew it would be a wrench to leave Torley, and it was something she did have to prepare for but she resolved to enjoy and savour every moment in her temporary home.

She was finding it easier now, to reflect on her marriage to Bryan. Clearly there had been a lot more to his relationship with his mistress than a simple illicit fling. Six years was more than just a flash in the pan. It involved a conscious commitment to cheating, and telling a lot of lies to cover it, and that hurt immeasurably. Maybe what Peg had suggested; that he too had been driven by a need to be validated, was at the heart of it all. It didn't excuse his years of lies to his entire family, but was Adie really in the best place to judge?

She decided that maybe she was, because what she'd done herself, in concealing a long-term secret, was geared more towards *protecting* the family, not gambling with it. She knew that didn't excuse her, but she hadn't risked their relationship in the same way Bryan had. For six years at least, every single time he'd climbed into bed with his mistress, he'd put their marriage directly on the line. But had she been more instrumental than she'd first thought, in driving him into the arms of a younger woman? Had they each taken the other for granted to the point of being oblivious to what they stood to lose?

When she'd first found out about Bryan's affair, she'd been devastated, angry, and hurt, but she realised now that she was none of those things anymore.

Adie also knew that Bryan really was aware of how much pain he'd caused. A letter had come from him, in the previous week, redirected through the post office with other mail. In that letter, he'd said that he lived with his guilt every day. "Please don't think I'm so insensitive as to not appreciate how much of this is my fault," he'd written. "I'm so sorry Adie, for everything I did, everything I said. I've been a selfish bastard."

Adie wrote back to him, thanking him for his words, and acknowledging that she'd been selfish too, in not trusting him with her secret. He'd texted her after that, for the first time in many weeks, asking if they could talk over the phone. She made the monumental decision to say 'yes' and speak with him again. She knew it was time to have the conversation. She also knew it wouldn't be an easy one, and it wasn't.

"You know, Adie, in spite of everything I did, I've always loved you, and I always will. If you ever want to come back to me, you only need to say the words. I'd be waiting with open arms, if you thought we could give it another shot."

"No," she said, sadly. "You can't love two people, Bryan. At least, if you do, you can't be really true to either of them, can you? We were on a hiding to nothing, well before my secrets came tumbling out, because half of your heart was already elsewhere. I just didn't know that, at the time."

"Would it have changed anything, if you'd known it?"

Adie considered Bryan's question. She spoke carefully. "Yes, absolutely. I'd have asked you to leave, if I'd known about your affair before everything else came to light. That way, when it did, I wouldn't have had to deal with your condemnation. That's been the worst of it all, really, the fact that you blamed me for our marriage going south, when you were taking a much bigger gamble with it yourself, for a long time before that. You still chose to try and hang everything on me."

"Are you sure you're not still angry? I wouldn't blame you one bit, if you were."

"No, I'm not angry. I'm just disappointed now, if I'm honest. And I'm no less so for you saying what you just did, that you still want me to come back." She felt infinitely sad now.

"You're with someone else now, Bryan, and the fact that you'd clearly dump her if I came back to you, or maybe still hope to keep her on the side, well, all it does is remind me what kind of man you really are. You don't care about anyone's feelings but your own." Adie shook her head as the all-too familiar tears welled up again.

"You've always been selfish, and you always will be. I've always known it, and I was prepared to put up with it, but not anymore. Not knowing what I know now, about how far that selfishness went. I was a pretty decent wife and mother. Despite my own secrets and shortcomings, I still deserved better than to have a cheat for a husband."

"We have no future together now. Too much has happened for both of us, and you need to move on properly from me, from us, because I'm at a point now where I just want the best for both of us, even though it's clear that it won't be as husband and wife. Or as anything, really," she added, almost to herself. *Because you're still every bit the self-serving pig you've always been.*

Bryan was quiet for few beats, on the phone, before he spoke again.

"You know, I think disappointment is actually worse. I could live with anger. But the fact that I disappointed you so badly, that's a harder thing for any man to live with. Anger flares and

191

burns out, in well-adjusted people at least. But disappointment, that's a lot more permanent, isn't it? An indicator of more lasting damage."

Adie shrugged. "Well, you set yourself up for it, and it's yours to own, and deal with as best you can."

They then talked a little about Matty and Teresa. Bryan was heartbroken that they hadn't tried to mend fences with him. He confessed to how much it had rankled, that they'd managed to forgive their mother, but couldn't seem to extend the same generosity to him. Adie had been the one to tell them about their father's double life, and they'd been predictably outraged and hurt, trying to get their heads around the fact that both of their parents had been outright, selfish liars for years.

"Give them time, Bryan. They're having a hard time, processing everything, and they're struggling to understand why you had a long-standing affair in the first place, because it means you lied consistently to all of us, not just me. The hypocrisy of it, after everything you've taught them about morals and respect, and after how you treated me, that's a big part of what they're grappling with. And don't forget, Matty is still feeling a lot of guilt and shame of his own that he still has to work through, about all that wretched escort stuff, and the death of that poor client."

Bryan sighed. "I know Adie, and if I could turn back the clock, I would. I'd love to go back to that time when we were a simple, happy, ordinary family. Everything seemed so comfortable and uncomplicated back then, didn't it?"

Adie felt a quick stab of anger. "It was comfortable and uncomplicated for *you*. I brought the kids up, more or less single-handedly. You were hardly ever around, always on site somewhere working. Or, as it transpires, busy in someone else's bed. I worked my arse off too, you know, to make sure that everything *would* be uncomplicated and comfortable for you when you did choose to come home. You never even noticed, let alone gave me any thanks for it. But as we know, for the last half decade and more, your commitment was only at half-mast."

Bryan conceded. "I know I took you for granted. I know I've ruined everything. Look, I didn't phone for a row, Adie, or to stir up the anguish again. I just wanted to reassure you that everything we agreed is being processed as promised, and to say goodbye, if that's what you really want, and wish you all the best."

Adie fought to swallow down the lump in her throat. Ending a relationship, even one you knew you no longer wanted to be in, was always a painful process. But Bryan had moved on, or at least he was trying to (at the same time as making sure he left the door open for her to walk back through if she felt so inclined), and she'd started a similar process.

"Well, Bryan, I have to go. Thanks for calling."

" Good luck, Adie, and I do mean that. I'm sorry I insulted your friend, that Northern bloke. And if he means more to you than just a friend, well I wish you luck with that too."

Adie had already promised herself that she wouldn't be drawn into any kind of discussion involving Mark. She'd been hoping it wouldn't come up at all, but now that it had, she simply chose to let it slide. It was no longer any of Bryan's business what she did, or with whom, and that point could make itself.

"Bye then. Try not to worry about the kids. Leave them for a bit, then try again. You're their dad. They'll come around, in time. Kiss Creole for me. I miss him, Bryan. I'd like to spend some time with him after I've finished up here, if that's ok?"

"Of course it is, Adie! He's your dog too. You can have him whenever you want, for as *long* as you want."

As calls went, it was better than expected. Civilized, with no mudslinging. What would have been the point of that anyway? Everything that had needed to be said had been, now, and there was nothing to be gained by raking over cold coals. She knew it, and so did Bryan.

Adie swallowed down her distaste at the fact that he would be callous enough to just cast aside his mistress of seven years or so (or girlfriend as she now apparently was), or keep her somewhere in the shadows as before, if Adie wanted to give their relationship another chance. He was a piece of work, but in saying what he had, he'd actually done her a big favour. It was clearer now than it had ever been that her decision to file for divorce, as painful as that had been, was absolutely the right one.

As the weeks went by, she continued to marvel at how effectively coming to stay at Teapot Cottage had moved her forward. Without even trying, she'd managed to get to a place of self-reliance and independence. After twenty-six years, she was finally free to make her own choices, and she was delighted to feel that she was being gently guided towards a new, more appealing way of life, where things were simpler, and people were more connected; where friendships and relationships mattered more than anything else.

Deep in her heart, Adie knew she could never again be involved with a man who was never at home, whose work took precedence over marriage and family, whose arrival at home was usually more disruptive than helpful to the routines she'd been forced to adopt in his absence.

Bryan had been an adequate husband. He'd also been a good enough father, when he was present, but for the most part Adie had done the job of parenting and raising their children alone. She could no longer imagine herself sitting at home, waiting for a man to make real time for her. She wasn't going to settle for that anymore.

Torley, for the brief time she'd been here, had shown her what was important. Adie knew that wherever she ended up after her time here, this straightforward, uncomplicated existence was exactly what she longed for. After a long year of almost unbearable loneliness and the deepest grief and sorrow imaginable, it felt good to be surfacing again, with renewed hope, and clarity at last, about the kind of future she wanted.

There really was something very special about Teapot Cottage. Adie felt *whole* here, in a way she'd never felt anywhere else.

She wondered, for the millionth time, if the restlessness she'd always felt in the past was to do with having given up her first baby. She'd found Ruth, yes, but she still felt that a huge part of herself was missing, because of the fear she had felt, of being harshly judged by everyone she loved. Only now was she able to understand and appreciate how lonely and isolated she had been, and for how long.

But look at me now! Just a year after my whole world imploded, I'm making a fresh start, all by myself.

Doing the Farmer's Market on Saturdays, selling eggs and marmalade had enabled Adie to get to know a lot more of the townsfolk. She'd lost a stone in weight with all the dancing and yoga she'd been doing, and she'd gone ahead and started a fortnightly book club. She seemed to be managing her menopause much better, *and I've learnt how to master an Aga!*

It wasn't as if she'd actively tried to change how she was feeling about her life. Being open to things and taking each day as it came definitely helped, but she knew that somehow, in a way she couldn't fully understand or explain, it had a lot to do with this lovely little house. There was a time when she would never have believed in auras, or energies, or anything 'woo-woo' like that. Teapot Cottage definitely had something special that couldn't be easily explained, even though Feen had tried, way back at the Christmas party, by saying that the cottage was on some kind of vibrating energy line.

Early one morning, about a week later, Adie got a surprise phone call from Ruth's wife, Gina. Adie had sent her and Ruth the jewellery gifts she'd bought from Feen, and Gina was over the moon about them.

"These are amazing pieces of jewellery, *A'dienne!* So interesting and unusual. I would very much like to meet the woman who makes these! Could you possibly put me in touch with her? I would love to talk to her about maybe making more."

So Adie had prompted Feen to get in touch with Gina, and it looked as if Gina was going to commission some pieces to complement her next winter clothing collection. It was far too late for anything to be included in the spring and summer collections, and probably too late for autumn as well now, but Gina was confident that a few bespoke pieces could be showcased late in the year. If the interest was high enough, it could lead to a lot of work for Feen, and she could potentially have her own cameo page on the GinGio website.

Gina had also offered to take Feen with her to Milan Fashion Week in September, if she wanted to go. Feen was beside herself. Adie couldn't recall ever having seen anyone so tied up in knots with excitement, nerves and disbelief, but she was thrilled for Feen, and delighted that Gina recognised her talent and was willing to give her a shot. Most women could only fantasise about being able to afford an item from Gina Giordano's highly exclusive brand, and for Feen, the chance to be involved with it was the opportunity of a lifetime.

Mark had made a point of telling Adie how grateful he was too, for the introduction Adie had made. He was thrilled that his daughter's talent had been recognised by someone so important and influential in the fashion world. Adie had waved away his thanks, saying that since talent always spoke for itself, Feen's chance was fully deserved.

Mark had a heart of gold, and not for the first time, Adie thanked her lucky stars to have found such a lovely friend. She would miss him a lot, when her time at Teapot Cottage eventually came to an end. Maybe there was some merit in seeing if a nice property might become available somewhere between the Lake District and where she used to live. It would be nice to have achievable access to both places. Her dog, Creole, was important to her, but several people were becoming ever more important to her too, as the weeks flew by. She was no longer too shy to admit that Mark Raven was definitely one of them.

Chapter 18

It was raining again. *Just for a soddin' change.*

Mark felt grumpy and frustrated at the rain clouds that didn't seem to know where else to drift off to, but hung like a saturated blanket over the entire Torley valley.

The meteorological start of spring was fast approaching, but the state of the weather had almost everyone in a bad mood. February had been terrible, with fog everywhere and endless drizzle continually soaking the ground. While there were signs of new life everywhere, and lambing was already starting early on a few local farms, everyone was longing for the sunshine that persistently stayed away.

Mark had fixed one of the leaks in the barn roof, but there was still a lot of work to be done on it. For over a decade now, he'd kept his fingers crossed, hoping to get away with not having to replace the whole thing. It had been patched up so many times over the years, it now resembled a crazy quilt. The second-hand corrugated iron he'd had to use in the beginning hadn't been in great condition to start with, but it had held up. He hadn't realised how bad it had got until the previous winter when he'd gone up there to look at where the water was coming through, and found more holes than the average kitchen colander.

The money to replace it wasn't an issue. It was the prospect of all the disruption that caused him to keep putting off the decision; having to get so much stuff out of there for the time it would take for the job to be done properly, because he suspected that it wasn't just the roof that needed replacing. He was fairly sure some of the old wooden beams would need to be replaced as well, and at least part of the back stone wall where the elements had eroded some of the pointing.

It all amounted to a major structural repair, and he was dreading it. Getting contractors quickly wouldn't be an easy thing either, since most were still booked up solid for months, after putting back so much of the work on their books when the pandemic stopped them from doing it. They were still catching up on their backlogs, as well as taking new bookings that pushed availability out for many months.

He supposed he'd have to hire a couple of lockable containers too, to put everything of real value into; the tools and machinery and the like, since there was nowhere else for it to go, and leaving anything sitting out was asking for trouble. It was a sad fact that hawk-eyed thieves routinely roamed the area, and many a farm had suffered when machinery, tools and other things accidentally left out overnight had mysteriously disappeared by morning.

Some bastards'd pinch the eye out of a bloody needle!

But the bald fact was that the roof wouldn't last another winter. Before the coming autumn, which was only six months away, it would all have to be replaced. The barn was a listed building, so whatever went wrong with the old hulk would always just have to be fixed, no matter what the cost, and the disruption simply went with the territory.

There's no use bendin' me arse about summat I can't change.

Mark made a mental note to contact a couple of contracting firms in the week, to get a few quotes. He wasn't as nimble as he used to be, and while the prospect of getting up on the barn roof hadn't daunted him even just five years ago, it wasn't something he felt keen to do anymore.

He sighed heavily, as the increasingly familiar feeling of distraction descended upon him again. As much as he hated to admit it, he felt like he'd been pitched into the middle of a mid-life crisis, with his thoughts all over the place about his life and his health and his future. He didn't really have much appetite for confronting his own reality, but there was no avoiding another bald and distressing fact – that his ageing body was starting to let him down significantly now, in ways he'd once never imagined it could.

Somewhere along the way, he'd developed a "clicky" knee, and he'd had two frozen shoulders at different times, which had hurt like hell and rendered him only halfway capable of working. A bad case of plantar fasciitis in his left foot hadn't helped in keeping active, and the constant prevailing damp was playing havoc with his aches and pains. Working outside in all weathers most of the time was starting to take its toll. One of his shoulders had become arthritic, and he no longer had full mobility in that arm. It wasn't enough to slow him down much, at least not yet, and he'd shrugged it all off for a long time. But the day was definitely coming, and probably sooner rather than later, when he'd have to get help on the farm.

Was there anything attractive at all, about a fifty-four-year-old man lurching ever-closer towards decrepitude? Probably not to a young woman, as Beth had been when he'd first met her. But maybe a woman in her forties or fifties might still find him interesting.

Casting aside the shadow of the God-awful Carla, Mark wondered if someone like Adie Bostock, for instance, would ever really give him more than a passing glance? Not that he was looking, he hastened to reassure himself, for the thousandth time. But what if someone did come along? Would anyone, anywhere, think he might still be worth having a kiss and a cuddle with, or maybe something more? Or was he now already relegated to the scrap heap, as he stumbled ever closer to old age and potential infirmity?

A quick wave of anger passed over him, and quickly dissipated into an all-too familiar sadness. He and Beth were supposed to have had the privilege of growing old *together*. She wasn't supposed to bail early, claimed by the cruellest of diseases. That wasn't the way the script was meant to run. He wasn't supposed to be left behind, with so much life left in front of him to face all alone. But how did you move on from the total devastation of losing your soul mate? How did you ever really come to terms with every last one of your dreams being dashed? What did you do when the 'forever' you'd banked on blew up in your face instead?

Well-meaning friends had told Mark, time and time again, that he'd find love again if he was open to it. But what did they know? To a man, every last one who'd said it still had their wives to go home to at night. They couldn't speak from a place of experience. They spoke from a place of hope, and a place of compassion, from a place of genuinely wanting him to feel better and more hopeful, and he understood that.

But they knew nothing of how he'd felt, back then or even how he felt now, getting into a cold bed every night, feeling the years rolling by, as bald and barren of love as anything could ever be? Was this it? Was this as good as his life was ever going to be? Unable to contemplate even the thought of meeting someone else, he'd imagined that it was, and he'd already gone a long way towards accepting it.

So where was all this longing coming from now, and what was it for, exactly? Something had stirred awake again in Mark; something he hadn't felt for a very long time. He couldn't even put a name to it. It wasn't anything he could even remember consciously feeling before, like love, or even attraction. It was just a simple awakening; an acknowledgement that his life wasn't what it should be, but in a different way from how he'd felt after Beth died.

His life back then, as a grieving widower, certainly *wasn't* what it should have been, but that had felt different. He hadn't wanted anything, except the one thing he couldn't have.

Mark knew he wasn't the most emotionally intelligent or self-aware bloke on the planet, and that had never seemed to matter much before. Now, suddenly it did. He needed, wanted *something*, but he couldn't articulate what it might be, and lately he'd been worried that he couldn't understand how he was feeling and would never be able to settle until he did. It was a spectacular understatement, to say that this sudden need to understand himself and figure out what needed to be different was completely at odds with how he normally felt about his life.

He felt restless now, and suddenly well beyond bored with his own reality.

Maybe it's an 'obby I need, other than't farm. Or maybe I need an 'olidy, change o' scene.

But curiously, neither of those prospects sparked a shred of enthusiasm. Clearly, those weren't the solutions. Whatever was waking itself up inside him, it wasn't the desire for anything as simple as a hobby or a holiday.

Wondering at his own attractiveness led him to consider if it might be time to seek some female companionship. He wasn't in the market for romance, and he couldn't imagine a time when he ever would be, but he did know one thing for sure. When Adie Bostock left her house-sit at Teapot Cottage and went off to pick up the pieces of her life somewhere else, he already knew that he would miss her more than he once thought possible.

200

He tried to imagine her already gone, and it was a horrible feeling. Maybe that was it. Maybe his psyche was trying to tell him that once Adie had gone, he would need to find a companion - someone to spend time with, so he wasn't so alone. Feen would one day get involved with someone, presumably, and her focus would switch from him to a partner (and hopefully children), and that would be right and proper, but where would it leave him?

A few short months ago, if he'd even thought to ask himself that, he'd probably have shrugged it off as unimportant. It didn't feel important then. But, in a funny way he so recently could never have anticipated, it was starting to feel important now.

The problem was, even if romance did come calling, could he face the prospect of giving his heart to another woman? For a long time now, he'd been telling himself that going through what he did with Beth, watching the cancer relentlessly rob her of her life, and rob him all-too slowly of the future he'd once believed in, he couldn't go through that again with anyone else. It had torn him apart. And sure, there were no guarantees for anyone, that something like that wouldn't happen, but to put yourself in the firing line for a second time? No. As unenlightened as he was about himself, Mark certainly felt that he could never face something like that again and survive it.

Maybe it's better to be a'feared than grievin'.

It hadn't occurred to him that it might be one and the same thing.

He looked up and smiled as Feen came into the barn, asking him what he might like for lunch. "Nah, lass. I'm 'avin lunch wi' Adie."

"Daddy, I love how you're spending so much time with Adie. She's so nice."

"Aye, that she is." Mark didn't know what else to say about it, and the notion that Feen was fishing a bit – yet again - didn't help his comfort levels.

"D'you think you'll stay in touch with her, you know, after she leaves?"

She was definitely fishing! He shrugged his shoulders, trying to keep off what suddenly felt like a dangerous hook, and appear nonchalant. "I dunno, kid. Mebbe, if she wants to. She might have other plans by then."

"That would be in just a month or so from now, wouldn't it, Daddy? The time is certainly flying. She'll be gone before we know it. I'll miss her, if she goes." Feen turned on her heel and walked off, calling in a sing-song voice over her shoulder, "Dinner will be lamb chops, at the usual time."

If she goes? If? What's Feen gettin' at? Why wouldn't Adie leave, when Senn and Glue get back? As much as Mark wanted to write his daughter's comment off as a simple slip of the tongue, he knew that it probably meant she knew something he didn't, as per bloody usual. *Maybe Adie'll buy a new 'ouse somewhere in the area.*

The thought of that made him feel quite warm, but he didn't allow himself to dwell on it. There was work to be done in here, and he needed to get on with it. Pushing his confused thoughts to the back of his mind, he turned his attention to the job at hand.

Chapter 19

After a full hour, Mark still hadn't turned up for lunch, nor had he texted Adie to say he'd be late. That was most unlike him. He was normally as good as his word, and a scrupulous timekeeper. He was definitely not the sort of man who'd stand somebody up without a word.

As the clock on the kitchen wall ticked inexorably onward, to a full hour past the time they'd agreed to have lunch, Adie decided that he must have simply forgotten. That wasn't like him either, but sometimes things just came up. No doubt she'd hear about it later.

Surprised at how infuriated she was, she drained her teacup and decided to forego her own lunch. *Well, bugger sitting around here waiting for him to turn up,* she fumed. *I think I'll have a drive into the town.*

Trudie had texted her that morning to let her know a much-anticipated new spring shipment of dresses and tops had finally arrived at GladRagz, and she could have first dibs if she got there quickly. There was also a newly set-up rail of sale items. It was mostly just what was left of the autumn and winter stock, now that the season was passing, but Adie thought everything would probably be worth a look. Whatever the weather, she was always a sucker for a woolly jumper.

She sent a quick text to Trudie, to say she was on her way, and grabbed her jacket from the back of one of the chairs in the kitchen. Maybe a bit of retail therapy would take her mind off the crushing disappointment of Mark not showing up for lunch. She'd decided against texting him to ask him where he was. As she knew well enough already, nothing annoyed a man more than feeling like a woman was trying to keep tabs on him, and if he had genuinely forgotten, he'd feel bad. She didn't want that either, in spite of being so annoyed about it herself.

What a minefield relationships could be, even when it was something as simple as a friendship!

The town was quiet, with very few people milling about. The weather wasn't helping, with the gathering dark clouds promising yet more heavy rain. A thunderstorm was forecast, and Adie would have cheerfully stayed at home if her disappointment over lunch hadn't driven her out of the house in a restless fit of annoyance.

Trudie gave her a warm welcome when she stepped into GladRagz. It really was a lovely store. Although quite small by city standards, it was bright, airy and well laid out, and jam-packed with clothes, shoes and accessories to die for.

The sublime smell of fresh coffee made Adie grin and she was delighted to find that she was the only person in the shop. She had everything - including Trudie - all to herself!

Three of the new tops had already been sold to one customer, but everything else from the new order was still there, freshly ironed and hung on pretty padded satin hangers, just waiting to be drooled over. Some of the dresses looked gorgeous, all bright spring and summer colours. Adie was delighted, being much more of a 'dresses' woman now than anything else. At least dresses stayed where they were meant to. Skirts had been her thing, for many years, until the loss of her waistline meant that most of them simply drifted north and ended up sitting straight under her bust like some sad A-line outfit gone horribly wrong.

Trudie unplugged her iron and started making them both a cup of coffee in the little alcove at the rear of the boutique. Adie indulged in trying on a couple of stunning spring frocks. One was a 1950's fit and flare style, in pale lemon cotton with a demure white cream bow at the scooped neckline and cream Rennie McIntosh-style roses printed all over it. The dress was knee-length, complete with capped sleeves and a net underskirt to give it fullness. It really suited Adie, and she decided that while she'd never worn yellow in her life, now was as good a time as any to start. The dress flattered what was left of her waist and accentuated her shapely lower legs. And this was definitely a fun, summery, happy dress. Feen would certainly approve of this one, being stuck in some kind of enchanting time-warp herself, with her fashion sense.

The other dress Adie fell in love with was a simple, sleeveless A-line in lavender silk with cream piping under the bust line.

Exquisitely tailored, it accentuated Adie's figure, which thanks to a couple of months of trekking over fields and eating a more healthy and organic diet had become more toned and firm. Her post-fertility torso was still thicker than she would have liked, and probably always would be now, but the ugly little muffin-top that had materialized above the waistband of her faded, baggy-bum jeans in the aftermath of her split with Bryan, when she was comfort-eating and wallowing in despair, was now well and truly gone.

"Coffee!" Trudie called from the counter. Adie stepped out of the fitting room in the lavender dress, and Trudie's eyes widened.

"Wow! Look at you! All that hill walking and yoga has really toned you up!"

At Trudie's insistence, Adie put the yellow dress back on, and again her friend's praise was fulsome. "Adie, you look amazing. You're in really good shape."

Adie laughed. "Don't sound so surprised." She was thrilled at how well the dresses fit her, with silhouettes which implied that she might still have the hint of a curve or two after all!

The tops that had just come in were all a bit too flowery and lacy for her taste, but she did spy a beautiful caramel-coloured cashmere boat-neck sweater on the sale rack that she didn't even bother to try on. She just knew she wanted it. It was probably a size too big for her now, but she didn't care. Having salivated over it a month or two earlier, and deciding she couldn't afford it at full price, she wasn't about to leave it behind now that it had a half-price label on it!

As Adie put her purchases on the counter, Trudie held up an index finger. She scurried to the rear of the shop, where the shoes were, and came back with a gorgeous pair of cream-coloured low-heeled retro-style sling-backs in buttery-soft leather. She placed them alongside both dresses, then showed them to Adie with her eyebrows raised and Adie simply nodded. They were perfect for both frocks, and they'd also go with a lot of other stuff Adie already had. Trudie looked at her sideways.

"I know I might be pushing my luck, but I do have a very nice handbag that would pull all that together. Do you need a new bag?"

Adie considered for a moment. Then she nodded. "Actually yes. I could do with a new one, just a small one to take essentials when I go out. It would have to be cheap though," she added, conscious that her bank account was now at real risk of bleeding to death.

"No problem. I've got one here from last summer. It didn't go in the last sale, for some reason but I've hung onto it. I usually send the rejected stuff to the charity shop, but I've kept this bag because it's just really sweet, and retro, and I think it's lovely. If you want it, you can have it as a gift from me."

She pulled out a small cream shoulder bag from a box in the alcove. It wasn't a perfect match with the new shoes, but it was close enough. "You'll be holding it far enough away from the shoes for it to look like a match," Trudie declared. Adie insisted on paying her friend what she'd paid for it herself wholesale, which Trudie admitted was ten pounds.

"You're such a good friend Trudie. Thank you so much for this opportunity, and for spoiling me with the extra discount. I know you only get one or two of each thing, so I'm grateful for the head's up. I really needed this today!"

Trudie gave her a quick hug. "You're very welcome, my darling. There's nothing like a bit of retail therapy to chase away the mind-winter blues, and you'll be the only gal in town with that yellow Rennie. I only ordered the one, and it's funny because I had you in mind when I put it on the list. I'm just glad it fits! That particular label does run small on sizing, but I figured you'd have lost a bit of weight since you've been here anyway, you've been that busy, with the dancing and the yoga, and chasing Sid across the fields."

Almost as an afterthought, she added, "Actually, I thought you might have gone for the navy dress with the musical notes on it. I got that one in with you in mind too."

Adie shook her head. "No, I don't think I even saw that."

Trudie shrugged. "Ah well, no obligation of course, because it will fly off the rail anyway, as soon as the sun comes along for more than a couple of hours, but here it is."

She pulled a few frocks across the rack, found what she was looking for, and held up a lovely navy dress, again in the 1950's style, with a full skirt, no sleeves, a scooped neckline, and an off-white print of little musical notes on a bar, dancing their way around the hemline and up across one shoulder. Adie took one look at it, and decided she absolutely had to have that too. It was the same size and label as the yellow Rennie, so she knew it would fit just as nicely. She whipped out her credit card, making up her mind to ignore it if it somehow physically screamed as she paid for her purchases. Trudie knocked a further ten percent off the final total, and Adie beamed. She picked up her mug of coffee and sipped it gratefully.

"My bank account might be in tatters, but this has cheered me up no end!"

Trudie frowned. "When you arrived today you looked like you'd lost a quid and found sixpence. Is everything alright?"

Adie debated about whether to confide in Trudie about feeling so let down by Mark's failure to show for lunch. She wasn't sure why it had upset her so much, and until she could figure that out, it really didn't feel right to tell anyone else about it. She shook her head.

"No, I'm fine. Just a bit tired from not sleeping as well as I should. I think it's just these rollercoaster hormones, still messing with me a bit when I least expect it. I'm so completely fed up with this endless grey weather, too. It'll be so good to finally see some sunshine. Then I can wear these gorgeous dresses!" She sipped her coffee.

Trudie sighed. "I know. Spring's nearly here, but it feels as far away as ever, today." She looked out at the darkening sky and frowned. "You know what? I think I'll close up early. There's nobody about. It's completely dead today, and I'd rather be back at home before this storm erupts. It's going to be a big one."

Trudie and her husband lived halfway between Torley and Carlisle, in a huge, rambling old cottage that had been extended at different times throughout its life, and fully renovated some years earlier. Full of quirky character and charm, it afforded panoramic views in all directions, but its access wasn't great. The driveway consisted of nearly half a mile of bumpy dirt track, which was rather poorly maintained by the farmer who owned the surrounding land, and it quickly became awash with mud from its overflowing potholes after any halfway heavy rainstorm.

Trudie drove a four-wheel drive as a basic requirement, and kept a pair of wellington boots and a small spade in the back at all times. She'd had to dig herself out of a mud-hole in her driveway enough times to know that it never paid to go very far without them.

"I think that's a good idea", Adie affirmed. "I'm pretty keen to get back myself, before it all starts. A good night to light the fire and snuggle down with a book, I think."

She drained her coffee cup and hugged Trudie tightly. The other woman handed her the bag with her dresses and jumper in it, and a separate one containing the bag and the box of shoes. As she left the store, Adie had all-but forgotten about her aborted lunch with Mark. At least, she was no longer as bent out of shape about it as she had been. Her anger was gone.

It's no big deal. He's so busy, it must have just slipped his mind. We can do it another day when he has a bit more time.

As she got to her car, the first fat, cold drops of rain were already starting to fall. The sky was heavy and black, and thunder growled across the valley. As she put her car into gear and pulled out of the car park, Adie had nothing else on her mind but getting home and lighting the fire. What she'd prepared for lunch - chilli-coated fillets of salmon with new potatoes and green veggies - would do perfectly for her dinner. She could reheat it in the Aga.

Just as she pulled up outside the front door of Teapot Cottage, the heavens properly opened and torrential rain started lashing down. Realising there was no point in trying to sit it out, she climbed out of her car, but had a sudden, unexplainable feeling of foreboding as she did so. She'd just opened the rear door to take out her shopping when suddenly, through the storm, she heard a long, loud, distant scream.

Feen! Somehow, she just knew it was Feen.

Adie jumped back into her car and quickly reversed it back to the point where she could turn and drive on up to Ravensdown House, reasoning it would be faster than trying to run up to the farm in the sheeting rain. At the front of the house, she jammed the brakes on and jumped out, calling Feen's name.

The wind whipped her words away from her, and they died before they could be heard. Adie battered on the front door but there was no answer. She ran around to the back of the house, and found the back door unlocked. She ran straight into the kitchen.

"Feen?" Silence greeted her. She ran from room to room, checking them all, and continuing to call Feen's name, and Mark's. The house appeared empty. Wherever Feen was, she wasn't in the house, and neither was Mark.

Adie ran back outside and looked around wildly. She caught sight of the open door to the big stone barn, just further up the rise from the house. There was a light on in there, and she tore up the driveway towards it as the rain drenched her thoroughly.

Just inside the barn door she called again "Feen?"

"Adie! Oh God, Adie, come quickly!" Feen's voice sounded almost hysterical. As Adie moved forward, she could see the young woman kneeling on the floor, scrabbling at her mobile phone. Lying motionless on the cold stone floor, with his head next to her knees, was Mark. And there was blood. Lots of it, dark and already congealing, all around him.

Adie's own blood ran cold. Feen looked up at her, with terror in her eyes. "Adie, he's unconscious. I can't wake him up, and I can't get a fucking signal on my fucking phone to call a fucking ambulance!" Her voice was steadily rising with panic and fear.

"Let me do it", Adie responded, holding her hand out for Feen's phone. Her own was still in the car. She ran to the open door of the barn and stomped around outside in the lashing rain while thunder clapped all around her. Finally, she managed to get a signal good enough to call the emergency services.

"999 - what's your emergency?" came the coolly efficient voice on the other end.

"Ambulance please," Adie shouted into it. "And hurry!"

As soon as she was connected with the ambulance service, Adie gave them the location of the farm and added that she wasn't sure what had happened, other than there had been an accident and the man involved - Mark Raven - was unconscious and bleeding heavily. She then supplied the other requested details, and was relieved to be reassured by the operator, part-way through that maddening, frustrating process, that the ambulance was already on its way.

She ended the call and ran back to Feen, to confirm that help was coming. Feen was shaking. Tears of terror and confusion were pouring down her face.

"Daddy! Daddy, please. Please wake up." Her voice was high-pitched with anguish. She was shaking hard and clearly in shock. Adie took one look at her and told her to go down to the house and get a blanket and a pillow for Mark. She knew Feen needed something else to focus on if she wasn't going to lapse into full hysteria.

Feen nodded and stood up, but didn't move again. Confusion clearly threatened to overwhelm her completely. "Go, Feen", Adie said sharply, wiping her own panicked tears away with the back of her hand. "Blanket. Pillow. I'll stay with him. The ambulance will be here soon, but he's ice cold. We need to cover him and warm him up. Go, quickly darling. Get what we need."

Feen snapped back into action then scurried off. Adie knelt on the floor and cradled Mark's motionless head. Fear flooded through her.

Oh, God. Oh, God. Mark! What happened? What the fuck happened?

She was shaking, herself, and almost blind with fear.

He can't die. Please Mark, please don't die!

"Mark? It's Adie. I've got you, my darling. Hang in there, my love. Help's coming. I've got you. I've got you. Feen's here too, and help's coming. We've got you." Tears were streaming down her own face again now, and she didn't bother to try and wipe them away.

Mark's breathing was so shallow and slight. He was alive, thank God, but in what state? What the hell had happened? Had he fallen? Adie looked up and around, and saw that a long, wide sheet of wood that comprised part of the mezzanine floor of the barn, was hanging down at a forty-five-degree angle, and a lot of the hay that was stored up there was now scattered around the floor where Mark lay.

It looked as if the mezzanine floor had given way under his footing and he'd crashed straight through it, twenty feet or more, to the stone floor below.

Adie felt physically sick. A fall, then, but so much blood! What did it mean? Had Mark cut his head wide open? Had he

210

broken his back? He was lying at such an angle that she couldn't see where the blood was coming from, and she was terrified of moving him to try and find out. All she could do was sit here on the icy stone floor, hold him as best she could without moving him, and pray.

After what seemed like an eternity but probably only was, in reality, a couple of minutes, Feen came rushing back into the barn with a heavy woollen blanket and a pillow. She was drenched to the skin, with her hair plastered to her face. She was only wearing a dress and cardigan and was now shivering with cold as well as shock.

Between the two of them they managed to wrap the blanket around Mark and prop the pillow under his head without moving him much. Adie stayed on the floor with him while Feen paced the barn, to and from the door.

The sound of an ambulance siren suddenly pierced the air and grew consistently louder. As it drew up at the door of the barn, its siren stopped, but its pulsating lights flooded the darkened sky, throwing surreal blue flashes all around the barn. Feen called to the paramedics, and they ran into the barn and crouched down beside Mark. Reluctantly, Adie let go of him, but stayed as close as she could. She didn't want to leave him for even the briefest of moments; didn't want to sever any connection between her own life-force energy and the man whose typically iron-strong hold on life suddenly seemed so fragile.

As the paramedics worked to assess Mark's injuries, feeling gently along his body and talking quietly among themselves, they decided they needed a stretcher and neck brace for him, and went to get them. Feen was trembling and silently weeping. She looked desolate, and clearly terrified. Adie wrapped her arms around the slight young woman and held her close. Feen was ice cold and rigid with fear and worry. She mumbled into Adie's shoulder.

"Adie, I-I d-don't know how long h-he'd b-been there. I just found him, you must have heard-heard me scream. I'd just f-found him. I -d-don't know what h-happened." Her teeth were chattering. "I c-can't l-lose him. Not him. Not him too, Adie. Not him too."

Adie felt Feen's anguish, but had no idea how to respond to it, other than to keep holding her as tightly as she could. She couldn't reassure Feen that her father would survive. She was no expert, but right now, it very much looked to be touch and go.

The paramedics expertly and efficiently secured Mark's head in place with the brace and deftly transferred him from the floor to the stretcher.

This is just routine for them. They've done this a hundred times before, maybe even a thousand times. They know exactly what they're doing. If anyone can save him, its them.

Feen and Adie answered the paramedics' questions as best they could, but with lamentably little information to offer. The medics did their best to be reassuring, saying Mark was in the best hands now and would be transferred to Cumberland infirmary in Carlisle, in the first instance, for a full assessment of his injuries, then on elsewhere to a more specialist unit if required. They weren't saying anything about his chances.

Feen decided to go in the ambulance with her father. Adie promised to secure everything at the farm before driving to the hospital to meet them. She needed to secure Teapot Cottage too, and put the chickens at both dwellings to bed and get Sid and Mittens fed, along with the dogs at the farm, before she could set off. It might be a long night. She might not be back before dawn. She still had to deal with her responsibilities, as much as she wanted to forget them and hurl herself into the back of the ambulance with Feen.

As the paramedics closed the ambulance doors in readiness for departure, the last thing Adie saw was Feen's pale, frightened face staring back at her.

Unused to praying, she suddenly found herself again bargaining with a God she seldom bothered to acknowledge, let along expect favours from.

Please. I know I'm no Christian, and I don't have the right to ask you for anything. But I'll do anything you want. Anything. I'll give up anything, everything I have, I'll do whatever you want me to do, just let him be ok.

Adie then went mechanically about the business of securing the barn and both houses, feeding the animals, peeling off her blood-drenched clothes and putting them in the washing machine to soak, and taking a very quick shower. She hurriedly got dressed again in black leggings, her grey boots and an over-sized black wool sweater. She picked up another pair of leggings and a jumper for Feen, who she remembered was soaked to the skin. They would swamp her, but she'd at least be warm. Adie didn't even bother to dry her hair or even run a comb through it before getting into her car and heading for the hospital.

Everything had been done on a peculiar kind of autopilot, as if stopping to think might derail the whole process of what needed to be done before she could leave home. But halfway to Carlisle, she had to pull over to the side of the road for a few minutes, as the inevitable delayed shock set in. Seeing Mark like that, badly injured and unconscious and surrounded by a pool of blood, had shaken her to the very core. She couldn't stop her tears from falling. Desperately she tried to convince herself that he would be ok.

Here, en-route to what suddenly felt like an impending execution, the reality of what had happened was starting to sink in. Adie didn't see how Mark could have survived such a big fall without horrific injuries. She knew that if she lived to be a hundred and forty, she would never forget the sight of her beloved, lying in a massive pool of blood.

And yes, he *was* her beloved. She loved him! It may not have been clear to her before tonight, but there was no doubt about it now. Realising how much she loved Mark Raven, how precious he was to her, and how precarious his life might now be thanks to this terrible accident, she allowed herself to cry hard, until the worst of the delayed reaction had passed.

Please, God. I'll do anything. Just don't let him die.

As her emotional outburst eventually tapered off to a hollow, dull despair, Adie took a few deep breaths, put the car into gear, and drove the rest of the way to Carlisle.

Chapter 20

Mark was in a medically induced sleep when Adie got to the hospital. He looked incredibly pale - almost translucent - as he lay there, mercifully in a private room, surrounded by a tangle of tubes and wires. His neck was encased in a rigid collar and his head was swathed in bandages. He had also cut his right ear and drops of blood had seeped through the bandage there. Two separate monitors beeped quietly, at regular intervals. Feen was sitting alongside him, with one of his hands encased in both of hers, but she sprang up to pull forward another chair for Adie.

Her voice was shaky. "Adie I'm so glad you're here." She looked at her father and picked up his hand again, massaging it lightly as she spoke. "He's just back from x-ray. I don't know anything yet, and I don't mind admitting I'm scared to death. Thank God you're here. I don't want to be alone when they tell me what's wrong with him."

Feen's voice hitched at the end. Clearly, she *was* scared to death. How deeply afraid had that poor girl felt, cradling her bleeding father, trying to make sense of what had happened, and all alone, unwilling to leave him and unable to call on her phone from where they were, for help? She'd already watched her mother die of cancer. Now she'd had to confront the prospect of watching her father's life ebb away too. No wonder she was shaking with fear. Adie wondered how long Mark had been there, lying unconscious on the cold stone floor, before Feen had found him.

Reading her mind in the usual off-beat way, Feen said "it must have been a long time, because I know he was looking forward to lunch, and I gather he hadn't made it down to you for one o'clock? I guessed that because he was still in the work clothes he'd put on thirst fing. So, it must have been since at least midday. That'd be the latest he'd work till, if he had an appointment to get cleaned up for."

Oh my God! Five hours! It's a miracle he's alive at all!

Adie shook her head and fought back her tears. "I did wonder what had happened. It's not like him to just not turn up, or say he wasn't coming. I wish to God I'd gone looking for him, instead of just thinking he'd stood me up, and getting all high and mighty, and going down into the town spending money I don't even really have, to try and cheer myself up. I should have known something was wrong. How stupid am I? He wouldn't just stand me up."

Feen shook her head. "There was no way of knowing. You mustn't blame yourself, or your reactions, Adie. It was just a terrible accident. I should have gone looking for him too. I just got so absorbed with my own work, and I didn't even notice what time it was until the thunder made me jump and I noticed it had started going dark."

"Oh, Feen!" Adie's tears welled up again. "I didn't want to chase after him. I thought he may have just forgotten, and I didn't want to remind him because then he'd feel bad, or think I was harping on, like nagging, like it was a proper date or something! It was just a bloody lunch, a light bite, like we so often have. I didn't want to put him on the spot, either way. I was disappointed though, and I just stomped off in a hissy fit down into the town and did my own thing. I shouldn't have done that. I should have gone looking for him like I really wanted to."

You and your stupid pride! He could have died in that bloody barn!

Adie knew it was silly to chastise herself over something she couldn't have known about, but she still felt wretched. Poor Mark. He really *could* have died. If he'd been there much longer...

Again, Feen was tuned into her thoughts. "He didn't though, at least he hasn't yet anyway. Where the hell are the bloody doctors?" she suddenly snapped, fear switching to anger in the blink of an eye. "Surely someone should know something by now? I can't believe they've just left us here alone. It's been nearly two hours."

Adie handed Feen the leggings and jumper, telling her to change if she wasn't going to get pneumonia and end up in a bed beside her father. The young woman obeyed.

215

As she came back, changed and now dry, the door to Mark's room opened and a young twenty-something doctor stepped in. He smiled gently. Despite his virtually adolescent appearance, he exuded an air of knowledge and competence that immediately reassured both women.

"Your Dad's going to be alright, Miss Raven", he announced. "It's a big shock, I know, seeing him like this, all trussed up and plugged in and everything. But the x-rays confirm two cracked ribs, a fractured eye socket, and a C2 Hangman's fracture, his second vertebra, near the top of his neck. We also did CT and MRI scans to see if there's anything else going on that we might have missed in the X-rays. Happily, there wasn't. The MRI scan showed no discernible nerve damage, which is all good news.

"He's been incredibly lucky, the way he managed to fall. With appropriate care and bed rest his neck fracture should heal well, and he probably won't need surgery, hopefully just a rigid collar to keep him immobile for a couple of months. He also has a small tear to his liver, thanks to the blunt force of the fall, and that's something we really need to keep a close eye on. Again, he should recover from it, but he does need complete bed rest. He won't be doing any gymnastics for a while."

Adie stepped forward. "But all the blood! There was so much of it! I - we - thought he was bleeding to death."

The doctor nodded. "Head-laceration, they do bleed a lot. Usually looks worse than it really is, to be honest, although it is a very deep cut, above his left eye, which we're guessing he sustained on impact with the stone floor, and we've stitched it, as you can see. But again it's good news. He doesn't appear to have any serious problems there, although I do expect him to have an almighty concussion when he does wake up because his brain's a bit banged around and swollen, which is kind of 'normal', for want of a better word, after an impact like that.

"He really will be like a bear with a sore head when he wakes, and he'll have a shiner to rival a heavyweight boxer's. But he's as fit as a butcher's dog, for his age. Extraordinary, really. I think the shape he's in is what's saved him from ending up any worse. We're keeping him very heavily sedated for now because even with the morphine he would still be in too much pain and nauseous from his concussion if he was awake. We'll gradually reduce the drugs as his brain swelling reduces, and eventually he should wake up on his own."

"When can I take him home?" Feen piped up.

"Oh, not for a long time yet, I'm afraid. We're fairly sure the fracture's stable but he needs to stay completely still for at least a month, until his brain and body start to recover from the physical trauma and the bones have started knitting back together."

He turned to Adie. "Your husband's a farmer, is that right?"

Adie was startled. "I - erm ... he's not -"

Feen swiftly interrupted. "Yes, that's right. Ravensdown Farm, over in Torley. Sheep, a few cattle and a bit of arable. We're about to start lambing, actually." She looked at Adie and smiled gently. Adie was grateful for the younger woman's insight and her quick alleviation of Adie's awkwardness.

The doctor frowned. "Well, I can tell you this much; he's not going to be doing any farming, or anything else for that matter, not for three months at least, maybe closer to four. I take it you have help on the farm, or can get some?"

Adie glanced at Feen before confirming, "Yes, we've got that covered, thanks." She determinedly ignored Feen's raised eyebrows and panic-filled eyes.

The doctor nodded. As he left the room, he added, almost as an afterthought; "you know, it's extraordinary. I've seen a lot of this sort of thing, and I have to say I've not seen anyone get away so lightly with a broken neck. He's incredibly lucky."

He also told them that although Mark was under heavy sedation for his brain and body's protection, there was every chance he could still hear what was being said. While in the room, it wouldn't hurt for all visitors to speak as if he was awake and listening.

"Adie!" Feen hissed, as the doctor disappeared, "Are you crazy? How can I possibly run the farm by myself for three whole months or more?"

Adie gently led her away from Mark's bed, mindful of the fact that he might well be able to hear every word. "You won't be by yourself, Feen", she murmured. "You'll have me. And Bob and Sheila will pitch in wherever they can, and I'm sure a lot of other people will too. Don't worry about it right now. And don't let him know you're worried about it." She nodded over towards Mark.

Feen nodded shortly. She spoke quietly. "Ok. I guess we have no choice, do we? We can't let the farm go to rack and ruin. We'll have to figure *something* out. I'll have to go over the insurance policies and see what might be offered there, if anything."

She dragged a deep breath up from within herself and let it out in a long, ragged stream. "Speaking of Bob and Sheila, I'd better go and call them. Will you sit with Daddy while I do?"

"Of course, I will!"

Adie hugged Feen tightly and whispered in her ear. "He'll get through this. You heard the doctor. He's as strong as a bloody ox, and he's twice as stubborn. He'll be just fine. We all will."

Feen left the room. Flooded with relief, Adie sat in the chair nearest to Mark, who appeared to be sleeping peacefully. His chest was rising and falling normally and his face, although battered, seemed serene. To an outsider, that's all it looked like. Nobody would realise he was really in a drug-induced coma to keep terrible pain at bay. Only the consistent, soft beeping of the monitors he was hooked up to told of the true reality. She sighed heavily, suddenly feeling desperately weary after what were now starting to feel like endless and uncontrollable traumatic events and emotional hurdles. She took hold of Mark's hand and spoke softly.

"It's Adie, Mark. You're in good hands, here at the hospital in Carlisle. You had a very nasty fall in the barn, and you've hurt yourself a lot, but you're going to be ok. Feen's here too. She's just stepped out for a moment, but she'll be right back, and Bob and Sheila are on their way."

She felt a little foolish, talking to a man she wasn't even sure was listening, but she ploughed on regardless.

"Well really, Mr Raven. You could have just said, if you didn't want lunch. You didn't have to go to these lengths, hurling yourself from the top floor of the barn, to get out of it. A simple 'no thanks' would have sufficed. I'm not that thin-skinned you know."

She chuckled lightly and squeezed his hand lightly. "But seriously, my darling, you gave us such a scare. I couldn't have borne this if it had been any worse, and it so easily could have been. The thought of not having you around ... well, I just never want to think about that. As you'd say yourself, y'owd bugger, yer've come to mean a lot to me."

She cringed at her own poor attempt at a Lancashire accent. But she needed to try and keep things light.

"Ah well", she continued. "I know my owd Lanky twang definitely needs work. But I'm willing to work on it if you're willing to help. Learning to talk like you do can be my reward for scraping you off the floor and chucking you in an ambulance."

She squeezed Mark's hand again and leaned forward close to his ear. "And you've left a right mess for us to clean up, but we'll save all that for later. For now, you being alive is the only thing that matters."

Feen came back in at that moment. "Bob and Sheila are coming. They're going to stop at the farm to pick up a few things. Sheila has a key."

Adie turned her attention to Mark again. "You hear that? Sorry but you don't get to wear this incredibly fetching pink and white floral hospital gown for much longer. I know it's disappointing, but you'll have to stop showing your bum to everyone, when your pyjamas get here."

Feen smirked and snorted. "Daddy, don't listen to her. It's pot nink. And it's flot noral. It's just grain pleen."

She looked at Adie and managed a grin. "He's never worn pyjamas in his life! A pair of boxers in winter's about as much as he'll ever wear. But he does have a ropey old purple towelling dressing gown I've been begging him to get rid of. It's a ghastly thing, truly horrible, but he's had it longer than I've been alive, and he loves it. I've told Sheila to bring it for him."

"Ah well, Mr Raven," Adie murmured, "bum to the world it is then, for now at least."

"Daddy, she's messing with you. It's a perfectly respectable gown they've got you in. Nobody can bee your sum!"

They sat together at either side of Mark's bed. Feen held one of his hands, while Adie held the other. After an hour, Bob arrived with Sheila, and they spoke with the doctor before coming into the room. Everyone exchanged hugs. Sheila kissed Mark on the forehead and stroked his hair.

"You daft sod. I can't leave you alone for five bloody minutes, can I?"

Her voice cracked. Adie could see how worried she was, even after being reassured by the doctor that with time, and the appropriate rest and care, Mark would be just fine. Bob was more stoic.

"The doc says he'll be right as rain, old girl! It'll take a bit of time, that's all. But you know how strong he is. He's a lion! It'd take a damn sight more than something like this to keep him down."

Feen still had some of Mark's blood on her arms. There were faint streaks of it on her face too, where she'd swept her hair out of her face and tried to wipe away tears and rain. There were bits of hay in her hair from the barn. She looked dirty, messy, and completely exhausted. Bob put his arm around her.

"Right, young lady. I think you need a bath and a brandy, in that order. Don't you worry about your dad. He won't be waking up tonight, and Sheila and I will stay with him until we get kicked out of here. I know you'll want to be here bright and early in the morning, but we'll come by the house first, if you don't mind, because we need to talk about how we'll manage the farm while he's out of action."

Adie piped up. "Feen can come home with me. And please include me in the plans for managing the farm. I'm very keen to do whatever I can to help."

She was aware of Sheila looking at her intently, but the other woman just smiled gently and said nothing. Bob nodded, and gave his niece a small squeeze.

"Yes, help will be needed. But we'll get it sorted. Everything will be fine, Feen, you'll see. Nothing will come unstuck."

As Adie and Feen were preparing to leave, Sheila touched Adie lightly on the elbow and led her to one side. She spoke quietly.

"Are you alright, Adie? You look done in too. Feen's not the only one to have had a bad shock. Why don't you stay up at the farm tonight? I imagine the best guest bedroom is all made up. It usually is. I think Feen might appreciate you stopping over, and maybe you shouldn't be on your own tonight either."

As Adie was considering this, Sheila leaned forward. Her voice was so low Adie could hardly hear it. "I know you love him, Adie. And for what it's worth, I think he loves you back. He'll come right from this. It will all be ok, I promise you, but for now, you and Feen, just stick together, ok? For both your sakes."

Adie nodded. Her eyes misted over. Sheila knew she loved Mark. Was she really that transparent? Was she wearing her heart on her sleeve like some silly teenager without even realising it? Did *everyone* know how she felt?

Under most circumstances she'd find the idea mortifying that everyone else knew before she'd even realised herself, how she felt about Mark, but right now it really didn't matter if anyone would choose to pity her for what they might see as a middle-aged crush on a man she'd only just met. All that mattered was him getting well again. He'd had an incredibly lucky escape. She refused to let her thoughts go to the place where she might have had to confront the fact that he'd died.

In the car, heading home, Feen was quiet. She said very little for the first few miles, and Adie didn't press her. Both women had to process what had happened, and that would take some time. Sometimes, talking just didn't feel appropriate, however after a short time Feen did clear her throat to speak.

"There's not so much to do right now at the farm but in a couple of weeks it will start getting busy. For now, there's just the faily deed to get out, and maybe moving the sheep around to different fields while the grass is growing, but by March lambing will be in full swing, and that's an incredibly busy time.

"Some of the ewes get into trouble giving birth so we'll have to have eyes on them all the time, and sometimes there are orphaned or sickly lambs that need fottle-beeding, or even round-the-clock care. Hopefully not too many this year", she added. "And there's only a handful of cows due to calve, and they do tend to run a bit later than the lambs. They're usually easy enough, but again we just have to get them into the barn when the time comes, keep an eye on troubled births, and do what's necessary."

She sighed wearily. "I'll contact the vet so he knows we may need support. I'll worry about the bills later. If there are too many animals with problems, I'm sure Uncle Bob will take some of them fack to his barn for Sheila to keep an eye on, so we won't have to worry about them. There'll be more than enough to do without that."

Adie reached across and grabbed her hand. "Don't worry, Feen. We'll figure this out. We'll manage."

"But you'll be leaving in another few weeks, Adie. Do we even know the date, yet? Whenever it is, Dad still won't be fit to work by then." She stared miserably out into the rain.

Adie shook her head, resolute. "The Robinsons haven't confirmed their return date yet, but even if I can't stay at Teapot Cottage, I'll find somewhere else. I'm not going anywhere. I've no pressing need to be anywhere else after here. I'll stick with this until I'm no longer wanted or needed."

Feen squeezed her hand. "Well, when you do have to give up the cottage you can come and fay at the starm. God knows there's enough room! The place is just enormous. Ten people can live in our house and never see each other. And as for not being needed, well I can assure you there will never be a day *ever*, when Daddy and I won't want or need you."

At a loss for how to respond, Adie simply said nothing. Instead, she concentrated on the road, and the beat of the windscreen wipers as they swept away the rain.

Feen spoke again. "I think Sheila's idea of you staying up at the farm tonight is a good one. I'd really like that, if you're up for it? It might be a supper of teans on boast, as I think we're both too exhausted to make anything more complicated."

Adie nodded. "We are, I think. And I have a better idea for dinner. Why don't we just grab something from Cat's Fish on the way through?"

Cat's Fish was the local chippy and it had won a couple of local awards for its food which, Adie had already discovered, was every bit as good as reports suggested. She had bought her dinner there a couple of times, enjoying some friendly banter with the shop's pretty and vivacious owner Cat Marshall, while her food was being freshly cooked.

"Ok", Feen announced. "Chish and fips, pushy meas and gravy."

Adie grinned. "Haddock, chips and curry sauce for me, and a small sausage for Sid."

"And we can keep it all warm in the Aga while I get cleaned up."

Feen phoned ahead for their order, which they picked up on their way through, just as the chippy was about to close. Adie couldn't believe it was already nine o'clock. The last few hours had been incredibly scary and traumatic.

Her stomach growled. She remembered that she'd forgone lunch, and her salmon meal was still sitting in the fridge. Since the vending machine slop that passed for drinks at the hospital had been virtually undrinkable, she was also hanging out for a decent cup of tea. As she drove up to the farmhouse, which was now in complete darkness, she apologised for not at least having put a light on inside.

"Of course, you didn't, lovely! There were far more important things. Anyway, the sensor lights are enough, until I get in. Are you heading back down?"

Adie nodded. "I want to just quickly grab a nightie and a toothbrush and say goodnight to Sid."

Oh, bring Siddy back with you, Adie! Don't leave him all alone. He's part of the family now. Please bring him back up here. I can cheak him some snips while you're not looking." She attempted a grin but was really too tired to pull it off.

Adie gave Feen the front door key, which she'd kept in her pocket, and waited until the young woman had unlocked it and waved, before carrying on around the circular drive to head back down to Teapot Cottage. Once there, she gathered up a few bits and pieces, including night things, toiletries, a pair of slippers and a change of clothes. She made sure there was food in Mittens' bowl and picked up Sid's bed and biscuit bowl, which was still half full.

He didn't need asking twice. The little dog was in the passenger seat of Adie's car, and wagging his tail madly, before she could even blink. Clearly, there was an adventure to be had, and he didn't want to miss a minute of it!

She heard the shower switch off upstairs just as she got back to the farmhouse. She set the kettle on the Aga's hotplate, pulled a couple of plates down from the wooden rack next to the oven, and set out the fish and chips, which Feen had put in the simmering oven.

Remembering where the drinks cabinet was, she went to it, poured a couple of hefty brandies into small crystal tumblers and took them back to the kitchen, just as Feen emerged in a pair of purple silk pyjamas and jewelled slippers, with her hair wrapped up in a huge towel. She looked like Aladdin, or some exotic Sultana from a faraway land.

They sat in the warmth of the kitchen, listening to the unrelenting rain as it lashed the windows, and ate their meal in silence. When they'd cleared their places, Feen offered, "D'you fancy taring a shin of rice pudding? "

Evidently, Feen wasn't quite finished with her desire for comfort food. Adie decided she wasn't either. She nodded enthusiastically. As Feen prepared the pudding she felt compelled to speak.

"Feen, I'm so sorry I didn't go looking for your dad. I should have. I knew there would have been a reason why he didn't show up. I wish I'd trusted my instincts. I don't know why I was so indignant about it, or why I felt driven to go out and bend my credit card virtually in half."

Feen turned from the task of preparing pudding and smiled gently.

"Adie it's ok. Stop beating yourself up. For what it's worth, I'm telling myself the exact same thing! I should have gone looking for him too. I was just so busy this afternoon, absorbed in doing the first commission pieces for Gina, I literally lost all track of time. It never even occurred to me that I hadn't heard him come in to get ready for your lunch date."

Adie protested. "It wasn't a date! Just a lunch. A silly, meaningless lunch." But even as she said the words, she knew they were a lie. Today's lunch she'd planned to have with Mark had meant everything to her. Only now could she see that.

Feen tutted and rolled her eyes, literally unable to hide her impatience. "Oh, for God's sake! You two are just bloody hopeless! If I was my grandmother, I'd sang your billy heads together! It wasn't 'just a meaningless lunch' Adie, we both know that. If it had been, you wouldn't have reacted the way you did. But it's ok." She stepped forward, took Adie's hands in her own, and looked her straight in the eye.

"It really is. It's ok to love him, Adie. And as much as we wish we'd done things differently today, we're not responsible for what happened. And beating ourselves up won't help him, will it? We can't dwell on what did or didn't happen. We have to focus on how we go forward. That's going to take enough energy just by itself, I should think."

Adie knew Feen was right. Sometimes the young woman's wisdom was stunning.

It's ok to love him, Adie.

"I do love him, Feen. I love him with all my heart," Adie confessed.

Feen hugged her tightly. "I know you do. I can feel it. I can feel how much you love him, and I can't tell you how happy that makes me."

Adie looked at her in amazement. *If there's one thing about this woman, it's her unfailing ability to surprise me.*

Feen just smiled. As she set the dishes of rice pudding on the table and sat down, she sipped her brandy and continued.

"After Mum died, I thought that was it, for Daddy. They were such a devoted couple, true soulmates. When she died, something in him did too, or at least I thought it did. He's spurned a fair number of advances over the years, let me tell you, including the ones from that frightful psychopath Carla Walton, as you know. Nobody's managed to even spark his interest, let alone light him up." She took another sip of her drink and smiled ruefully.

Is that what I do? Light him up?

"Yes, you do, Adie. I've often wondered if he'd ever find love again and it's always worried me that he might not because he's just too nice, and far too young really, to be on his own for the rest of his life. But it would have to be somebody pretty special," she added, "to fit into our funny little life. Because I'm a big part of Daddy's life, and I kind of go with the territory really, as far as he's concerned. And a lot of people think I'm a nutcase, which doesn't help.

"But since you've been here, he's been happier than I've seen him since before Mum got sick. It's like he's woken up again from some kind of slumber. He's been functioning absolutely fine of course, all this time, but not really living. Not in the true sense of engaging with life and enjoying it, like we're all supposed to."

She took a deep breath and carried on. "He hasn't talked about you, so please don't think we've been sitting around discussing you or anything. He's not like that. He'd never tell me what he was thinking. He probably wouldn't talk to anyone else about it either, really. He's a bit of a blosed cook about his feelings. But he doesn't need to tell me anything. I already know what goes on in that head of his."

She grinned. "He's an *open* book to me. I know him in ways he doesn't even know himself, and I can see the change in him. You've done the most extraordinary thing, Adie Bostock. You've breathed new life into us - both of us - up here in this tucked-away part of the world. I know it's only been a few short months, but I can't imagine life without you now, and I'd be willing to bet that Daddy can't either."

At a loss for words, Adie set about clearing and washing the dishes. Feen said nothing further, but simply picked up a tea towel. Before long, the kitchen was back to its usual clean, pristine state.

"I love your Aga," Adie mused. "It's three times the size of the one at Teapot Cottage. And I love that it's dark blue. So full of character."

Feen nodded. "I love it too. I can't imagine cooking on one of those new-fangled, multi-ringed gas things like you said you had in your house. I'd take this over one of those, any day. If I ever have an ace of my plown, I'm definitely having one. I don't care how much it costs."

She then showed Adie to her room for the night, a lovely front-facing one on the first floor, with a king-sized sleigh bed and heavy drapes that matched the bed's sumptuous quilt. Like Feen's work room directly below it, it had a lovely big bay window. In daylight, Adie knew, it would provide a wonderful view of the top end of the valley. Tonight however, only the odd half-hearted flash of lightning gave any illumination at all. The storm was still raging, albeit further in the distance now.

Fortunately, Sid wasn't worried about storms. After settling his bed in a corner by the window and directing him into it, Adie prepared for bed herself. She was bone-weary and still worried, and her head was spinning. She turned out the light, not expecting for one moment that she would really sleep. But the next thing she knew, it was morning. Sid was curled up in the curved space between her chest and her knees, snoring peacefully. The violent storm of the night before had gone, and a glorious ray of sunshine has successfully fought its way into the room through the chink at the top of the curtains.

Chapter 21

Mark slowly opened his eyes. Where was all that bloody noise coming from?

His vision was blurred, and he could barely make anything out, at first; just vague shapes - a chair, a window, a curtain around his bed. As he blinked a few times and everything came more into focus, he could see that he was in a hospital room. He tried to lift his head off the pillow but couldn't. Pain seared through his brain, leaving him breathless and gasping. He tried to move but couldn't. He wiggled his toes and fingers, and was relieved to realise he had full movement, but his head and neck were encased in a brace which literally left him unable to turn or shift position.

He lay there for a few moments, determined not to panic. He managed to call a feeble, gruff "'ello?" but there was no answer. He was by himself.

There was a lot going on, outside of the room. The hustle and bustle of a hospital ward, with people talking and walking, machines beeping, phones ringing, and the clatter of items hitting trays.

Standard stuff, he supposed. He tried to cast his mind backwards, to try and understand why he was here, encased in a way that prevented him from moving. Much seemed hazy, but he did remember looking at his watch, and realising that if he didn't get moving quickly, he'd end up being late for lunch.

He'd been in the barn, planning on getting some feed and old tools down from the top floor. Being suddenly mindful of time slipping by, he'd bounded up the steps to the mezzanine floor with the idea of quickly throwing a couple of bales of hay down, so he could pop back later in the afternoon and load them into the trailer for disbursement among the sheep, and then make a start on refurbishing his dad's old rake. He vaguely remembered getting to the top, then losing his footing, but everything after that was a complete blank. Judging by the rigid encasement that held him in position here in bed, Mark deduced that he must have somehow fallen.

'Ave I broke me bloody neck?

He wondered who'd found him, and decided it was probably his daughter Feen. She'd likely gone to remind him not to be late for his lunch with Adie.

Adie! Did she know he was here? Did she know what had happened? What exactly *had* happened? Mark managed to look down at his left hand and saw there was a buzzer to press, so he did just that, and waited.

In less than fifteen seconds, his room was full of people. Two doctors, two nurses, and his sister Sheila, who was crying, but smiling. All five stood staring at him for a few uncomfortable beats, as if he'd grown an extra head. Then one of the doctors cleared his throat and stepped forward.

"Good afternoon, Mr Raven! Welcome back. We're all delighted to see you awake at last. You're in Cumberland Infirmary. You've had a serious accident, and you've been asleep for just over a week, but you're going to be alright, so don't worry. We just have to keep you braced for a while yet, because you've got what we call a Hangman's fracture. It's a break at the base of your neck that affects a part of the vertebrae called the pars interarticularis. That's a part of the bone that connects your skull to the main part of your spinal column.

"Luckily, it's fairly close to the top, so we can sort it out without too many problems, as long as we can keep you still. You've also torn your liver though, and banged yourself around a bit, so it's all going to take a bit of time to heal."

He looked at Mark's chart for a minute and came over and shone a light from a small torch into his eyes. Satisfied, he stepped back.

"You look ok to me, sir. All things considered, you've bounced surprisingly well from a twenty-foot fall onto a stone floor. The brace is uncomfortable, I know, but please bear with it. Keeping your body rigid is what's allowing the fracture to start knitting back together. I'll stop by again early this evening, before I finish for the day, see how you're feeling."

He spoke to one of the nurses about monitoring Mark's pain levels.

Mark tried to speak, but his voice was too hoarse. Sheila stepped forward and placed a glass of water to his lips with a straw. He took a long drink, and then tried again. His voice was husky.

"What about farm?"

Sheila patted his shoulder. "Farm's all in 'and, love. Everything's under control. Everything's just fine."

"Who?" Mark's throat felt like it was full of sand and gravel.

"Bob, Feen and Adie. They've got it all sorted. They're the lean, mean farming machine. They're amazing, Mark, and they're doing you really proud, with the lambing about to begin an' everything else. I'm pitching in too, of course, whenever I can. You mustn't worry. Just get better, that's what you 'ave to think about now."

One of the nurses asked Mark if he was hungry, and he nodded. She came and unhooked the intravenous drip from his arm and told him she would organise some soup and a sandwich. He croaked at her.

"Murder a cup o' bloody tea."

Sheila literally shouted with laughter, and the nurse grinned widely. "There you go, Mr Raven!" she exclaimed. "Sounds to me like you're going to be hunky dory in no time!"

Chuckling to herself, she promptly left the room.

Mark looked up at Sheila as she squeezed his hand and grinned at him. "Yes, you bloody are. Two seconds awake and already shouting an' bawling for tea. I don't think we've much to worry about, have we? You daft bugger."

She sat down in the nearest chair. "But you had us pretty scared for a while. We've all been worried sick. Feen's been beside herself. It was she who found you, and it wasn't pretty. There was blood everywhere - and I mean *everywhere*. She thought you were dead, Mark."

Mark closed his eyes as Sheila recounted events as best she could from what Feen and Adie had told her, that he had indeed fallen through a rotten floor panel on the mezzanine and had lain unconscious on the barn floor for five hours until he was found. It all sounded horrendous, and his heart ached for poor Feen, who'd found him and probably imagined the worst. He could imagine how distraught she must have been.

"Ow long am I gonna be laid up for, with this 'angman's bloody fracture?" Mark growled.

Sheila inwardly cringed, and Mark could see it. He knew she'd be honest with him, but he also knew he wasn't going to like it. Not one bit.

"They're saying three months, Mark." She didn't bother to try and reassure him that the farm would be in good hands for all that time. She knew it wouldn't have made any difference.

"What? Are you fuckin' kiddin' me?"

"'fraid not, brother dear. That's what they're sayin', and it's important that you *do* take the time to heal properly, that's if you ever want to be fit enough to run the farm again yourself. It's not just your neck, it's your liver as well. Concussion, banged-up ribs and the like. It all needs real time to heal."

Sheila didn't mention Adie at all. She was probably curious to see whether Mark would, himself. He had a feeling she already suspected how he felt about Adie Bostock, even though it was only becoming clear to himself. He'd never said anything, but he didn't have to.

Unfortunately, very few of his thoughts were safe from his sister. Sheila could read him like an open book and, as far as his daughter was concerned, even fewer of his thoughts were sacred, thanks to her own vision, through her own peculiar window, clear into his brain.

He'd long since stopped being unnerved by Feen's uncanny ability to read minds, but he was often frustrated by the fact that sometimes even his most innermost thoughts couldn't be classed as private. Even when he didn't fully understand what they were, the women in his life apparently did. It was excruciating.

Mark was fairly sure both women understood his feelings for his new neighbour, but he was grateful for the respect they gave him in not making comment or prompting any discussion about it.

He understood the farm to be in hand, for now at least, and he just had to trust that it would remain so until he was fit. But he literally couldn't help himself; he couldn't wait another minute. He simply had to ask.

"'Ow's Adie? 'As she been in, at all?"

Sheila nodded. "Adie's just fine, and she's been here as much as anyone. Regular as clockwork, every day the same. She phones here first thing, to ask how you are, then she puts a full day in at the farm, and every evening she's been driving over here with Feen to sit with you until they literally get thrown out."

Mark could feel Sheila watching his face carefully, as she chose her words. "She's a real trooper, that woman. She's 'ad her sleeves rolled up at Ravensdown right from day one. Every day's a Groundhog Day right now for Adie, but she doesn't seem to mind one bit. All she cares about is keeping that farm going an' you getting well again."

Mark merely nodded, aware that he was giving his sister no more than what she'd expect. The fact that he'd asked at all would have confirmed enough for her. He wasn't a man who wore his heart on his sleeve, and he never felt like saying more than he needed to, even to family, particularly when it wasn't necessary. Besides, he was exhausted. There was a lot to come to terms with, not least of which was being laid up for at least three months while his battered body healed itself, but he was glad to hear that Adie had been very much a part of everything since the accident. He would have been surprised if she hadn't been, but it was reassuring nonetheless to know for sure.

A nurse arrived with a tray, and Mark's nostrils immediately picked up the welcome smell of tomato soup. His stomach growled. He was ravenous.

With Sheila's help, the nurse managed to manoeuvre his neck and head into position with pillows, to allow him the dignity of feeding himself. He appreciated that and felt lucky, under the circumstances, to have the full use of his arms. He quickly set about demolishing the chicken salad sandwich, expecting it to taste like cardboard but being pleasantly surprised at how delicious it was.

His soup had been served in a mug, to make it easier for him to get down, and he jumped at how hot it was as he sipped it.

But real food, after a full week on a bloody drip, this is exactly what me system's in need of.

There were two cups of tea on the tray as well, also both piping hot, and he was touched at the hospitality that allowed for his sister to have one too. Hospitals usually weren't this accommodating. When Beth had been dying, he'd still had to get his own tea, and he knew from experience how foul it usually was, from those infernal vending machines. *Lukewarm stew, and that's bein' bloody kind to it.*

Mark managed to polish off his food, but he really felt too weak to make conversation. In truth, it was an effort to even listen to someone. Having been told what had happened and realising the extent of his injuries, he felt he had a lot to process, and really just wanted to be left alone to make sense of it all.

Right on cue, Sheila drained her cup and stood up to leave. She kissed Mark lightly on the forehead. "Right, face-ache. I'm off. Places to be, people to see. I'll give Feen a quick call an' tell her you've woken up demanding tea. No doubt she'll be keen to see you, as I'm sure will Adie. Bob will get in as soon as he can. He's got his hands full, with shuttling back an' forth between farms, but you really would be surprised at 'ow well they're managin'."

As she left the room, she turned back. "Behave yourself, and by that, I mean go easy on the nurses!"

Mark raised a hand in farewell, then slumped back against the pillows. His head was hurting like hell, throbbing fit to burst, and just as he was about to call for someone another nurse appeared, smiling, and waving a tiny plastic pot at him. She wrote something on his chart, looked up and smiled.

"Right, Mr Raven! Now you've had some food, we can give you some pain relief." She handed him the little pot containing two tablets, and Mark swilled them down with the last of his tea, which by now had gone cold. As she left, the nurse reminded him to press the buzzer near his left hand if he needed assistance.

Suddenly, everything went quiet. He was on his own again. It dawned on him that being bed-ridden meant he couldn't get up to pee or poo. He was in bed-pan city.

Wonderful. Bloody sparklin'. Peein' into a bottle, I can do. Havin' a crap on a soddin' bedpan, well that's gonna be interestin', to say't bloody least.

He remembered there'd been something vague said at some point about a pink floral hospital gown and having his arse on show, but when he looked down, he was vastly relieved to find himself in a pair of his own modest boxers and one of his t-shirts, probably stuff that Feen had brought in. The t-shirt was the one with the unicorn on it, which she'd given him for Christmas a year or two earlier. He supposed it was his daughter's way of having a laugh at his expense while he was unconscious but ever-thankful for small mercies, he reasoned that while it might have a cringe-worthy smattering of dark blue glitter on it, at least it wasn't a pink floral nightgown.

What did trouble him though, was the farm. Feen, Bob and Adie had things well in hand, according to Sheila, who'd done her best to reassure him without going over the top about it, and he knew beyond all doubt that she would tell him straight if there were any problems with anything. He trusted her word completely. But he felt bad for his family and his friend. They were all busy enough with their own stuff.

Feen had a lot of new work commissioned by Adie's daughter-in-law, and she needed to get on with meeting her order, which she'd struggle to do if she was running the farm as well. Although Mark had no doubt that his indomitable daughter was capable of dealing with almost anything Ravensdown threw at her, he wondered what price she was paying in terms of her own business project, for doing that.

Gina Giordano was a famous dress designer. Her commission work for Feen's unique jewellery could literally put the girl on the map, and she really did deserve that kind of break. Mark worried that she'd miss out if the farm became too demanding. If that happened, he'd never forgive himself.

Bob was busy enough too, on his own farm, without having to deal with Ravensdown as well. Mark knew his sister and brother-in-law wouldn't allow things to fall apart up there. They'd do everything they could to lessen the impact on Feen. Bob was too good a man to stand by and watch while anyone else flogged themselves into the ground. But Mark knew what that meant. Bob would be running *himself* ragged, in the months to come, with lambing in full swing on both farms, and Ravensdown's big top field needing seeing to. Spring was nearly underway. It was about to get blindingly busy, and Mark would be out of action at the worst possible time.

And then there was Adie, who had Teapot Cottage and its pets to take care of, and who was just finding her feet in the area,

233

making friends, and getting connected to local activities for the time she would be here. Mark was aware that she would be leaving Torley in a few short weeks when her house sitting ended. That would be well before he'd be up and about, if the doctors were right.

I bloody hate the thought o't poor lass feelin' like she has to work 'er backside off, instead of enjoyin' whatever time she has left in Torley. She's come 'ere to heal and rebuild 'er broken life, not to end up a skivvy on some bugger else's bloody farm!

No. This wasn't fair to any of them. It was clear to Mark that he had to hire some solid, reliable help. He resolved to talk to Bob about it straight away. Bringing in a caretaker/manager was the most logical solution. He pressed his buzzer again, and when a nurse appeared, he asked her for his mobile phone, which was fully charged, thanks to Sheila's foresight in bringing in the charger. She knew how lost he'd be without it.

He called Bob, not expecting an answer but preparing himself to leave a message, and he was surprised when his brother-in-law picked up on the second ring.

"What y'bloody doin', answerin't phone? 'Ave yer not got enough to friggin' do, man?"

Bob bellowed with laughter at the other end, and Mark had to hold the phone away from his ear.

"Well, hello there, sleeping beauty! Who's kissed you awake, then?"

" Smell o' food, I reckon! Me stomach thinks me throat's been cut."

Bob explained that he was on his way to Torley to help Feen repair one of the fences that had somehow sprung a wire and was now posing a hazard to the sheep. Mark got straight to the point.

"Get on to't agency an' get a couple o' staff up there at farm, if yer would please, Bob. A manager an' a farm 'and. Quick as yer can, like. Preferably someone to start tomorrow." As Feen was co-signatory on all farm-related matters, Mark knew the bills would be taken care of.

"Well, I can if you like, old boy," came Bob's gruff response, "but we're managing ok up there."

Mark couldn't contain his exasperation. "I've no doubt. I know yer not as green as yer bloody cabbage lookin', but yer'll not manage for long, once lambin's in full swing. Get it sorted please Bob, get the 'eat off them lasses. They've enough o' their own to do wi'out 'avin to run't bloody farm as well!"

He could almost feel his brother in law's shrug of defeat. "Okay, if that's what you really want, will do. Tomorrow might be a bit soon, if we want someone decent, but I'll get a couple of bods up there as quick as I can. And I'll pop over and see you tonight with the details. Any food requests?"

Mark thought for a moment. "Yeah, pizza. Pick us up a meat-laden pizza, would yer, wi' extra cheese? And yer can try for a couple o' cans o' lager, an' all."

"I'll see what I can do", Bob chuckled, and rang off.

Mark lay back against his pillows. Now he really *was* exhausted. Weak as a kitten, he felt frustrated and powerless. But he knew Bob would be as good as his word, in getting people up to the farm. They'd both used agency staff in the past, and they'd both had mostly good experiences with whoever came. Having a manager in place would be a little different, as that meant handing over a much greater level of responsibility, but Bob wasn't going anywhere. He'd certainly keep an eye on things, making sure whoever was up there was competent and trustworthy. Hopefully they'd be fairly local, so they wouldn't need accommodation. If they did, it would be up to Feen to decide whether or not she wanted them in the house.

With that sorted, Mark could relax a bit more. A fractured neck and a torn liver were nasty injuries. As much as he wanted to get up and get going, he knew the doctors were right. The healing process was exactly that - a process - and he had to comply if he wanted to get back to the level he was at before.

They'd said he'd be fine, but Mark knew it would all be conditional on him toeing the line. Doing as he was told. With the farm being managed, healing would be a far less stressful process than it would be if he was lying here worrying about Bob, Feen and Adie all working themselves into the ground on his behalf.

Adie! Mark felt a smile playing around his lips, as he thought about her. Since she'd come into his life, he'd felt lighter, happier, and more positive about life in general. He couldn't put his finger on what it actually was, but something about Adie

Bostock just drew people in. Without even trying, she had a way of making people feel important, and comfortable around her. When you were talking to her, she treated you like you were the only person in the world that mattered, and that was a rare gift. Not many people made you feel like that. The woman was solid, straight up, and genuine, with an open face and an open heart. He'd also come to realise that he loved her for it.

The idea of ever meeting someone else and developing a relationship had always been an uncomfortable one. Not only had he never imagined ever feeling for any other woman what he'd felt for his wife, he'd also felt that even if he *were* capable of that, it would feel like a betrayal to the woman who'd loved him, shared his bed, given him a child and worked like a Trojan herself, to help him turn his derelict wreck of a farm into a profitable going concern.

But then Adie Bostock had turned up. And somehow, even though there had never been the vaguest hint from either of them to the other, of anything other than a simple friendship, Mark had of course already sensed a subtle change in his own thinking, about the way he wanted to live his life.

A lot of people maintain that a man and a woman can't be just friends. Many say there's always the spectre of sex involved and until you get that out of the way, there will always be a spark, or a fear, a denial, or some other sub-conscious barrier that will complicate things to the point where a 'simple friendship' just won't work.

Mark wasn't sure about that, and he knew he didn't have the patience or insight to really analyse it fully, but he also knew that his 'simple friendship' with Adie Bostock had slowly but surely evolved into something else.

The problem was, he didn't for one moment presume that she felt the same way. How could she? She was still climbing out of a marriage she'd fought incredibly hard to salvage, because it meant so much to her. Even if she no longer felt the marriage to be worth fighting for, as she'd said more than once, the hurt must surely still be there? Even though she'd decided she no longer wanted her lying, cheating husband, how ready would she really be, to embrace someone else? Did he really want romance with a woman on the rebound?

Adie's marriage had only collapsed just over a year ago, after twenty-six years! It could be a very long time before she'd be ready to consider a new mate. And, as he'd already asked himself before, even when she did, would it be someone like him?

She came from a different world. He'd met the snake she'd been married to, and he'd seen the places where she was comfortable and familiar. Posh department stores, stately homes, hustle and bustle, big, detached houses in quiet tree-lined streets that silently screamed of affluence. It was all about as far a cry from a remote and windswept Lake District sheep farm as you'd ever find.

Mark imagined Adie dating smooth, sophisticated golf pros, or well-heeled investment bankers. An educated man of substance would be more her kind of guy than a rough and ready farmer who got his hands dirty for a living, usually stank of sheep, and spoke like a common peasant.

He wasn't generally a man prone to self-comparisons, but nor was he under any illusions about himself. An examination of his own shortcomings had never been an issue for him before, but now he was more acutely aware than he'd ever been, of what he couldn't offer to a woman like Adie Bostock.

It hadn't occurred to Mark that his assessment might be doing Adie a grave injustice. The thought hadn't crossed his mind that she might have made some big emotional adjustments of her own recently, and reached the conclusion all by herself that Mark was *exactly* the kind of man she wanted.

It was Adie herself that put him straight. Later that evening, after Bob had popped in, alas with no beer, but bringing a very impressive pizza and good news about staff for the farm, Adie and Feen rushed into the room, both panting as if they'd run a marathon. As soon as they clapped eyes on him, both promptly dissolved in tears. Mark shook his head. Women crying, even for good reasons, always left him feeling inept and frustrated.

"Stop yer mytherin', the bloody pair o'yer. I'm alright. At least, I will be. Save the 'istronics for some poor sod who's dead!"

Feen hugged his upper body as best she could, and he patted her on the back. Adie hung back a little, more nervous than he recalled ever having seen her, so he beckoned her forward and took her hand. He squeezed it gently and gave her a wink. She smiled. Boom! There it was! That smile, the only thing he'd really been interested in seeing since the minute he woke up.

After the usual pleasantries, Feen got down to business.

"Bob says you've got a manager to start next week. It's not necessary, Daddy. We've got it under control, me and Bob and Adie. If you'd asked, we'd have told you."

She sounded defensive, but Mark was adamant.

"No! It's the only practical solution. You lot 'ave to get back to yer own lives. An' anyway, 'ow the dickens d'you think I could 'ave asked yer anything, yer daft bugger? I were bloody asleep until this mornin'."

Adie laughed. "I think we just wondered if you were doubting us, that's all."

She hadn't let go of his hand, which Mark thought was a very good sign. He shook his head.

"No, lass. It's not that. I know you're all doin' a grand job on't farm. But there's money for a good manager an' a decent farm 'and, so I'm going to use it. I think the insurance will cover it, any road, so I'd be mad not to 'ave someone there who can just get on with it. Someone who doesn't have owt else to do but that."

Both women knew it made sense and the subject was duly dropped. An awkward silence then prevailed, so Mark cleared his throat and asked Feen if she wouldn't mind going and fetching him a newspaper or two and a couple of bags of boiled sweets from the shop across the road from the hospital.

"I can see the bloody place from't winda. It's a proper tease, that. Get me some goodies will yer please, lass?" He looked sheepish. "I do love a bit o' tuck."

Feen just grinned and rolled her eyes. "That you do" she muttered good-naturedly and headed for the door. After she left, Mark turned to Adie and said softly; "Now then, you're a lovely sight for sore eyes. The best thing I've seen in a week."

She pulled up a chair and sat down. "More like the *only* thing you've seen in a week, sleepyhead!"

Her face became serious. "Honestly though, I've never been so worried in my life. When we were waiting for the ambulance, it felt like hours. It wasn't, of course. They got there really quickly, but it felt like forever, sitting there, wondering how bad things were. You scared us to death." She squeezed his hand. "But you're a tough old boot, aren't you?"

Mark grinned at her. "Oy, less o' the owd! An' I'll be right as bloody rain in a few months." His face fell, realising what he'd said. Adie would be gone by then, gone from his and Feen's lives, and the thought made him sick with sorrow. He shook it off and told her how grateful he was for the fact that she'd stepped up, working on the farm like a real trooper. She waved away his thanks.

"To be honest, Mark, I think it's been the best thing that could have happened to me." Adie nodded, almost to herself, and continued. "Yes. It really has. It's given me a real focus, and there's a lot to be said for a hard day's graft and a good night's sleep at the end of it. It translates to a simple life, but a wholesome, meaningful one. It's so rewarding. I can see exactly why you love your farm. I think I'm coming to love it too."

D'you think you could come to love me?

Mark was astonished at his own thought. It had popped into his head so quickly, and so emphatically, he was actually worried he might've said it out loud without meaning to. He held his breath and looked at Adie, but her face didn't change. She didn't startle, or look embarrassed or affected, in any way at all. Relieved that Feen hadn't been in the room, he let his breath out with relief. That wasn't a thought that would've sailed past his daughter.

But he realised it hadn't come from nowhere. That wishful thought (and he had to admit it was wishful) was the culmination of many weeks of growing friendship, of sticking his head above the parapet and allowing a woman part-way into his life for the first time since Beth had died. And although they'd started off just as friends, and he'd had every intention of remaining that way, ever-so subtly the dynamics had changed. Adie herself hadn't changed and neither, he supposed, had he. But the *situation* had, somehow, without him realising it was happening. And Mark knew one thing for certain; this was not just any ordinary woman, though she'd described herself as such, many times. Adie Bostock was a lot of things, but 'ordinary' definitely wasn't one of them, and it was time she knew it.

He cleared his throat. "Yer've settled well into Torley. Yer almost part o't furniture, and it's not taken long, 'as it? It's like yer've always been 'ere. I feel like I've known yer for a lot longer than just a couple o' months."

Adie smiled gently. "I feel like I've been here a lot longer. And I love it. I love Teapot Cottage, and Sid, and Mittens. The thought of leaving, well, that's something I can't bring myself to think about. Not just yet. I've got a few weeks to go, I think, before I have to face it."

"Aye. Although if you wanted to stick about for a bit after't 'ouse sittin's over, you could still stay locally. Maybe rent a place for a bit, see 'ow you get on. Maybe get a long-term deal on an 'oliday cottage or summat. There's no need to rush off, is there?"

Mark's heart was in his mouth. What if Adie *had* made new plans for after she left Teapot Cottage? Was she already arranging to pick up her life again back in Guildford? Anything could have happened in the past week to cause her to make new plans. The looming deadline on Teapot Cottage would be enough by itself, to make her contemplate what she'd be headed for next.

Adie shrugged. "I suppose not. The Guildford flat's not exactly a magnet, is it? And quite frankly, after Bryan coming round and tainting the place, shouting the odds at me and spilling his own dirty little secrets, I'm a hundred percent sure I don't want to live there again, as I've told you before, I think."

"Aye, you did. Well, yer kids are all managin' okay, so you might not 'ave to rush back down south for anythin', although that flat's a bloody expensive storage unit" Mark observed. "I'm sure a lot of people around 'ere would be glad to see you stay a bit longer."

Or maybe permanently?

At that moment, Feen came bursting back in, with a white plastic bag. She proceeded to lay a variety of treats on the bed for Mark; salt and vinegar crisps, a box of Roses chocolates, a packet of blueberry muffins, two bottles of cordial, a newspaper and a book of crossword puzzles. Only then did she think to ask Mark if he had a pen.

As he shook his head, Adie rummaged in her bag and found one for him.

At that moment, a nurse came in and asked them, very nicely, to leave so that Mr Raven could get some much-needed rest. Outraged, Mark barked at her.

"Fer God's sake, woman! I've just *been* asleep, fer an entire bloody week!"

Adie doubled over with laughter. Feen just stood there, shaking her head at him.

The nurse stepped forward. "Now then, Mr Raven. An induced coma's not the same thing as good quality sleep, and you know it. That's definitely what your banged-up body needs, and right now. And no arguing!" she added firmly as Mark opened his mouth.

Helpless, furious, he could do nothing but lie there. He *was* exhausted, he *did* need to sleep. He couldn't deny that. But Feen and Adie had only just arrived, and he was desperate for more time.

The nurse looked at them all and signed heavily. "Five more minutes, then" she announced, "and I mean five. Not fifteen. Not even ten."

"Skedaddle, will yer? Bloody Gestapo!" Mark muttered as she left the room.

Feen looked at her watch. "We'd better go before we're physically turfed out of here and banned from coming back. We'll be back tomorrow, Daddy. The nurse is right. You do look wiped out. Get some good rest, and don't eat all that tuck at once! I'm not going back for more tomorrow, you know!"

"Bloody women, tellin' me what to bloody do!"

Adie leaned forward and gave him a kiss on the cheek.

Well, that'll do for starters, lass!

She stood up. "See you tomorrow. Is there anything else you need from home?"

Mark thought for a moment, then shook his head. The only thing he really wanted was one person, and she was just about to walk out the door. Exhaustion battled with indignation, and finally won the toss. He slumped back against his pillows.

The two women said their final goodbyes, and suddenly he was alone again.

Chapter 22

"That's the last lot for today, I think", Adie panted, as she heaved a bale of hay onto the tiny trailer attached to the back of the quad bike. Feen gave her the thumbs up and drove away from the barn and down to the west corner field where they'd put the ewes with their early lambs, to deliver the last bale.

They'd already given out a trailer-load of turnips to the sheep, earlier in the week, and another delivery of silage was being sorted in a day or two, but hopefully not before the temporary Manager and farm labourer turned up on Monday. For today, the end of work was in sight, and now that Mark was awake, and Adie had seen him with her own eyes, the load somehow seemed a lot lighter.

She'd miss all this, though, now that she was no longer needed. There was something really basic about farming. Something that spoke to her heart. She couldn't really put it into words, or describe how stopping would make her feel, but she reasoned she could still pitch in a bit, if the new Manager would let her. That decision would be largely up to Mark, of course, and she hadn't wanted to bother him with it last night. Maybe tonight she could ask him. Along with finding out for once and for all, maybe, what 'britches arse steam' was.

One of these days I'll remember to ask him.

Feen seemed happy enough to be stopping, but of course she had all Gina's commission work to be getting on with. There was no arguing the week's intense work on the farm had got in the way of that. She knew that Feen had fallen behind a little, trying but failing to stay awake at nights, in an effort to try and crack on with the order. Adie knew how torn Feen was, between wanting to help her dad and wanting to please Gina, whose commissions could give her an enormous boost towards becoming better known as a craftswoman jeweller, and of course very well paid for her work.

Bob had been coming over every morning, sometimes before daybreak, so he could get a few of Ravensdown's heavier chores done before he started on his own farm. Sheila had come with him a few times, and Adie was impressed to see how adept she was at driving a tractor and ploughing the field that Mark had pulled winter cabbages from, back in late January. Bob and Sheila were just keen to tidy it up and get it ready for the next round of planting.

Ravensdown also had a pair of pigs, away in their own field up towards the rear boundary of the farm. Adie adored them. Having named them Pinky and Stinky, she talked to them every day, and simply laughed when Feen had caught her telling them about what the weather was going to do for the next 24 hours and had strongly admonished her.

"Adie, you mustn't talk to them! They're food for our freezer, eventually. It doesn't pay to get too attached. Please tell me you haven't niven them games!"

Adie had shaken her head solemnly, poker faced. She thereafter always made a point of making sure Feen was nowhere in sight when she told Pinky and Stinky whether or not it was going to rain.

And that was the other important thing to do with farming - the weather! Some days, it literally dictated the order in which they did most of the work on the farm. Adie's new morning routine consisted of getting up, getting showered and dressed, taking Sid for his morning walk, feeding him and Mittens, letting the chickens out at Teapot Cottage and giving them their morning mash, then bolting up to the farmhouse, where Feen would have a hearty breakfast waiting. The two women would listen intently to the weather report as they ate, and Adie got into the habit of tapping the barometer glass just inside the front door, before she went out each morning, up to the barn to don boots and overalls. The weather became the all-important driver, every single day.

Rain or shine, every day was blindingly busy from start to finish. Whether it was helping to deliver breached baby lambs, bottle-feeding one orphan and a set of rejected twins several times a day and keeping them warm, moving livestock about, checking hooves for foot-rot, inspecting chickens for mites, taking scraps up to the pigs or checking fences and gates and repairing any damage to either, Adie and Feen were never short of things to do.

Planning each day to also allow them time to go over to Carlisle to visit Mark was sometimes a bit of a challenge, and they found it easier to stagger their visits. Bob, Sheila, Adie and Feen could all go on different days, which took the pressure off a bit. As much as Adie was desperate to do nothing else but sit by Mark's bedside and feel close to him, she knew she was of much more help to him here at his farm.

Feen was missing him terribly, and Adie was concerned that she might be feeling very isolated up at the farmhouse on her own, so she spent as much time there as she could, between shuttling back and forth from Teapot Cottage, making sure her own responsibilities were met there, with the house itself and her 'charges'. The two women had grown very close in that first week, bouncing well off one another and being focussed on getting jobs done, and sharing meals together at the Farmhouse table well after the sun went down.

Mercifully, they hadn't had to do much cooking. Word had quickly spread around Torley about Mark's accident, and the fact that Feen and Adie were running Ravensdown as best they could without him. In the usual spirit of support that seemed to be indelibly woven into the culture of the town, a steady stream of people kept turning up with casseroles, baked goods, and produce from the Saturday Farmer's Market, which had temporarily fallen by the wayside for Adie, as there simply hadn't been time to make the marmalade, but Peg had promised to pop up every Friday night, and collect the eggs to sell at her own stand, on Adie's behalf.

Although Adie and Feen had gently refused Peg's incredibly kind offer to help out on the farm in the evenings during that first week, Peg did insist on doing some cleaning and laundry at both the farmhouse and Teapot Cottage. On the first Monday morning after Mark's accident, she had arrived at the farm proclaiming that her assistant was perfectly capable of opening the cafe and running it single-handedly for the first half of the cafe's quietest weekday.

Peg's small act of domestic kindness, in making kitchens and bathrooms presentable, was a massive help, because at the end of each day, neither Feen nor Adie had been able to summon enough energy to do much more than eat a reheated casserole. Scrubbing down the shower or wielding a mop wasn't on the radar for either of them.

In many ways, Adie was sorry Mark had employed a Manager. While she understood Feen's need to get back to her own work, she herself had been very happy with the initial arrangement, thinking they all had everything well in hand. She fully understood Mark's decision had been made out of concern for her and Feen, and for Bob too, particularly as it was now obvious that things were going to get a lot busier and they really *would* have struggled to cope, but she'd been looking forward to the arrangement they'd agreed to with Peg, who'd offered to bring a takeaway every Friday night when she came to collect the eggs for the market.

Peg had seemed disappointed too, and suggested that maybe they should still have a Friday night meet-up anyway. Adie and Feen had readily agreed that the three women would all chip in each week for a takeaway and a bottle of wine. All three of them looked forward to it immensely, particularly Feen, who'd had little in the way of regular female company before Adie had arrived on the scene.

Feen had spoken to Bob about the mezzanine floor, which he had already inspected, and had proclaimed to be a death trap, with rotting floorboards, unstable stairs and rickety handrails. The decision was made to replace the floor, with the insurance company meeting the cost. Since Feen's name was there with her father's, on all of the various policies for the farm, it meant they could proceed with a claim straight away. Both women were very keen to have the new floor finished before Mark came home from the hospital. Two neighbours had offered to come over and fix it for them, but Feen had assured them both that it was well covered by insurance.

Adie marvelled again at how sweet and generous everyone was. In times of adversity, the people in this community really stepped up and pulled together. It was the kind of spirit that had prevailed during the war. She doubted very much if such community involvement would rear its head in a place like Guildford! Nowhere in the world felt further away to her now than the town she'd so recently called home. It would never feel like home again. She knew that for a fact.

The day after Mark's accident, Adie had taken on the deeply unpleasant task of cleaning up the barn. It wasn't at all fair to expect poor Feen to do it, and it needed to be done, so with tears streaming down her face, Adie had found a mop, filled a big bucket with cold water and set about scrubbing away the stubborn, heavy, congealed bloodstains from the stone floor. Once she'd got the worst of it up, she then filled the bucket with boiling hot water and a good half a bottle of strong disinfectant and had gone on to wash the floor thoroughly. Only when every last trace of blood had been removed did she proclaim it to be clean.

After that grisly clean-up task, the barn became Adie's responsibility, more or less by default. She'd had no trouble finding whatever they needed and after that first week she knew the layout of the barn like the back of her hand. It had been easy enough to keep tidy, much as it already had been. Mark had set everything up in there very well, and it was an efficient building to operate from. Everything had a rightful place of its own, and good access.

She'd been scared beyond description, in the first few days after Mark's fall, at the prospect of him being permanently hurt. Nobody knew, at that point, when he might wake up or what state he'd be in when he did. After the realisation had come to Adie that she loved him, she'd been plagued by the prospect that he might not recognise her, or he might be changed in some way that rendered their friendship meaningless to him. All kinds of scenarios went through her head, and more than once she had to stop and admonish herself for fearing the worst.

Being told that Mark was awake and demanding cups of tea felt like the best news she'd ever heard in her life, and her heart soared when Sheila had told her he'd been asking for her. That day, she couldn't wait for the work on the farm to be finished so she could get cleaned up and rush to his bedside to see and hear him for herself.

He's going to be alright!

Seeing him for herself had confirmed that he was, in fact, going to be as right as rain. He was still 'her' Mark, and after leaving him on that first night, and dropping Feen at home, she had pulled into her own driveway and sobbed for a full five minutes with relief.

They still weren't talking at the hospital, about letting him come home, but Feen had already prepared a ground-floor reception room for her father that had access to a shower and toilet. With Bob's help she'd changed the bed in there for Mark's own, and had even changed the curtains and rugs, and put Mark's personal things around the room, to make it feel more like home for him.

Adie marvelled again at how sensitive Feen was. The younger woman was wise in her knowledge that Mark needed to feel properly at home and familiar. Just being back home but ensconced at the other end of the house by himself would not be fair, because the accident had been traumatic, not just to his body, but to his mind as well. Feeling laid-up and powerless was going to frustrate him enough, without feeling isolated to boot. Being in his own bed, with his own things around him, but close to the heart of the house instead of stuck upstairs away from everything and everyone, he'd feel a lot less disconnected. In a downstairs room, where he could actually be heard if he needed something, he could at least feel like he was part of daily life as it all carried on around the house.

The day after Mark woke up, Feen also did what she referred to as a healing and cleansing ritual for her father as well, to "eliminate any impediments to his healing." She invited Adie to witness it, knowing that Adie was curious about her beliefs and customs. Adie sat on the floor in one corner of the room and watched with real fascination as Feen peeled back the big carpet and set down in the centre of her Intentions mosaic, directly on top of the red heart, a selection of crystals, candles, some yellow daffodils with orange centres, and Mark's wedding ring. She then poured a trail of sea salt around the outside of the circle, lit her candles, and sat next to it all with her head bowed. She whispered gently;

"By divine intention, hold at bay all negative thought and action. By divine intention, bring forth the power of healing energy to this house and the next, and to whoever dwells within. Spirit, heal my father. Spirit, bless my mother. Spirit, hold me and all who I hold dear safe in your hand."

All Adie could hear in those moments was a clock ticking in the hallway, and the sighing sound of wind through the trees. Feen looked to be meditating, sitting in a kind of half trance and breathing quietly but deeply. Adie decided to breathe deeply too and as she did so, she became increasingly aware of a very deep sense of calm in the room. She thought she could hear a woman's voice, far away, gently and quietly singing a song she couldn't quite identify, and she found herself relaxing into the sounds in her head.

After a time, Feen opened her eyes fully and blew out the candles. She looked at Adie and spoke quietly.

"I don't want to freak you out, Adie, but I'm sure my mother was here with us just now."

Adie ventured hesitantly, "I heard a woman singing, very softly. At least I think I did. It almost wasn't there, but it kind of was. It's very hard to describe. Fragmented. Almost like it was in my head but not quite."

She felt silly, admitting to hearing what she still wasn't sure had been real.

"What was the tune? I don't suppose it was that song by Medley and Warner, was it, "I've Had the Time of My Life"?

Adie felt the hair prickle gently at the back of her neck. She stared at Feen.

"Actually, it was. I couldn't place it while I was hearing it, but now you've said it... yes, that was it. A lovely, uplifting old song."

Feen nodded, her eyes wet with unshed tears. "Yes, that was Mum. She loved that song, and when she organised her funeral, she asked for it to be slayed after her plervice, for Daddy. It was her last gift to him."

She said nothing further, but she was clearly moved by Adie's experience. Adie wasn't sure what to say, so she continued to sit mutely on the floor, slightly confused herself, and feeling more than a little unnerved.

After Feen cleared everything away and rolled the carpet back over the top of the mosaic, the two women went back to the kitchen. Adie set about making a pot of tea but was profoundly startled, on turning around, to see that Feen was weeping silently but profusely. She was sitting at the table, with her head in her hands, and her shoulders were shaking.

"Oh Feen!" she cried. "What is it? What can I do to help you?"

Feen shook her head. "Nothing, Adie. It's fine, truly. Sometimes even white magic comes with a bit of a backlash, and it looks like this is my day for it."

Adie felt completely inadequate. She didn't have a clue what to say. Feen knew she felt uncomfortable, and sought to reassure her, but her explanation left Adie completely floored.

"I'm sorry. I had no idea you'd be affected by the ritual, Adie. You weren't supposed to be. But you've been given a very big message. A really important one. Mum has stood aside for you. She's cleared your path. Your path to Daddy."

Adie stood staring at Feen, dumbstruck.

"You heard her singing. That was her message to you. I didn't hear it, Adie. I didn't hear her at all. I *sensed* her, like I always do, but I never heard her singing! And that song, I've Had the Time of My Life? That was her message. She was saying goodbye. She was stepping aside, Adie, so that you can go to Daddy."

Adie's mind struggled to make sense of what Feen was saying. Saying goodbye? Stepping aside? She felt compelled to ask poor Feen a difficult question.

"But you never heard her. Does that mean you've lost your connection to her?"

Feen smiled through her tears and shook her head. "No, Adie. I'll never lose my connection to her. She and I will always be tethered by something much bigger and stronger than the two of us, so please don't worry about that. But her connection to Daddy is gone. He's never felt it, but I always have." She paused for a moment. "I can't feel it anymore."

"But what does it all mean?" Adie felt more confused than ever.

"It means that she herself has broken her connection to him. She has severed it. She has said goodbye, and in doing so through you she is bliving her gessing to you - to find love with him."

Feen was crying still. "Adie, she wouldn't do that if she didn't think it was right. She's kept her connection because she couldn't stand him being so lonely. He's been so terribly lonely without her, even though he'd never admit that, and it hasn't even dawned on him in fact, until recently."

She managed a watery smile. "And even now, he's still fighting it. She's never wanted to leave him that way. But she trusts you, Adie, and she knows he doesn't feel bereft anymore. Her singing to you was her way of telling you that she knows it's time for her to step aside. She can let go now, and she's okay about doing that, because she knows he's in good hands with you. It's finally time for her to leave him, to say goodbye and let him find his own way now. With you."

Adie was crying herself, now. Feen was so sad, yet so philosophical, and suddenly it did make sense. A gentle voice, from another world, a woman handing over her dearest treasure into the safe keeping of another.

She trusts you, Adie. She knows he's in good hands with you.

Adie walked over to Feen and held out her arms. The younger woman rose from her chair and stepped into them. The two just hugged, for a long time, then Feen finally released her and sniffed hard.

"I know you're in love with him, Adie. And I also know he's in love with you. I've known this day was coming, even before I knocked on your door that first day at Teapot Cottage. It's such a bittersweet thing, seeing it come together like this. Feeling Mum letting go like this, it's such a funny feeling, like nothing I've felt before, but it's good for her, to finally feel she can say goodbye. It's good for all of us."

She thought for a moment, and continued; "and for what it's worth, I'm happy for you both, that you've found one another. The fact that Mum is happy too, well, that's very special. And to my knowledge, she's never communicated with anyone other than me, so that makes *you* very special too. And you are. Please know that you are, and not just to Daddy. You're special to quite a few people around here, Adie, including me."

She hugged Adie again. "So, what are you waiting for? Go and get him. Run to him as fast as your legs will carry you. Make him happy, Adie. I once thought nobody would, ever again, but I know you can, and I know you will."

Chapter 23

Darkness had fallen by the time Adie made it back to Teapot Cottage. After taking Sid out for a short run across the fields, there was barely time to get showered and changed and grab a bit to eat before she needed to be on the road to go and see Mark.

She decided to check her emails, for the first time in five days, as her food was warming in the oven. Someone had sent over a small fish pie with a delicious-looking cheesy mash topping. It wasn't quite big enough for two, really, so Feen had told her to take it home with her. Normally the two women grabbed a bite together at the end of the working day, but on this day, after the extraordinary revelations up at Ravensdown House, Adie felt that both women probably needed some time alone to process everything. Feen agreed, and sent her off with the fish pie and a warm hug.

As she sat reading through the list of emails, she saw that one of them, from Glenn and Sue, was marked as urgent. Adie only had something like three weeks left on her house-sit, and her heart leapt at the prospect that the email would offer some kind of extension; something she'd secretly been praying for.

But Glenn and Sue's email made her sit up with a start.

Dear Adrienne,

We hope you've been enjoying your time at Teapot Cottage, and thank you again, for taking such good care of our home and treasures. Your regular updates on how Sid, Mittens and the chooks are doing have been very reassuring to us. To have everything held in such capable hands has been a godsend at a really difficult time.

Glenn's dad passed away a couple of days ago. It was all very peaceful. He was surrounded by his family, and we were able to say goodbye to him properly and tell him how much we loved him. But since then, we've been trying to figure out what to do about coming back to Torley, because neither of us feels it's appropriate yet, and after a long discussion we've made the very big decision to stay here for the foreseeable future. Purely by chance, Glenn has been offered a good job, with good benefits, and staying means we can keep an eye on his mum. She's struggling to come to terms with everything, and she's not getting any younger either. She's lost her confidence and she's not as steady on her pins as she used to be, before all this happened.

We'll be buying a place of our own, but sadly it means we have to sell Teapot Cottage. So, since your stay is due to finish next month, we wondered if you could use that time left to prepare the cottage for sale for us? We'll arrange to have it valued in the next week or so and will get the valuation consultants to contact you to arrange a time to come. We'll also instruct an estate agent as soon as the valuation is in, and let Mr Raven know, up at Ravensdown House.

We've also done some research into what's required for shipping a cat and a dog to Australia, and we'd like to go ahead with that, so if you feel up to arranging that for us for Mittens and Sid, we'd be very grateful. Of course, my friend Madeleine can do it if you'd rather not be involved. She will also find a new home for the chooks if the new owner doesn't want them. We'll be sad to say goodbye to our lovely special little cottage, but we do have to be practical. This decision has been a really big one, but we feel it's the right one. Wish us luck!

You're welcome to stay until the place sells, but we do understand fully if you wish to leave next month as arranged. Please let us know what you'd like to do.
All best wishes,
Glenn and Sue Robinson

Adie was gobsmacked. Teapot Cottage was to be sold! Her very first thought was that she desperately wanted to buy it herself. She really, really did. Would it be possible? Would her share of the matrimonial settlement come through in enough time? Thoughts suddenly crowded her head. It would mean moving to Torley and staying here. Was she ready for that? She suspected she probably was. In less than three months, she'd felt more at home here than she had anywhere else, for a very long time. Already, there were people here she already regarded as good friends; people like Peg, Feen, Sheila, Bob and Trudie. And, of course, Mark.

What if things went south with Mark? Would that make living here too awkward? As quickly as the thought had entered her head, she quashed it. They weren't children. They were both mature adults who could deal with a falling-out, if it came to that.

What if the kids needed her? Well, they were all on the same land mass, for most of the time at least, and it was no more than a day's drive at worst to reach any of them. They'd be able to visit too, of course. Having them all here at once, like for Christmas or something, could be a little tricky, but she could always buy a cheap caravan to put at the back, to serve as another bedroom...

Suddenly, Adie was too excited to eat. She quickly fired back an email to her hosts.

Dear Glenn and Sue

I am so very, very sorry for your loss.

Not much time to write a decent response so forgive me, will do so later, but for now, yes get valuation, but please don't put house on market yet as I'm interested in buying, would like first refusal please.

All best,

Adie B

P.S. Happy to sort transportation of Mittens and Sid for you but will miss them terribly.

She quickly grabbed her bag, coat and car keys, and headed for the door. In the car, her mind continued to race. All thoughts of her strange afternoon with Feen were temporarily forgotten as her mind focussed on the possibility of buying Teapot Cottage. If her settlement didn't come through in time, she could possibly get a bridging loan, or maybe Ruth and Gina would help out. That would be a lot to ask, but if anyone was in a position to help, it would be them. Money certainly wasn't a problem for Gina Giordano and so, by default, not for Ruth either. But did they have that kind of money just floating around? And even if they did, would they help out? Adie wouldn't blame them if they refused. But like people often say, if you don't ask, you don't get.

And, as audacious as it probably was to even ask, you could often go a long way on an ounce of cheek.

Matty had no money to speak of, and she knew Teresa was coming home flat broke from her travels, so they'd be out of the question. Bryan might help, but Adie doubted that, and in any case, asking him for help was the last thing she *ever* wanted to do.

She had no idea what the cottage might be worth, or whether she could afford it at all. Despite having a fair idea of how much she'd end up with after the sale of the family home, and various other joint assets that would go under the hammer as part of the divorce settlement, without knowing how much the cottage would likely sell for it was difficult to say if it could be within her grasp. But Adie wasn't about to give up on such a heart-warming plan before she'd even started, and she certainly needed something to aim for as she moved on with her life. This might be it! Maybe Mark could offer some insight as to the true value of the property.

Mark. Adie's mind came back to her afternoon with Feen, which had been unsettling, to say the least. If Feen was right, and Mark did love Adie as much as she loved him, what did that mean for the future? Did it mean marriage? If so, what would be the point of buying herself a house at this stage? But there again, was she really ready to forgo her new-found independence and go back to being someone's wife? Her thoughts were a complete jumble as she opened the door to Mark's room.

Her turmoil must have shown on her face, because as soon as he saw her, Mark did a double take.

"What's up, lass? Yer look worried."

"It's been a rather strange afternoon, "Adie admitted, sitting down beside him. "I'm still trying to collect my thoughts about it all."

Mark raised his eyebrows. "Well, tell me what's been 'appenin'. I may be able to 'elp."

Putting aside her thoughts about the two of them, Adie launched straight into talking about Teapot Cottage. She told Mark about the email from the Robinsons, and then confessed.

"I'm thinking maybe I could buy it, if it's not too expensive. Would you have any idea how much it might be worth?"

Mark thought for a moment, then cleared his throat.

"Aye, I've an idea, an' I'm willin' to bet it's well within yer means." He chuckled softly, winked at her, and took a deep breath, but he winced as his broken ribs protested. His face grew serious. "But Adie, there's summat I need to ask yer, if yer don't mind? "

Adie suddenly felt wary. She nodded, reluctantly.

"If yer don't mind me askin', 'ow are yer feelin' about Bryan now? "

It was an unexpected question. She grimaced. "Well, you know he texted me, saying he wanted us to talk. I didn't really want to but I thought it would have felt a bit mean to say no. He needed proper closure, I think, and to be honest, I thought it might help me too."

Mark nodded, so she continued.

"So, he rang me, and we talked everything through. It was all very amicable, and it did help. It really was the best thing, for both of us."

"So 'e wasn't beggin' you to go back to 'im then?" Mark asked quietly.

Adie reluctantly nodded. "He did say I could always go back if I wanted to, yes."

"An' what did yer think about that? Were yer tempted at all?"

Adie shook her head emphatically. "No, not even remotely, and it's so ironic really, because when I arrived here, just a few months ago, that was the *only* thing I wanted. I was *living* to hear those words from him. I wanted to go back, and I wanted him to want me back, more than anything. But I don't anymore."

"What's changed?"

Adie thought for a moment. "I dunno, really. Finding out that he'd had a mistress for so long was a big part of it I think, because it was clear that the marriage hadn't been what I always thought it was for a long time anyway, and there was no real hope of going back and starting again with a clean slate after that. Besides, she's still in the picture. He loves her. He wouldn't say it at first, but he admitted it at the end."

Adie shook her head, sadly. "The trust went a long time ago, for him, and it's gone on both sides now. I now feel like he felt, after the whole Ruth business blew up. Betrayed, let down, confused about so much that I never knew and didn't see, all that kind of stuff."

She took a tissue from the table next to the bed and dabbed her eyes with it before continuing. "And the rest of it? Well, it was just a gradual process of change, within me, I think. A new environment gave me a new perspective. I started having to be responsible again, for the pets, and for myself. I had to stop wallowing, tough out my first Christmas on my own, take on the Aga!" She grinned, and Mark did too.

"And I've survived. I've made it through all the things I first though I wouldn't, and the horrible spectre of Christmas, that was such a huge obstacle in my mind, to get through, when I arrived here. But it turned out to be nothing major at all, in the end. It just came and went, like most other days." Adie gazed out of the window, thoughtfully.

"And over the weeks, I've started making friendships here that feel meaningful. I've begun to see glimpses of what my future could be like; tranquil, happy, filled with good people and real purpose. I've realised I didn't have to be that woman anymore, the one who'd fucked up her whole life, who before that had more or less *spent* her whole life just waiting for her husband to come home from work and have time for her."

She took a deep breath and continued, "Don't get me wrong, it wasn't always awful. We had a lot of good times, over the years, and that counted for a lot. All that history we'd shared! I didn't want to let go of it all. I was in a place where even that existence, of being an endlessly expectant, unfulfilled wife, still seemed preferable to being alone and ostracized, and I was desperate to be forgiven."

She faltered, but Mark nodded for her to continue.

"But that was then, and this is now. When Bryan and I spoke on the phone, all I felt was sad. And kind of relieved, if I'm honest. Then when he asked me to go back, even though they were the words I'd been longing to hear for so long, I didn't feel anything. And when we said goodbye, I knew it *was* goodbye, and so did he. And there's a very deep sadness, of course, but it's not all-consuming, like the end of the marriage itself was. I now find it hard to believe that I wallowed, drowning in despair and self-pity, for an entire year!"

Adie shook her head, literally unable to believe her own, earlier self.

"In this environment, with different things to focus on, I've somehow managed to heal, and the really strange part is that I haven't even noticed it happening. I look back on all that wreckage now, though, and it really *is* looking back. I'm not in the middle of it anymore. I'm grieving for what's been lost, but I don't want it back. Now, I'm just readjusting my sails, and looking forward to whatever comes next."

Mark took hold of her hand.

"And what do you want to come next, Adie?"

She thought for a moment. "I don't know", she confessed, looking out the window again, into another rainy night. "I have no idea what the future holds, but I do know I'm excited about it, which is a complete about-face to how I felt when I first arrived here - sick with misery, unable to imagine any kind of future at all. But Bryan's sticking to his agreement not to contest anything, so it's all going through, tickety-boo. I'll get my divorce settlement in another few months, so I'll be ok financially as long as I don't make any stupid decisions. The world's my oyster, so to speak."

Adie's voice was a little wobbly, but Mark took her hand and squeezed it gently.

"I do know I'd be desperately sad to leave Torley," she went on. "I've been dreading the house-sit coming to an end. In fact, I'd already started grieving for it. You've all been so kind to me. Torley, and Teapot Cottage - *especially* the cottage - is so gentle, and healing. It's worked some kind of magic on me. It's hard to explain. Feen gets it, and I think I'm starting to, but it does all sound a bit air-fairy, and I don't think I could do a decent job of trying to explain it. What I do know is that I never want to leave such an amazing place. I've been longing to feel like I belong somewhere again, and I feel like I've found that here."

Adie was astonished to find herself properly crying, and she knew it wasn't just because of her topsy-turvy, wildly fluctuating oestrogen levels. It was mostly the thought of leaving Mark that made her so tearful. So far, she'd survived everything life had thrown at her, but if she couldn't buy the cottage and had to move away and leave Mark - how would she get over that? Would he keep in contact, once she'd left town? Would she really come back for the next Christmas party, or had it all been just wishful thinking? The thought of losing touch with him, and with Feen, was more than she could bear.

Do you love me? Please say you do!

Mark squeezed her hand gently but didn't let it go.

"Adie", he said softly. "There's a reason why I've asked yer to tell me all that. I needed to know 'ow things stood wi' you and Bryan, and what you want from life now, before I made a fool o' meself, which I may just do anyroad, but 'ere goes."

He gripped her hand a little tighter. "Adie, you know 'ow I feel about you, at least I 'ope yer do."

Adie went still, holding her breath, as Mark took a deep breath of his own and continued, quietly.

"It's been a long while since Beth passed on, an' I were alright, just gettin ' on wi' things, and I'm sure I would've carried on that way. But you turned up, Adie, and yer made me realise I were lonely. You made me feel like I were back in the world proper, an' I'd not even realised I'd been out of it."

He sighed. "It's 'ard to explain. I'm not a man o' great words, as yer know already. But when Beth went, it were like a door slammed on me for good. I couldn't imagine ever 'avin' love in me life again. I thought I'd 'ad me one go at it, the one great love we're all supposed to 'ave, and that were it, I were done. An' I were ok about it, I really was, and forever grateful I'd been that lucky, because some people don't even get *one* big love, do they?

"No. But you bein' 'ere, it's woken summat up in me, Adie. You've made me feel alive again, like maybe it's possible to be truly 'appy again."

He was breathing hard now. She didn't take her eyes off him, as he ploughed on.

"I'm in love with yer, Adie. An' I think you might love me too. But I do need yer to be honest, because I'm just a bloody farmer wi' dirty 'ands and face most o't time, who talks better to cows an' sheep than people, an' I can only say all this once."

Adie felt the tears prick her eyes again. Feen and Sheila had been right. This wonderful, salt-of-the-earth, rough and ready, gold-hearted man really was in love with her. And, finally, it felt safe to openly admit that she loved him back, with all her heart and soul.

It's okay to love him, Adie.

She'd hardly dared to explore the fact, in her own mind. In spite of how close the two of them had become in the recent weeks, and how much she cherished the fact, she had to acknowledge that she'd deliberately shied away from examining her true feelings, probably from the fear of being rejected, or falsely hoping for something that could never be. She knew Mark was fond of her, but as many people had already told her, he'd been devoted to Beth, and had locked his heart away forever after her devastating death. His daughter and sister had both said something different, though, and now he was saying it himself.

Things had moved so fast, and yet so gently, evolving from a friendship into something much more meaningful. It had been less than three months since they'd met, but there was no denying how quickly their bond had formed.

Mark's horrific accident, which he'd been so profoundly lucky to survive, had turned everything on its head. Life was short. Nobody knew what was round the corner. You had to make the most of every chance for happiness you could find. Adie recalled how she'd felt when she was faced, that day in the barn, with that first terrifying thought that Mark was dead. The shock and fear had been overwhelming. Losing him was the biggest fear of her life in that moment, and she now knew that it probably always would be. What was that, if it wasn't love?

So, Adie sat there, weeping quietly, and admitted that she was completely in love with him too, and she adored Feen. Something within all of that suddenly felt safe, secure and wonderful. Now that she could admit how she felt, she wanted nothing more than to shower this amazing, grounded, tolerant, handsome, rough diamond of a man with all the love in her heart.

"Oh, Mark! I've been afraid to face my own feelings, because I wasn't sure how *you* felt, and I couldn't bear it if you didn't feel the same. People have told me you've got feelings for me, but I wasn't ready to believe it. Since everything in my home life blew up, and since I started the menopause, my confidence has just kind of evaporated."

She then talked to Mark about her strange, 'otherworld' experience with Feen that very afternoon, and how Beth Raven had, according to Feen's interpretation, stepped aside to make way for Adie. Mark nodded sagely. Adie hadn't expected outrage, denial or disbelief, but neither was she expecting his immediate acceptance of what she'd told him.

"Well, ecky thump. You've been Feen'd." He said it so quietly, and so seriously, Adie just burst out laughing, and the uncertainty that had filled the air was suddenly gone.

"Yes, it feels like I definitely have been Feen'd!"

"Then welcome to *my* world. Our world. Please, Adie, stay in our world. Don't leave. Very few people in the world get Feen'd. It means you 'ave to stay."

She was crying properly now, tears of joy, and letting it all out, knowing that trying to stop them would be futile.

Here I am, in all my emotional, soggy, red-nosed glory! If you can still want me after seeing me like this, you're a great man indeed!

At that moment, Sheila came in. She looked at Adie's red-rimmed, weeping eyes and runny nose, and Mark's broad, beaming smile. She saw his hand holding Adie's. She saw how he looked at Adie, and she saw how Adie looked at him.

"Ah! So, you've sorted yourselves out then, 'ave you, lovebirds?"

Adie and Mark both nodded.

"Well, good. It's about bloody time! Do I need to buy a hat?"

Adie didn't know what to say. They hadn't quite got that far.

Mark winked at her, then beamed at his sister. "Aye, reckon you might. Not that I've asked 'er yet. Yer timin's bloody appallin' as usual."

Sheila looked distressed. "Oh, no! God, I'm so sorry! Please tell me I 'aven't barged in on a special moment?"

"Yer bloody 'ave, as it 'appens. But don't worry. Like our Feen would probably say, it's just the way o't universe, tellin' me to find a more appropriate moment. Right now, the intention's clear, an' that's all that's needed fer today." He squeezed Adie's hand, and she squeezed back. "An 'ospital bed's not what yer'd call the epitome o' romance, any road. 'Appen I'll find a more fittin' place fer't big proposal. Reckon it can wait until I'm capable o' gettin' down on one knee, what d'you think, lass?" he winked again at Adie.

She laughed at him. "That suits me just fine."

Sheila kissed her brother, then came around the bed and scooped Adie into the biggest hug she'd ever been given. "Welcome to the family. It's more than slightly bonkers, in our daft little world, but I think you'll fit in just fine."

Adie laughed again. "Thanks - I think!"

Sheila winked at her too. Just then, Adie's phone beeped. It was a simple, one-word message from Feen. "*Congratulations.*"

She showed it to Mark, who just rolled his eyes and nodded.

Realising her brother and his new fiancée had much to talk about, Sheila didn't stay long. As she left, she asked their permission to tell Bob their news, and they both readily agreed.

"But let's just keep it within't family for now, okay?"

"Yes, of course. But we'll be back tomorrow with champagne, and the nurses can say what they like but you'll be 'aving some."

"Aye, too right. Bloody Gestapo, they can take a runnin' jump if they think they'll stop me from sippin' some champers."

Adie thought for a moment then quickly ran after Sheila, and caught her in the corridor. "Hey, hold up! Something's really been bugging me for ages. It's something kind of funny, that Mark said a while back, and I've just kept forgetting to asking him what he meant. Sheila, for the love of God, can you *please* tell me what the hell 'britches-arse-steam' is?"

Sheila rolled her eyes and grinned. "It's work, Adie. Dedicated hard work. The kind you've been doing, on Ravensdown farm!"

Adie and Mark talked some more about Teapot Cottage, eventually settling on the decision that Adie would buy it if she could. Mark was pretty confident that the price would be within her means, and he was happy to bridge the purchase if the Robinson's couldn't wait.

When Adie was ready, she would eventually move into Ravensdown House with him, after which point Teapot Cottage would be used as a guest house, or a holiday let. She pointed out that she would quite like to have the rental income from it, when it wasn't being used for family stays, so she could have a degree of financial independence.

Mark assured her there was no need, which was sweet of him. He said there was already more than enough money for them both to live very comfortably, but he fully understood why she still insisted on having an income stream of her own. Having learned to stand on her own two feet, Adie was now her own person, with her own dreams and desires. Her independence had been hard won. She was no longer interested in 'just' being someone's wife, and he was quick to reassure her he had no quarrel with that.

Chapter 24

Mark was really fed up. It was official; it would be another three weeks before he'd be allowed to go home. The news was crushing. His injuries were slow to heal, and while the doctors were convinced he would be fine eventually, they were not about to risk the healing process by allowing him to go home before they were fully satisfied that he'd be safe there.

Three *more* weeks! Clearly, the doctors didn't trust him to remain on bed rest at home, and as much as he hated to admit it, Mark knew it was fair for them to wonder, since he was fidgety and made no secret of champing at the bit to get back to work. Adie didn't trust him to stay still either, and she'd said as much. She seemed relieved he couldn't go home quite yet. But the fact that he was still stuck in the hospital, miles away, was still frustrating for everyone.

Eric Tripper, the new Manager, had gone in as arranged, with his farmhand Luke Morris, and the two men had rolled up their sleeves and got stuck in straightaway on the farm. Adie had asked Mark if she could still pitch in, and he'd said as long as it was okay with Eric, she could certainly do some light duties as required. Mark was thrilled that she enjoyed farming, and Eric had proved very obliging in finding her a few light but important things to do, mainly feeding the livestock and continuing to take care of the orphaned and rejected lambs. There weren't many, and she said she was still able to make her marmalade for the Saturday Farmers Market. She had apparently mastered the art of baking in the Aga and had found a glorious recipe for lavender shortbread, and various other delicious cakes and biscuits with which to regularly tempt Mark, Feen, Eric and Luke. Mark liked the sound of that!

Eric seemed like a good egg. He was a semi-retired, divorced man with a shock of steel-grey hair and an easy-going manner that most people warmed to. He had a dry sense of humour that Bob liked, and that was good enough for Mark. Luke, by all accounts, was a shy young man in his mid-twenties, who hardly said boo when spoken to, but he worked very well on the farm, according to Bob. Both men lived about fifteen miles away, so were happy to go home at night. Mark knew Feen would be glad she didn't have to put them up.

The Robinsons had accepted Adie's offer on Teapot Cottage, for the exact valuation given. Since there were no agents involved, and no chain to deal with, the transaction looked like it would be straightforward enough. Buying and selling houses could be a lengthy and stressful process but Adie was excited, and had resolved to simply let things take their course, having no reason to believe there would be any hiccups. As she'd pointed out to Mark, she had the time for the process to rumble on in its own way, and the longer it took, the greater the likelihood of her settlement money being through by the time contracts were due to be exchanged so she wouldn't have to borrow the money from him. It wasn't going to be a problem if he had to bridge a short gap between a proposed completion date and Adie's settlement coming through, but he knew she wanted to do the deal independently if she could. He understood how important that was to her.

She'd advised her kids about buying the house and was relieved that they all seemed relatively unsurprised that she'd decided to settle in the Lake District. They'd all said they were happy about it if she was, and they'd be keen to come and stay at some point in the near future, after everything was settled. It was as good an outcome as Adie could have hoped for, Mark decided.

She hadn't told them about him yet. He wasn't bothered by that either. There would be plenty of time for all that, later. Besides, they both wanted to keep the delicious news about their new relationship to themselves for a while, and savour it. Only Feen, Bob and Sheila knew about it so far. Mark also understood that Adie was also keen to avoid any criticism from her kids, about it all being 'far too soon'. She wasn't ready to confront any resistance yet, to the plans she was making,

It didn't feel too soon for Adie and Mark. The small matter of him being incapacitated was a hindrance they simply had to live with, for the time being. Mark loved to watch Adie's cheeks burn though, whenever he made mischievous, twinkle-eyed promises of exactly what she could expect from him when his back had fully healed. He thought she seemed a bit shy about sex, and he reasoned that his situation would give her the time she needed, to get used to the idea of becoming intimate with another man.

Adie had started the vet checks for Mittens and Sid, and although they still had a few other procedures to go through, their flights to Sydney had already been booked. A courier would collect them when it was time and take them to the airport.

The Robinsons were deeply attached to their pets and it would be great for them all to be reunited, but Mark knew Adie missed her own dog mightily, and was certainly going to miss the Robinson's little critters very much. They were such loveable, happy little characters, and they meant a lot to her. She'd admitted that Teapot Cottage wouldn't feel quite the same without them. Mark wondered if maybe Adie could get a kitten or a puppy of her own. Maybe she could have one of each. If they grew up together, they'd likely get on as well as Sid and Mittens did. Mark wouldn't mind a few more pets around the place. That's what made it a home, as far as he was concerned.

The Robinsons had also arranged for their furniture to be collected for shipping. They'd sent Adie a list of what they wanted, which was mainly personal effects, books, and bedding and just a few bits of the larger furniture. They'd told her she was welcome to keep or get rid of whatever was left.

Peg was still cleaning the bathrooms up at the houses on Monday mornings, and going up to Ravensdown on Friday nights with takeaways. Adie had told Mark that on the last occasion when Eric had finished later than usual and come into the kitchen to let Feen know he was leaving, Peg had unexpectedly blushed like a teenage girl. Eric had seemed quite taken with her too, by all accounts, asking her about her cafe in the town, and whether she enjoyed a good trade there. He told her his own little town on the other side of the hill could do with a decent cafe and vowed to call in and try Peg's famous pies, as soon as time permitted. He'd seemed torn between wanting to keep chatting to Peg and needing to get away, so Adie decided the pair needed a bit of a shove in the right direction. She invited him to stay for a drink this coming Friday so he could plan to stick around for a bit.

Eric was a good bloke, and Peg was a good woman; kind and helpful. Adie had suspected that Peg wasn't quite as done with relationships and perfectly happy on her own, as she wanted people to think, and Mark was inclined to agree. He chuckled to himself. *When yer put two single people together who 'ave a connection to start wi', yer just never know what might 'appen!*

All in all, Mark was happy with the way things were going for the people he cared about. Feen had apparently been squirreled away in her work room for most of the time, fulfilling the order for Adie's daughter in law, Gina, and surfacing only for meals, and the odd household chore. Her work seemed to be going well, punctuated with periodic dashes down to the post office with parcelled up boxes of beautiful jewellery.

Adie had seen some of it, and thought the pieces were exquisite. Mark knew they would be, and he hoped Gina would be happy with it all. A courier had delivered a large box of tiny lime green and slightly larger purple jewel cases, all with black satin inserts, that Feen had ordered from a company that had printed her name, 'Seraphine Raven' in black lettering on the lids with a black raven flying above it. As a logo, Mark thought it was just perfect in its simplicity. His daughter was on the verge of making a real name for herself, with her strictly limited pieces, and he couldn't have been more proud.

She'd told him that Gina was planning to launch Seraphine Raven Jewellery in around six months, to coincide with the release of her winter collection. There would be a new page on the website, dedicated to Feen's work, and Feen was to be interviewed, complete with a photo shoot, which was to take place next week. It involved going to London, and she was really excited about it. Adie had decided to go with her, and Mark was glad about that. Feen was nervous about her upcoming exposure, but thrilled at the thought of a couple of days in the capital with Adie.

He knew the two women planned to do some sightseeing, since Feen had never spent any real time there before. She was keen to see the Tower of London, and of course it's famous ravens. Camden Market was also on her list, along with Buckingham Palace and a particularly well-appointed herb shop near the Elephant and Castle. Since Ruth and Gina were only forty minutes from London by train, they'd invited Adie and Feen to stay at their house, which thrilled them both, especially

Adie. Getting to spend a little time with her daughter and gorgeous granddaughter Chiara was a wonderful bonus, on top of everything else, and it marked a definite step in the right direction for Adie and Ruth.

"It'll be a wrench leaving you", she'd told him, but he'd reminded her that it was only for a few days, and it wasn't like he could get up to much mischief without her. He did add that he was very much looking forward to getting up to mischief *with* her, when the time came, and she'd gone all pink again, rolled her eyes at him, laughing, and told him he had a one-track mind. She'd confessed to him then, that she was getting more used to the idea and was just as keen to get into some serious mischief with *him*! That put a smile on his dial for a whole day!

Being able to stay put at Teapot Cottage as its new owner was hugely exciting for Adie. Mark was thrilled to see how happy she was when the house-sit deadline sailed by, and she'd already started rattling away to him about new curtains, a set of bunk beds and a pull-out double sofa bed for the spare bedroom, and planting a bigger herb garden. She planned to enlist Feen's help with ideas of what to grow, with the main focus on flowering herbs that would attract more bees into the garden.

She was also keen to start a couple of beehives, and she'd already put a note up on the community notice board at the church hall to ask if anyone locally could give her some advice about how to start. Nobody had replied yet, but Mark felt sure some help would come. It was all just going to happen in its own time, that was all, and on that basis, Adie seemed content to wait.

Her divorce was still in process, and would take a few more months to become finalised, and although Mark had made it clear to her that he intended to ask for her hand when the time was right, he wanted to be fully healed, and able to take her to a romantic location to propose. Adie was fine about it, saying that with so many other things going on around them both, this too would fall into place when the time was right.

Adie seemed to be very much at peace with herself now. Mark could feel that the anxiety about the future that had virtually paralysed her just a few months ago was now almost completely gone. Now, she knew she was safe and loved and accepted, and the future was no longer something to be feared.

Feen had put it all in perspective the last time she'd popped in to make sure Mark wasn't driving the nurses mad. "If anyone had told either of you, in the widdle of minter, that by the middle of spring you'd both be in a new place, with a new life to look forward to, and new love in your lives, you'd have thought they were bark raving stonkers. It just goes to show, doesn't it, Daddy? If you let a little magic grab you by the hand, there's no telling where it might take you. Love changes everything."

ONE YEAR LATER

Traditional AGA-baked Wedding Cake

115g (4 oz) wholemeal flour
2 tsp baking powder
75g (3 oz) butter
175g (6 oz) sultanas
50g (2 oz) glace cherries
2 free range eggs, beaten

115g (4 oz) plain white flour
1 tsp nutmeg, grated
75g (3 oz) soft brown sugar
50g (2 oz) mixed peel
½ lemon
150ml (¼ pint) milk

- *Mix together the flours, baking powder and nutmeg.*
- *Rub in the butter until the mixture resembles breadcrumbs, or use a food processor to do this.*
- *Stir in the sugar, sultanas, peel, cherries and the rind and juice of the half a lemon.*
- *Make a well in the mixture and add the eggs and milk, mix together.*
- *Spoon the cake mixture into a greased and lined 18cm (7 inch) cake tin.*
- *Cook in the AGA Baking Oven for about 1 hour, until the cake is browned and firm to the touch.*
- *Replicate the procedure for a second tier, and cut to a different size if required. Ice and decorate as desired.*

The sun streamed in through the open curtains. Adie rolled over to find a cup of tea sitting on her bedside table. It was still steaming. Mark must have brought it in, and maybe it had been the sound of him leaving the room again that had woken her. She stretched and sat up in bed, and let the sun warm her face, feeling once more the profound sense of happiness she once thought she'd never have again.

Marrying Mark early last autumn had been the best decision she could have made. After deciding it was what they both wanted, there didn't seem much point in delaying things. The minute Adie's decree absolute had come through they'd organised a simple ceremony on the first available date, in the town's beautiful church, and well-wishers had packed it to the rafters. A party had followed, in a marquee they'd put up in the gardens at Ravensdown House. Peg and her staff had catered the event, and Sheila Shalloe had baked their two-tier wedding cake – in her Aga of course - and iced it very simply with a band of blue ribbon at the middle of each tier and a small spray of miniature cream and yellow roses on the top, fresh from her own garden.

Adie had worn a beautiful peacock blue, calf-length, 1950's style off-the-shoulder heavy satin dress that hugged her slimmed-down figure to the waist, then fanned out like a voluminous dance frock, with lots of netting beneath it and sequins dotted randomly all over the skirt. Thanks to Trudie, who'd searched for and finally found Adie's dream - a real "Come Dancing" gown - the bride looked absolutely stunning. Her headdress of miniature cream and yellow roses stitched to a peacock blue band were a perfect match with her bouquet of slightly bigger blooms. Both had been made by Feen, and when Adie had thrown the bouquet, Feen had caught it, with a look of surprise that had made both newlyweds laugh out loud. Their photographer had captured that moment of pure delight, and it had become the most treasured picture in the entire wedding album. Did anyone really have the right to look that happy?

There hadn't been any bridesmaids, only little Chiara as a flower-girl. Adie's best friend Miranda had served as Matron of Honour, and Bob had served as Best Man.

Adie and Mark had wanted to keep things very simple. There were so many people who could have been asked to 'stand' at the wedding, as Mark described it, and to have left any one of them out would have been unfair. They both decided they just didn't want that big a fuss. Luckily everyone understood that having just one attendant each from their own generation felt entirely fitting for what was, after all, a second marriage for them both.

The weather had been ridiculously kind, that day. They'd had the marquee set up with a dance floor inside, being ever-mindful of the lightning-fast weather changes that commonly plagued the district, especially in the autumn. But, in the end, everyone had simply danced barefoot on the lawn. The sun's warm rays, so rare at that time of year, had felt like a divine blessing, and a beautiful starry night had been the perfect end to a perfect day.

After everyone had gone, Adie had swapped her peacock satin heels for a pair of trainers, and she and Mark had gone up to the Tor with a blanket and a tilly lamp, and the very last bottle of champagne that he'd had the good sense to squirrel away before the guests had got their hands on it. As dark as the night sky was, the path to the tor had been clear and dry, and they sat watching the lights twinkle in the valley far below, savouring their first few moments truly alone as husband and wife.

Mark had made love to Adie up there that night, for the very first time, beneath the stars. They'd wanted to do things the old-fashioned way and wait until their wedding night, which made it all the sweeter. Adie quietly rejoiced that the menopausal loss of libido she'd experienced with Bryan hadn't extended to wanting to rebuff her new husband. Whether she could still be considered sexually desirable in her fifties was something she'd fretted about so much, in the run-up to the wedding, but Mark clearly cherished her body and hadn't been afraid to show it, right from the start. He was a surprisingly tender and considerate lover, who paid real attention to her needs and desires, and her doubts had been gently but firmly swept aside. Making love in menopausal midlife was suddenly something she didn't have to be anxious about anymore, and to her great surprise, she enjoyed being intimate with him, in a way she'd never experienced before. It was like a curtain had been pulled back on a window she hadn't even known was there.

Mark also had divulged the extent of his wealth to her, on the second night of their honeymoon in Bali. As it turned out, Ravensdown Farm was merely a hobby for him. He ran it as if it were a business, and was fully committed to keeping it turning a profit, but he did it to stay active and healthy.

The true love he had for his land and his animals meant that farming was a joy to him, but he didn't need the income from it. Wise investments in stocks and shares over many years, overseen by the family's long-standing family friend and financial wizard Kevin Sangster, had yielded very comfortable profits.

When Mark told Adie the extent of his savings and income, she was speechless. Her ex-husband Bryan had written him off as a "north-arsed, inbred halfwit", but he'd be choking on his words if he knew just how well-off Mark Raven really was. You don't make that sort of money by being *any* kind of halfwit.

Still, as much as it amused Mark, Adie was determined to enjoy a degree of financial independence. She kept up her Saturday Farmers Market stall, and had recently taken on the responsibility for running the entire event, in exchange for a small commission. The rent from Teapot Cottage was fairly constant, since walkers and ramblers used the Lake District all year round. Adie wasn't greedy about the rent she charged, and thanks to advertising on a few ramblers and accommodation internet sites, the cottage was usually occupied and booked well in advance.

She was fascinated to learn, in her role as landlady, that the cottage seemed to regularly attract people who were at some kind of crossroads in their lives. Many of them told her, when they left again, that being at Teapot Cottage had significantly helped them in ways far beyond what they'd expected when they first arrived. It was becoming a familiar story that really resonated with Adie, and even more so with Feen, who said that yes, the energy within the cottage walls *did* attract people who needed to sort themselves out, and it really was as simple as that.

Adie stopped trying to find explanations for the fact that whenever there was a cancellation that left a good block of time free at Teapot Cottage, it was invariably taken up by someone who genuinely needed extended time there. It was one of the miracles of the ethereal realm that she was still learning about, with Feen's help, and she couldn't yet describe it any better than that. She decided not to try and over-think it, and simply be grateful that the cottage was fulfilling an important spiritual function, even if it was one she didn't fully understand.

She ran the bookings diary meticulously, and blocked off any time when family and friends wanted to visit. Almost everyone had done so. Even Miranda had come up for a week, with her latest toyboy. Adie had also installed a small bench-top oven-grill for those who really couldn't face trying to get to grips with the Aga.

Her own relationship with the much bigger Aga at Ravensdown had developed nicely too, and she was now proficient with it, to the extent where she had added large batches of her organic lavender shortbread to her Farmers Market offerings. After checking with Peg first, who hadn't minded a bit of baked-goods competition, Adie had decided that the milk and cream/butter from Freesia, the farm's one and only dairy cow, would be perfect ingredients for home-made cakes, particularly the shortbread. Feen's crop of lavender bushes ensured enough for supply, and the two women had recently planted a lot more.

The lavender shortbread was an unusual offering, but the locals loved it, and Adie found herself barely able to keep up with the orders. On one morning at the market, two women had virtually come to blows over the last packet on the table, and only calmed down after Adie had faithfully promised to make more that very night, to ensure they could both have some!

Peg had been seeing a lot of Eric Tripper, who had remained a good friend to the Ravens after his time managing Ravensdown had ended. As much as Eric had enjoyed his time at the farm, he was genuinely pleased when Mark was declared fit enough to work again. Eric had made good on his promise to keep in touch, and it was at one of the Friday night takeaways (which had continued for a long time after Mark had come home and got back on his feet) that he'd turned up at the farm and come into the kitchen, as tense as a wound-up spring, quivering with nerves, but brave enough to formally asked Peg if he could take her out to dinner.

"No," she'd said, gruffly. "But you can come over to my place for a meal. I'll make you one of my pies, since you keep saying you want one. And you'd better like cats, because I've got three."

As nonchalant as Peg had tried to be about getting together with Eric, Adie knew she was thrilled. They'd been dating for several months now, and were all set to head to the registry office to make things official. Peg would never be drawn on many of the details of her new relationship, but she did manage to let it slip, after one-too-many glasses of wine on one particular takeaway night, that she had no complaints about Eric in the sex department. Feen had been aghast at hearing such a comment from a woman who she clearly considered to be well past any kind of sexual capability or interest, but she eventually saw the funny side and joined in the laughter. She then dubbed the pair 'Egg and Peric', and they'd been known as such ever since.

Bryan was also planning to get married again, to Nikki, the woman he'd cheated on Adie with, although Adie suspected it wouldn't be a particularly happy marriage. As Mark said, when they heard the news, a cheat will always be a cheat, and when a man marries a mistress, he simply creates a vacancy. In Feen-like style, Mark had laughingly referred to them as 'Nyan and Brikki'. Laughing herself, Adie had asked him if he thought of her and himself as 'Ark and Madie'.

Adie hoped Mark was wrong about Bryan, and she wondered if her ex-husband would finally find real happiness but, in her heart of hearts, she doubted it. Bryan was never satisfied with what he had, and always wanted more. He'd sent a telegram for Adie's wedding, wishing her and Mark a happy life together. She'd been very surprised by the gesture, but she appreciated it, as Bryan's way of letting her know he'd moved on too, and that the past really was the past for both of them.

Teresa had returned from Australia and managed to get some temporary research work in London. She was sharing a flat with a couple of the girls she'd been at university with, and admitted that after her gap year travelling around, she was finding it hard to settle into a normal routine. Adie assured her it would take a little time, and as the months progressed, Teresa did seem to be more settled, and was hoping her temporary contract would go permanent once she'd proved herself.

Teresa's wedding gift to the happy couple was a beautifully painted, authentic Aboriginal didgeridoo that she'd brought back from Australia. Adie decided that it was probably a bit ambitious to try and learn how to play it, but it would make a nice conversation piece, hung above the fireplace in the main living room

Matty and his wife Marie were pregnant again, and thrilled about it. They'd managed to come up on the train, for the wedding, but it hadn't been an easy journey with a fractious little Millie, so she didn't imagine they'd be making another trip any time soon.

Matty had initially been outraged at his mother's plan to remarry so soon, calling it a selfish act, and disrespectful to the family. He'd refused to come to the wedding at first, but oddly enough it was Bryan who'd told him in no uncertain terms to grow the hell up and be the kind of son his mother needed him to be! Matty therefore swallowed his pride and reluctantly agreed to come, which was no small thing.

To Mark's credit, he'd told Matty at the wedding how much he loved Adie, and would make it his life's commitment to make her happy. When Matty saw how real Mark was, how down-to-earth and straight-shooting he was, and he also saw how happy Adie was, he started to thaw a little. Grudgingly, with Marie's encouragement, he agreed to bring his family back to Ravensdown for the first new family Christmas.

And what a Christmas it had been! It was about as far removed from the previous one as Adie could ever have imagined. All of her family were there, she was newly married, her husband and stepdaughter did everything they could to make everyone welcome, and even though Matty stayed mostly aloof and non-committal, it had been a wonderful time, especially since Adie had vowed to carry on with Beth's tradition of holding the Christmas night drinks party.

After the wedding, she had lost no time in redecorating the living room, before going on to do the entire downstairs floor of the house. Mark had laughingly told her how Feen had reassured him, the Christmas before, that it would all be done within a year. She'd been absolutely right about that, he conceded, even if it was in a completely different way than he'd imagined! At the

Christmas party they'd just had, nobody had to wonder at the shabbiness of the house. It was glorious now; sumptuous and fresh, in soft creams, beiges and golds, with different coloured accents such as gentle duck-egg blue, warm convivial orange, or rich regal purple, in different rooms.

The party also meant that Adie's family could meet some more of her new friends and start getting to know them a little. It felt important that her children related to at least some of the new people in her life, because this *was* her life now, and she never wanted them to feel shut out or cut off from it. When she spoke to Teresa on facetime, she wanted her daughter to know who Peg Wilde (soon to be Peg Tripper) was. When she chatted to Matty, and mentioned the Shalloes, she wanted him to know who she was talking about.

The night before Matty, Marie and Millie left for home again after Christmas, Adie realised that it had been almost two full years since they'd last sat together and had a halfway decent conversation. It was clear that her son had real issues with the way his parents had split up over the secrets his mother had kept for his whole life, and even more with the fact that his father had been having a clandestine affair for six years. He was also still struggling with the shame of his time working as a male escort, a "gigolo", as his father had disdainfully described it.

Messed up and unwilling to communicate, he was still bitter towards Adie and Bryan, and had consistently tried to avoid having any kind of discussion with either of them, about anything meaningful. But, after deciding she'd had enough of his aloofness Adie was determined to try to put a stop to it one way or another. She sought him out, demanding that they finally have a decent talk, even if it meant continued disruption to their relationship. Secrets and failure to communicate didn't help anyone, and it was the first thing she said when she confronted him.

Matty confessed that meeting Marie had saved him from himself, and Adie knew that to be true. Their romance had been unexpected and short too, before they got married. But Marie was the anchor Matty needed. She gave him love, support, encouragement and stability. She was a fairly plain girl with few major aspirations in life; what most people would call a 'reliable plodder', content with having a husband, a part time job, a comfortable home, and the chance to raise a family. Marie would never set the world on fire, but she was sweet, honest and caring. They'd met when Matty had gone for a job interview at her father's company. She worked there as a receptionist/typist. Matty had been offered the job and seeing Marie every morning when he arrived soon led to him noticing her properly. It became clear to him that she fancied him like mad, so he asked her out and the rest, as they say, is history.

They loved one another totally, and the birth of their daughter Amelia only brought them closer. Adie was profoundly grateful that Matty had finally started to find some peace. He was still on his journey, but he was moving forward.

His life seemed settled, and it looked to Adie like he was going to be just fine. Having married the boss' daughter was something a guarantee of continued employment, as long as he kept his nose clean, which it looked like he was managing to do, and fatherhood had brought out something truly tender in him. She no longer had to worry for him.

As they talked, Matty had admitted to how much he'd struggled with everything and was even now still trying to come to terms with a lot of what had happened. He had a particular problem accepting his father's prolonged infidelity. Adie's own subterfuge had been easier for him to understand in the end, and he said he had to credit his wife and baby with his perspective on that.

"Marie made me realise, Mum, that you were so young, and so vulnerable. And after Millie was born and I realised the lengths I'd go to, to protect her, I understood how tough it must have been for you to give Ruth up. If we lost Millie, I don't think I'd ever get over that. I'd kill anyone who tried to force me or Marie to give her up, so I totally understand what you carried, for all that time. I wish you'd told us all, though, years before."

He shrugged his shoulders. "I dunno. I'm not saying we could have been much help, but it might have made things easier for you, not having to bear that burden by yourself. And maybe we could have found her sooner."

"I know," Adie admitted. "It's a scenario I've played out in my own head, so many times. But I was a coward back then,

Matty. Pure and simple. I adored your father. I didn't like myself much, and I couldn't believe it was me he wanted to marry. I'd already been forced to give up my baby. The thought of losing him too was more than I could bear. I was *still* young then, and still grieving, although I didn't really know that at the time, and I was still naive enough to believe that if I told him the truth, he'd think I was a slag and he'd dump me.

"Things were a bit different back then, remember. It was better than the previous generation, I'll grant you, but there still wasn't the kind of help that young girls in trouble can get now, and there isn't the same stigma attached to young teenage pregnancy as there was when I was fifteen. It's still very few people's preference, but it's no longer the end of life as we know it."

"I know, Mum, and I get it. All of it. Becoming a father has taught me so much." Matty took a deep breath. "I was so angry with you, I just didn't know what to do about it. But Marie told me I was being a hypocrite, and she was right, and considering my own moral standards, as they used to be, working as an escort, shagging old women for money, I was hardly in the best place to be judging you, was I?"

Matty had gone on to say how much his life changed when the woman he loved was effortlessly able to accept him despite his past. It made him realise how important forgiveness was. If Marie could forgive him for his moral aberrations and see the man he was in spite of them, he could forgive his own mother. The moment he did, he realised how much it mattered, and his attitude towards everything changed. Life got better.

"I still have a real problem with Dad though, Mum. I always thought it was you who'd ruined our family but finding out that we were probably doomed anyway because of *him*, well, that's been pretty hard to stomach." Matty shook his head.

"The worst of it was him letting you take the blame, and that first awful Christmas, or should I say the last one, when we all tried so hard to be normal, he was sitting there at the table with a filthy bloody secret of his own, yet he spent the whole day crucifying you for yours. Why did he have an affair in the first place? That was a conscious choice, to put his whole family on the line."

Adie shrugged. "I dunno, Matty. I've asked myself that many times. I've asked him too, but I don't think he even had the answer himself.

"Maybe I just wasn't the best wife I could've been to him. I'm going through the change, and maybe he found that hard, you know, the fact that I didn't control my emotions too well at times, and wasn't interested in certain things."

She didn't want to embarrass her son by supplying specific details, such as her waning sexual interest in her husband, and her inability to stop herself from randomly sobbing uncontrollably when she'd failed to control the hormonal chaos that had started overwhelming her more and more.

Matty shook his head. "No. That's not a good enough excuse for him to do what he did. Any of it. He's just a sneaky, two-faced bastard, who *chose* to lead a double life. Nobody put a gun to his head, did they? I just can't respect him, Mum. I'm ashamed of him. More so than he is of me, I'll wager."

Matty went on to ask the same questions Adie had always asked herself. If her secret had never come to light, how much longer would Bryan's affair have lasted? Another six years? Ten? Would any of them *ever* have found out?

Adie sighed deeply. "That's something we'll never know. But it's in the past, Matty. If you can find a way to forgive your father, I know it will help you in the same way that forgiving *me* has helped you. He's not ashamed of you, darling. Far from it! He misses you terribly." She'd grabbed Matty by the hand at that point.

"Forgiveness would help him too, and that's important because despite what he's done he's still your dad, and he wasn't a bad one, was he? Despite what he is - a liar, an adulterer, a sneaky bastard – whatever you want to call him, he gave you everything he could, and he never abused you or abandoned you. He loves you more than life itself. He's always been there for you, and he will *still* be a good father to you, if you'll let him."

Matty had swallowed hard. "I know. I'm working on it Mum, and that's the best I can say for now."

He'd then changed tack, clearly at the end of his ability to keep discussing Bryan. "But I'm glad you're happy. Mark seems like a decent sort, but I do hope he knows I'll have his severed head on a platter if he ever lets you down."

Adie had hugged her son tightly. "Thank you for forgiving me. It means more than I could ever tell you. I hope, in time, we can all be a family in the real sense again. Especially since you have a new stepdad *and* a new stepsister, as well as a fairly new half-sister, half-sister-in-law and a niece."

Matty had looked at her with crossed eyes for a second. "Yeah, I'm still getting my head around the new family tree. Seems a bit skewed in the feminine sense though. Quite a lot of girls in there. Might even things up a bit if Marie pops a boy out this time. Feen seems cool, although I do find her a tad strange."

Adie had laughed. "Yes. Feen's rather unique. I don't think there's another soul in the world quite like her. Most people haven't a clue how to take Feen, until they get to know her a bit. But you'll soon find out she's lovely. She has a solid gold heart, and she'll be a great sister if you give her the chance."

Her son had just nodded.

"And there's one other thing," Adie had added. "I want you to know how much I love you, and how proud I am of you. How proud I've *always* been of you. You're an amazing young man. You've been through a fire, but you've come out just fine. You really are going to be fine, Matty. Just give everything the time it needs and keep your heart open."

So, things were on an even keel with her son, and with the new baby on the way, he and Marie had accepted Adie's offer to go down and spend the first two weeks with them after the birth, to give them some initial support. That was something to look forward to!

Adie's new relationship with Ruth was still a work in progress, but they too were heading slowly in the right direction. Sometimes all you could do was let time take its course. Ruth had come through an even bigger fire than Matty, and she was going to be fine too, but she did still have a lot of issues to resolve, including allowing herself to grieve for what had been a pretty messed-up childhood with her abusive adoptive parents.

Adie had high hopes that eventually Ruth could regard her as the mother figure she'd never really had. She was still learning how to trust and respond to Adie's positive overtures. Adie knew she had to be patient, knowing in her heart that with enough time and enough love, Ruth would get there, and no matter how long it might take, Adie wasn't going anywhere. She would never abandon Ruth again.

She grinned to herself as her beloved shepherd Creole came bounding into the bedroom. The old dog never let her lie in for long. Bryan had returned him to her a few months ago, after securing a new work contract that meant he'd have to start spending a lot more time away from home. It was clear to them both that it wasn't fair to Creole to leave him alone for so long, and Adie was overjoyed when her ex-husband had offered her "sole custody" of her cherished boy. She would never have to miss him again.

After getting up, showered and dressed, she prepared the coffee and sat the percolator on the Aga hotplate. Feen wasn't up yet, and with it being a Sunday, Adie didn't disturb her stepdaughter, who had got in very late the night before. Feen had just fallen head over heels in love with a very nice young man called Gavin Black, a gifted musician from London.

Gavin had just moved into Teapot Cottage for a few weeks, to be close to Feen, but like many of Adie's previous tenants, he also needed to resolve some serious issues that were casting a shadow across his life. It meant that his and Feen's budding romance was not without serious family complications, which were quite uncomfortable for Adie and Mark, as it turned out.

But that was another story, and Feen was deliriously happy, which was all they really wanted for her. She was definitely at an age where she should have male company in her life. It would be an extraordinary man indeed who could ever hope to win the heart of such an ethereal, unique woman who usually only had one of her feet and only about half of her focus in the real world, but it was clear to anyone with half an eye that Gavin was that man. He kind of 'got' Feen, in a way that Mark had spent more than a decade hoping someone one day would, against what had felt like insurmountable odds. Despite their relationship being barely a few weeks old, Feen and Gavin were already excitedly planning their future together.

Mark was a bit tied up in knots that it was all a tad too soon, but the young couple were clearly made for each other, and having been the unwitting 'victim' of love at first sight himself with Feen's mother, there was a limit to how much protest the poor man could really make about his daughter being snagged by the very same hook.

Feen's jewellery was gaining profile, thanks to her work providing exclusive lines of her resin floral pieces for the Giordano collections. Within just one year, Feen had gone from being relatively unknown to being a 'jeweller du jour'. She was currently experimenting with different designs, all with nature at their core, and she was excited about a few new concepts. Adie admired how Feen's new-found recognition hadn't affected her ability to stay focussed on what really was the most important thing to her - the natural and spiritual worlds.

And Adie had her bees! Mark's wedding gift to her had been two beehives, a beekeeper's suit, a diploma-level tuition course, and a quarter acre of land on the farm where she could plant flowers for bees. Adie had opted for a traditional English meadow, and the flowers were already in their full, late-summer glory, lending a riot of colour to her small portion of the south-facing hillside. Mark had helped her choose the best, most sheltered location for the hives, and the bees had settled nicely into their colony. She loved nothing more than to sit and watch them work. They were already producing lovely honey, and Adie was hopeful that very soon she would be able to offer it for sale at the Farmers Market too.

To Mark's dismay, she'd admitted to befriending and naming the two pigs, Pinky and Stinky. He'd groaned with frustration. "Ah, bloody 'ell, Adie! I can't slaughter the buggers fer't freezer now, can I?"

"No, you most certainly cannot. Pork is mostly off the menu around here. It does us no good at all," she'd added, as he'd opened his mouth to speak again. "It's too close to our own DNA, chemically. Its effectively cannibalism."

Mark had shut his mouth firmly at that point and blinked hard, a couple of times, with a look of confusion on his face that left Adie struggling mightily not to laugh.

"Right, so we're raisin' a pair o' pigs to bloody owd age, then. As well as Beth's God-forsaken sheep and that bloody cow! And no more friggin' bacon." he'd muttered.

"Yes we are, and no there won't be, except on the weekends, and only if you're very, very good. So you'd better get used to it."

"A'right then, Miss bloody bossy-boots. But don't think this is the start of owt else. I'll not be bullied into owt else, by a slip of a thing like you!"

She'd stepped forward and hugged him, at that point, and he'd pulled her into a bear-like embrace. She'd muttered into his ear, "Oh, yes you will, my darling. And its *Mrs* bloody bossy-boots, thank you very much."

Coming soon:

THE POWER OF NOTES AND SPELLS
A Teapot Cottage Tale (#2)

Every woman dreams of finding the love of her life. But what do you do when yours brings baggage that can hurt you and your family?

Feen Raven is often described as more than just a little bit barmy. The young "white witch" has finally found her soulmate, but old family wounds are opened again when she finds out who he's involved with.

Gavin Black is on an unhappy errand that forces him to reconnect with his estranged mother. Staying temporarily at Teapot Cottage, all he wants is to claim what's his and go home again. He doesn't need any complications.

Carla Walton can't let go of a grudge. After a lifetime of pushing everyone away, she is isolated, bitter, and blaming everyone else for her problems. She wants to be left alone so she can keep ignoring her demons.

But Teapot Cottage, with its mysterious ability to heal the broken-hearted, always has a more complicated agenda for people who don't want to rake up the past. Pretty soon, Gavin, Feen and Carla come to question everything they think they do and don't want in life.

Will love and a little bit of magic help them find a way forward? Or will old family fractures be too hard to heal?

Milton Keynes UK
Ingram Content Group UK Ltd.
UKHW022336260824
447357UK00009B/143

9 781915 889942